The End of Innocence . . .
The Dawn of Desire

Young and beautiful, Dahlia and Cassie became friends just as they left girlhood behind to become women . . . just as they discovered the white-hot passions of loving to the limit . . . and the ecstasies that lay beyond.

DAHLIA, born to money and class, led a glittering life of chic all-night parties and casual affairs. But her secret inheritance was a shocking scandal . . . her destiny was a dangerous liaison of punishing kisses and illicit love.

CASSIE, haunted by a poor Southern childhood, fought her way to power in a New York publishing dynasty, craving success the way she savored the fire left by her lover's hands.

They were friends. They were rivals. They were two fascinating women about to pay the price of . . .

SEDUCTIONS

SEDUCTIONS

GEORGIA HAMPTON

A JOVE BOOK

SEDUCTIONS

A Jove Book/published by arrangement with
the author

PRINTING HISTORY
Jove edition/June 1986

ISBN: 0-515-08576-6

Jove Books are published by The Berkley Publishing Group,
200 Madison Avenue, New York, N.Y. 10016.
The words "A JOVE BOOK" and the "J" with sunburst
are trademarks belonging to Jove Publications, Inc.

PRINTED IN THE UNITED STATES OF AMERICA

Prologue

SOME FOURTEEN YEARS before our story actually begins, on a small island in the Aegean Sea, a woman is up at dawn. She climbs quickly up the steep path behind her stone cottage to a meadow where flowers and grasses bend their heads with the weight of the morning dew. A blood-red sun emerges from the dark sea and paints the whitewashed houses of the village below in shades of pink and rose. She pulls up stalks of wild oregano, clumps of purple thyme, and bunches of pungent mint. Back in her kitchen, the herbs perfume the air as she ties them into bouquets with string she had saved in a drawer.

The same drawer yields up a tiny bar of Ivory soap, a gift from an American lady, saved for a special day. She uses it to wash her face and arms in frigid water from the well. Foreigners, it is well-known, like everything to be very clean.

She puts on a gray dress, black stockings, black shoes. A square of blue cotton tied tightly around her head is the only spot of color. A crisp white apron and the fragrant herbs are tucked into her satchel, and she kneels before an icon. In murmuring tones she implores the placid Madonna for blessings on her enterprise, then, signing the cross three times, she rises and reaches behind the Holy Mother for a small leather pouch. In it are the coins that are her life's savings. She tucks the pouch into her bosom, picks up her bag, and leaves the cottage.

It takes her almost an hour to walk to the market square, but the morning is still cool and her step is light. Her cousin who works on the Athens steamer and who always knows

1

first about rich foreigners has told her the news: two ladies, English, very rich, have taken the big villa on the east end of the island. They have brought *ten* trunks.

At the market she buys only the freshest and the best: sardines just hours from the sea, spinach with garden soil still clinging to the roots, black olives, eggs, cheese, bread, green olive oil, coffee, a handful of fresh figs.

It is a long walk to the villa on the other side of the island, and the path climbs steadily up. All the dew has dried, and the road is hot and dusty. At the high gates of the villa she stops, wiping away the sweat on her face. At last she is in the cool shade of the garden, winding her way to the back of the house. Two tall women stand on the end of the large terrace, looking out at the Aegean far below. She waits quietly for them to notice her, and, when they do, she smiles and nods repeatedly to reassure them. "I cook you good," she says and repeats it slowly as if she were speaking to a stupid child. The ladies speak to each other and then to her, and all the time she smiles and nods. At last they are silent and she leaves them, finding her own way to the kitchen.

Now everything is simple. She knows how to prepare delicious food that even thin ladies will like to eat. They are pleased. Their voices are soft as they eat and sip the cool, pink wine. She brings them tiny cups of thick black coffee, sweet juicy figs, and brandy. The ladies smile, nod, and press money into her hands. A lot of money, enough to pay for what she has bought, to buy for tomorrow, and to live for a month. Tomorrow she will bring the boy.

The boy stands on a high, rocky ledge, a dark silhouette in the hot, white light. He leaps and falls straight as an arrow into the sea. The violent shock of cool water on burning skin takes his breath away, but still he can stay underwater longer than any boy on the island. He waits calmly for his eyes to adjust to the green darkness as he swims along the sandy bottom. There was a time when he needed to bring up octopus and shells to sell in town, but life is better now.

He works for the English ladies. In the early morning he tends the garden; late in the day he runs errands, does odd jobs. The midday hours are his own.

Sometimes in the evening he wears new clothes and walks among the ladies and their guests. He carries trays of food, pours wine, lights candles. He has learned to open the wine bottles that have come from France, to pour out bubbly, frothing wine without spilling a drop. He knows now where to place the silver knives and forks and which glasses to bring with brandy. These evenings are splendid. Musicians from the village play *bouzouki* music, and everyone dresses in fine clothes and sparkling jewelry. Always the two English ladies are the most beautiful, especially the pale one with the golden hair. He has never seen a woman so beautiful, and he has no words to describe her. Sometimes she walks in the garden where he is working, but he cannot look at her—he keeps his eyes lowered in her presence, and she walks past him. He is invisible, but her silk gown brushes his arm like a soft breeze.

One night the music is wild, with pulsing rhythm and wailing strings. A man from Athens leaps from his chair and begins to dance. He does not want to dance alone and beckons the boy to join him. It is an ancient dance—music and motion proclaim joy and virility, grace and beauty. Proudly the boy seeks out her gaze. She reclines on a sofa, a vision of white satin and glittering gold; her eyes look past him at the moon. The dance is done, and he must bring more wine.

The other woman, the one he calls the dark one although her skin is pale and only her hair is dark, paints pictures. Not pretty pastel drawings of the sea, the hills, the towns, for tourists to buy in harborside tavernas. Her pictures are of people, mostly women. She lines them up in the large room she calls the studio and shows them to the boy. He moves quickly past this gallery of female faces and lingers only at the three large portraits of the woman with golden hair. In one she holds a baby in her arms and looks like the Madonna in his mother's kitchen. The dark one wants to paint his picture, and she will pay him for the time that he stands and does nothing. It is agreed, and he arrives the next day dressed carefully in his fine new clothes. The golden one is there drinking coffee. He climbs onto the little platform and stands stiffly, looking straight before him. All is silent, and then the large room rings with laughter. Please, the dark one says, the clothes must go. Yes, yes, please, he must remove everything. The boy's eyes are hard and black with fury as he leaps off the platform and rushes from the room. In the kitchen, his mother is angry, and, though she is shorter than her son, her arm is long enough to land three sharp blows on the back of his neck. Lazy, stupid oaf. Do you think anyone cares for your little worm of a pecker! Go! Now! Crawl on your belly. You will do as the ladies want. Ignorant son of an ass! Do you know how much they are paying you? The boy goes and stands naked like a statue to be painted.

He swims to shore and plummets again through air and water like a sea bird. He spots a shell, a perfect one, its pink and white spirals closing in on themselves. It will fetch a good price at the marketplace. For the first time in his life, he has money—a pile of coins hidden under a loose tile—and he wants more. Carefully, he extricates the shell from its sandy bed and swims to shore. Exhausted but pleased, he flings himself on the warm sand in the shadow of a big boulder. Puffy white clouds are motionless in the blue sky, but the earth beneath him is spinning. He closes his eyes, and it spins faster still, until it can no longer hold him, and he is hurled into space. He is a bird soaring through the air, a fish playing in the blue waves, a boy diving into a sea of gold coins. There are mermaids, lovely creatures who tease him and laugh in high, silver voices or murmur seductive words he cannot understand.

Slowly he comes awake and is surprised that he has been asleep. But still he hears the laughter, the husky, intimate voices. How can he dream when he is not asleep? Suddenly he sits up. The voices are real. He peers through a tiny crack between the boulders and stifles a gasp. The beautiful golden-haired woman lies naked on a white rug. Beside her, the dark one pours oil from a small bottle onto the pale, smooth belly. She spreads the oil around, up between the small breasts and down again to the white thighs. The boy is on his knees, pressed to the stone. A sweet, dark pleasure fills his heart. Has he not stood for days while they looked on him without shame? Now he can look as he pleases, not to the left or right or up or down, but straight ahead at their white bodies gleaming in the sun. The dark-haired woman leans closer; her head moves down to kiss the other's open mouth. The kiss lasts an eternity. A gull screams overhead. The boy's heart pounds against the rock; his mouth is dry; there is a strange sensation in his groin. Something is happening. The golden one lies motionless; the dark head moves—a mouth closes on a nipple, a hand moves down and hides between the gleaming thighs. The bodies merge— a tangle of limbs, buttocks, breasts. He thinks suddenly of the doe who comes early in the morning and licks the salt from his open palm. The pure delight of a wild creature's caress. All is a jumble now. Time passes or stands still. Is he alone or is he one of them? Another cry pierces the silence, but there is no bird. An instant of sharp pleasure and all is still. A little breeze stirs and dries the sticky moisture on the stone.

A woman and a boy rise at dawn. They lock the door to their stone cottage and walk down the steep path to the village. The air is cool, but they walk slowly because their suitcases are heavy. The steamer is waiting for them in the harbor. They are going far away, thousands of miles to a house on the sea coast of England.

BOOK ONE

Chapter 1

"RISE AND SHINE!" the irritatingly cheerful voice pierced the layers of sleep. The magazine cover with Cassie's picture and the headline naming her Woman of the Year evaporated into thin air. "You don't want to lie slugabed on Christmas morning, do you, honey? And such a perfect day. I declare, it's almost sweater weather." Shades snapped smartly into place and the casement windows of the tiny bedroom flew open to let in a flood of fresh air and sunshine. Cassie glared evilly at her mother, but Blue Litton paid her no mind as she set down a tray laden with coffee, orange juice, and hot cinnamon rolls. The rich, sweet smells were irresistible, and Cassie sat up fully awake and very hungry.

"Merry Christmas, Mama. What time is it?" Cassie sipped the steaming coffee. "I was having the nicest dream."

Blue sat on the edge of the bed only half listening. It was an old, familiar ritual. She loved pampering her daughter when she came home from school, and every holiday began with breakfast in bed. Sometimes they would tuck up for hours talking about everything in the world, everything from the dreams they had had the night before to the dreams they had for the future.

Cassie sipped her coffee again and smiled at her mother. "God, Mom, how can you sleep in those? Doesn't it hurt?" Blue patted the tightly rolled curlers that covered her head. "Oh, I don't know. I guess I'm used to it. Anyway, what's a little pain . . . for beauty?" She bit carefully into her muffin. Even this early, wearing her faded chenille robe and with her hair still set, Blue had rouge on her high cheekbones and bright-coral lipstick on her wide mouth. "I could no more let myself be seen without my face on than without my clothes," she told Cassie long ago as the little girl had watched her making up. Anyone could see that Blue had been a beauty once—that she had cause for her small vanities. Cassie tried to imagine how the quick, nervous gestures had once been youthfully eager and vivacious, how the incurable optimism had been a large part of her girlish appeal. Is this what happened to eager young girls when they grew up? Did everyone end up twenty years later thrilled to be bringing coffee to a visiting daughter? Was that all that would be left? Well, it wasn't going to happen to her. She would do anything, anything it took, to lead a different life.

"This is so nice, Mama. But you shouldn't spoil me. *I* should have brought *you* breakfast in bed."

"Nonsense. It's so rare I get to fuss over you. And now . . ." she paused, overcoming a tiny hesitation, "I don't even get to have you the whole time. 'Course, I'm thrilled that you're going to visit your friend, but, still . . . we've hardly had any time together." Blue turned away to pour herself another cup of coffee.

Cassie tried to fight down the rising tide of guilt. "Mama, tell me the truth, are you very upset because I'm going to visit Dahlia?" She asked in bad faith, and she knew it. She had no intention of changing her plans.

"Well, the truth is I am excited for you. Maybe I am feeling just a mite sorry for myself, but I wouldn't stand in your way for anything. A week in Washington will certainly be more exciting than anything here." Blue forced one of her smiles. "You know, honey, I just can't help it. It does get lonely with you off at that school."

Cassie was determined not to get herself started, but it was exactly this sort of conversation, this melodramatic needling, with her mother in the role of the brave and self-sacrificing widow, that drove her to unwilling malice. "But, Mama," she said, feigning innocence, "I thought you were so happy for me when I got that scholarship. Remember how you kept saying that the Bennett Academy is the best girls' school in Virginia? In the whole South?"

"Mmm," Blue agreed reluctantly, flicking away invisible lint from the quilt. She had in fact been sorely doubtful about the wisdom of sending her daughter off to the la-di-da Bennett Academy for Young Women.

Blue was slowly adding cream and sugar to her coffee, stirring attentively as if she were making a complicated sauce that might suddenly curdle.

"Of course I'm thrilled for you," she lied, smiling brightly. "And I can't help thinking how proud your daddy would have been. He always did say that you were goin' to grow up to be the smartest one of all the Littons . . . and the prettiest, too."

Blue was proud of her daughter, and she did rejoice in her accomplishments. But then, too, she had always harbored a secret wish that Cassie could have been just a little *less* smart and a little more like a normal girl—a girl who liked to play with dolls, dress up, and go dancing—instead of ruining her eyes and posture, always poring over books. Almost as soon as Cassie had learned to talk, people had been taking Blue aside and telling her how gifted and intelligent her little girl was. And they had never much bothered to hide their surprise that a common hillbilly like Blue had produced a precocious child who knew how to read at the age of two.

"Mama, I am sorry about not being with you for the whole vacation. I truly am," Cassie said evenly. Then she softened her voice to an appeal. "But please try to understand. I've never known *anyone* like Dahlia. She's so different . . . we're so different . . . oh, I don't know. Sometimes I can't quite believe she actually likes me."

"That's ridiculous, Cassie! Why in the world wouldn't she like you?" Blue was genuinely indignant, even angry at the thought that this girl might not like Cassie. "If you ask me," she continued, "you've been altogether too taken with all their money—their titles. I don't think that gives them any right to—"

"Mama, pleeeeese!" Cassie had to grit her teeth to keep

control. She tossed the blankets aside and burst out of bed. "Let's do go for a walk. I want to get all the fresh air I can before facing the ghouls on the hill." Blue pursed her lips in mock disapproval, and they both broke out in laughter. For now, at least, the tension had passed, and mother and daughter were in total agreement.

"Seriously, Cassie, I want you to behave yourself up there. No sour looks or smart-alecky remarks. I don't want our nice time ruined picking over a lot of useless family gripes. Winthrop is Winthrop, and that's that. If you could accept him the way he is, you might even see a few nice qualities peeping through."

"Sure, Mom, you mean the nice way he treats his dogs better than his own family?"

"Shush now, Cassie. I mean it. He does no such thing." But it was unclear whether she was shushing Cassie or herself. "You first in the bathroom, and I'll carry these things down. Go on, now."

"Okay, Mama, but please leave the dishes for me." It was Cassie's peace offering.

Chapter 2

IN THE SHOWER, Cassie's thoughts drifted back to simpler times. Until her father died, when she was twelve years old, she had led an ordinary childhood, a happy and secure childhood. Her parents adored her, her teachers loved and favored her, her schoolmates admired and liked her. Oh, she had known that the other Littons were a bit—well, apart, she had called it then. Her Uncle Winthrop, Aunt Lucille, Cousin Peachie, and Granny Litton—all of them lived in a much grander house with servants and fancy heirloom furniture—but, in fact, she had preferred her own family's smaller cottage on the Litton estate. Everything there was cozier and a lot more relaxed.

But then her father died. Right from the start, Cassie had been aware of the bad feelings borne by the Littons for her poor, weeping mother. They blamed her mother for Bobby's death, she knew they did, though she never could understand why or how. They thought he had married beneath his station. He had abandoned all his healthy ambition for a hick, and she had encouraged him to do it, claiming to love him for his dreamer's way. She had dragged him down and seduced the very life force from him, they said. And they had no scruples about laying the blame.

After weeks of bitter tears and loud recriminations, Blue had packed up to leave. They would go to another city, another state, another country if necessary, where no one had ever heard of the Littons.

But Blue had not reckoned with the power of her mother-in-law, who was not about to let the daughter of her favorite son disappear. Augusta Litton had ignored Blue and spoken directly to Cassie: "Your mother no doubt means well, child, but that is not enough," she had said bluntly. "You are a Litton, and I will not have you growing up entirely outside our influence. You may tell your mother that you and she will be properly taken care of, but I don't want to hear any more talk about leaving Winston-Salem. You may think me tyrannical, I know your mother does, but this is how it must be, and she must know that. Now give me a kiss, dear, and run along."

They had stayed, but nothing had ever been simple again. In time, Cassie had gone off to Miss Bennett's Academy, and, somewhere along the line, she had grown to despise the cottage and all that it represented. She had learned to live with a divided heart. Part of her loved her mother— so much so that sometimes she thought her heart would break. What on earth made the Littons think they were better than her guileless mama, who tried so hard to make things happy and fun and carefree? Yet another part of her guiltily, secretly, admired the Littons—their strength, their power, their haughty breeding, even their condescending ways. That part of her had learned to be ashamed of her mother.

In the past, this conflict had trapped her into endless late-night bouts of "if only." If only her mother had come from a good family instead of those nobodies from the hills. If only her father's trust fund had come due before he died instead of reverting, as it did, to the Littons. If only his newspaper had been allowed to flourish as she knew it would have. If only he hadn't died.

But now Cassie was no longer interested in "if onlys." A letter of acceptance from Smith College had changed all that. That letter was her ticket to life. That college was to be her salvation. The poor girl from the wrong side of the family stood in the shower, her vision misted over by a combination of steam and tears, and she thought not "if only," but "how."

"Can I come in, darlin'?" Blue popped her head through the door without waiting for an answer. "Oh my, how nice you look. Turn around so I can see." She turned Cassie around and then held her by the shoulders at arm's length. "What a pretty sweater."

"Dahlia gave it to me."

"She did?" Blue looked more closely at it. "Was it something she didn't want? It looks brand-new, Cassie. It looks very expensive."

"I'm sure it is very expensive, Mama, but Dahlia wouldn't care about that. Money means absolutely nothing to her."

"That sounds very foolish if it's true." Blue regarded her seriously. "Really, Cassie, isn't that a bit extravagant? What will her parents say? Honey, do you think you should have accepted it?"

"Mother, please stop it!" Cassie's voice rose. "Haven't you listened to a word I've said all week? Don't you realize who her parents are? Don't you read the magazines? Here— here, look." Cassie dug out a copy of *Time* she had saved since the fall and started flipping the pages. "Baron Guy de Ginsburgh is in banking. I mean, he *owns* banks all over the world. The baroness is one of the most beautiful women in Europe—her photographs are everywhere, like Jackie Kennedy. Do you really think they're sitting around worrying about a sweater?"

Blue was working to control herself. Without a word, she took the magazine that Cassie thrust in front of her and disappeared with it down the stairs to the living room. She found a cigarette and sat down to read.

It was an article about Baron Guy de Ginsburgh, of the illustrious French banking family. He had recently accepted a position as consultant to the World Bank and had brought his family to live with him in Washington for a year. Blue skimmed quickly over the details, and her eyes came to rest on the photographs that accompanied the story. One was of a fourteenth-century château in Epernay, the baron's ancestral home. Another was of the de Ginsburghs, mother, father, and daughter, grouped in a rather formal pose in front of a massive stone fireplace. The mother and daughter were seated on a small sofa; the father stood behind. The baron was obviously a good deal older than his wife, and looked as if he could have been the girl's grandfather. He was, however, handsome and distinguished looking, like that French movie actor whose name Blue couldn't remember. The woman was very fair and had that kind of sculptured face that always photographed well. The girl, Dahlia, sat stiffly, looking straight at the camera. She was breathtakingly beautiful. But the photograph that held Blue's attention the longest was of the mother, "Baroness Camilla Baring de Ginsburgh," the caption read, "arriving at La Maisonette for lunch." Blue studied the image. It was one thing to see pictures of movie stars and celebrities, but quite another, she thought, when there was, well, a connection. She *was* very beautiful, and expensively dressed in a gold-trimmed white Chanel suit, but it was the expression on her face that intrigued. It was so completely oblivious to the photographer and to the attention she was getting from the bystanders. Oblivious and profoundly bored.

Blue sighed. She didn't at all like the way she was feeling—a little jealous, a little dowdy, a little threatened, and very confused. Clearly, Cassie and this girl were becoming good friends, and for that Blue was happy. Cassie needed a friend; she had always kept too much to herself. But what would this friendship mean? The world of the rich was not an easy one to enter—if there was one thing Blue knew about, it was that. Cassie was sure to be disappointed, even hurt. She could never keep up with a girl like Dahlia de Ginsburgh, a girl who had everything, a girl who could order what she liked from an expensive catalogue and then give it away.

"These pictures make your friend's family look very glamorous. Don't they mind being photographed and written about?" Blue looked up as Cassie came to sit beside her.

"I don't know . . . I think the baron might. Dahlia says he's very private. But you know," Cassie laughed, "Dahlia only minds because it's her mother that gets written about all the time . . . she'd much rather it was she."

"Well, she is a pretty little thing, isn't she? I think she

looks a bit like Audrey Hepburn . . . those big eyes in that small face, and that long neck—"

"Great! I'll have to remember to tell her that. She'd love you for it."

"Well, you know, honey, I think you should invite your friend home with you for your next vacation. I bet she'd just love a bit of plain, ordinary family life." Blue was all smiles, warming to this idea. "We could have some real good times together . . ."

Cassie quickly agreed, anxious to preserve the peace. Easter was a long way off, and something would surely come up . . . Her mind reeled as she tried to imagine sophisticated, glamorous Dahlia de Ginsburgh coming to visit. What on earth would they do? Go bowling with her mother's bowling team?

Chapter 3

IT MAY, PERHAPS, have been through no fault of her own, but the simple fact was that Dahlia de Ginsburgh had not the slightest idea what it meant to be without money. Every Saturday morning at school she routinely tucked an alarming number of fifty-dollar bills into her pocket and set off for the tiny town of Greenville for shopping. In the afternoon she would stagger back under a mountain of parcels. The fault, if any, lay in her generosity. Dahlia's gift-giving had embarrassed Cassie at first; indeed, it always did, but Cassie soon learned that once Dahlia had made up her mind to do something, it was as good as done; and there was no talking her out of it.

Cassie had never seen anyone as excited or happy as Dahlia had been giving the sweater. She had jumped up and down, clapping her hands. "I just knew it would be perfect for you. Do you like it? Really like it?" Cassie was speechless. It was the most beautiful thing she had ever owned in her life.

The blue of the wool and the blue of her eyes matched perfectly, and her hair was positively golden against it. All her life she had thought of herself as an ugly duckling. "Four eyes," other children had called her, "bean pole." But Dahlia dismissed her insecurities with a wave of the hand. "But, darling," she said, and Cassie had never heard the word sound so right from anyone but a movie star, "darling, you're perfect. Thin. You can't be too thin. Tall. You can't be too tall. Or blond. You can never be too blond. All you need are a few tiny touches of makeup here and there. Let me show you." And she had. Dahlia transformed her.

Through Dahlia, Cassie felt as if she were awakening from a long sleep—awaking to her own potential, her own beauty, and all that the world had to offer. Dahlia, with all her worldliness and sophistication, was central to it all, but it had started the year before, Cassie remembered, smiling, with Candy and the blow-job.

If Cassie was even now a bit on the prim side, she had been a thoroughgoing prig in her junior year. A scholarship student and fiercely determined obeyer of rules, she had considered it her duty to remind transgressors of their responsibilities, and on a few occasions her own sense of responsibility had included the reporting of various misdoings to Miss Jefferson, the headmistress.

Straight-A, straight-arrow Cassie prompted Miss Jefferson to pair Cassie as roommate with a girl named Candy Lescaux. Candy was a senator's daughter with the sluttish good looks and matching character to give any headmistress a bad case of insomnia. The year, a trying one for both girls, had produced a kind of nervous détente. Candy continued to indulge in a precocious sexual career, and Cassie, with equal effort, learned to ignore it.

All that changed on the eve of final examinations, when Cassie returned late to her dorm from the library. In the glare of the bedroom light, Candy and a young man of African ancestry were creating a most unusual profile and, incidentally, affording Cassie her first glimpse of an erect penis.

Under the circumstances, one might have expected Candy, in alarm, to have ceased; the young man, out of embarrassment, to have subsided; and Cassie, given her reputation, to have screamed and run for help. None of that happened.

The young man, though startled, was in such a state of urgency that he promptly grabbed Candy's ears as if to remind her that there was work as yet undone. Candy, looking up and engaging Cassie's eye, seemed to shrug, "What the hell," before applying herself to the task. Cassie's ears burned, her eyes bugged, but she remained firmly rooted to the spot and watched. And when it was over, and the boy left without so much as an awkward good-bye, Cassie quietly said, "Don't worry," and, feeling oddly pleased with herself and somehow subtly changed, she went directly to sleep.

Though Cassie never said a word about Candy's indiscretions, nevertheless Candy failed to return to the Bennett Academy in the fall. And so it was that Miss Jefferson announced to her that she would be rooming with Dahlia de Ginsburgh, daughter of *the* de Ginsburghs, and for once Cassie had been on the verge of rebellion. Senior honor students had first chance at the small number of single dorm rooms, and Cassie had been determined to have one to herself. She was fed up with serving as a good example to spoiled princesses, and she wouldn't have it.

Nevertheless, three weeks later Cassie stood, her mouth slightly agape, and watched a never-ending procession of Hermès luggage arrive in her room. Outside a silver Rolls-Royce sat parked in the drive complete with Maurice, the quintessential French chauffeur, his Gallic disdain and fussiness honed to a fine degree. In the midst of this, and apparently totally unaware that her arrival was anything but normal, came one of the prettiest girls Cassie had ever seen.

They spent their first night as roommates making small talk and sizing each other up. Dahlia unpacked. Cassie longed for a cigarette, a vice she had picked up over the summer and which she indulged in furtively and illegally in her room alone.

Suddenly, Dahlia dipped down deep into her trunk, announcing that what was needed was a picnic.

"A picnic?" Cassie raised her brows. "Uh . . . well, you see this is actually the study period and we're not allowed out of our rooms until the ten-o'clock bell. And even then we're not allowed outside at all. Besides, it's awfully cold and, uh . . . well, maybe we could plan a picnic over the weekend."

"Of course we can't go outside. What a revolting thought. No, I'll show you what I mean." In minutes, a silk blanket was spread on the floor and candles were produced as if by magic from her voluminous trunk. The lights were turned out. In the middle of the silken spread stood a bottle of red wine and a huge bag of Wise potato chips. Cassie watched with fascination as Dahlia carefully removed the heavy foil from around the neck of the bottle and expertly decorked it. They had to use their simple water tumblers, but Dahlia rinsed and dried each one before pouring out the wine.

"First, inhale," she said, bringing the glass to her nose. "I think this is the one that smells like violets in about ten minutes. Anyway..." She raised her glass and looked directly into Cassie's eyes, "Here's to...decadence!"

Cassie said nothing but raised her glass to clink it gently against Dahlia's. Just a few minutes before, she had been ready to put a stop to all this. A picnic, indeed! This girl was crazy...But there was also something about her enthusiasm that was hard to resist. In fact, much to Cassie's surprise, she didn't want to resist, and, feeling reckless as anything, she took a small sip.

She had never really liked drinking wine—it made her mouth pucker and her stomach upset—but she knew immediately that she had never tasted anything like this before. She sipped again and again, trying to identify the soft, velvety taste. There were no violets, but it no longer seemed insane to look for them.

"Do you like it?" Dahlia asked, almost shyly. "It's about as old as we are. Papa thinks that only the finest wines should pass a young girl's lips. I think he enjoys choosing for me even more than for himself."

Years later, Cassie found that she agreed with Baron Guy de Ginsburgh. In the best of all possible worlds, every young girl's introduction to wine should be the Château Petrus 1953 that they drank that night.

Cassie smiled now, remembering Dahlia's bright, chirpy voice exclaiming, "But of course, you must smoke!" when Cassie, emboldened by the wine, had asked if she minded. "I love smoking," Dahlia prattled on. "It's so...so pointless. It makes one look so, well, occupied, don't you think?"

She hopped up and was again rummaging through her trunk. "I wish I could smoke. I've tried dozens and dozens of times, but I can't. It makes me go all purple, coughing and choking. Here, you should have this." She held out what looked like a short, expensive pen, enameled in a deep burgundy color. "Go on," she commanded, "take it! I can't possibly use it." She flicked the top, and a small flame appeared. "Someone who really smokes should have a pretty lighter."

Cassie didn't know what to think. She lit her cigarette and examined the lighter closely. "This is beautiful, Dahlia. I've never seen anything like it."

"It is pretty, isn't it? My mother bought two dozen of them back from . . . somewhere, and set one at each place for a dinner party she was giving. I sneaked down afterward and nicked one for myself. But now you must have it as a favor for my party."

Cassie looked at this strange girl in the flickering candlelight. She felt giddy from the wine. She was drunk with a kind of excitement that was totally new to her. Never had she met a girl so eager to please, so childish in her friendliness, and yet so arrogant and aristocratic at the same time. She was beautiful, with a kind of delicacy that made ordinarily pretty girls look coarse by comparison. Certainly, Cassie felt gross beside this five-foot-two-inch princess whose thick braid of honey-colored hair fell to well below her knees. Rapunzel, Cassie thought, but clearly a Rapunzel who had never been locked away in an ivory tower. She was enthralled. Had she been a boy, she would surely have fallen in love.

"You know," she said, sipping more of the delicious wine, "I think we've broken about enough rules tonight to get us thrown out of here six times over."

"Oh good," Dahlia nodded, stuffing potato chips in her mouth, "I love living on the edge. Here." She generously poured the last of the wine into Cassie's glass. "Now, tell me, are you still a virgin?"

Chapter 4

DAHLIA WAS EXTREMELY pleased with herself. So far the holiday had been perfect, even cozy. She had not missed the endless parade of aunts, uncles, cousins, and other more remote relatives, and she had certainly not missed the cold English country houses or the boring village in France where there was nothing but nothing to do.

She liked the hustle and bustle of M Street and Wisconsin. She liked the radio stations, and she liked pizza, hamburgers, milkshakes, and best of all, french fries. Even Maurice, her father's valet cum chauffeur, liked to go with her to Fat Boys for the fries. She knew her father liked America. The brisk pace and informality suited him, he said. The Baron Guy de Ginsburgh, a true aristocrat, a skillful and successful banker, and an old-world diplomat found American politics, particularly as they were played out in Washington, extremely amusing. "They are like eager children," he'd confided to his wife, "some are greedy and ambitious, some are truly altruistic and concerned with doing good, but all are quite touchingly naive."

The Baroness Camilla Baring de Ginsburgh did not share either her husband's interest in American business and politics nor her daughter's fascination with the more popular aspects of American culture. As far as Camilla was concerned there were only two civilized places in America— New York City and Palm Beach. However, when it had become clear to her that a year in Washington was unavoidable, Camilla graciously took charge of the move. From her suite at the Carlyle she telephoned a "few special friends" and set them scurrying to find a suitable house in

Georgetown. She rejected various residences over the telephone and only ventured south when she was sure the right house had been found. Dahlia, who was supposed to start school weeks earlier, was held hostage by her mother. "Darling, you can't leave me now," she'd told a completely agreeable Dahlia. "Surely your school can wait a few more days. I have heard," Camilla confided in her most gossipy voice, "that American children are very slow."

The house was originally built to house the ambassador from Imperial Russia, but Camilla rushed through it shuddering and declaring each room more ghastly than the last. Then, telling the agent to arrange things with her lawyer, she called Billy Baldwin from the airport. "It's too awful— dark, gloomy rooms . . . red velvet . . . I can't go on. Imagine the worst. You've simply got to help me . . . You can? How kind . . . You know just what I like. White, ivory, magnolia . . . Yes, that's it. And something pretty for Dahlia. I'll leave it all in your hands and will ring you from Bangkok in a few weeks, just to see how you're getting on."

Camilla returned in early December. "We'll stay put for the holidays," she told Dahlia over the telephone. "Your father is exhausted and so am I, and anyway I have a wonderful surprise. Charlotte is joining us . . . yes, darling. I promise. She's in New York setting up her show at the Museum of Modern Art. She's free until the fifteenth."

This was the rarest of treats. Her mother and father both at home, and Charlotte—even Charlotte arriving mid-week.

It wasn't until late Wednesday, after a last-minute dash for Christmas gifts, that Dahlia returned to find Charlotte upstairs, conversing idly with Camilla. "Hullo, kitten," Charlotte hugged her, kissed her, tweaked her braid, and kissed her again. "Happy Christmas."

Camilla's bedroom, whether at Epernay, Membland, or now in Washington, was always the best room in the house. The soft, pale colors; the deep, cushioned furniture; the ever-present scent of freesias—all arranged like a stage setting for Camilla. Dahlia loved her mother's room, even though she felt obscured by it. Often she went there when

Camilla was away just to walk among her things, touch her possessions, imagine herself the mistress of the room. But even without the physical presence of Camilla herself, the room always belonged to her and Dahlia felt herself a trespasser.

Only Charlotte seemed unaware of the spell of the fragrant bedroom, and now Dahlia curled up contentedly next to her on the floor.

"Well, now, I've been hearing the most awful rumors about you," Charlotte teased. "They say you've reformed, given up your wild and woolly ways, that you're doing well in school . . . Is this true? Is this your uniform?"

Dahlia leaped up to show off her orange tights, white boots, and purple mini-skirt.

"Dahlia, do stop," Camilla held her fingers to her temple. "Where *did* you get that costume? You look like one of those hippies. Now do stand still so I can look at you."

Dahlia stood as still as a wooden Indian and submitted to her mother's scrutiny.

"The clothes must go, of course." Camilla's voice was firm. "But really, it's the hair. Definitely the hair. Wouldn't you say so, Charlotte?"

"Well, yes, the hair must go." Charlotte squinted at Dahlia, who was crossing her eyes in the manner of a village idiot. "But why take half measures? Off with her head, while we're at it."

Camilla ignored this and reached out, gently lifting Dahlia's heavy honey-colored braid. "Yes, I think a cut to just below the shoulders . . . long enough to play with, short enough to control." She let the braid drop and then, ever so gently, trailed her open palm across Dahlia's brow and cheek.

Dahlia thrilled to the soft touch. Caresses from Camilla were rare and fleeting, for she was not a hugging and kissing sort of mother. She rarely seemed to touch anyone or anything.

Dahlia turned back to Charlotte, who was trying, unsuccessfully, to blow a smoke ring. She couldn't remember a time when she had ever seen Charlotte in the winter. Charlotte was summer. Summers and Membland, her mother's house in Kent. Lazy warm days, the house filled with amusing people. Swimming, picnics, croquet tournaments, sailing. Camilla was happiest there, her restlessness gone, her hauteur and reserve relaxed. She was almost gay. And every summer, Charlotte Soames came, from Italy or Spain, or New York or wherever she had spent the winter painting the portraits that had made her famous. It had always been the best of times, the happiest and silliest times when Charlotte came.

But summers always came to an end, and then trunks were packed and itineraries were discussed. The house was shuttered and the furniture shrouded. Dahlia would be sent back to school; Camilla would return to the apartments in Paris or the château in Epernay, and Charlotte to her winter studio. That was why it was so special to have Charlotte here for Christmas. Dahlia couldn't possibly have wished for anything better.

"Haven't you mastered that yet? You should meet Cassie. She can blow a smoke ring inside a ring."

"Can she?"

"You will meet her, too. If you're staying, that is. You're staying, aren't you, Charlotte? For the entire holiday . . . ?"

"Dahlia, please." Camilla and Charlotte exchanged a brief glance. "Don't be tedious, darling. Charlotte's only just arrived, and I'm sure could do without this badgering."

"Relax, kitten." Charlotte winked at Dahlia. "I'll be here so long you'll get bored with me."

That had been a week ago, and so far the holiday had been splendid. Only now that Christmas was all but over, Dahlia could hardly wait for Cassie to come. She had always wanted a friend like Cassie, a truly best friend, someone just as important to her as Charlotte was to her mother.

Cassie was an unusual experience for Dahlia. At all the other schools she had been to, the girls had been just like her. Rich girls with rich parents and rich lives. But Cassie was poor, and Dahlia had a very romantic notion of poor.

Forced into difficult circumstance by the whim of fate, Cassie was just like the heroine of a nineteenth-century novel. Dahlia lost no time in casting herself in the role of benefactress, and it pleased her more than she could say to treat Cassie to some of the nicer things in life. Charlotte had been poor, too. A struggling, unknown artist on the Left Bank of Paris until she had painted the young Camilla Baring and got all famous. Well, Dahlia concluded, Cassie needed the same sort of help, and for starters this holiday in Washington was going to be the best time Cassie had ever had. Dahlia would see to it.

Chapter 5

PROMPTLY AT THREE o'clock, Cassie and her mother started up the long drive to the big house that overlooked their cottage as well as most of the town. Rhododendrons, tall as trees, lined the way, and the silence was broken only by the *click-clack* of Blue's high heels. The house, as it came into view, was not inviting. Like the Littons themselves, it was stiff and austere, a great red brick rectangle embellished with heavy Victorian balustrades.

Easily the most prominent family in the State of North Carolina, the Littons had been prosperous planters from the very earliest colonial times, cannily emerging from the debacle of the Civil War as even wealthier industrialists, owners and operators of more than half the cotton mills in the state, major investors in a wide and varied number of carefully chosen enterprises.

"Well, here we go again. Go ahead, you knock." Blue and her daughter stood for a moment grinning at each other. It was not the first time they had made a pretense of indecision at the doorstep, as if they might spontaneously just turn around and race back home. For years, the heavy brass knocker high up on the door had been their measuring stick for Cassie's growth. But now the door was opening, and there stood old Sam, as plump and bald and black as ever, smiling his warmest welcome.

"Miz Litton, Miz Cassie. Come in, come in. Merry Christmas."

"Merry Christmas to you, Sam." Cassie smiled with sincere pleasure. Sam and his wife Sarah, who did the cooking, had been working for the Littons since before Cassie was born. They were quiet, dignified, and deeply religious people. Winthrop Litton had a jest, of sorts, which he repeated with tedious regularity. "Did you pray for me today, Sam?" he would ask. "I could sure use it." And Sam would unfailingly answer, "Yes, sir, I did. I prayed a good prayer for you." Then Winthrop would give a hearty laugh and wink to his white audience. Oh, what a good joke, the wink said—imagine, the prayers of a black servant for Winthrop Litton.

Cassie knew a secret about Uncle Winthrop though. Sarah had told it to her one day when she was sitting in the kitchen waiting for Blue to pick her up. Sarah's sister Lottie had just died. Lottie had nursed Winthrop when he was a boy and stayed on long after. Even when she had gotten very old and not quite right in her mind, Winthrop had kept her on in the house, giving her all the care she needed. Sarah was full of the funeral that day, telling Cassie all the details. But the part that had embedded itself in her memory had come when Sarah lowered her voice to tell her that, "Mistah Win, he sat to the back of the church for the preachin' and then he drove all the way out to Wayne's Corner, where we laid her to rest. You know, honey, that man just stood by Lottie's grave for the longest time, then his face kinda puckered up... an' he started to cry. He looked like a little boy ... real hurt, like he was lost..."

Cassie had studied her uncle ever since, trying to imagine him crying at Lottie's grave, but she could never see it. He went on, though, making as many jokes about Negroes as he could. Not cruel jokes, exactly; he was just determined to get his good laugh out of them.

Sam took their coats now. "Miz Cassie, you all grown up. Yes, ma'am, if you don't look the image of Mistah Bobby. Ain't that right, Miz Litton?"

Blue smiled in agreement and her eyes misted over.

"Thank you, Sam. I feel grown up." Cassie tried to cover up for her mother. "Please tell Sarah I'll come see her after dinner."

Sam led them down the hall to the big room that was

still called the library though all the books had been removed years ago.

A large Christmas tree in the corner was covered with lacy angels, and assorted family members stood around, holding drinks and eyeing the brightly wrapped packages.

"Merry Christmas. Merry Christmas," Lucille greeted them. "Blue, honey, don't you look nice in that pretty paisley. I've loved it for years. And Cassie—look at you! Win! Oh, Win. Would you come look at your niece. She's as pretty as a picture!"

Winthrop, in his favorite role as jovial host, greeted them heartily and steered them deftly to the bar.

"What'll it be, Blue? Bourbon, right? Egg nog's for children and invalids."

Cassie suppressed a groan as he filled a silver julep cup to the brim with liquor. Her mother always drank too much at these gatherings, and with each drink her laugh became louder, her good cheer more forced.

"Come get some egg nog, Cass darlin'," Winthrop boomed.

Many greetings and kisses were exchanged. The women all looked beautiful; the men all looked fit as well-to-do fiddles, and the children, my, how they'd grown. Well, thought Cassie, here they all were, gathered for yet another Christmas, high on the hill, high on the hog, and most of them just plain high. She watched the chattering group and spotted her mother, smiling, smoking, pretending.

Was everyone pretending? The two brats, Allison and Tommy, should have been happy. God knows, there were enough toys around to brighten the faces of every urchin in all of Dickens, yet there they were, already fighting over who would play with what. Their father, Hoyt, was over by the bar with the men, of course, talking horses and sports. Hoyt was certainly the ideal Litton son-in-law—tall, fair, good-looking; he was an odds-on favorite to take over the helm of Litton Manufacturing one day. Peachie, his wife, sat talking to Blue, interrupting herself from time to time to hush her squalling children. Poor, fat, silly Peachie. She had gone to the best schools, worn the best clothes, attended the best dances, and all for what? Twenty-two years old and her life was over. Cassie could hear her now. "We went to see that movie th'other night, that Bonnie and Clyde thing . . . Hush, Allison! You may not! The idea! Well, I wanted to ask for my money back 'cause I couldn't look at most of it anyhow. It was that bloody. Ask Hoyt. Hoyt, honey, didn't they blow her brains clear out of her skull at the end of that movie?"

Blue clucked, and Rosa Litton turned pale. Greyson and Rosa were not much interested in anything but horses—and at that only the horses they raised themselves on their farm. Of course Rosa was always good on diseases: "I never go to films anymore. You know these color films, they send out rays . . . some kind of electromagnetic thing . . . well, these rays penetrate your skin. If you get enough of them, they give you cancer!"

Just when Cassie was thinking she might have to ask for a bourbon, Granny Litton appeared in the doorway.

This was the time-honored signal that dinner was about to be served. Augusta Litton never joined the family for cocktails—she did not drink and she detested smoking. She stood now just inside the double doors—a tall, elegant old lady, wearing her thick white hair in a braid on top of her head like a coronet. Cassie had never seen her with her hair down, nor had she ever seen her in anything other than the black silk crepe dresses she had worn since her husband's death in 1940. No one had any doubt that this ageless, graceful woman was the matriarch of the Litton clan.

Drinks were put down, cigarettes extinguished, and everyone rose to greet and be greeted by their hostess. It is amazing, thought Cassie, how everyone pulls themselves together and acts almost dignified in Granny's presence. Even the brats had stopped their squabbling and looked angelic while Granny patted their heads. Blue and Cassie stood back, waiting their turn.

"I always feel like she's going to ask me if my ears are clean," Blue whispered, while Cassie blushed and felt her hard-won detachment start to slip away. Her mother had managed to down two stiff bourbons and was already not a little tipsy. But, although her cheeks were flushed and her voice a touch too loud, Blue greeted her mother-in-law with fair dignity.

Granny murmured an acknowledgment and turned to Cassie. "Come here, child. Let me look at you." The old woman surveyed her granddaughter carefully, and her blue eyes softened with approval. "How nice you look. That color is very becoming. I dare say you are prettier every time I see you."

"Isn't she?" Blue burst in, unable to keep herself in check. "Can you believe how tall she's gotten? I told her..." Blue's hand was busy tugging away at the hem of Cassie's sweater, "I said, honey, if you dare grow another inch, I'm going to pack you off to live with the Amazons!" She let out a hoot of laughter. Cassie wished heartily that the earth would open up and swallow the entire State of North Carolina.

"Yes." Granny Litton did not look at Blue. "The Littons are tall. Well now, we mustn't keep dinner waiting. You may take my arm, Cassandra." But Augusta Litton detained her granddaughter a moment longer. "I want to have a talk with you after dinner, my dear," she said. "Please don't make any plans. Sam will come for you when I'm ready. Now, let's join the others."

The Littons' Christmas dinner was much like other well-heeled Christmas dinners all over America. Silver sparkled, candles gleamed, Granny said grace, Winthrop carved, Sam served. Everyone praised the food. Blue tossed back her wine. Sarah was brought in to be thanked. Hoyt pinched Cassie's knee under the table. Greyson told a long, pointless story about a man who had worn the wrong boots at the last hunt. The children kept a careful eye on Granny Litton and, when she wasn't looking, played a game called show, which had to do with stuffing the mouth with food and at just the opportune moment showing as much partially chewed mess as possible. Cassie felt sick.

At last the pies, pecan and pumpkin, were brought out, and everyone had a little piece of each. When coffee appeared, Augusta Litton wished everyone well and excused herself. Once again, the gathering was transformed. Chairs were shuffled around, the air hung thick with smoke, children raced madly around the room, and the talk became louder and looser. Cassie waited nervously to be called upstairs.

Chapter 6

THE BARON GUY DE GINSBURGH stood on the stairs looking down through the wide, mirrored hall of the house in Georgetown. The two women sitting on either side of the green felt backgammon table had not yet heard him come down. He saw them as statues—his wife, delicate and pale, her ash-blond hair swept high away from the finely chiseled features. Opposite her, the remarkable contrasting face of her gaming partner, whose short, dark hair framed an angular jaw and wide-set almond-shaped eyes. To his view they made a design, the faces profile upon profile, the heads blond and dark, the erect yet vaguely lounging bodies, the hands moving in sure but unhurried motions over the board. Behind and around them the lights from the Christmas tree and the fire burning low in the grate bathed the room in a warm glow that rendered him immobile, almost as if he were viewing a priceless painting. Then, suddenly, Charlotte Soames moved a red piece several spaces and removed a white one. This evidently pleased her, and she looked up to grin at her opponent. Camilla grimaced slightly and then shrugged in a gesture of friendly defeat. The stillness of the *tableau vivant* was broken, and the baron quickly descended and entered the room.

"There you are, de Ginsburgh," Camilla leaned back in her chair, her long, slim fingers passing lightly over her eyes. "Have you been on the telephone all this time?"

"Yes. I am sorry to say I have." The baron crossed to the silver tray holding a selection of liqueurs and brandies. He poured himself a cognac and then rather absently asked if Dahlia was in for the evening.

"Yes, darling. She came in hours ago. She seems to have gone to bed."

Charlotte lit a cigarette. "What is it, Guy? Bad news?"

"Unfortunately so. There appears to be a rather messy situation brewing. I must leave for the Netherlands in the morning—a meeting of the executive council at the Hague. Then it's back to Africa, I'm afraid."

"Africa! You can't be serious. You were just there in October. Can't they manage without you this once?"

"I wish they could, my dear. How I wish they could. But distressing facts have come to light and it's important that I see to them."

Camilla sighed and stifled a yawn. "I can't imagine why these ridiculous countries all go rushing about clamoring for independence when they can't even remotely manage their own affairs and must come crying to you to bail them out!"

The baron smiled indulgently at his wife. "I should have anticipated that there would be problems. But let us hope for the best and the quickest solution. My greatest regret is that I am leaving you. We'd have done better to plan our holiday in Palm Beach after all. At least you would have had the sun."

"Don't give us a thought, darling. One way or another we're sure to survive this barren outpost." Camilla rose languidly and crossed to stand beside her husband. Her long, slim hand brushed his cheek lightly and came to rest, like a fine, exotic bird, upon his shoulder. "Do you have any idea when you'll be returning?"

"No. None whatever. But, of course, I'll cable as soon as I know something definite. Could you ask Maurice to see to my clothes?" The baron took his wife's hand tenderly and turned it to kiss the inside of her palm. It was a gesture at once submissive and masterly, and it conveyed a total sense of love and devotion. Camilla accepted her husband's tribute by leaning toward him and pressing her cheek to his. "I'll go supervise the packing myself."

Both Charlotte and the baron watched her drift gracefully

out of the room. They remained silent, listening to the soft rustle of Camilla's gown as she went up the stairs, the crackling fire in the hearth, and the distant chimes of the cathedral.

Finally, Charlotte spoke, looking at the baron with a sharp gimlet eye, "Forgive me, Guy, but is this really necessary? Surely even an important banker might be allowed to enjoy Christmas with his family. Dahlia will be very disappointed, and I know how much Camilla counted on arranging this cozy *en famille* holiday."

The baron regarded her affectionately. "Ah, Charlotte, whatever would we do without you? You're a marvel! You remind me of a fierce lioness protecting her brood. Unfortunately, circumstances are sufficiently serious that I have no other choice. Still—"

"Still, it's damned exciting and you can't tell me that you're not actually looking forward to getting over there and pulling off some major coup. I'll join you in a cognac, Guy."

The baron laughed. "Charlotte, I'm afraid you know me only too well. Frankly, I've been prepared for this development for some time. I'd only hoped we'd be able to get through the holidays before . . . well . . . before events took the turn they did." He handed her a crystal brandy snifter, a slight conspiratorial smile playing on his lips. "And now that you know my little secret, you can do me a great favor."

"Oh?"

"I know Washington is dull for Camilla, and for you, too, I think. Now that Christmas is over, I can see no reason why you must stay. Muriel Whitney rang me last week to say her house in Hawaii was free, and part of that long telephone conference just now was to make arrangements for you three ladies to fly there tomorrow night. You can stay as long as you like, and Dahlia can come back after the New Year. What do you say, eh?"

"Guy! What a splendid plan. I don't have to be back in New York until the fifteenth. And I was beginning to think I would never see the sun again. You *are* thoughtful. And you have always been more than generous..."

"Tut, tut!" the baron raised his finger to his lips to stop her. "That is a subject where we can only disagree. In truth, I consider myself to be the most selfish of men. I have denied myself nothing in the way of luxuries. I allowed myself the privilege of marriage and paternity and yet I always knew I would never be fully able to fulfill the obligations and responsibilities that are a part of these joys. I know full well that the notion of public service, yes, even the notion of *noblesse oblige*, have an archaic, almost comical connotation today. And yet, you see, that is what I was born to do. I have it in my blood and in my genes, and always my first obligation is toward the world in which I live, in which I have the competence and knowledge to effect some change, some tiny increment toward the common good.

"Perhaps I never should have married, but in all truth, I could not have denied myself the pleasures of being even such a poor husband and father as I have been. And I have never for a single moment lost sight, dear Charlotte, of how much I owe to you for all the happiness that I possess. So do not speak of generosity to me."

They were silent for several moments, and then the baron raised his glass to Charlotte in an unspoken toast. "Then may I count on you to see to it that all goes as planned tomorrow? I've arranged for a car to meet you at Waikiki. From there you may take a private plane whenever you like. Muriel has left the house fully staffed, and she has arranged for an authentic luau for New Year's Eve. Otherwise it will probably be fairly quiet. Dahlia may miss her young friends—"

"Now, Guy, if you're going to leave everything to me, then don't start worrying about Dahlia. She'll probably be doing cartwheels. I've never known a child so feet first and ready for action." Charlotte stubbed out her cigarette. "Come play billiards with me, Guy. It will sharpen those killer instincts you'll need tomorrow."

They went through the double doors into the billiards room. Charlotte kicked off her shoes and rubbed her hands together gleefully. The baron lit a cigar. "Ah, yes. A killer game."

The cigar smoke, the amiable chatter, the pleasant *click-clack* of the billiard balls continued late into the night.

Chapter 7

CASSIE SAT QUIETLY on her grandmother's green velvet sofa. It was, she knew, a rare distinction to be invited here. She had always felt a kind of magic in these rooms, as if she were stepping into another time that had nothing to do with the room downstairs. The last bit of afternoon light filled the room with a warm glow, and Cassie's ears hummed with the quiet. Her grandmother's pen scratching across the paper and the ticking of the Seth Thomas clock in the corner were the only sounds. She remembered trying to describe the room to her mother, and, having just read the phrase in Dickens, she'd called it a place "untouched by time."

"You mean untouched by money," Blue had retorted, dismissing Cassie's romantic notion. "Why that woman would rather die, and I do mean lie down in her grave, than spend a nickel updating herself. Just look at her! Where on earth do you suppose she finds those clothes?"

Cassie had let it pass, but she didn't agree. Secretly and timidly, she admired her grandmother. She thought now what a comfort it was that no matter what changed, what upheavals took place in the world outside, they would have no effect on this room or on the stern decorum of her lovely old grandmother. Cassie loved the old polished furniture, the ever-present scent of violets and verbena, the fussy but beautifully embroidered pillows, the gallery of photographs—each in its elaborate gold or silver frame—that stood lovingly arranged on the marble table by the window. Here, among others, were pictures of her father. Bobby: a grinning baby in a pram; a young boy in short pants and funny sandals, hugging a golden retriever; a schoolboy in uniform; Bobby in white tie; in a convertible; Bobby and Winthrop wearing black arm bands in front of the Litton building . . .

"Well now, that's done." Granny got up from her desk and came to sit in a chair facing her granddaughter, looking at her silently for a long time. Cassie smiled, looked up, looked down, smiled again, and would have fidgeted had she dared. Finally, Granny sighed, "Forgive me, I didn't mean to make you uncomfortable. I'm afraid I fell into a reverie . . . easy to do at my age." She raised a hand to stop Cassie's remonstrances. "I was thinking, my dear, how very much you look like your father . . . However . . ." She had collected herself and was now all business. "There is something very specific I want to discuss with you. You're quite grown up now, and I must say that I am very pleased with the way you've turned out."

Cassie was silent, feeling somewhat like a potted plant that has bloomed after all.

"I understand that you will soon be completing your studies at the Bennett Academy, and that your performance there has been excellent. I'm very proud of you. I'm glad to see that you have a good head on your shoulders and that you haven't taken up the frivolous notions of young people today."

Cassie murmured a modest thank you and wished she could smoke a cigarette.

"Therefore," Granny continued, "I've been thinking about what I can best do for you now that you're a grown girl."

Cassie was all attention now. There *was* something Granny could do—something very important, something very necessary. "Granny, please, there's something I want to tell—"

"Don't interrupt, dear." Granny was having none of it. "I wasn't finished." Cassie chalked up a major mistake—very few people ever interrupted Augusta Goodfellow Litton.

Having registered her disapproval, Granny went on. "I have considered a variety of possibilities, and I've finally settled on what I believe would be the most appropriate gift for your graduation." She paused. Cassie, on the edge of the sofa, waited expectantly, silently praying, Please, let it be money. Please, let it be money.

"I intend to give you a coming out. A debut. It will not be anything ostentatious, but it will be done correctly. I do not approve of excessive expenditures on the young, but it is important for a young lady to be properly presented to the society of her people. In my day this was accomplished quite simply at a tea, but it is not my day any longer. I'll be quite frank with you, my dear," she confided to a stupefied Cassie, "I did not approve of the way Winthrop executed Peachie's debut. It was quite unnecessarily vulgar. Yours will be much quieter. I've given it quite a lot of thought." Granny reached into the drawer of a nearby table and removed a small notebook. "We will start your season with a formal afternoon tea here at the house. After that there will be a series of luncheons to be sponsored by your uncle and cousins. Finally, there will be a presentation ball at the country club. I will, of course, see to your clothes, including the gown."

Cassie stared at her grandmother. She was mute with horror. A debut! Cassie Litton, debutante! It was the most ridiculous, preposterous, grotesque notion she had ever encountered. What's more, it was so unwanted—so silly, stupid, meaningless—that it quite literally took her breath away. Granny, however, took her shocked expression as one of grateful surprise. "I thought you would be pleased, my dear. I'm glad. We'll say no more about it now, but I want you to come stay here with me on your next holiday. I'm sure your mother will understand—"

"*Stop*. Please . . . just stop for a minute!" Cassie was on her feet. "Granny, this is not what I want! Oh! I'm sorry to be rude . . . I know you're trying to help me, and, believe me, I need help. But not a debut! Granny, please listen to me . . ." She made an attempt to control her emotions and went on. "I've been accepted to Smith. I want to go there. More than anything, I want to go there. But it's not like the Bennett Academy . . . I need money for tuition, for books, living ... for everything! I won't be able to go unless I get the money. Oh, I've worked so hard for this. Don't you understand that to spend all that money on parties and ball-gowns ... well, it's just ridiculous!" Her throat was making strange noises, and her knees buckled under her. Cassie had broken the two cardinal rules of being a lady and a Litton: thou shalt not make a fuss and thou shalt never, never, ask for money!

"Sit down, Cassandra, and be quiet."

Cassie sat, covered her face with her hands, and cried, not at all quietly.

"Cassandra!" Granny spoke in a voice that brooked no disobedience. "You are to march into my bedroom immediately and close the door behind you. You will find smelling salts in the medicine cabinet in my bathroom. Use them. Wash your face and do not come out again until you have taken hold of yourself."

Cassie marched.

When she emerged, some ten minutes later, she found her grandmother standing, looking at the photographs on the marble table. Cassie joined her. She picked up the picture of her father dressed in formal clothes to look at it more closely. "I've always wanted to know where he was going that night, all dressed and looking so handsome."

Granny took the picture from her and studied it. "He was handsome. My sweet, handsome Bobby." She handed the photograph back to Cassie and stared through the parted curtains into the twilight, into the past. "I remember that night very well. We were having a grand evening to celebrate Winthrop's engagement to Lucille. It was early spring, the magnolias had only just blossomed, but that night was as warm as summer. So many people came. There was a big buffet supper on the west terrace, and, oh, the music was so lovely. Your grandfather was quite ill, but he came down-stairs all the same and sat in his big chair telling all the old stories. He couldn't dance, of course, but Bobby danced with me. Oh, my dear, how we waltzed! I hadn't danced like that since I was a girl."

Once again the room was silent but for the ticking of the clock.

"You're grandfather died shortly after that." Granny sighed, pulled the curtains shut on the window, and went to sit down. Cassie followed. "We've never had a dance in the house since then. Since my husband died. Since Bobby left me . . . to marry. But . . . here you are, and all's well that ends well, isn't it?" Granny smiled a small, stern smile. "I'm sorry, Cassie, that the debut isn't what you wanted. I had looked forward to it—the planning of it. However, I'm not going to force you into something that would be quite costly of time and money and that you obviously wouldn't appreciate. I must tell you, however, that I fail to see why you wish to go north to school. The Littons have always attended schools in the south." Granny's voice conveyed in no uncertain terms that the very notion of going north was distinctly distasteful and unsavory.

"But Smith is one of the best schools in—"

"I know all about Smith, Cassandra. It is an excellent school. I am aware of that. After the holidays I will write to your headmistress. Constance Jefferson is an old acquaintance. I knew her family. If she supports this idea of yours, I will not stand in your way. If she approves, I will bow to her judgment and you shall have your tuition for Smith College."

It was all Cassie could do to keep her composure as she thanked her grandmother. Miss Jefferson would approve, all right. Miss Jefferson had been as excited as Cassie herself when the letter from Smith arrived. Indeed, Cassie was her star pupil.

Granny Litton rose from her seat. "You must forgive me, Cassie. I'm very tired." The audience was over.

She could never quite remember how she left the house and managed her way down the dark, winding drive. Perhaps her feet never touched the ground. She had the money she needed for college, and she was on her way to visit Dahlia. As she raced home she felt as if she had been touched by magic. A wonderful world lay before her.

Chapter 8

"HAWAII!" DAHLIA STOOD sleepily in the doorway of the breakfast room. "But . . . I don't want to go to Hawaii."

"Don't be silly, darling. Of course you want to go." Camilla eyed her daughter impatiently. "We've only a few hours to get ready, so hurry along with your breakfast and then pack. You needn't take many things. We can buy what we need when we get there. You'll love it, Dahlia. Muriel's house is splendid. It's perched on the side of a mountain with a view of the sea that's breathtaking."

"But, Mummy, what about Cassie? What about our plans? She'll be here tonight. I can't just ring up and tell her we're off to Hawaii."

"Yes, you can. Tell her our plans have changed. We'll have her to stay in Nassau over Easter. So much nicer than this cold, dreary Washington. She'll understand, darling. Now hurry up."

Dahlia stayed put. "I invited her weeks ago. I can't . . . I won't call her and tell her not to come. I won't! I don't want to go to Hawaii. Papa didn't understand."

"Dahlia," Camilla's voice was testy. "I don't want to hear another word. You are being childish and difficult. Papa is halfway around the world, with more important things on his mind than whether you and your friend have a visit. It's not as if Casey—"

"Cassie."

"—Cassie is coming such a long way. What possible difference could it make? If you like I will ring her mother."

"It does make a difference, and I'm not going. I don't

want to go. If you're so hot to go, then go. But I'm staying here."

"Do not speak to me in that tone of voice, Dahlia. Your manner is appalling."

"I'm old enough to stay here by myself. The servants are here. Maurice is here. You and Charlotte go. I'm old enough to take care of myself and so is Cassie."

And so it began. Like two proud divas in an operatic duel, each of them pushing her emotional range to the limit, neither willing to budge an inch. In exasperation, Camilla pulled rank and sent Dahlia to her room.

"Gladly." Dahlia huffed up the stairway, not unaware that her mother would straight-away consult with Charlotte, as she often did when Dahlia was too much to handle.

Once in her room, Dahlia quickly changed into a pair of jeans and her old school sweater. She tied her hair back in a bunch, and then glancing around at the chairs and bed strewn with clothes, she decided to tidy her room herself. She was all but finished when there was a light rap at the door.

"Come in."

Charlotte leaned at the door frame and yawned. "And your mother promised me it would be a quiet holiday."

"Please, Charlotte, you're not going to side with Mummy just because she got to you first? She's being mean and selfish and unreasonable."

"Funny, that's exactly what she just said about you. Must run in the blood."

"It's not funny. At least not to me. You and Mummy can do anything you want. You always do. But this time I don't want to be dragged along. I mean it. I'm sorry to disappoint Papa, but it will be almost the same thing if you two go. I know you want to, but I don't."

"But your father would be very unhappy if he thought we had just gone off and left you alone."

"But I won't be alone. We've been planning this holiday all term. Cassie just hates it where she is, and she's so ex-

cited about coming here. Don't you see?" Dahlia's voice
was pleading.

Charlotte came in and sat down on the bed. "Cassie
means a lot to you, doesn't she?"

"Well, yes, I guess she does. She really is my best friend
besides you."

"Why, Dahlia, what a nice thing to say."

"But it's true. You've never treated me like a child. I'm
sure you won't start now. Besides, it so happens I'm not a
child anymore. I'm almost eighteen, and next year I'll be
completely on my own. I can't possibly see why Cassie and
I can't stay here by ourselves for a week."

Charlotte stared at the ceiling in silence for a long moment. At length she said, "I see your point, I really do."
Her words were noncommittal, but the smile that followed
was enough to make Dahlia jump up and hug her. "Oh,
Charlotte, you're wonderful. If anyone can change Mummy's mind, it's you."

Charlotte laughed. "Darling, no one has ever changed
your mother's mind. But perhaps she's willing to change it
herself. We'll see."

An hour later the three of them stood in the front hall as
Maurice carried the luggage to the car. Camilla surveyed
herself in the glass. She was immaculate in a soft dove-
gray corduroy skirt and cashmere sweater. Dahlia watched
her closely, as she often did, but doubted there would be a
break in the aloof expression that had settled on her mother's
face. She had neither agreed nor disagreed with Charlotte's
elegant argument on Dahlia's behalf. She had merely, and
quite completely, removed herself from the situation.

It was a side to her mother that was as mysterious and
as exasperating as anything Dahlia had known. As a child
it had frightened her, as if her mother had gone away, leaving
in her place a blank stranger. To allay the real distress it
had caused her, Dahlia had started collecting bits and pieces
of her mother's things, hoarding them in a box. She called
it The Mother Box, and over the years it had grown from
a simple shoe container to a silk-lined miniature chest. In

it were things belonging to Camilla—mainly discarded objects: a broken Spanish comb, a torn Hermès scarf, empty scent bottles, feathers from a shooting hat. There were letters written to Dahlia from all over the world, and souvenir trinkets. Photographs, old invitations, news clippings, all carefully preserved in envelopes and thin tissue. The Mother Box had traveled faithfully with Dahlia from school to school, but she had not brought it to America. Now it was safely tucked in the deepest recesses of her closet in the bedroom at Membland.

"We won't worry about your father just now, Dahlia." Camilla was adjusting the drape of the St. Laurent cape on her shoulders. "There is no way to reach him by telephone, and I can't put it all in a cable."

Dahlia nodded.

"I'll ring you in the morning."

Silence.

"Good-bye, Dahlia."

"Good-bye, Mummy." And she was gone.

Dahlia stood alone. Her mother would never change. If she'd learned anything by now it should have been that. Damn her anyway. She wasn't going to ruin this holiday!

Charlotte had disappeared into the drawing room, and now she reappeared with a package. "It arrived this morning. A belated Christmas present."

Dahlia took the package. "It's a book. Oh, Charlotte, it's your book. The catalogue from the exhibit. It's beautiful, and it's so big." She fingered the deep-blue linen cover and the gold letters of Charlotte's name stamped on the front. "Are we all in here?"

"Oh, yes. They've selected a good number from every period. Even some very early things from the studio in Paris. You can look at it later, but I wanted you to have the very first copy." She hugged Dahlia. "You're sure about this, aren't you, baby? You're not regretting your decision?"

"I only regret you won't get to meet Cassie. You'd really like her. I know you would."

"I'm sure I will, darling. I may even break my hard and

fast rule about school fetes." Dahlia looked puzzled.

"You know. June? Daisy chains? Tea on the front lawn? All that good fun. I'll meet Cassie then. At graduation."

Charlotte winked and the heavy door closed with a decisive thud. Dahlia ran quickly up the stairs. There was so much to do. Cassie was coming tomorrow.

Chapter 9

IF CASSIE WAS disappointed to discover that the baron, baroness, and Charlotte Soames were all gone when she arrived, she was also vastly relieved. Two sleepless nights and a recurring stomachache bespoke her nervousness at the prospect of spending almost a week with Dahlia's aristocratic family. Dahlia, too, treated their absence with a cool matter-of-factness, and the friends settled in for what promised to be a lazy, hedonistic, and unsupervised holiday.

The week's serious activities had begun at Arden's, and it was there, sitting with her hair in rollers the size of beer cans, watching Dahlia with her long hair tumbling almost to the ground, that Cassie first began to notice the manic edge to Dahlia's gaiety. The stylist was hovering around Dahlia, carefully lifting thick strands of her hair and draping it one way and another, waiting, like a doubtful artist, for some inspiration. He was nervous. Dahlia was clearly "someone," and her extravagantly long and very beautiful hair had caused a sensation, so that other employees had gathered to watch what would finally be done. Dahlia herself was quiet and completely unresponsive to questions or suggestions, until suddenly her face broke into a wickedest of grins and she declared that she would have it entirely off—not shoulder length, not chin length—but short as Joan of Arc's, short as Mia Farrow's, short as Twiggy's. Moments later, when Cassie realized that Dahlia was not joking, that she was, in fact, deadly serious, she was aghast. But there was nothing to be done, and indeed, the stylist, delighted with so dramatic a decision, flew into action. In a matter of moments, Dahlia's beautiful tresses lay in heaps on the floor. Cassie was speechless and near tears.

The final effect, however, was not nearly as awful as Cassie had expected, and she had to admit that the severity of the haircut gave Dahlia's beautiful features a kind of highlighted purity and seriousness that had not been evident before. Dahlia was delighted. Over and over she ran her fingers through her short curls, tossed her head from side to side, and exclaimed that her head felt pounds lighter. "Mummy was absolutely right about getting rid of that hair. I can't wait till she sees me! Don't you think she'll be pleased?"

Cassie felt confused and more than a little uncomfortable. She hadn't the faintest idea what Camilla de Ginsburgh would or would not like. She doubted that Camilla had wanted her daughter to come out looking like a sexy Peter Pan, but on the other hand, who could tell anything about a family that . . .

It was, however, Dahlia's reckless and relentless spending that caused the first real flare-up, the first serious disagreement between the two girls. As they left Arden's, Dahlia insisted they go shopping. "We look so different." She was admiring Cassie's belled and bouffanted hair. "We've simply got to have something new and wonderful to wear." And off they went, Dahlia firmly in the lead.

They traipsed from Magnin's to Woody's—to a dozen or more smart young boutiques that seemed like outposts from Mars, with their Mylar walls and ear-splitting sound systems. They tried on everything, costuming themselves in a dozen different looks—from simple country lass to a rather decadent Barbarella—but bought nothing and returned home exhausted and happy.

It wasn't until the following morning, when the doorbells started ringing for one delivery after another, that Cassie began to smell a rat. Everything she had so much as cast a sidelong glance at, no less openly admired, was now piling up on the living room furniture.

"Dahlia, what have you done?" she asked, and by way of answer Dahlia did a ballerina's deep curtsy and smiled so broadly that in spite of Cassie's anxiety, which was mounting to the point of panic, she couldn't help being profoundly touched. Dahlia danced around the room, opening box after box, tossing sweaters, blouses, skirts, and dresses at Cassie's feet, draping them over her head and shoulders, completely ignoring the dismay that was so clearly written on Cassie face.

"I can't keep these, Dahlia. You've lost your mind." Her voice was dazed, as if she were still clinging to the faint hope that perhaps she actually could.

"Why ever not? You liked it all yesterday," Dahlia's manner was breezy. "Here put on this leather skirt—it made you look super sexy..."

"Dahlia, please, listen to me. We've got to send all this back. This must cost..." she looked around helplessly, "hundreds... maybe thousands of dollars. Who's going to pay for it? Your parents will be furious..."

"Don't be silly. They won't even notice. Anyway, I'm sure it would have cost much more to go to stupid Hawaii."

Cassie watched her friend thoughtfully. "Were you supposed to go to Hawaii? Did you stay here," she hesitated, "because of me? Oh Dahlia, did you?"

"Of course not!" Dahlia would not stand still. "Anyway, what if I did? I didn't want to go to Hawaii. We weren't supposed to go to Hawaii. We were all going to stay here ... for the holidays." She was plucking tinsel off the tree, crumpling up the strands into little silver bullets. "Don't you remember? When I invited you? The wonderful family Christmas we were going to have ... because for once, she wanted to stay put." Dahlia stared at the portrait over the fireplace—a mother, a father, a little girl—then burst out angrily, "She never stays put! And she always, always, always does exactly as she likes. Do you know, it never even occurred to her that my plans mattered? Well, fuck her, fuck Hawaii, and fuck them all! We're going to have a good time, just as *we* planned!" She flung herself onto a pile of skirts, sweaters, lingerie and glared defiantly at Cassie.

"We've still got to send all this back." Cassie's voice was gentle but firm. "It's just too much money. I could never pay you back." The minute she said it, she knew she had somehow done wrong, despite the fact that she was trying so hard, so hard that she could almost feel the weight of her virtue pressing down on her, to do right. Even so, she was shocked by Dahlia's fury.

"Oh please," her voice was hard, her gray eyes shining like polished steel, "don't start your boring little speech about money. I don't *want* you to pay me back! I thought you'd be happy to have some nice clothes for a change—" She stopped, suddenly horrified by the shocked look on Cassie's face. "Oh, damn it!" she flung a pile of boxes onto the floor, "Who gives a shit about money, anyway!"

Cassie got up. She was pale and her voice was unsteady as she struggled to control the self-righteous anger she felt, which kept being undermined by the equally strong feeling of self-pity. "I'm sorry if my clothes have embarrassed you." She sniffed and was mortified to hear herself sounding just like her mother, but she couldn't stop, "Of course I want to have nice new clothes . . . and someday, when I can pay for them, I will!" She rushed blindly out of the room but stopped in the doorway for a final burst of choking anger, "Spoiled rotten little brat!" Then the house was still with their shocked silence.

In the bedroom, Dahlia's bedroom, Cassie sprawled on the bed. A confounding number of emotions crowded in on her and left her inert and powerless to do anything but lie there occasionally hiccupping forth a small sob. She hated Dahlia, she hated herself, she hated Blue, she hated Camilla—at the same time that she knew that the leather skirt did look good on her, and, in fact, she lusted (as much as she ever had for anything or anybody in her life) for all the goodies with which Dahlia had tempted her. She felt as limp as old celery and about as principled. There was a soft knock on the door, and Dahlia came in with a bottle of brandy and two glasses.

"Here." Dahlia handed her a balloon glass half-filled with

amber liquid, "You'd better have some of this." Cassie gulped it back and felt better almost immediately as the heat spread through her body.

"Look," Dahlia sat at the edge of the bed, looking at Cassie's splotchy, swollen face, "I know I can be an awful bitch . . . and I'm sorry, but don't let's ruin everything . . ."

Cassie's eyes were swelling up again, and she could only nod her response, but she raised her glass in a salute, and both girls drank again.

"Only just one thing." Dahlia's voice was deadly serious. "Don't *ever* call me little again!"

They refilled their glasses and, pledging eternal and undying friendship in a cold and hostile world, drained them again. By the end of the third round, Cassie had agreed to keep a few of the things Dahlia had bought, and by the time they finished toasting and drinking yet another round, they were both horribly, helplessly, revoltingly sick.

Chapter 10

WHEN CASSIE WOKE up it was five o'clock in the afternoon, and it was dark outside her window. She groaned, realizing that almost two entire days of their holiday had been lost. Downstairs, she gratefully accepted the maid's offer of tea. She curled up on the sofa and stared at the flames dancing cheerfully in the fireplace.

A second cup of tea and three buttered muffins later, she noticed a large square book bound in a rich-looking blue fabric on the table beside her. It looked new, and she picked it up, wondering vaguely why it did not have a dust jacket.

Inside were pictures, reproductions of the paintings of Charlotte Soames. Cassie turned the pages over one by one, only half paying attention until a picture of a young girl, perhaps nine or ten years old, caught her eye and brought her fully awake. It was unmistakably Dahlia, and, as she studied the portrait, Cassie marveled at the talent that had captured both the impish innocence of the young girl and the beguiling beauty of the woman who would one day emerge.

"There you are. God, I'm starving." Dahlia stood in the doorway, wearing, Cassie was amused to see, Cassie's own ancient green plaid bathrobe. "What are you doing?" Dahlia stuffed the remains of a muffin in her mouth and sat on the sofa beside Cassie.

"I'm looking at you." Cassie shifted the book so her friend could see. "And wondering how a sweet girl like this could grow up to be such a—"

"Charlotte's book!" Her surprise was happy and genuine.

"I'd forgotten all about it. Oooh, let's see . . . she's awfully good, isn't she?"

"She sure is." Cassie turned the pages carefully, trying to guess at the proper speed to move on from one picture to the next. Dahlia, however, seemed content to let Cassie set the pace.

"Who's this? She looks like she's about to kill someone."

Dahlia peered at the stern face of a woman whose dark eyes seemed to burn with a lively anger. "Oh my God! That's Evangelina! She was Mummy's cook at Membland. How amazing!" Dahlia looked more closely. "You know, she did look like that . . . except I never noticed that she was, you know, like that."

Cassie gave her a puzzled look. Dahlia giggled and tried to explain. "I guess I never realized that she was, well, so *fierce*. She was just cook . . ." she ended lamely but added in a dreamy voice, "She did make the most delicious things— little flaky turnovers stuffed with cheese and spinach, little tiny meatballs in a kind of lemon gravy . . ." She groaned and jumped up, pulling Cassie with her. "Come on! If I don't get something to eat, I'm going to be sick again."

They stuffed themselves with scrambled eggs and steak, toast and fried potatoes, gallons of orange juice and Coca-Cola, and argued amiably about whether they were eating breakfast for dinner or dinner for breakfast. Then, settling back on the same sofa, they continued to peruse Charlotte's book. They were both surprised to see a youthful male nude posed like a classical statue.

"Well now," Cassie attempted a risqué note, "that's what I call good-looking. Do you know him, or did Charlotte keep him to herself?"

"Oh, no you don't!" Dahlia pulled the book onto her own lap. "I saw him first. Actually," she grinned, "he was even better-looking by the time I knew him. Although . . ."

"What?" Cassie was impatient.

Dahlia looked at the picture a minute longer and looked up at Cassie. "Well, actually, nothing happened. By the time

I knew him he was almost twenty, and, alas, I was only ten."

Cassie groaned.

"I thought I was really in love with him. I never saw him again, though . . . and after that . . . I don't know what happened to him after that."

"After what?"

"Oh, well, if you must know—"

"I must," said Cassie, "I really must."

"Well, actually, he was my first kiss," said Dahlia, "and the plain truth is it was a rather embarrassing experiment."

"Oh." Cassie, who had idly turned over another page of the book, suddenly found her attention riveted.

They had been leafing through the book from back to front, and this last picture, actually the first, was hypnotic. It was also a nude, but a woman this time, a beautiful young woman on a sofa, gazing directly into the eyes of the viewer. Cassie lacked the knowledge of technique to say why the painting was extraordinary, but she had the sensitivity to feel the power of the portrait. Long moments of silence passed as the girls studied the beautiful woman reclining so provocatively before them.

"Jeez," Cassie broke the silence. "Talk about sexy."

"That's me Mum!" Dahlia affected a carefree Cockney accent. "Yup, she's a looker, she is."

"Wow! Your mother! I guess she was pretty young. Still it must be . . ." She searched for a way to ask her question, finally settling on the straightforward. "Does it bother you? I mean, how does it feel having such a beautiful, sexy mother?"

Dahlia was all nonchalance. "I don't know," she shrugged, "I guess I'm used to her." She continued to study the portrait. "Only, it's funny. I never think of her as sexy. I sort of see what you mean here . . . but I don't think she is sexy. I mean I don't think she ever does it. I certainly can't imagine her . . . oh, well," she shut the book. "Can you imagine your mother, you know, in the throes of passion?"

"Well, no." To her surprise, Cassie found this question almost irritating. "But then for years I never had to."

"Had to?"

Cassie found she was annoyed. Not at Dahlia, though, but at the unexpected turn of events in her mother's life. "She's going out," Cassie explained brusquely, "with this guy, Bud, who runs a bowling alley. She told me, when I was home, she thought it might be getting serious. Whatever that means!"

"What do you think it means, you goose? It probably means they're sleeping together, and I, for one, say good for them!"

Cassie didn't feel that way at all, but she didn't want to talk about it, either. "I thought you were going to teach me how to shoot pool?" she demanded.

"Billiards, my dear. Billiards. Let's go."

But later, after Cassie had gone to bed, Dahlia sat by the fire, Charlotte's book opened to the portrait of the boy. Thinking of him, she could once again feel the stirrings of excitement and the longing, the wild longing for romance— and sex.

It was at Membland, the summer she turned eleven, that Dahlia had fully realized what romance, and sex, were all about. That was the summer her best friend, Carrots, had come to stay. Worldly, wise, thirteen-year-old Carrots had known all about the large, indefinable "it." "It" was what separated grown-ups from children, and "it" was something Carrots and Dahlia decided to find out more about.

Underneath the calm, organized surface life at Membland, where meals were formal, where guests never wore to tea what they had worn to breakfast, where dinner glittered with fashion and jewels in the candlelight, where everything from croquet to afternoon walks were rituals of subtlety and refinement, there teemed a life of intrigue, passion, and adventure. The two girls learned to listen when voices dropped to gossipy whispers, to watch for the slight, lingering touches that led to pointed absences, to spy in the corridors, to see who was going to be "naughty in the night" and with whom.

But the game of spying soon bored them, and Carrots decided that they, too, must "fall in love." The problem was that the boys, such as they were, seemed discouragingly unattractive, while the men were far too old and treated the little girls with the same good humor and detached affection they offered their dogs.

"Lean and mean," Carrots stated. "That's what we want. Lean, mean, and moody." Dahlia thrilled to the sound of it all.

Still, the quest seemed doomed, until one day, while eavesdropping in the pool house, two of Camilla's house guests unwittingly provided them with an inspiration.

"Have you noticed the young Adonis?"

"Hasn't everyone?"

"He seems a bit wasted in the kitchen, don't you agree?"

"Hmm. Pity you're stuck with Rex."

"Yes, but you're not stuck with anyone. Do nab him, Diana. He's frightfully good-looking and just that randy age..."

"Oh, no. Not me. This is much more your sort of thing. How on earth would I lure that cook's son into my bed?"

"Not the bedroom, silly. Charlotte's gone off to London. Why not the studio—you know, a bohemian sort of thing."

Carrots pinched Dahlia and they crept silently away. The cook's son! Yanni! It had never occurred to them to think about the servants. Well, they would take a good look at him now. And they were not disappointed. The dark-eyed, slender, solemn youth of seventeen, in his white steward's jacket, seemed the epitome of all that Carrots had envisioned. Smitten, they embarked on an absurd campaign of seduction. They rolled their eyes, giggled uncontrollably, and followed him about. They spied on him and made a nuisance of themselves in the kitchen. Evangelina, his mother, laughed and blushed, flattered by their eager attentions to her cooking, but Yanni Stavropolis ignored them completely, speaking to his mother in rapid Greek whenever they were about.

Finally, Carrots decided on another strategy. "Look," she said, "we're getting nowhere. I'm going to *make* him notice us. After all, he's only a servant, so he must do as we tell him."

"What do you mean?" Dahlia was interested.

"Watch me," Carrots tossed her head confidently.

At tea that afternoon, Lady Caroline became an imperious demanding bitch. "Yanni, I've dropped my napkin." "Yanni, I'd like another sort of biscuit." "Yanni, please close the window." "Yanni, I've left my book in the rose garden." His face flushed with anger, and Carrots nodded a triumphant look to Dahlia. After tea they followed him into the hothouse at the end of the kitchen garden, where he was cutting grapes. They watched him silently for a few minutes from behind a row of large avocado plants, and then Carrots abruptly pushed Dahlia toward him and said, "Yanni, Miss Dahlia wants you to kiss her." Laughing hysterically, she then turned and fled. Dahlia stood rooted, staring openmouthed at the angry youth. The moist hot air was heavy with the scent of fruit, and she felt her face flush and her skin prickle. Yanni said nothing but walked deliberately to her, pulling her roughly to his chest. Holding her hard, he forced his taut mouth on hers, his hands bruising her arms as his tongue harshly invaded her childish mouth. A moment later, he released her and their eyes met briefly. Fear and excitement swept over her. She touched her swollen mouth in wonder, gasped, and ran away. Moments later, her feet pounding down the path, she felt the strangest sensations between her legs, and then it was as if her body were bursting into a million little pieces. It was something Dahlia never forgot.

Chapter 11

CANDY LESCAUX ALWAYS traveled first class. Thanks to the miracle of credit, her luxurious style of living remained unaffected by annoying fluctuations in cash flow. Her daddy had given her her very own credit cards when she turned fourteen, a little starter set that she outgrew in a mere four years. After that, she used her daddy's gilded cards. A quick call to Senator Lescaux's office always secured the approval necessary to charge whatever Candy wanted, because Candy's daddy always paid. He paid for travel, clothes, cars, and hotels. He paid for drama lessons, photographic portfolios—he paid for anything, in fact, that kept her occupied and happy, that kept her name out of the papers and her flamboyant presence out of the State of North Carolina and away from the scrutiny of his constituency. The only thing her daddy didn't pay for were the illegal drugs she liked to have in quantity. Unfortunately, the people who supplied these items were in the habit of accepting hard cash as payment for their wares, in amounts that were difficult for Candy to come up with. It was this last circumstance more than any other that had propelled Candy out of the leisured, idle life of a debutante and into the hurly-burly of entrepreneurship. Candy had become a businesswoman almost by accident. For a gram of the purest cocaine Candy had ever snorted, she agreed to smuggle a freelance photographer into the ladies' room at her father's annual Tarheel Ball. Hidden behind an improvised screen, Neil Straker had taken and subsequently sold to the tabloids some of the funniest candid shots ever of Washington's political and social elite. Thereafter, Candy and Neil worked as a team in the highly competitive but often quite lucrative paparazzi trade.

Now, as she sat in the crowded restaurant in Georgetown, Candy's brain was clicking like a ticker tape. Dahlia de Ginsburgh was there having lunch. She recognized the little twit, having seen her often enough in the past week. Candy and Neil had just about frozen their bums off staking out the de Ginsburgh mansion, hoping to get a shot of Camilla. There was a guy in London rumored to pay big bucks for anything on the la-di-da baroness. But what really interested Candy now was not Dahlia but the girl opposite her, that prig of a roommate from the dreary Bennett Academy. When Candy smelled money, bells went off in her head. Now she licked her lips. Cassie Litton was going to get her and Neil inside that house.

.

"Why, Cassie Litton. If this don't beat all." A well-dressed young woman stepped briskly up to Cassie's booth. "Don't tell me you've already forgotten the bad girl of Miss Bennett's?"

Cassie was not likely to have forgotten her former roommate, although she was a little surprised, considering the circumstances under which they had last seen each other, at her breezy, self-assured manner.

"Umm, Candy—Candy Lescaux—uh, this is Dahlia de Ginsburgh. We're about to have lunch," she added, somewhat stupidly.

"Well, hi, Dahlia, it's lovely to meet you, but I can see I picked just a terrible time to bust in and say 'howdie.' It's just that it's so nice to see a face that you know when you're out alone in a crowd." Candy fixed an appealing smile on her face and commenced a lopsided contest of wills that Cassie lost no time in losing: "Oh, you must join us, please."

Witty, charming, and inquisitive, Candy allowed nearly all of lunch to pass before allowing the conversation to turn to herself. "Oh, I've been so lucky, I must say. For a while I was sort of floating around the fashion business, doing a little modeling, a little styling, a little this, a little that. But then I got a job with Neil Straker, and now I'm his first assistant. Isn't that fabulous?"

Cassie and Dahlia smiled to indicate their willingness to assume that it was indeed fabulous, though in truth they were a bit unsure just who Neil Straker might be. Cassie, ever the more straightforward, was bold enough to ask.

"Oh, how silly of me to assume you'd know. I must sound terribly obnoxious, but I forget how small the fashion world is. You can be quite famous in that world, you know, I mean even very famous like Neil, and for outsiders—I mean for people who don't really follow fashion, as a business, that is—of course no one's ever heard of you. I mean, you saw the Napoli perfume ads in *Vogue*, I know you did, they've been running all year—the one with the girl and the dove in the forest? Everyone in the world has seen that photograph, but how in the world would you know that it was Neil's. I mean, you wouldn't."

Despite the vague impression they had that they had just been insulted, Cassie and Dahlia were entranced. The photograph in question was indeed one that both girls had mooned over at some length. A ravishingly beautiful yet softly innocent nude figure in a misty sylvan glade extends her arms, ballerinalike, to a snow-white dove that has just taken wing—an image so unabashedly romantic that it had invaded both girls' most intimate fantasies of themselves.

Such is the power of fantasy that at three in the afternoon on the following day, Neil Straker was setting up his photographic equipment in the drawing room of the de Ginsburgh house, while upstairs, Candy explained to the girls that it would be best to remove their underthings now, since marks from the elastics would remain visible for at least half an hour. "Why don't you two share this joint while I go help Neil set up?" She offered the slim cigarette to Dahlia, who made a brave effort at accepting nonchalantly. "Hey, loosen up," she said, smiling warmly, "This is a natural thing you're doing. You're both beautiful, you know, and Neil's an artist. Be cool and let yourselves go."

The smoke had been harsh; the resulting moods were mellow. The awkwardness of being naked passed quickly; the session proceeded in a blur. The room was warm, the heavy drapes were drawn, the darkness stabbed by strobe light. Suggestions were whispered, encouragements, "Nice, oh, nice, that's lovely, good, yes, good, that's right, head back, yes, part your lips a bit, love. Now Cassie, yes, love, come sit, yes, you're beautiful, just there, exactly, touch her if you like, kiss her, yes, that's beautiful, lovely, more, yes."

And suddenly they were done, gone, and the girls retired to Dahlia's room to hash it all over and, of course, to giggle.

"Can you believe we did it?"

"You were fantastic."

"God, really? But you were the one he liked..."

"Wasn't it weird?"

"Know what I think? I think we forget about school and run away to New York and be models and have affairs, dozens and dozens of them."

Cassie's eyes were shining. "I don't want this to stop. I've never had so much fun in my life. Oh, I wish...I wish..."

"I wish we had a man," Dahlia interjected. "Right now. Right here. Don't you? We could take turns."

"Or do it together. That would be kinky, wouldn't it?"

"Kinky? Well, aren't you the expert," Dahlia teased.

"Oh God, Dahlia, I wish I was an expert. I wish I even knew for sure what a stupid orgasm really is. I mean I've thought about it, I've read about it, sometimes I even get kind of sweated up about it, but how do you know, I mean..."

Dahlia rolled over on the bed. "Do you mean to say that you've never...don't you masturbate?"

Cassie felt herself blush and become suddenly uncomfortably aware that neither of them had much in the way of clothes on. "No, I guess I don't. I mean I sort of have, but I don't think..."

"Well, my poor, poor innocent. I'm just going to have to show you what to do."

"Are you kidding?"

"Of course not." Dahlia was all business. "I never knew you were so deprived. I mean, I just assumed everyone . . ."

"Dahlia, I can't do this . . ." But Dahlia was pushing her back on the bed.

"Imagine you're with the most divine man . . . imagine *Neil* has come back. He was turned on by you, I could tell. He was all hard. Now he's back in the room . . ." She had switched on the radio to a rock station and was turning the lights down. All except one. Cassie lay there like a stiff board, horribly embarrassed, but Dahlia was cheerfully persistent.

"And you're all alone with him. He doesn't say anything, but you can hear him undressing. He's all hot, and his eyes are burning down on you. He has a terrific body . . . tangles of black hair and his muscles are hard . . . hard . . ." Slowly her slim fingers began to circle Cassie's nipples.

Cassie bit her lip, wanting to pull away but not wanting to. She was so curious . . . so desperately curious to know. She could feel her nipples harden, and she started to concentrate, to concentrate with all her might on all the sensations there. The heat spread over her body until she could feel herself melting, relaxing onto the cool satin sheets of the bed. Now Dahlia's hands trailed down her naked tummy, lightly brushing her pubic hairs but only for a teasing instant, then they continued down the inside of her thighs, her knees, her calves, all the way down to her feet. The gentle stroking of the soles of her feet sent arrows and fiery darts up, up to a spot deep inside her. And then Dahlia's presence faded altogether, and this spot, this mysterious part of her, commanded all her attention. She allowed it to expand and grow so that it became a larger and larger pool, radiating warmth, taking over her entire body. Her legs parted, and then those magic fingers reached higher and higher up her legs until they were fluttering just at the rim of her pubic tangle. Cassie could feel her swollen clitoris, and her body strained upward, desperate to press against something, her own hand,

and now her fingers reached and probed, rubbing harder, faster, on that part of her that was wet and aching. Waves of pleasure rolled over her until she felt herself poised on the edge, her nerves taut with energy. Sensation closed in like a beam of light drawn down to pinpoint focus, and she came in one glorious, bursting, breathtaking rush.

Chapter 12

New Year's Eve—a time of transition. A year ends and another begins. It is a kind of death! And a re-birth. Death of what? Bad habits, bad temper, laziness, envy, etc. It is a time to think about one's life, to make plans and resolve again to become a better person. My resolutions for the coming year are:

"DAHLIA!" CASSIE STOOD in the doorway to the kitchen. Dahlia was sitting on a high wooden stool monitoring a batch of brownies baking in the oven. "You're reading my journal!"

Dahlia looked up and grinned. "You haven't filled in your resolutions yet."

"How much of this have you read?" Cassie demanded, relieved to note that it was her new journal and had very few entries.

"Oh, I've read all your journals," Dahlia announced blithely. "I saw you scribbling away one night, and when you went to study hall I had a peek. Then I got hooked. They're really quite good, Cassie. I mean you write very well. I could never get everything down like that. Things go right out of my mind the minute I think of them. You don't mind, do you?"

Cassie sat down. Part of her was pleased with the compliment; secretly she admired her own observations and heartfelt comments, but the other part of her was horribly embarrassed. Her cheeks went red remembering the long passages she had written about Dahlia.

"I was really flattered by all those things you said about

me," Dahlia continued, as if reading her mind. "I'm not sure I agree, exactly, on some points, but it doesn't matter. It's rather fun seeing what you think of me. Someday..." she struck an imperious pose, "I may even allow you to write my life story." A buzzer went off by the oven. "Hey, I think these things are done." She peered into the oven. "What now?"

"Take them out, you dope," Cassie said, tossing two pot holders to her.

"Right." Dahlia had totally dismissed the diary incident. "We've got the brownies and the champagne. That's just starters. I've ordered the biggest, gooiest pizza in all of Washington, which should be arriving," she looked at the kitchen clock, "in about three-quarters of an hour, so we better look sharp."

In the library Dahlia sprawled in front of the fire. The close harmonies of Crosby, Stills, Nash and Young filled the room. Cassie plopped down beside her and carefully poured the champagne. She handed Dahlia a glass and held her own up for a toast. The pale bubbly liquid caught the light from the fire, and for a moment Cassie felt as if she were holding a burning torch. It dazzled her. "Here's to ... to us," she said simply, though she meant something far more complex.

"Exactly," Dahlia leaned forward and touched her glass. "To us." She smiled happily, and taking a big gulp she managed to spill half the contents of the glass on herself.

Through their laughter and the music, they were surprised by the ringing of the doorbell, and they looked at each other, momentarily bewildered. Dahlia jumped up. "It's the pizza. Forgot all about it."

"Shall I go ... ?"

"No, I'll do it. It's my treat."

She started out the door, but Cassie called after her. "You're in your bathrobe, you know."

Cassie lay back on the thick carpet and closed her eyes. She heard the bell ring again—and then some sort of commotion—one, two, many voices. She got up quickly and crossed the room, a feeling of urgency creeping around the edges of her stomach.

"Dahlia?" she called down the sweeping staircase. She could hear the voices clearly now. Men's voices . . . and all talking, shouting at the same time. Cassie ran down the stairs.

Dahlia was standing still in the middle of the hall, a stunned look on her face. Gathered around the door were news reporters with cameras and microphones. Cassie grabbed Dahlia's arm. "What is it? What's going on? Dahlia . . . ?"

But Dahlia looked blank. Then she whispered, "Something's happened . . . an accident. I don't . . . oh, God! Get them out . . ."

Cassie turned to the door. Two reporters had stepped inside, and one of the photographers was kneeling to get a better shot of Dahlia. "Are you the daughter . . . ?" "Can we get shots of the living room . . . ?" "How did you feel when you heard . . . ?" "Over here, sweetie."

Cassie reached out and pushed the photographer off balance. "You jerk." Her voice was strong and threatening— although later she would remember it as a disembodied voice that seemed to come from a long way off. "All of you, get out! Do you hear me? Get out of this house this instant! I don't know what you want, and I don't care. Just get out!" She slammed the door and turned back to Dahlia, grabbing her arm and propelling her up the stairs to the library.

"Dahlia, what in God's name is this all about? What did they say?" She put her hands on Dahlia's shoulders and gave her a shake.

"I don't know. I honestly don't know," Dahlia whispered. "But there's been an accident. My mother . . . Charlotte."

The telephone rang and Cassie answered it.

"Yes . . . yes, this is the Baron de Ginsburgh's residence. Who are you? I see. Yes, well, this is, this is, uh . . . the housekeeper and there's no member of the family here to talk to you. No, I *don't* have a statement . . . I don't even know what you're talking about. We . . . I mean, I just heard something but . . . can you tell me what you know?"

Cassie listened, keeping one eye on Dahlia, who was still standing where she had left her. Dahlia seemed to be staring right through her.

Dahlia saw Cassie's hand tremble. She saw a wave of shock and pain cross her face . . . and she knew. She knew without question or doubt. Her mother and Charlotte were . . .

Cassie hung up the telephone. "Oh, my God, it's bad, Dahlia. It's very bad."

"They're dead." It was a statement, not a question.

Cassie's eyes blurred and she nodded, crossing to Dahlia. Dahlia clutched at her arm. "What did they say?"

"It was a lady from CBS. They're going on the air in just a minute and they really didn't have . . . the details. But, oh God, Dahlia, I can't . . ." Cassie held on to Dahlia's arm tightly as she leaned down to turn the television on. She flipped from channel to channel. Canned laughter and New Year's Eve variety shows spilled their silliness into the stilled room.

Finally the familiar face of Walter Cronkite appeared on the screen. There was a piece on the war in Vietnam. Another on student riots at the Sorbonne in Paris with footage of overturned, burning cars and bleeding people. Then there was a commercial. A sleek cougar jumped in and out of a sports car. Then, maddeningly, another commercial. A man was attempting, wrongly, to wax his car. The news came back on again:

What appears to have been a tragic accident has claimed the life of painter Charlotte Soames, an artist considered to be in the vanguard of post-war modernists. At ten A.M. *Eastern Standard Time today, Soames and the Baroness de Ginsburgh, wife of banker Guy de Ginsburgh, fell to their deaths when the rock ledge on which they were standing collapsed. The accident took place on a remote island of Hawaii. Eyewitnesses reported seeing the ledge crack and one*

of the two women fall to the rocks and the ocean below.
The second woman, who appeared at first to be on
safe ground, fell moments later. The Baron de Gins-
burgh could not be reached for comment. CBS will
have further details on the late news.

In Oregon, the Republican Party . . .

Cassie reached down and turned the television off. Gently
she pushed Dahlia down into a chair and then knelt before
her. Dahlia's hands were like ice.

"Dahlia," Cassie insisted, "we've got to call someone.
We can't stay here alone. Listen to me, Dahlia. Who can I
call?"

"Call Papa . . . You must call Papa."

Cassie's heart sank. She had no idea how to reach the
baron. She didn't know where in Africa he was. She rubbed
Dahlia's hands, trying to be as gentle as she could. "Someone else, Dahlia. Who can I call?" But she could see by
the numbed look on her friend's face and by the rigid posture
of her body that Dahlia could be of no help. Cassie was
frightened. More frightened than she had ever been. Her
body felt like lead. Surely there was an office number, but
no one was likely to be there at this time of night, and on
New Year's Eve. Surely, when the baron's staff heard the
news, someone would call. Or would they? Did anyone
know that Dahlia was in the house? No. They would assume
that no one was here but the servants. But the servants were
gone, too. Cassie felt a growing panic in the deepest part
of her belly.

The telephone rang again, and she raced to answer it. It
was another news station. She curtly refused to comment
and hung up. She knew that she'd have to keep answering
the phone, hoping for someone to come and take charge.
But who would that be? Cassie's mind raced and she fought
down the hopelessness that was washing over her. In the
desk by the telephone was a leather-bound address book,

but most of the numbers, as she flipped from page to page, were in Paris and London.

Dahlia continued to sit in the chair, staring blankly at nothing. The telephone rang again. This time, tears welled up in Cassie's eyes and she couldn't answer it. Damn it! She mustn't lose control. She sat staring at the phone and taking in great gulps of air as she fought to get a hold of herself. Suddenly, she felt a hand on her shoulder, and she literally jumped out of her seat.

"Maurice!" She practically fell into his arms. "Thank God, you're here. Have you heard . . ."

"Yes. I heard a report on the car radio on my way to Baltimore. There are reporters outside. I came in the back entrance." He looked from Cassie to Dahlia and back. "Miss Dahlia . . . ?"

"She's . . . she's in shock, I think. Those men were awful. They just shouted the whole thing at her."

Maurice shook his head angrily. *"Cochons!"* he muttered. "They are inhuman!"

"Maurice, I don't know who to call. I don't know how to reach the baron. I don't know what to do."

He nodded and went to the telephone. She watched as he dialed a number, and, though he spoke in rapid French, she felt relief spread through her body.

After interminable minutes, Maurice hung up. "The ambassador is in Paris, but his attaché will be here within an hour. The baron has been informed of his wife's death. And now," once again his sad eyes lit on the tiny figure of Dahlia huddled in her chair, "now, I think you must assist Miss Dahlia."

BOOK TWO

Chapter 13

IT WAS FOUR-THIRTY, and the street lamps had only just come on when Angus Braxton left the pub to return to his desk at London's *Daily Comet*. On every corner in the drizzly rain, in almost every doorway, stood shivering, red-nosed boys hawking news, scandal, and disaster. In years past, Braxton had patronized them regularly, occasionally offering a word of advice, occasionally rewarding a good show with an extra coin. A very long time ago, he had himself been one of them—a boy with holes in his shoes and an empty stomach, who worked fourteen hours at a stretch and was still tough enough to bloody the nose of an impertinent competitor. Over the years, as he worked his way through the apprenticeships and jobs of the newspaper profession, this unchanging, rag-tag army of news brats endlessly crying out their lurid messages became as much a part of his life as the smell of printer's ink and the taste of his midday bitter. He passed them now without a glance, and he hurried back to the warmth of his office. There, his secretary, the efficient, maternal Miss Greenspoon, would have all the afternoon papers already arranged on his desk, arranged in exactly the order he liked to read them. With surprising nimbleness, considering her size and weight, Miss Greenspoon would leap from her chair and rush to help him remove his scarf, overcoat, and galoshes, clucking all the while like a big, bosomy hen about the horrid chill, the dreadful damp. As she followed him into his office, she recited the afternoon's telephone messages. Finally, she would leave, quietly shutting the door to his private office, to let him get on with his work—the cozy little made-up jobs that were the only thing for him left to do as the elderly but greatly respected publisher of the very successful *Daily Comet*.

Braxton glanced through the headlines, trying to ignore the sense of déjà vu that came upon him with increasing regularity these days. They were like so many whores, he thought, all trying to outdo each other in their gaudy vulgarity, so that in the end they were indistinguishable. As always, he saved his own paper for the last. It was a tough test, one that he had applied stringently over the years to whatever paper he was working on at the time. Did it have anything fresh to say to a reader surfeited on newsprint? No, of course it did not.

This afternoon's front page, screaming the word EXCLUSIVE in red, provided a pleasant surprise, but the headline that followed was a disappointment: LOVERS LEAP (followed by smaller type) *to watery grave!* He yawned. A couple of socialites had fallen off a cliff. The rest of the page was given over to smudges—photos of women dressed up in fancy clothes. Braxton sighed, imagining what Oscar would say if he could see this, and he pushed the tabloid aside. He leaned back and let himself remember a leaner, hungrier, much more exciting time.

Oscar Bendel and Angus Braxton had been more than just friends, more than good newspapermen. They had been socialists, reformers. They were men who'd had a vision of a world of social justice where poverty would be unknown and the class system dismantled. Their unlikely partnership—a fiery, stubborn Scotsman and a smart, determined Jew—had given birth those many years ago to the *Daily Comet,* a paper to inform and stir the working class, to help them rise up and take their due. Oh what a dream it had been! A dream big enough to sustain a man through many a hungry time, through many a bitter disappointment.

Somehow the *Comet* had survived. Year after year it struggled along, denouncing injustice and proclaiming a message of equality and opportunity for the working classes. The friendship of the two men endured, through lean times and leaner still, as youth and finally middle age passed them by. But one morning they found Oscar Bendel dead at his desk, keeled over onto the galleys he'd stayed late to read.

Angus Braxton was left the sole owner of a newspaper that was by then barely surviving in a rapidly changing and even more competitive marketplace. The old left was dying off, and the new left, the young people who picked up the banner, the ones who marched and sang, who railed against injustice, against capitalism, racism, facism, imperialism, and war—well, there was no mistaking the fact that they considered the *Comet* a relic, an irrelevant dinosaur. They were reinventing the wheel, Braxton told his wife sadly, and they wanted everything their own way.

He often wondered what would have happened had he refused to meet with John Stavros. What was it? Three years ago? It seemed like more. Stavros, the absurdly precocious, frighteningly impatient young man with no past and all that money. He had known about the *Comet;* he had done his homework, there was no doubt about that. Aye, and he was well-spoken, too, a real silver-tongued devil, he was. He had spoken with respect of what Angus and his late partner had done. He knew all about the "youth market" and he was brimming with ideas about how to bring them to the fold. More to the point, Angus had to admit, he was prepared to pay off the debts that had been multiplying exponentially as the *Comet*'s readership had dwindled. More than that, he was willing (and able!) to spend lavishly on the kind of promotions that would, he said, make the *Comet* a force to be reckoned with in the journalistic community.

Well, that much at least had proven to be true. The *Comet* was certainly a force to be reckoned with. It was spectacularly successful now, with circulation expected to exceed two million by the end of the year. But at what price? Oh, yes, the paper was still as anti-establishment as ever, but only in the sense that, like all the others, it trumpeted— no, reveled—in the decadence of the upper classes. Yes, it was widely read by the common people, but instead of challenging them to build a better world, it pandered to their lowest instincts; it wallowed in prurience and scandal.

But, Braxton thought philosophically, it was, after all, out of his hands at last. Though he retained the nominal title of publisher, it was the majority owner and executive publisher, John Stavros, who held the cards now. And if it was not a righteous passion that burned in John Stavros's breast, it was at least a fiery passion. Braxton's own fires were burning low of late. He was a wealthy man for the first time in his hard-working life, and, if truth be told, he was more content than he might have liked to admit.

Chapter 14

JOHN STAVROS SAT in his darkened office, his hands alternately gripping and caressing the arms of his leather chair. The telephone rang incessantly, but he ignored it and so at last the sound receded and merged with the faraway noises of evening traffic nine floors below. Outside the misting rain made ghostly halos of the street lamps. Before him, in the gloom, the grainy image of Camilla de Ginsburgh's lovely face gazed up at him. Her visage was, as always, calm and unperturbed. She was dead, the headlines insisted, yet her eyes still mocked him, as they had always done, as they had mocked him on that terrible night when he had gone to offer up his life to her. He looked at the photograph hoping to find some sign, some clue to the mystery of his enchantment. Her eyes were laser beams that burned into the deepest vaults of his soul, where hate and desire were so cruelly mixed, but they offered up no answer, no salve for all the pain and humiliation that he had endured. She wore her famous little smile as if to show him how amusing all this was, and at any moment he might hear the peals of crystal laughter that had been the joy and torment of his heart...

He had loved Camilla de Ginsburgh from the first moment he saw her when he was barely twelve years old. Before her there was nothing—only the mountains, sea, and sky—and though he played and ate and ran and swam, he was more like one of the wild little mountain goats than like a human boy. But when she came, she lit the spark that set his mind and heart aflame. He had adored her; worshiped her with an intensity that was beyond his powers to describe or understand. He had never before seen any woman so wondrously beautiful, with hair of such palest gold and skin so alabaster white. She was so calmly, luminously aristocratic that for the longest time he couldn't even bring himself to look at her directly, much less approach her with his clumsy boyish ways. But there had come a time when he had also learned to hate her, not only her but all her world and all she stood for. The hate he felt was just as strong and unremitting as his love, and so the conflict grew until there was a never-ending battle in his heart.

It seemed impossible that she was dead. Without her, how could he go on? Without her, life was a tangled web with no center, no beginning, no end, and there was no way to unravel the confusion that he felt. From the moment she appeared on Spetsai, and plucked him out of the throng of ordinary mortals to serve her, she had influenced every aspect of his life. And later, when she so cruelly thrust him out of paradise, when she ordered him to leave her house forever, she continued to exert her influence on him, perhaps even more than before. Not only did he learn to love and hate because of her, but he transformed himself a thousand times. Only for her. He traveled round the world, learned to face danger and survive. Only for her. He entered into the heart of darkness, walked hand in hand with evil, learned how to kill and rape and plunder. Only for her. He acquired the trappings of culture and civilization, so that his clothes, his bearing, and his speech were those of a gentleman. Only for her. And he was rich now, richer by far than many blood-born kings. His houses, cars, paintings, and women were envied by all who saw them. All this he'd done for her. But she had tricked him once again, and she had had the final laugh. The lovely pale Camilla; long-necked, swanlike Camilla; cool-skinned Camilla of the feathery touch; Camilla of the dove-gray mocking eyes, the silvery laughter, and the whispery voice had plunged like Icarus into the sea. Now she was dead and lost to him forever. He sat and stared and felt his heart grow cold as ice, as if some part of him were dying too. He felt as old as mountain stone yet he was only twenty-six.

On the surface of it, he should have been grateful, grateful that Camilla de Ginsburgh had changed his life so dramatically. Certainly it had been his mother's incessant chant. But somehow it had not turned out that way and gratitude had never played a very large part either in his growing up or in his life as a man. It was a boy he thought of now, a rough and tumble boy named Yanni Stavropolis who was twelve years old when he first came to Membland in the county of Kent in England. Until then he had not owned a pair of shoes, seen the Atlantic Ocean, traveled on a train, or ever, in fact, been off the tiny island of Spetsai. His initial response to England was instinctive—he hated it. The climate and the people were equally cold and hostile. He had been poor in Spetsai, but it was the kind of poverty that mattered little to a boy—he had no need for clothes when the sun warmed him and there was always food enough. The sea, the earth, provided. On that hilly, sun-drenched island, he had been king of all that he surveyed. He could run across the rough terrain as fast as any mountain goat, could dive as deep as any sea bird, and swim as easily as any fish. In England he was earthbound, chilled to the marrow and damp as his mother's kitchen rags. His feet were shod in heavy boots that pinched his toes and he wore woolly clothes that smelled of mold and made him itch. At school he was an outcast and a stranger, a lowly foreigner for all to laugh at and despise.

From the very beginning his life was divided into two very distinct and different parts, like night and day—Camilla was either there or she was not. The winter months were always worse, for then she rarely ever came and he was like Persephone condemned to suffer out these barren months in hell. Everywhere he went, around the parks of Membland, throughout the gardens, meadows, and the woods, it seemed to him that life had stopped and all was sere and gray. But everything could change at once, no matter what the season, with the arrival of the purring motor car delivering Camilla and her entourage. She was the life force and the sun, and when she came it was as if the shrouded skies had parted and everything would come alive. The very air was sweet and all the countryside was brushed with vibrant colors.

Yanni and his mother lived in the gate house. From the window in his bedroom the boy could watch the sleek, expensive cars of his mistress and her guests sweep by and disappear around the curves of the long drive. They came and went and lived according to a rhythm of their own, never once suspecting the stir that their appearance caused within the cozy cottage by the gate.

Camilla kept few servants at her country house. A man from the village looked after the grounds and gardens, and his wife came in to do the cleaning and the wash. Evangelina and her son were the only live-in staff. Evangelina shopped, cooked, and did the fine sewing. Yanni helped in the gardens and tended the greenhouse. For a long time his only indoor chore was to provide the house with flowers. No matter what the season, flowers—camellias, freesias, roses, lilies —were always in the house. Camilla did not like the feel of a deserted house, of rooms musty from long months of disuse, and so even if she were away for as much as a half a year, she wanted each room to look and feel and smell as if she had only stepped out for an instant or so. Everything was always ready, the fires laid, the cupboards stocked, and the vases filled with blooms.

Their own cottage, while not luxurious, was extremely comfortable. To Evangelina it seemed a palace. She and her son had separate rooms to sleep in, there was a modern, ample kitchen, and an entire separate room in which to sit after a day's work had been done.

Every morning and every night before she went to bed, Evangelina sank heavily to her knees before her treasured picture of the Madonna. "Come, Yanni," she implored her son, "kneel and pray with me. We must be grateful for all the blessings the Holy Mother has bestowed on us."

His first conscious act against his mother had been to refuse to participate in her religious rituals. It made him sick to watch her, humbling and prostrating herself, the smell of garlic clinging to her ample bosom. He would have none of it.

Evangelina bullied, pleaded, and poured forth a never-ending stream of unwanted advice. Her voice was shrill as she called to him to bring him to the house to perform some task. "Yanni! Yanni! *Eletho* . . . Yaniiiiii!" Dark shame and anger would fill his heart. His mother had grown stupider, it seemed to him, with every passing year. Why had she never tried to learn the quiet ways, the civilized behavior that separated the better class of people from the brutish peasants. Why did she always come screaming after him as if they were still back in the rocky hills of Spetsai? There, her speech had blended naturally with bleating goats and screaming crows. But in the soft well-bred English land-scape, she seemed to him a vulgar, rough intruder. And he had tried so hard to teach her, to smooth away some of the rougher edges, all to no avail.

"My name is John now," he had told her countless times. "We live in England now, and here my name is John. Not Yanni. John." But even this, Evangelina never learned. She clung, like a gnarled and ancient olive tree on rocky, barren ground, to her own ways and the things she knew.

Evangelina had a dream, a very big, important dream. It suited her to have her son educated in a proper English school, so that he would acquire some of the polish and the manners that would distinguish him back home. She had never intended that they stay in England. Oh no. Evange-lina's plan was to return to Greece, even to Spetsai. For there, she knew, they would be rich, and there her son would be important, grand, and cultured. They would buy a tav-erna, and that would make them richer still. Then she would find her son a wife, a good, obedient, and modest girl, and with the large dowry she would bring, perhaps they'd buy a small hotel . . . Her son would wear a good white suit and look very handsome and distinguished, speaking perfect

English to the rich tourists from America . . .

He tried to tell her that he had other dreams, dreams that were bigger than anything she could imagine. But after a while he didn't bother anymore. She never listened to anything he had to say anyway, but only closed her eyes and played with her worry beads and went on telling him how it would be, as though she could convince him with sheer determination and monotony.

Yanni Stavropolis did well in school. He was insatiably curious and quick-witted, a good observer and a gifted mimic. His grades were the highest in the class, though this did not endear him to his teachers. He was too foreign and reserved and oddly condescending. He made them feel as if they were his inferiors, and so the honors he earned were given grudgingly. He made no friends at all because he never tried to, but what did win him the respect of his schoolmates was his physical courage and skill at sports. Yanni Stavropolis cared for nothing but that he be the first, the best, the winner. Everything he did was with a purpose. Everything he learned, every bit of knowledge, skill, wisdom, or gossip he acquired was toward one goal—that he be worthy of Camilla.

In time he was brought to work inside the house, waiting at table, serving drinks, attending to the endless needs and whims of his employers and their house guests. It was a strange life for a boy. Unconsciously at first, and then with ever-increasing attention and purpose, he learned the ways and habits of these rich, polished people he served, absorbing, as it were, the nuances of their speech and their gestures. Invisible behind his servant's mask, he could come and go at will, listen to conversations of the most private sort, enter a bed chamber to bring some wanted object or to take something away and be privy to the various, and often unusual, couplings.

With growing fascination he studied their idiosyncrasies, their hypocracies, large and small. No article of dress, no covert glance, no laugh or intonation was lost to his inquisitive eye. And always, always the one he watched and studied and admired and adored was the beautiful golden-haired woman who was the center of this world, and central to his heart. He swore one day he would be one of them. One day he would be master and she, cruel mistress, she would be . . .

Chapter 15

As THE YEARS went by, his obsession grew. The summer that the young misses Dahlia and Caroline came to Membland was a particularly trying one for him. For one thing, at seventeen, he was really no longer a boy. He was tall, handsome, and virile, with all the needs of a man. All summer long women had been trying to seduce him, even the wretched little girls had played their games with him. The afternoon that they had followed him into the hothouse and he had kissed the little bitch, it had been purely to teach her a lesson—like teaching a baby not to play with fire.

As he stood watching her run away, he felt nothing but hatred and defeat. He was trapped here in the greenhouse. He was nothing. How could he ever hope to compete in the world Camilla ruled. The women flirting with him, the little girls teasing him, they played with him as if he were a toy bought in the shops. He was a man. He was not a toy. He felt a fury rise up in him, and when he heard a voice behind him he spun around as though he were about to be attacked. Only it was she . . .

"There you are, Yanni. I've been looking for you." She smiled and walked to where he stood. So close he could smell the scent of her. She was so white, so incredibly white. He could see the outline of her breast against the soft fabric of her blouse. She was talking to him, ". . . the flowers, yes? . . . could you be so kind as to change them today, and oh, yes, Yanni, in my room . . . please only the white freesias. Everything else has so heavy a scent . . . do you understand?" He nodded. "Good." For the briefest of moments her hand rested on his arm.

How was it possible he could feel so strongly about her and she herself seemed not to know? Did she not feel any of the overwhelming chemistry that surged through him as she touched his arm? She must know her powers of seduction, and yet, was it possible that she remained unaware of her power over him?

The effect she had on him lingered even after she had gone, and for the next few hours he moved as if in a dream as he cut the flowers and arranged them in the crystal vases. He saved the delicate, sweetly scented freesias for last and carried them carefully to her bedroom. It was a room he knew well, for during Camilla's many long absences from Membland, Yanni had taken to spending long, solitary hours here enveloped in her aura. He liked to touch her things—the silver brush on her dressing table, soft slippers on the floor, the glittering gold-embroidered cushions on the expanse of her bed. Sometimes he would open the large armoire that housed her wardrobe and simply stand and inhale the expensive scent that clung to her clothes. But most of all he liked to look at the beautiful portrait of his mistress that hung over the bed. Even though he knew little of art, the power of the painting was clear. And of all the works of Charlotte Soames, it was the best. In it Camilla was nude, but classically, chastely so. The real nakedness was in the expression on her remarkable face. There was a restless hunger in the eyes—a desperate longing that was unmistakable. It was a passionate work of art, but its true subject was passion undiscovered, passion unfulfilled. It was like an erotic dream only half remembered and it haunted Yanni so that he was drawn to it over and over again.

He felt himself grow hard, felt the blood rushing to engorge his groin, and again the feeling of despair swept over him. As he turned to go, a small moan escaped his lips. She was there! Standing in the doorway watching him!

"I was very young when that was painted." Did her eyes flicker in amusement? Could she see the swell in his trousers? "I daresay not really much older than you are now. Do you like it?"

He nodded. "Yes, m'lady."

She entered the room, shutting the door behind her. "Ah, yes. The flowers look lovely. I shall find it very difficult to find someone with your special eye, Yanni, when you go."

Go? What was she talking about. His mouth went very dry. Was she dismissing him?

"Oh, dear. Don't look so stricken," she said, reading his thoughts. "It's only that surely a young man of your intelligence and," again her eyes seemed to sweep over his body, "your appearance should be thinking about a future. I can't think that arranging flowers and serving drinks holds much appeal. Evangelina tells me you have excelled in your studies. Really, quite the cleverest boy in the village." There was a certain amused tone in her voice, as if she were challenging him in some way. "And naturally I thought you would be leaving us...oh dear." She had crossed to her dressing table. "How very tiresome. The clasp on my necklace is caught. Can you see the problem?"

And now he was standing behind her as she bowed her head to expose the long, swanlike neck. His hands were trembling as he tried to deal with the tiny jeweled clasp of her pearls. His fingers would not obey him; his hands were like large, clumsy paws. He fumbled and silently cursed himself. She was growing impatient. He tried again, and this time his hands were so urgent that before he knew what had happened the clasp had broken and so had the necklace. Dozens of pearls scattered on the carpet.

"Oh, for heaven's sake," she sighed. He was kneeling now, scrambling to pick them up. "It's all right, Yanni. Leave it be and please tell Evangelina to come."

But Yanni didn't move. All of a sudden he could not hold himself back. He wrapped his arms around her waist and pressed his head against her stomach. A sob choked his words, but they came pouring out nonetheless. He loved her. He had loved her from the first moment he had seen her. "Never in my life was there anyone like you, who looked like you, who wore such clothes, who laughed as you do, or who is so soft." He held tightly to her.

She was startled, yes, but she didn't move away from him. "Yanni, get up and stop all of this. Do you hear me?" she said quietly.

He shook his head and clung on to her dress as if it were a life line. She must know of his love. He could not bear another moment of her not knowing. "I will do anything for you. I will give my life to you, only please, please..."

"If you don't get up and leave my room immediately, I shall be as angry as I ought to be already." But she did not sound angry, and even if she had there was no way he could stop himself now. He didn't loosen his grip on her but boldly held her even tighter. Now his arms were embracing her and he rose, lifting her effortlessly with him. Then he buried his face in her neck and tasted for the first time the delicious soft skin. She did nothing to stop him and he gasped for the pleasure of her. Could it be that she wanted him as much as he wanted her? It was all so sweet, so incredibly sweet—

She burst out laughing. Yanni froze. "Really, you are an impertinent boy. Take your hands off of me and go away." And all this she said as if he were a joke.

Something exploded inside him. He was suffocating with rage. His muscles tensed and he felt he could crush her. He was literally shaking with an unleashed passion and anger he did not know he had. If she screamed, if she struggled, he knew he would knock her senseless. But she made no sound.

He carried her to the bed and pushed her savagely down, his hands ripping open her blouse, tearing at her skirt. Somewhere in his mind he knew he should stop, should beg her forgiveness, should run as fast as he could from the room, from the house. But he could not. No reason or sanity was possible. He was the master. Now he did not look at her lying on the bed but saw only the beautiful face of Camilla in the portrait. The desire in her face, the longing and passion were for him. Only he could satisfy her. His urgency was so intense he could not hold back any longer. He bore down on her, forcing her legs apart with his knee, and now his body pressed hard against her. But then, a cold terror enveloped him. He was limp. He was powerless to take her. He was physically helpless. Her eyes once again filled with amusement. Neither triumph nor pity; only that irritating, maddening, frustrating, impenetrable, droll expression that could so swiftly and cruelly render everything impotent.

With a roar of fury, of frustration and panic, he rushed from the room, not daring to look back, humiliated by the expression he had seen on her face.

Chapter 16

HE WAS dismissed. It was intolerable to Camilla that he stay. Of course he had to go. At once. Charlotte spoke to him in the morning. "I don't think we need to discuss it. It's simply better that you leave. Tell your mother anything you like. Naturally, no blame will be attached to her, poor woman." She gave him fifty pounds and sent him on his way. Evangelina wept, not understanding anything, pleading with him not to go. Then he was gone.

Only he didn't leave at once. When darkness fell he stole back and, hidden in the shadows, watched the house. He was like a ghost, a shade, walking between life and death. Yanni Stavropolis was gone—disappeared never to be seen again—and no new personality had come to take his place. The boy was dead, the man was not yet born, only a lonely creature filled with hatred, confusion, shame, and scorn haunted Membland in the night.

The lights were on inside and all the rooms were gleaming. Rich, lovely, distinguished, and important guests were gathered in the drawing room to have their cocktail hour. Tonight there was no boy to serve them and so they helped themselves from an arrangement of bottles and glasses on the sideboard. And he was on the outside looking in. When he thought about it, he realized nothing had really changed. It was the same as it ever was. He had always been on the outside looking in. Only now it was clear and defined. He was a Greek peasant boy on the edges of an ancient class system, and there was no way in for him. Invisible behind his servant's mask, he had seen and heard everything that would have otherwise been hidden from him. But no one had ever seen him, because to them he did not exist except to serve and cater to their whims.

Camilla was late, as she always was. She had to make her entrance. She had to capture and hold everyone's attention. When at last she entered the room in a black gown that set off the whiteness of her skin and the shimmering golden hair, all the heads turned in her direction. She paused a moment to let everyone fully drink in her beauty. But the pause is not a moment too long, and then she smiled and greeted her guests.

He moved in closer, pressing himself against the window. She took his breath away, even now when he had sworn to have revenge on her, to frighten her, yes, and destroy her insulated little world that cared for nothing and nobody but itself. His entire being had been turned into a vessel filled with bitterness and hate. How could he have been so stupid? He had fallen into the age-old trap of believing that because his love for her was so overwhelming, he must have power over her. He had allowed himself to read a million meanings into a glance, a touch, a gesture. Even a half smile from her, one little glance from her in his direction, had been enough to lift him out of the realm of ordinary life. And because she could do things to him without even half trying, he had come to believe that she looked at him in a different way than she looked at anyone else. His love had turned into obsession and his obsession had made him blind.

Now he saw everything clearly. He could never be one of them and she could never really belong to him. The hatred burned like a fire in his soul, and as it burned he felt a purifying kind of strength from it. At last he could see them for the shallow, selfish, artificial wretches that they were. Everything they said meant something else. Every look, every smile, every gesture was a lie. Their favorite game was called humiliation. Theirs were arts of beguilement, temptation, and seduction, and when they'd conquered you with secret promises and hidden smiles, when you had once exposed your weakest and most fragile underbelly, they cut you down with laughter like a knife. He had played the fool for her and given her the biggest joke, and she had laughed, oh how she'd laughed at him, while he stood naked and exposed and felt his manhood shriveling and dying like a worm.

When they went in to dinner, he felt himself released from watching them. Then quickly, silently he climbed onto the roof and within seconds he was through her open bedroom window. The fragrance of her perfume assaulted his senses mercilessly. That penetrating scent, that subtle and elusive smell of her, was almost his undoing. His vision blurred as tears sprang to his eyes, but in the end his anger proved to be much stronger than his pain. He strode purposefully to her closets, flinging aside clothes, and reached inside for the leather box that held her letters and her photographs. These he would take and nothing else. It was enough, they were her secret life and he would use them to torture, torment, and expose her. He held under his arm the playing card that would let him be a master at their own kind of game. A few quick steps, a quick climb down, and he was gone into the dark night. Yanni Stavropolis was no more.

Four years later a man named John Stavros began to make his presence felt in London business and social circles. No one seemed to know anything about him except that he was young, very ambitious, and extremely rich. No one knew anything at all about his past, and as he was, in addition, extremely handsome, he provoked much gossip, talk, and speculation. He had made his mark on Fleet Street by elevating the dying *Daily Comet* to one of the brashest and highly controversial tabloids ever to be seen. The word on publishing row was this John Starvos was a comer.

The sensational world of tabloid journalism suited him perfectly. Here was where the money was — flash and trash and gutter gold. His papers appealed to the basest sort of emotions and they were bought in the millions. Numbers, ever increasing numbers, was the name of the game. And this was only the beginning. John Stavros was building a media empire.

His papers allowed him to keep tabs on her. He always knew exactly where she was and usually with whom. Her comings and her goings were regularly reported and photographically documented in his papers. He was still on the outside looking in, despite his riches, his new name, and his position, but he felt a growing sense of power and a gradual change in the balance of the scales. He knew now how to watch and wait until his time had come.

But her dying was the one thing he had never counted on.

So in the end she'd cheated him and won again. She'd left him sitting with the winning hand and no one left to play with. He rubbed his eyes for several minutes, as if that could erase the grainy image of her face, then turned the page to study the other pictures detailing this tragedy in the upper echelons of international society. One photograph made him sit up and take notice. It was a picture of a young girl in a bathrobe, her arms extended before her as if she were trying to push something unpleasant away from her. *Dahlia de Ginsburgh*, the caption read . . . He'd almost forgotten her existence. Camilla had a daughter . . . a very grown-up, lovely daughter, a girl whose face looked as distraught on being told the news of her mother's death as he now felt . . .

Chapter 17

"I CANNOT CONTROL what you girls choose to read on your holiday, but I can, and do, forbid your bringing these ... these scandal sheets into the school." Constance Jefferson's hand came firmly down on the newspapers on her desk, but she did not allow her eyes to waver from the two girls standing before her. Gray, like a flat, calm sea on a cloudy day, her gaze was shrewd and unillusioned. Ten years as the Bennett Academy's headmistress had taught her the realities of the hard, often vicious ways of schoolgirls caught up in gossip, hearsay, and slander.

"These publications are intrusive and cruel. They thrive on misfortune and tragedy in a most despicable way, and most certainly they are beneath the standards of a Bennett girl."

Without doubt, the tabloid version of Camilla de Ginsburgh's life with Charlotte Soames was priority reading throughout the school. In the three weeks since the accident, the student body had buzzed about nothing else. Now Dahlia herself and even Cassie Litton had become the brunt of cruel and malicious speculation. It was an intolerable situation, and one that could not be ignored any longer. Miss Jefferson felt the familiar stab of pain at the center of her forehead. Handled incorrectly, this was a situation that could very well get out of hand.

"I think that you, Malinda, and you, Heather, had better return to study hall and concentrate on your mid-term exams. I will expect to see no more of this contemptible material in circulation." The two girls glanced quickly at one another, and the headmistress caught the tiny flicker of triumph that flashed between them, but she chose to ignore it. Regrettably, she had little choice.

Constance Jefferson had been pleased when Cassie Litton and Dahlia de Ginsburgh had established an obvious and genuine friendship. It was one of the rewards of being headmistress, these little surprises, the special friendships that sprang up between girls when you least expect it. Girls that would grow together, become women together. Surely that was one of the most satisfying relationships to be had in the whole symphony of human relationships. Miss Jefferson had always believed this.

The intercom buzzed. "A telegram has just arrived from the Baron de Ginsburgh," her secretary said. "Dahlia will be returning tomorrow night."

Now it would begin. "Thank you, Miss Peters." The smirks, the freeze-outs, and deliberate tauntings. "Please see that a car is arranged to meet her at Dulles Airport." She had seen it before—many times—and it was not pretty.

In the aftermath of the scandal, the girls at Miss Bennett's behaved no better than Miss Jefferson had feared, yet her concern for Cassie and Dahlia was, in the event, misplaced. If anything, the atmosphere at school served only to strengthen the bond between the two. Cassie had even been persuaded to accept a trip to the de Ginsburgh family compound in Nassau over spring break, now just three days away.

"Mail call!" Cassie handed Dahlia six letters, five of them from France or England on thick bond with addresses and crests embossed on the envelopes. The sixth was from a Washington travel agency and contained, Cassie was sure, their airline tickets to Nassau.

"Throw them on my desk. I'm tired of reading condolences."

"The tickets are here, I think."

"Great!"

"Going to the gym?"

"No."

"Why not?"

"Because I don't feel like it. The school rules state quite precisely that one needn't engage in the physical education program if one is incapacitated," Dahlia quoted, smiling brightly. "And I'm incapacitated. See?" She ran her finger across her throat. "I've just cut off my head."

Cassie made a wry face. There was no point in arguing with Dahlia. She was in one of her moods. Cassie began to leaf through her own mail, mostly college catalogues, thinking she was getting a bit tired of Dahlia's moods. Not that she didn't have a right to them . . .

Her hand stopped on a large manila envelope. It was addressed to her in a messy scrawl of handwriting, and there was no return address. She turned it over a few times before opening it. The photographs caught her eye first. Three black and white prints—as stark and ugly as anything Cassie had ever seen. In each were two female figures so harshly lit, so grotesquely, so absurdly naked that she shivered uncomprehendingly before forcing herself to focus on the blankly anonymous-looking faces. When she did, the breath left her body in a soundless, fluttering groan, and for a brief, panicky moment, she forgot how to draw another. The brutal, nauseating fact was that these two ridiculous, pathetically, grossly exposed creatures were Cassie and Dahlia themselves—in the flesh.

Yet, dumbfounded as she was, it took her a moment to connect these squalid images with the romantic, sophisticated "art" photographs they were to have been.

"I don't believe it. It's Candy," she managed to stutter, "Oh, my God, it's that girl Candy and that bastard photographer. My God, Dahlia, look what they've done to us. I don't believe it!" She threw the pictures down on the bed.

Dahlia crossed the room in slow motion, it seemed to Cassie, and stared at the offending objects one after another for a maddening length of time. Then she lightly tossed them on the bed.

"Well, they're hideous," she said, "perfectly hideous. And we were absolute twits to be seduced into something so . . . cheap. It's only embarrassing because they're vulgar, and, of course, no one must ever see them, but, really, I think it's not the end of the world. We must simply get in touch with Candy whatever-her-name-is and explain to her that this is not the sort of thing we had in mind, you know, not at *all* the sort of thing we had in mind, and say that, no, *demand* that they give us back everything, you know, the negatives and all, and that will be that. Here now, give me the envelope and we'll ring her up right now."

There was, of course, no return address on the envelope, but there was a note inside, and its contents completely toppled Dahlia's brave composure so that she, too, felt the heat at her temples, the gall in the pit of her stomach.

Cassie, honey!

Proper young ladies should never go out among the street people without knowing how to live on the street. I learned that a long time ago, and it cost me plenty. Now it's going to cost you too. Think about it. I'll be in touch soon.

They both floundered in that blind space between knowledge and belief, until Cassie made it final. "She's going to blackmail us. She *is* blackmailing us."

Dahlia fought on, reflexively, but without heart. "But she can't . . . they can't publish anything. We never signed anything. Nobody's going to . . ."

"Don't be so dense. They don't have to publish them. All they have to do is send them to our families and we're ruined. And besides, they can do anything they want. What about the filth they're printing about your mother? Do you think anybody needed a signature for that?"

Dahlia stared at the photographs with an intensity that might have set them aflame. An icy nausea enveloped her.

Was that how it started? Two good friends pretending it was a lark? Alone in a house, in a bed, turned on? She flushed hot, remembering the scene after Candy and Neil had left. Was she attracted to Cassie *that way?* Were her feelings really the sexual yearnings of one girl for another? She had wanted a friend, as good a friend as her mother had had in Charlotte, and now, from the looks of the photographs, it was just such a friend she had. They were grossly entwined, Dahlia's hand reaching for Cassie, her mouth wet, her eyes eager. But that wasn't the way it had been! Camilla and Charlotte. What did *they* do to each other in bed?

Dahlia felt sick. So sick and tired and disgusted. Why hadn't she known about her mother? All those years, all that time spent in the same house, under one roof. All the trips and holidays and jolly good times... Why had she been so naive? The last to know... She had loved them and lived with them and envied them and admired them. And she had been the last to know. Her beautiful mother and her wonderful Charlotte. Dykes!

Cassie got up and paced back and forth in the room. She was unable to speak. If Uncle Winthrop... her grandmother ... "Just like her mother. Just like her mother..." She could hear them now. Cassie Litton's no better than that cheap, vulgar, common woman, and we were fools to expect anything else.

Was she like her mother? Was that how her mother had gotten Bobby to marry her? She had wanted so much to be a Litton. A lady and a Litton. But there was nothing ladylike in that face, that exposed body, that lewd spread of her legs. Vulgar, common, and cheap. That was Cassie Litton. Her grief was devastating.

"Don't cry, Cassie. *Just don't cry.*" Dahlia gritted her teeth. "We've got to think of something."

"You think of something. You've got the money!"

"Don't be a ninny. We can't pay her. She'll just come back for more and more. I can't get my hands on any real money anyway. It's all tied up in trusts..."

"Oh God, Dahlia. You've just got to do something. She's trouble, Dahlia. She's really big trouble. If my family ever sees this . . ."

"We can't let her blackmail us, Cassie. We just can't. I . . . I think I'm just going to have to tell Papa. He won't let this happen to us. He'll hate it, but he'll fix it. He has to." Bitter tears welled up. Her poor papa. So sad. So sad and silent at the funeral. He didn't deserve this.

"Cassie, let's just get to Nassau and everything will be all right. I promise you. Don't cry. Please don't cry."

Cassie believed her. Dahlia could do anything. Cassie had to believe her. She had no choice.

Three days later, Cassie stood on the balcony of her bedroom, looking out over the beach at Lyford Cay. It was a special kind of wealth, she was thinking, that made a place like this possible.

Lyford Cay, once a swampy tangle of jungle overgrowth, was now a splendid compound of grand houses with rolling, emerald lawns, exuberant flower beds, and stands of manicured palm groves, tennis courts, gazebos, and lily ponds, all edged by perfect, white sandy beaches and the deep-blue horizons of sea and sky. It was indeed old money that paid for the armies of uniformed servants. And it was old money that dictated the aimless, though hardly dull, ambiance of days spent in no greater or other pursuit than that of pleasure and amusement.

Surely here, Cassie reasoned, among these people, I am insulated from the tawdriness of the world. Surely Dahlia's father, the head of this kingdom of peaceful luxury, knows how to deal with the likes of Candy and her pornographer friend. If only the baron would arrive.

"He's delayed," Dahlia said as the two of them settled into their rooms at Lord and Lady Hamilton's large pink-stuccoed house. "Aunt Delphine says it's business. Cassie, relax. Candy's the criminal, not us. Blackmail is illegal, and she's just trying to scare us. Papa will fix it. I promise."

"I guess you're right," Cassie said with a slight pang.

She wished she had a papa of her own to fix things for her.

"So. Let's enjoy ourselves—have a good time. I don't want those pictures shown around anymore than you do, but I'm not about to spend my whole holiday quaking in my boots over that second-rate little tramp and her threats."

And in the days and nights that followed, Cassie did try to relax. The three beachfront houses owned by Dahlia's aunts were crawling with people. Flirtations were everywhere. Older women had much younger men in tow, and older men were not the least inhibited about flirting with the girls who only a few days before had been under the strict protection of the Bennett Academy. Everyone, of course, was terribly rich. They had castles, villas, lodges, country and town houses all over the world. Had Cassie been to Tuscany? To St. Tropez? Surely she had spent time in London? In Biarritz? No, no, no she had not, Cassie was forced to admit a hundred times over, and she would smile and say, "Thank you, how lovely" to the invitations that would invariably follow.

"How lovely" was a phrase that Cassie had quickly learned. It came to her as easily as having breakfast served in bed or drinks brought in at the cocktail hour. It was a pleasant enough remark, yet so vague as to be apt in virtually any situation. Would one like to have a swim? A drink? Luncheon? An affair? One simply murmured, "How lovely." It could mean "yes," it could mean "no," it could mean "maybe." No one seemed to expect a direct answer to anything.

It was an unreal world inhabited by a cast of characters that seemed to Cassie to have walked right out of the pages of Somerset Maugham, Noël Coward and Oscar Wilde. They made her shy in a way she had never been before, and increasingly she felt as if she were being drawn more and more into a looking-glass world where nothing quite made sense. Alice at the tea party, she thought. That's me.

Dahlia was no help. She was everywhere, laughing, chattering, apparently having the time of her life. But Cassie could see there was a nervous edge to her gaiety, frantic overtones to her flirtatiousness, as if she were trying to prove to the world that she wasn't like her mother. All this left Cassie feeling unhinged, and she longed for some footing on sure ground, something or someone familiar to her, something that made sense. The aristocracy at play made no sense at all. And still there was no Baron de Ginsburgh.

"But *when*, Dahlia? Doesn't he know? We've only got ten days..."

"Cassie, *please*. You've just got to trust me. There is nothing to worry about. Absolutely and finally... Now, tell me how I look." Dahlia stepped back from the mirror in her bedroom and turned to face Cassie.

"God. Smashing. You really do." Cassie viewed her friend with genuine admiration. Her slender figure was perfectly revealed in a simple white dress, and a band of lilies charmingly restrained the mass of golden curls that framed her face. "A new man?"

"Clever girl." Dahlia adjusted the line of her bodice so that it fell squarely from her shoulders. "His name is Desmond Lovell. He was here playing golf with Uncle Charlie this afternoon, and he's coming to the dinner tonight. I met him at the clubhouse, and Cassie," she turned to her with flushed cheeks, "he's ages older than all these *boys*. And he's so elegant and graceful. He actually bowed when he met me. I've got myself placed next to him at dinner."

"But, Dahlia, who is he? Is he staying here?"

"I have no idea. But I certainly intend to find out."

"Poor Desmond Lovell." Cassie made a face of mock concern. "I'd say he doesn't stand a chance."

"Me too," Dahlia agreed.

Damn it all, Cassie thought. Why shouldn't she be like Dahlia, chasing after a man, falling in love, acting silly? Why was the weight of the world always hanging on her shoulders? Dahlia was right. The baron would fix everything. And in the meantime who knew when she would ever find herself in such a setting as this again. Ahead of her was school and more school. The thought of books, graduation, the real world seemed distant, but she knew it was there waiting for her. Granny Litton's money was waiting for her, Smith College . . . a neat, structured world was there for her. Why shouldn't she relax now—and have fun?

"It's early yet, Cassie. Let's go down by the water. It's such a pretty evening."

The two girls drifted off across the lawn toward the shimmering bay that lay bathed in the pink light of the setting sun. For an instant they paused as they seemed to debate on something. Then, in obvious agreement, they each kicked off their shoes and ran barefoot in the sand, down the beach, and out of sight.

Chapter 18

WHEN THE LIMOUSINE emerged from the Midtown Tunnel, a few wet snowflakes splattered on the windshield. By the time it pulled into Kennedy Airport, almost three hours later, there were eight inches of snow on the ground, and the air was impenetrably thick with falling flakes. The chauffeur had tried to convince his passenger as they inched toward the Van Wyck Expressway that the airport would probably be shut down. But the man insisted, in his cool, precise English accent, that they go on.

"So wadda I care," the driver muttered. "Time is money." And this guy had it. In the past week he'd been hired to drive him all over New York, and he'd never seen anything like it . . . the most expensive restaurants, dames dripping in furs and jewels, fat-cat businessmen, doormen snapping to and fro like mechanical toys. It was like out of a movie. And look at him now. Coulda cared less about the snow. The driver peered into his rear-view mirror. Like a goddamn king he was, having his nails manicured by a little blond cutie, right there, in the back of the car, on his way to catch a plane.

John Stavros pulled a crisp one-hundred-dollar bill out of his wallet and waited for the man to bring his luggage around. At the last moment, he added a twenty and, handing the bills to the driver, walked away quickly, ignoring the thanks. He liked the feel of American money in the same way he liked the feel of American business negotiations— brisk, to the point, and no embarrassment at wanting to come out on top. The intensity of the past week in New York had engaged him totally. It had been a gambler's game, a game of wits and skill, and Stavros knew it had been his hard, competitive drive that had finally won him the victory.

He turned into the large British Airways terminal, ignoring the sea of disgruntled passengers and their ineffectual complaints about the weather. All flights were canceled, and ground transportation to or from anywhere was doubtful. Stavros presented his ticket at the first-class counter, and immediately a trim, pretty hostess detached herself from a knot of people and led him briskly down a corridor and through an unmarked gray door. Another narrow corridor, another door, and they were in the large, quiet, softly lit VIP lounge.

The hostess greeted him, took his coat, asked him what he would like to drink, and then pointed to a young girl reading a magazine in a corner. "Miss Lescaux has been waiting for you. Let me know when you are ready, and I will have a car to take you to the Sheraton Hotel. I'm afraid everything is grounded until tomorrow morning at the earliest."

Candy had worked hard to arrange this meeting, and she hadn't minded the wait. She was feeling good. Once she'd seen the contacts of the photographs Neil had taken, her course had been clear. Neil, she knew, was distinctly lacking in initiative—he was a small-time jerk and always would be. With initiative of her own to spare, Candy boarded a plane for Winston-Salem, prepared for a bit of straight forward talk with Winthrop Litton, owner and president of Litton Manufacturing.

"Well, now, darlin', what happy circumstance brings a fresh young thing like you to see a tired old man like me?" Winston greeted her with the warmth and easy condescension that powerful men reserve for the children of their peers. Graceful compliments were offered, her daddy's health was asked after.

Candy was the very picture of innocence, batting her long eyelashes and recrossing her long legs. She was thinking, she said, of taking up a career as a photographer, "You know, freelance sort of thing, where I might come up and show you pictures that you might want to buy."

Winthrop was relieved. He had feared she might have been asking for a job. "Certainly, my dear. I'm sure you're very talented. You go on out there and snap those pictures. Come up with something interesting to the folks of Winston-Salem, and Tom Waring at the *Courier* is just bound to jump on 'em. I'll see to it." Winthrop beamed at her.

When Candy finally pulled the photographs from her portfolio and spread them on his desk, Winthrop's smile vanished quite suddenly, as she had known it would. Cynic though he was, he was unprepared for such hardened corruption in one so young. He was putty in her hands, unwilling or unable to muster more than a few indignant splutterings.

A scant fifteen minutes later, Candy left his office with a check for five thousand dollars.

Well pleased with herself and the immediate success that the first half of her plan had met with, she was eager to meet this John Stavros, whoever he was. She had done her homework, but she was totally unprepared for the sight of the very young and very good-looking man who tossed a gray cashmere coat onto the chair beside her and held out a slim, perfectly manicured hand to her, saying, "Miss Lescaux? Sorry to keep you waiting. I'm John Stavros."

He, too, was pleasantly surprised, for Candy Lescaux was a strikingly attractive girl with deep-blue eyes, straight jet-black hair, and pale-white skin. She had the long-limbed body of a model, and she dressed with the expensive, throwaway flair of someone who might be in show business—a short, black leather tunic that barely qualified as a dress showed off her very long and shapely legs; a pair of silver snakeskin boots matched the large, shapeless pouch she carried as her bag and baggage; over it all she wore a silver fox fur as casually as if it were an army blanket.

"Miss Lescaux, I'll be frank with you. You are the first attractive development in an otherwise dreary day." He gestured at the blustery weather outside. "I understand that we have some business to do . . . and as we seem to have time on our hands, why don't you join me in a drink? What will you have? Scotch? Vodka? Cognac?"

Once they had gotten their drinks, he raised his glass, "Now my attention is all yours. Tell me about yourself. Why are you here and what do you want?"

Candy sipped her bourbon and gave herself a long moment to study the man before answering. He exuded an aura of power, money, and self-confidence. Something in his manner made her feel that he knew all about her, knew exactly who and what she was, and that he was not displeased. There was a very palpable contradiction between his manners, in all ways impeccable, and the bold, unabashedly sexual way he looked at her.

"I have some pictures," she got right to the point. "I heard that you buy pictures . . . for your paper."

"Indeed? What sort of pictures?"

She pulled an envelope out of her pouch and handed it to him. He sat back and quickly flipped through the snapshots, pausing briefly at a close-up of a young girl's face.

"Dahlia de Ginsburgh," Candy said needlessly.

Stavros gave her a brief, hard stare, finished flipping through the photos, returned them to their manila envelope, and tossed them aside.

"Where did you get these?"

Candy shrugged. "Does it matter? I got them, that's all. Do you want them?"

Stavros reached into his pocket and removed his wallet, extracting five one-hundred-dollar bills. He folded them in half and handed them to Candy. Her look told him that she was disappointed.

John Stavros sipped his drink. "Miss Lescaux, these pictures are quite worthless to me. I appreciate that you've gone to some trouble to get them here, and for that I am paying you five hundred dollars. But it's a cold and dreary afternoon, and I am feeling out of sorts and bored. Why don't you amuse me. Why don't you tell me a story, Miss Lescaux. Tell me how these pictures came about, tell me about yourself, who you are and what you want . . . only remember, the truth is always more interesting than fiction. If your story interests me, perhaps these—snapshots will increase in value . . ."

Candy thought it over for a moment, and, realizing that she had nothing to lose and possibly something to gain, she launched into a nearly true story, ending up two bourbons and a half hour later with a hilarious account of her meeting with Winthrop Litton.

John Stavros smiled. "I can see that you are a resourceful young woman with energy and imagination. But, tell me, why are you doing all this? I have the distinct impression that there is very little your father or any other man would deny you . . ."

An enigmatic smile played on Candy's pretty lips. "Let's just say I have expensive tastes."

"Expensive tastes. Yes. All women should have expensive tastes, and beautiful women should get what they want. But you are frightfully naive. You've gone to a great deal of trouble for . . . what? How much did you hope to realize from this transaction? A thousand? Two thousand? I spend more than that on an evening's entertainment. You see, I, too, have expensive tastes."

Candy licked her lips, suspecting, quite rightly, that the conversation was about to take an interesting turn.

Stavros lightly tapped the envelope of photographs before putting them in his briefcase. "You seem an admirably nasty-minded young lady," he said, smiling at her. "Your approach is a bit crude, but I recognize, shall we say, an uncompromising ambition. I find that amusing." He gestured toward the window. "This storm seems to have presented me with an unexpected evening of leisure, and I would like to pass it in pleasant and stimulating company. I think you might find it worth your while to join me in, oh, an hour's time. The hostess will tell you which room I'm in. You could, if you like, consider it an audition of sorts."

"Something tells me it's a part I'm a natural for."

"A natural, yes, no doubt. But why don't you see what

you can do about a supporting cast. My guess is that you're just the girl to arrange something like that. A blonde, let us say, to set off your ebony features. Am I wrong?"

Candy grinned. "Not about me, Johnny boy."

"Good. Resourceful, enterprising girls can go far with me. As far as their imaginations and 'expensive tastes' take them."

Candy gathered up her coat. "See ya later, boss. I gotta Swedish girl I think you'd like to meet."

He watched her walk away, but this time his eyes were not dwelling on her body. He didn't seem to see her at all. At length he reached into his briefcase and extracted the envelope she had given him. Sipping on his drink, he flipped once more through the pictures until he came to a close-up shot of Dahlia. He studied it without expression—and then a little smile began to play on his face.

Chapter 19

DESMOND LOVELL DID not know quite what to make of his dinner partner. The halo of hair framing her face and the simple, white gauzy dress gave her an aura of innocence so that one was tempted to treat her almost as if she were a child. And yet... And yet here she was flirting with him as if he were a schoolboy to be teased and played with. There was mischief in her eyes and a light, breathless quality to her banter that delighted him.

"And so, Lord Lovell, you've kept me chattering for the whole of dinner and now I know nothing about you, except you won at golf today and put Uncle Charlie in a terrible mood."

"Oh, dear. I hope not. It was just luck, anyway. Do you golf, Miss de Ginsburgh?"

"No." She leaned to him intimately. "I'm quite lazy. I would have been much better off in another century, where women weren't expected to *do* anything."

Desmond laughed. "Quite right. In London you can't find a girl who isn't about to open some terribly clever and useless boutique. They dance all night in those discotheques and rush about all day fitting out little shops in Chelsea. It's quite mad, really."

London, Desmond informed the attentive Dahlia, had turned into a carnival of decadence and revolution. As for himself, he was a traditionalist and could not for the life of him understand why all the attractive daughters of good families were tossing out the old values and virtues as lightly as they tossed out old clothes. Girls who should be pursuing gentle lives were now going about with hairdressers and nightclub owners and movie stars. Parasitic fringe elements were suddenly all the rage in fashionable society. Desmond shuddered.

Dahlia nodded, looking very demure. "Then I shall be a terrible washout in London, I'm afraid."

"You're going to London? To live?" Desmond felt immediately protective of her.

"Yes. Well, at least that was my plan." In truth the idea had just popped into her head. London sounded fun.

Desmond made no comment. It would take so little time for this beautiful, fragile, innocent girl to fall prey to the London scene. Suddenly, instinctively, he took her small, warm hand in his and felt an inexplicable tightness in his throat. "Would you care to dance, Miss de Ginsburgh ... Dahlia?"

Cassie watched them from her seat a few tables away. Dahlia certainly seemed to have made her conquest, she thought, and then she turned back to Teddy Cameron, the attentive young man on her right. She had every intention of making him her own conquest.

"Not Bats Cameron!" Dahlia collapsed in amazement on the bed. "You can't be serious. He's weird and I don't think he's ever had a girl friend in his life."

"Good. Then I'll be the first." Cassie brushed her hair up into a knot on her head and pulled on an old, comfortable pair of jeans. She had met him on the beach. He was sitting under a large umbrella, wearing a Panama hat and fiddling with a tape deck. "Listen to that!" he said excitedly, motioning her to sit down. "It's a very rare gecko, very hard to find." Cassie listened to the faint squeaks and rustlings coming from the tape. "Such a pretty song," Teddy said, nodding his head as if in time to music. Cassie liked him immediately.

The name "Bats" had come to him via his schoolmates at Eton where he had been a brilliant biology student. His passion was night animals, and now he roamed the globe in search of specimens.

"He's asked me to go out taping with him tonight."

"Oh, no," Dahlia winked knowingly. "Well, now, perhaps we've misjudged old Bats. Perhaps it's all a ploy of his, these *bugs* and things, just to lure innocent young maidens into the night, where, under the cloak of darkness, he ravishes their bodies."

"Speaking of which, I thought Desmond Lovell was practically going to devour you last night. The man is in love."

"Yes, he is, isn't he?" Dahlia looked pleased with herself. "Which is why I think I'll make him my lover."

"Are you serious?"

"Never seriouser. I think an older man is essential, so much more experience and finesse, and I certainly don't want my first time to be with some hot, sweaty boy. I want to be made love to, not jumped on and mauled to death."

"Well, who does?" Cassie wondered to herself what Teddy would be like to touch, to kiss. It excited her.

"Don't worry. I'll tell you all about it," Dahlia said airily.

"Or maybe *I'll* tell *you* all about it."

Dahlia's eyes widened. "Why, Cassie Litton, I do believe you have a wanton streak in you after all. So it's to be a race?"

Cassie attempted a saucy wink as she went out the door. "May the best woman win," she called back.

In the following days, Desmond was the prime if not exclusive object of Dahlia's attentions, and he in turn pursued her passionately. They went everywhere together and most often alone.

"I honestly don't know, Vi. It's not as if Dahlia confides in me, goodness knows. I think it's simply a matter of a young girl having a bit of a fling. Though I wouldn't have bet on Desmond Lovell in a million years, would you?"

"Well, I for one am glad she has someone to play with for a while. Desmond seems a nice enough sort..."

"Mmm. Too nice if you ask me. Not that Dahlia isn't a charming girl, but she's far too young for him. What could a grown man of thirty possibly see in a seventeen-year-old schoolgirl. It's no secret that Dahlia has come into a great deal of money and property from Camilla, and next year she'll probably have control of her entire trust from her father. She's absolutely a sitting duck for fortune hunters."

"I doubt Desmond is a fortune hunter. He doesn't have the imagination." The "aunts," Delphine and Violet, were sunning themselves on the terrace. Their voices drifted up through Cassie's window.

"But he's land poor. Everyone knows that his father left him with little more than a title. Glinveagh Castle is a shambles and Desmond is not making a very good show for himself in London. Now I ask you, does that sound like a suitable match for Dahlia?"

"Violet, *really*. I hardly think we're talking about a suitable match. Dahlia is a baby. This is her school holiday. He's simply squiring her about. It's harmless. No doubt Desmond appeals to her because he has . . . well, he's got . . ."

"A foot fettish?" The two of them fell to laughing.

Upstairs, Cassie, who while trying not to eavesdrop had nevertheless heard the entire conversation, started to giggle, too. She had been looking for Dahlia the night before and had found her sitting in a far corner of the veranda. She had been reclining in a large wicker armchair, looking for all the world like a fairy-tale princess—an impression that was only heightened by the almost comical sight of Desmond kneeling on the floor before her, holding her bare foot in his hands. He spoke in a voice so low that no one but Dahlia could have heard, yet so intense that no one, certainly not Cassie, would have dared to interrupt.

Meanwhile, Cassie could feel herself growing more and more attracted to Teddy. She felt comfortable with him and she admired the intensity of his interests. For three nights running she had gone out on his nocturnal ramblings with him. He had rented a golf cart, and with the tape deck positioned like a duenna between them had driven slowly and silently along the roads as he listened for the barely perceptible sounds he was seeking.

Tonight, however, she knew would be different. There was a blanket and a bottle of wine in place of the tape deck, and overhead there was a great splendid and starry night.

Cassie could feel the growing excitement inside her as Teddy led her to a small cove surrounded by trees. They walked hand in hand to the edge of the sea and stood listening to the soft sounds of the waves lapping on the shore. Then he turned, touching first her hair and then her cheek. "My night girl," he whispered, kissing her gently. Their mouths opened and their bodies pressed together.

It was all so sweet. So exquisitely sweet. Cassie took his hand and placed it under her blouse. Slowly, lovingly, she inched it toward her breasts. She wanted to feel his hands on her body, and though she had never done anything remotely like this before, it seemed to come as naturally as breathing. They undressed and stared at each other in the pale moonlight, and then Cassie lay down on the blanket— the sand was still warm from the sun. There were endless discoveries to be made in the closeness of their naked bodies—long, searching caresses—and again and again the other's lips and the kissing that sent waves of desire to the pit of her stomach.

Cassie could have gone on like this forever, but she could feel his tension and his need. He rolled on top of her and she opened herself to him. For an instant, a mere second, she was frightened; then she opened her eyes, and a million stars shone overhead. She bit her lip as he entered her.

It was not painful, as she had expected, but uncomfortable until she willed herself to relax, to meet his body with her own. He was groaning now—his passion rising up and his breath caught and strangled. Cassie's eyes blurred and she hugged him tighter. And then it was over. His body relaxed and his face burrowed into her neck. She could feel his warm breath and she was afraid to move—afraid to shatter the moment. Gently her fingers stroked his neck. He sighed and snuggled closer to her. Cassie smiled.

They swam in the inlet before dressing and heading back.

Teddy stood awkwardly when they reached the house, not knowing what to say. For Cassie, however, it was simple. "Thank you," she said, kissing him once more. "I had a lovely time."

Chapter 20

"WELL, WELL. SOMETHING *has* happened, hasn't it?" Dahlia said.

Cassie nodded.

"Oh, Cassie. You . . . you were the first! What was it like? Can you talk? Did he really . . . ?"

Cassie didn't know why, but suddenly she felt like crying. Dahlia hugged her and began to rail against Teddy, but Cassie stopped her. "No, no, please. He was wonderful. It's only just that, well, I feel as if I've left something . . . become something else . . ." She smiled helplessly.

Dahlia nodded solemnly. They sat letting the enormity of the event fill the room. But, like a cat, Dahlia was overcome with curiosity. "But what was it like? Did it hurt? Did you . . . did the earth move?"

"Well . . . no . . . not exactly," Cassie stammered, not wanting her big moment to go by completely without drama. "He's very sweet. I don't think . . . well, I'm not in love with him. I guess I should be . . . but, well, it was just a nice . . . oh, I don't know . . ." And she truly didn't.

Dahlia looked perplexed. "God, Cassie," she confessed, "I've just spent the last few hours, begging—begging— mind you, for Desmond to do the same thing, but he won't. I thought that's all men ever wanted. Do you suppose there's something wrong with him? He kisses my hand. My God, he even kisses my foot, but he hardly dares kiss me, really kiss me. And tonight I did everything short of ripping off my clothes and attacking him. What do you think it means?"

Cassie shook her head. What did it mean? She was sleepy now, but she fought her drowsiness, knowing that Dahlia wanted to talk. She could heard Dahlia's words, but the sentences didn't come together very well in her mind.

She awoke with a start. She had fallen asleep, but Dahlia, she saw, was sitting in the window seat staring out at the dawn, which was just then breaking. Cassie rubbed her eyes. Something about Dahlia's look, the intensity of her gaze, kept Cassie from speaking, and she lay miserably on the bed. She had failed her friend . . . somehow.

That day, Dahlia disappeared with Desmond for a trip into town. Cassie swam by herself all afternoon, lazily doing lap after lap, and then half-heartedly returned to the house to change for dinner. Dahlia had called, saying that she and Desmond were having dinner in town and would be back late. Cassie spent a quiet evening playing Scrabble with Aunt Delphine, but she had little enthusiasm for the game in the hot, still night.

Delphine threw up her hands.

"I can't concentrate, can you? Shall we call it a night?" Cassie agreed, relieved, and started to get up to go to her room, but Aunt Delphine detained her.

"You know, Cassie, we're all very concerned for Dahlia. I haven't wanted to intrude on you girls this holiday. I wanted you both to feel free to do as you pleased, but frankly I haven't liked this turn with Desmond Lovell. It worries me."

"Oh, I wouldn't worry, really I wouldn't. Dahlia's just trying to have a romance, and Desmond is, well . . . he appears to be very romantic."

Delphine smiled. "Yes, of course. Then you don't think she's gone and taken him seriously, do you?"

Cassie swallowed. "Well," she weighed her words, remembering Dahlia's troubled face the night before, "I would say Dahlia has things in control. I mean, I don't think Desmond means very much more to her than . . . you know, a fun time."

"I see." Delphine patted Cassie's arm absently. "I hope you're right. I'm sure you are."

Cassie nodded and turned to go, but then she remembered

to ask. "I was just wondering, Lady Hamilton, I mean, Dahlia's been expecting her father ever since we arrived. Do you know when he's coming?"

"Guy? Coming here? Why, whatever gave her that idea? I doubt that Guy de Ginsburgh would ever find Nassau amusing, and certainly not now. He's in mourning. Surely you misunderstood."

Cassie's mouth went dry and she knew she looked like a gaping fool. But she managed to leave and go to her bedroom. There she waited for an hour before going downstairs to see if Dahlia was in. But she was not.

She returned to her room in an agitated state, having left a note on Dahlia's bed to come see her, "no matter how late."

Cassie woke up just before dawn, drenched in sweat, having had a terrible nightmare. In her dream she had been a little girl and she was sitting on her daddy's lap. Everything was warm and secure and wonderful—she, Bobby, and Blue were all back together again. Then, suddenly, he was sick and gasping for air and she was running through an enormous castle calling for help, "My father is sick . . . please, he's dying." And all around her were elegantly dressed people who smiled at her and said, "How lovely, dear, you must come to Provence."

Cassie waited until she could hear the house stirring and then went to knock on Dahlia's door. When there was no answer, she pushed it open carefully. She could see that the bed was unused, her note unread. Worried and confused, she went to the dining room. Aunt Delphine was sitting at the breakfast table, a telegram in her hand. Without greeting, she handed it to Cassie.

DARLING AUNT: WE'VE ELOPED. DON'T BE ANGRY.
I'M VERY HAPPY. LOVE, DAHLIA
P.S. TELL CASSIE I'LL WRITE.

Chapter 21

BUT DAHLIA DIDN'T write. No letter was waiting when Cassie returned to school, and she found herself by turns forlorn, anxious, angry, and depressed. She felt stripped of the security that the de Ginsburgh wealth and power promised. Yes, "stripped" was the word, all right, she thought, as she allowed herself to envision the black and white horrors that were the source of at least part of her agony.

But, more important, there was Dahlia. Or rather, there was *not* Dahlia, and that, perhaps, was the bitterest pill. How could her best friend in the world have lied to her, have abandoned her so blithely, changed her stripes so abruptly, disappeared so completely? No. It was impossible. Tomorrow there would be a letter. Or the next day. In it, a contrite Dahlia would beg Cassie's forgiveness, invoke the imperishability of their friendship, hint at circumstances far beyond her control, and announce her imminent arrival back at school to share and explain these mysteries in person. Oh, and there would be a P.S.: Cassie would be advised not to give a further thought to those pictures. The baron would have made a few well-chosen phone calls. Neil would be in jail; Candy—who knows—in a convent; the photographs, destroyed. Forever.

The absence of such a letter in each successive day's mail was in each case a blow, and, as one lonely and anxious week of study melted inexorably into the next, Cassie squandered ever greater quantities of energy on maintaining her flagging hopes.

One rainy spring morning, Cassie sat in the library working on her final term paper, consoling herself with the thought that soon this particular and very hateful phase of her life would be over. Just a few more weeks and she would graduate from the Bennett Academy and leave behind forever this awful, adolescent world of stupid, giggling, pimply girls. She knew that college would be different—a world of serious, ambitious, worldly women all busily engaged in purposeful intellectual pursuits. She stared out the window at the gray, wet campus and imagined herself in a cozy, book-filled room, a Turkish carpet on the floor, a cheerful fire in the grate, a group of women gathered to discuss the influence of Kierkegaard on modern life as they sipped sherry and endlessly smoked cigarettes.

A lone figure appeared on the deserted lawns outside the library and made its way hurriedly toward the library building. Cassie turned so she could see her as she came through the heavy doors. The girl whispered something to Miss McGrath, and suddenly Cassie knew they were talking about her. She watched, immobilized by a strange and chilling curiosity as the librarian glanced around and pointed in Cassie's direction.

"Excuse me." The girl was still a little out of breath. "Please, you're to come to Miss Jefferson's office at once. There's an important phone call."

Dahlia! It simply had to be, thought Cassie, trying to conceal a little giggle of amazement at her friend's audacious ways. Whatever had she said to Miss Jefferson to make the headmistress break all her own rules and summon Cassie from her studies.

The girls walked quickly through the teeming rain, and, although Cassie was longing to know more, she held her tongue so as not to ruin whatever crazy scheme Dahlia had managed to cook up. She was ushered directly into the headmistress's office and left alone with Constance Jefferson.

"Sit down, Cassie." Miss Jefferson pointed to the padded green leather chair beside her desk, but she herself stood up and walked across the room to shut the door. "I'm afraid, my dear, that I have some rather bad news for you."

Cassie felt her heart leap up to her throat, and an image formed itself spontaneously in her mind's eye. Dahlia was standing high up on a cliff, at the very edge of a dangerous precipice. Her arms were stretched out to the sky and her white dress blew about her in gauzy billows, and then . . . One step and she was in air, plummeting, to be dashed upon the stones below, a heap of broken bones and spattered blood.

"Your grandmother . . ." Miss Jefferson's kind, thoughtful voice broke through the horrifying vision, "she died last night."

Cassie stared dumbly at Miss Jefferson. Granny Litton? Dead? But she had been so sure that Dahlia had called at last that she could not think what one had to do with the other. Nor could she imagine Granny Litton dying. It just didn't seem the kind of thing that Granny would allow herself to do.

"I knew Augusta Goodfellow quite well," Miss Jefferson was saying, "and she was a remarkable woman. I know she was very fond of you and very proud of you too. You must try to take what comfort you can in that. In many ways you bear a remarkable resemblance to your grandmother. And now you must draw on the fortitude and dignity that are your legacy from that great woman."

Cassie said nothing and continued to sit motionless as if waiting for something further to happen.

"Of course, you will want to go home at once. The funeral will be tomorrow. Can you be ready in an hour? Shall I have one of the girls help you to pack? Do you want Melissa to walk back with you to your room? Cassie?"

Cassie shook her head, and, with a great effort of will, she pulled herself together. "Thank you, Miss Jefferson." She felt the tremor in her voice as she spoke. "I can pack by myself, so there's no need to disturb anyone. I'm all right, I really am. It's only that . . . well, it's a shock."

"I know, dear, I know." The older woman placed her arm around Cassie's thin shoulders and gave her a rare, uncharacteristic embrace.

Cassie moved to the door, but then paused for a moment. She wanted to ask the question that had been uppermost in her mind for the past several weeks, but in the end she changed her mind. Granny Litton was dead, and, as far as Cassie was concerned, Dahlia de Ginsburgh might as well be dead, too.

Chapter 22

GRANNY LITTON WAS buried the next day, in the old hilltop cemetery, flanked by her husband, Cornelius Litton, on the left, and her son, Robert Augustus Litton, on the right. The church service, the long cortege, the funeral, and the following reception were a carefully choreographed and elaborate display of the Littons' rank and position as the leading family in Winston-Salem. Hundreds turned out, dressed to the nines in their darkest, gloomiest finery, to pay their final respects to the woman whom Senator Lescaux called in his eulogy, "Our greatest lady and our finest friend. Augusta Goodfellow Litton."

Throughout the long day, Cassie went about her ceremonial obligations feeling strangely invisible and only remotely connected to the surrounding people and events. She felt as if she had somehow turned to stone, and the more she tried to dredge up some semblance of feeling or emotion, the colder and more removed she felt. She wondered if everyone felt that way, and at the reception she studied her relatives. It was all too obvious that Aunt Lucille felt only relief and excitement at this liberation from her mother-in-law's rule and that she was wasting no time in stepping into the role of reigning matriarch of Winston-Salem society. Cousin Peachie burst into wet and copious tears regularly and on cue—just as she did when she watched afternoon soap operas. Winthrop looked splendidly somber and convincingly sad as he allowed the fluttering, lace-bedecked ladies to comfort and kiss him even as he heartily accepted the tributes, back slaps, and handshakes bestowed by the men. He looks, thought Cassie, like he's having the time of his life. Only old Sam and Sarah look as though they've suffered a loss.

At length, having calculated that she would probably not be missed and that her mother had downed about as many bourbons as she could handle in public, Cassie was preparing to leave when she felt a hand on her shoulder and turned to face Uncle Winthrop.

"I'm so terribly sad and sorry . . ." she started to say, as this was the first time she'd had a chance to speak to her uncle, but he stopped her with a gesture.

"I'd like to see you in my office tomorrow at ten. Ten sharp. We've got some serious talking to do."

Cassie started to nod, but Winthrop walked away as abruptly as he had appeared.

By the time she had gotten to his office the next morning, she was sure she had figured out what the meeting was about. It just had to be money. Granny Litton had promised she would take care of her favorite son's daughter, and, though she felt a little guilty, Cassie had let her imagination run through the night. Her little inheritance had grown by leaps and bounds, and now Cassie's heart raced with excitement.

Once she was in the office, with the door shut firmly behind her, she waited until Winthrop swiveled his chair around to face her. He nodded curtly at her greeting but did not ask her to sit down. Well, thought Cassie, if he's this angry it must be a tidy sum indeed! No doubt he disapproved of his mother's generosity.

"Do you have any idea why I've called you here?" His voice was unpleasant.

"I believe I do, Uncle Winthrop," Cassie answered quietly. "Is it about my inheritance?"

"Your inheritance! Well, I call that a brassy piece of business!" Winthrop's face had turned red, and he slammed his hand down on the desk. "What makes you think that there's a single penny of my sainted mother's money coming to the likes of you?"

Cassie was confused now and not a little frightened, but

everything that mattered in the world was at stake and she knew she had to call on all her courage to stand up to her uncle.

"Uncle Winthrop," she kept her voice steady and quiet, "I don't know if inheritance is the right word, but I do know that Granny promised me, just last Christmas, that she would pay for my college education. We talked about it . . . she and I. She knew I'd been accepted at Smith College, and she knew that it cost a lot of money to go there . . . and she said that she was setting the money aside so that I could have it to go to school . . . instead of a debut." She knew it was a weak ending, but she felt herself running out of steam.

"Is that right, Missy? And what do you think your grandmother would have said if she'd seen these?" He pulled six glossy black and white photographs out of a manila envelope and spread them out on top of the desk. One glance was enough. All the color drained out of Cassie's face.

"Where did you get those, Uncle Winthrop?" she asked weakly. "What are you going to do?"

"I don't rightly know, Cassie, and that's the truth of it. But I'll tell you this. The Litton family will not be exposed to the threats posed by this kind of scandalous behavior. My God! I've heard of youthful indiscretions in my day, but these . . . This is pornographic trash! How could you do this? Have you no shame? No consideration for our side of the family? I always knew there was bad blood on your mother's side . . ." He spat out the words, "But I never expected this! Don't you have anything to say for yourself? Were you drugged? Just what in God's name prompted you to display yourself in this obscene manner?"

"I'm sorry, Uncle Winthrop. I have absolutely nothing to say. If I tried to explain, I don't think you would understand."

"No, I doubt that I would." He was silent for a minute, as if he thought she might come up with an excuse yet. "Well, at least you're not trying to weasel out of this. I'll give you that much credit."

Cassie said nothing.

"All right, then. I've given this painful, disgraceful matter a great deal of thought, and here is what I propose to do. I will attend to the problem of eliminating these . . . things," he pointed to the photos. "And I don't mind telling you that it will cost me a great deal of money not to mention embarrassment, but, in the interest of the family, I will see to it that they are destroyed. After that I wash my hands of you. Do you understand? I want not a single reminder of the depths to which a member of the Litton family has stooped."

Cassie bit her lip. It was trembling uncontrollably. She knew he was talking about the photographs and yet, deep within her, she suspected that it was his own brother, her father, whom Winthrop could not forgive. She could only guess at what her father's offense might have been, but she knew her own and she was genuinely sorry, though something else, something very like anger, was beginning to buzz in her ears. "Yes, sir," she mumbled. "I understand."

Winthrop went on, though less pompously, in a more businesslike way. "You're aware, I suppose, that my brother, before he died, made over to your name five hundred shares of voting stock in the *Salem Chronicle*—the last of his harebrained schemes?"

"Yes, I know that."

"I trust you have no illusions about its value. It is, purely and simply, voting stock in a failed company. It cannot be sold to anyone outside the family and it confers nothing more than the right to attend our stockholders' meetings— a right that properly only belongs to members in good standing of the Litton family, a right you have abused with your shameful behavior."

By now all feelings of shock and contrition had fled from Cassie's trembling frame. She was angry. "No, Uncle Winthrop. I have no illusions about anything. Your lawyer, Mr. Potts, made it abundantly clear what that stock was worth after you and the others allowed Daddy's dream to fall apart just because it was his and not yours. Do you really think I would have taken money from Granny, the only one of you with an ounce of love and dignity in her soul, if that stock was worth anything? Do you think that Mama and I would have put up with the humiliation you Littons love to dish out if we had anything of our own?"

"Well now, young lady, that's quite a display of temper. But if you're being so high and mighty, I think we might just have the makings of a deal. You go ahead and sign these worthless stock certificates over to the family, and I'll undertake to preserve your equally worthless reputation." He tapped the photographs with his pudgy forefinger. "Then we're quits of one another, and I take it that will be to your liking."

Cassie was shocked by her own boldness, and even the hide-bound Winthrop was taken aback. "What about my college education?"

"What about it?"

"It may not be in her will, or maybe it is, I don't know, but Granny Litton promised to put me through college, Smith College, and she knew it and I know it and you know it, too. It's my birthright—the only one I had—because she loved Bobby even if you didn't. You can show those damned pictures to anyone you like. I don't really care. They're not nearly as ugly as the way you've treated Mama and me all these years. But if you want your precious voting stock back, you'll have to make good on Granny's promise. You do that, or so help me I'll show up stark naked at every stockholders' meeting from now until doomsday, just to shame you. Because it's you, Uncle Winthrop, who needs to be ashamed. Not me. It's you!"

As the plane taxied down the runway at Winston-Salem airport, Cassie slipped her hand into her purse to assure herself, for the hundredth time, that the cashier's check was still there. She smiled bitterly. Ten thousand dollars would get her through Smith College, albeit with no frills. Almost as important, it tokened her release from bondage to the hateful Litton clan. It was her quitclaim and her freedom. With Granny Litton dead and gone, there wasn't one of them she would miss.

Perhaps she ought to be grateful to Candy Lescaux. Cassie laughed aloud mirthlessly, startling the woman in the seat next to hers. Perhaps *grateful* wasn't exactly the right word, but it was odd, she thought, how things worked out. She was, in fact, less angry at Candy, who had plotted against her, than she was at Dahlia, who had let her down. So much for family and friends. Easy come, easy go. Well, she could do it on her own. She would make something of herself, that much she was sure of. They could all go hang themselves.

There was, of course, another six weeks of school to get through. She would wait a bit, then tell Blue that she'd won a scholarship. And, by God, she would not go back to Winston-Salem for the summer. Or ever again, for that matter.

Chapter 23

A BRIEF CEREMONY in the offices of the governor general transformed a smiling Dahlia de Ginsburgh into a triumphant Lady Lovell. No one threw rice as they dashed off into a waiting car, but six hours later, as they descended from the plane in London, Dahlia turned and impulsively tossed her small, crumpled bouquet to an astonished air hostess. It was not until they closed the door of their suite at Claridge's that they began to feel that they had successfully pulled off some sort of miraculous caper. They toasted each other with champagne and giggled idiotically as they composed telegrams that told their news but not their whereabouts. At last they fell exhausted into a long, deep sleep.

It was on the second night of her marriage that Dahlia discovered that as a lover Desmond was every bit as inexperienced as she. She had expected to be swept off her feet and masterfully transformed from girl into woman. She had longed for passion, but there was nothing in the least passionate about the man who came to her bed in a suit of striped pajamas, turned off the light, and awkwardly consummated their marriage.

But if Desmond was disappointing in bed, he was at least affectionate at all other times, and if Dahlia had married him in order to drastically change her life, then in that regard she was not disappointed at all. She had plunged headlong into the merry-go-round that was London in 1969, a city alive as it hadn't been since the war—leading the world in fashion, art, music—all at a tempo that left one breathless.

It all seemed tailor-made for Dahlia. She simply stepped in and became, almost overnight, a luminous presence on the social scene. Her days were a frenzy of shopping, her nights an exhausting round of drink parties, dinners, dances, and midnight appearances. She was the new, best-loved darling of society. *Vogue* photographed her wearing the latest clothes from Zandra Rhodes and said that Lady Lovell stood for everything that was happening in the latest fashion renaissance of London: she was young, she was beautiful, and she had that little extra something that went beyond. Lady Dahlia Lovell was NOW.

The hectic pace also allowed her to avoid thinking about certain unpleasantnesses, certain feelings and nagging questions that had plagued her since her mother's death. She could forget about those nauseating photographs, and she could put off the guilt she felt when she thought of Cassie. With every passing, busy day it seemed harder and harder to recall the times with Cassie, in Washington, at school, in Nassau. It all seemed to be from another life, one that was very far away and somehow not quite real.

At the center of her new life now was an old friend. She had not seen her childhood chum, Caroline, now married to Sir Nicholas Keyes, since those long-ago days at Membland.

Lady Caroline Keyes, a brunette, was the most unlikely person to have acquired the nickname of Carrots. She was six feet tall with long, long legs and arms that floated about her as if she was in a perpetual production of *Swan Lake*. Her long, aquiline nose and deep-set slate-gray eyes gave her an ageless, aristocratic look that belied her twenty years. The name had come about as a result of a nursery costume party when all the children had been invited to come as "something from the garden." Tall, even at seven, Lady Caroline had insisted on wearing a shocking-orange sheath found on the bargain tables of Marks and Spencer's, topped by an enormous headdress of ostrich plumes. She had looked so preposterous next to the other children dressed as adorable flowers and Farmer Browns, that the name Carrots had stuck.

Everything about Carrots was melodramatic and extreme,

from the large, jeweled combs she wore to secure her jet-black chignon and the vintage clothes she collected with a passion, to her outrageous and loudly voiced opinions on almost any subject at all. Lady Caroline considered it her sacred obligation to avoid, whenever possible, anything even remotely serious or significant. Pious to a fault in that one regard, she pursued the trivial pleasures of life with assiduous discipline and unfailing energy.

With Carrots at her side, Dahlia was kept extremely busy, ongoingly amused, and well supplied with outré advice on every possible subject.

"But, darling, what you don't understand," said Carrots, after Dahlia had finally confronted her friend with the information that she might have made a terrible mistake by marrying Desmond, "is that no woman actually *likes* her husband."

They were tucked up in the cozy sitting room of Caroline's elegant house in Belgravia, sipping tea and brandy after an exhausting afternoon of shopping. Dahlia giggled, tipsy from the brandy.

"Oh, come on, Carrots, you can't mean that! Surely there are *some* good marriages. What about Nicky? He's adorable and awfully kind."

"Of course he's adorable, and I adore him. But you mistake my meaning. You've obviously spent a great deal too much time in America, and you've picked up some of their shallow, vulgar notions about what a marriage is supposed to be. Wasn't it Somerset Maugham who said that American women expect the sort of perfection from their husbands that English women only look for in their butlers? Well, there you are! And you know how hard it is to find an even tolerable butler these days. But it's obvious that you've got yourself in a muddle. We'll analyze your situation point by point, and I guarantee that there is absolutely nothing wrong with you except your way of looking at things. So you've gone and married Desmond Lovell. Fact. Why did you do it?"

"I suppose because I couldn't bear my life as it was and

I thought that by marrying Desmond everything would change." Dahlia felt herself blushing at hearing the truth so plainly for the first time.

Carrots was nonplussed. "And as far as I can see, you *have* changed your life. You've gone from being a schoolgirl in some dreary American backwater to a rather jolly life in London. I'd say your marriage is working unbelievably well. It's true, Desmond is a bit of a bore, and I suppose you might have done better to marry Rupert Howard or better yet Henry Brooks, but, then, they weren't around when the need arose, were they? Really, *cheri,* everything has worked out for the best, *n'est-ce pas?*"

"Carrots, how can you be so cynical?" Dahlia wailed. "Here I am married to a man I hardly know..."

"Quite right, darling, and I should keep it that way if I were you. Desmond Lovell is not the sort of man about whom one wants to know very much at all. Ask anyone. And, believe me, it's much the best sort of domestic arrangement. I've spent the last three years not getting to know Nicky. And, you know, I don't. I hardly recognize him sometimes."

Dahlia couldn't help laughing at her friend's preposterous way of putting things, and yet there was something comforting and reassuring about Carrot's point of view. "But what about romance, passion, love?" Dahlia demanded. "Oh, Carrots, remember the summers at Membland? Sex and romance seemed so exciting then. So intriguing. Was it all a sham? All those elegantly got-up guests whispering their little secrets and sneaking about. You used to say they were all being naughty in the night. God, what images that phrase used to conjure up for me. It still does. Don't you remember the time—"

"God, but we were monsters. Wasn't it fun?" Caroline said, remembering.

"Yes. Yes! That's just my point. It *was* fun; it was exciting and intriguing. I mooned about that poor kitchen boy forever, I was so turned on by it all. What's happened to all that? Desmond and I make love . . . often enough, I guess but it's—"

Carrots interrupted. "Ah, but now you're talking about love—*l'amour, l'amour.* Nothing's happened to that at all, I assure you. Love is alive and doing well, but that's an entirely different subject. We were speaking of marriage."

Chapter 24

In the year that followed, Dahlia and her friend spoke very little of marriage and a great deal about love—love with viscounts and dukes, with French soccer players and Italian bicyclists, with American businessmen and Arab oilmen, love with friends, love with strangers, and, just once, love with the chauffeur. Of course, it was Carrots who did all the talking, and Dahlia who listened in wide-eyed amazement.

It was following a particularly juicy true-confessions luncheon that it happened. Dahlia and Carrots had gone on to a fitting at Jean Muir's and were now browsing at the food counter at Harrod's. As the man handed Dahlia a bit of Stilton for a taste, she became suddenly and intensely nauseated and fainted dead away. An hour later she was stretched out on Lady Caroline's bed. Dr. Appleby attended her and reassured her that absolutely nothing was wrong. She was simply pregnant.

Dahlia was stunned. "I'm going to have a baby," she repeated in a dazed voice. "How can I have a baby? I've never even once thought about having a baby."

"Thinking, as I understand it, has nothing to do with it. According to the most reliable sources . . ."

"Carrots, please! Aren't you thrilled? I think it's wonderful that I'm going to have a baby. Don't you think it's wonderful?"

"I should rather have said it was amazing. Frankly, I didn't think Desmond had it in him. It is Desmond's, isn't it?"

"Don't be ridiculous, of course it's Desmond's. I wonder what he'll say."

"Oh, darling, he'll be as pleased as anything. It'll give him something to talk about at his club."

As Carrots chattered on about babies and doctors and charming little French dresses and silver cups, Dahlia could feel herself being carried away with this wonderful change in her life. Her happiness was boundless, and for the first time in a year she could hardly wait to see Desmond.

But Desmond was gone for the day, in France seeing about a horse, or was it a dog? She could never quite gather what it was that he did, but it involved endless trips in search of studs and bitches. In fact, he had spent more time away from her than with her, and she could not say that she had minded much—until now. But a baby—a baby was supposed to be one of the high points of a marriage—not exactly the kind of news to be blurted out over the telephone.

"Is it change tonight?" Desmond asked when he returned.

Dahlia nodded, "Black tie. But first, darling," she said, not wanting to wait one moment longer, "come and sit down. There's something wonderful I want to tell you."

Desmond dropped a kiss on her forehead. "Have you now?" he said indulgently. "Well you'll have to hold on to it for just a little while longer. I've simply got to bathe— I smell as ripe as the kennels. There's a good girl." He patted her hand. "I'll be with you in an hour." He hopped up the stairs to his dressing room. Dahlia marched along behind him and rapped on the door.

"Desmond. I have something *important* to tell you." But the bathwater drowned out her voice. "Bastard," she said. When he emerged an hour to the minute later, Dahlia was sitting in a chair, blocking the door, holding two glasses of champagne. She smiled prettily at him. "Desmond, I'm going to have a baby." She waited.

Desmond stared at her. "Are you sure?" he finally asked.

"Of course, silly. I even fainted at Harrod's."

"I mean, have you been to the doctor? Is it all officially confirmed?"

Dahlia nodded, her eyes brimming with pleasure. But Desmond's thoughts seemed elsewhere. She watched him, waiting for the news to sink in. Finally he looked at her, his face flushed now with happiness and pride. He nodded several times, took her hand and said, "We'll leave for Ireland in three weeks."

"Is that all you have to say?" Dahlia exploded. "Well, it so happens I don't want to leave for Ireland in three weeks—or three years, for that matter. Can't you even say you're pleased?" She burst into tears and spilled the champagne all over her dress.

"But of course I'm pleased, darling. There, there," Desmond said. "Don't cry, Dahlia. It's simply time we went home. It's only right that my son be born on the land that will be his some day. Hush, now. You knew we'd be going home to Glinveagh eventually."

She could see by the look on his face, by his stance, and his entire manner that the news had somehow transformed him. He was now the man of property and responsibility, returning to the ancestral home with his bride, ready to produce the next lord of Glinveagh Castle.

Desmond took her to lunch the next day, and she found a small box from Cartier's under her napkin. In it was a fine gold chain from which suspended an opal, the biggest she had ever seen, like a shimmering sparrow's egg.

"Ireland," Carrots moaned. "I detest Ireland. All those smiling eyes and everyone bursting into song. I don't care if he owns ten castles, there is nothing, but nothing, interesting or amusing anywhere in Ireland. You're not going, are you? I mean, green is not your color. Remember that gown at Saint Laurent?"

"Darling Carrots! What would I do without you?" Dahlia smiled indulgently. "But there are worse things to endure than a castle in Ireland. I mean, it's really not all that far away."

"Then you actually are thinking of going?" Carrots was appalled.

"Yes, darling, I am."

"But why, for heaven's sake?"

"Oh, I suppose a part of me is curious. And it does mean so much to Desmond. He's so firm about the whole thing, so sure of himself and what we've got to do. It's an altogether new side of him. I rather like it. Anyway, it really isn't as if we're moving to the North Pole. We'll keep the flat, and as soon as the baby is born, Glinveagh will be just a nice country retreat. Nothing will change very much at all."

But Dahlia was wrong. Everything changed.

Chapter 25

CASSIE LOVED HER life at Smith. For the first two years she immersed herself in her studies to the exclusion of everything else. Classes and schedules were challenging enough to fully occupy her time and mind, while her teachers and classmates were as interesting a group of people as she had ever hoped to meet. The campus was a beehive of activity, and the competition for excellence was fierce. There were times when Cassie felt like a long-distance swimmer in a race of mammoth proportions. Yes, she had skill, strength, and endurance, but every time she finished a lap and came up for air, a new challenge loomed before her and so she quickly gulped another lungful and dove back in.

She got to know the campus and she came to love it. Nowhere, it seemed to her, was there a lovelier place on earth. The old stone buildings with their turrets, towers, and leaded-glass windows were surely the equals of any castle in the world, while every massive tree and rambling walk and every sparkling clapboard house seemed to her eyes the perfect specimen of its type. Even when she felt lonely and melancholy, as happened inevitably from time to time, it seemed somehow appropriate here. The feelings were in perfect harmony with the sharp bite of the autumn air and the *swoosh-swoosh* of rustling leaves beneath the never-ending rush of feet. The times she loved best were the dark November afternoons when she lingered in the cold outdoors to watch the lights come on in the halls and cozy little rooms, until all the windows were ablaze and every light burned with a purpose of its own.

By her junior year, she felt ready to expand her world

to include more extracurricular activities. She eagerly accepted an invitation to join the staff of the *Smith Review* and immediately embraced the cause of contemporary belles lettres. She also began to take a serious interest in meeting men. Meeting men and getting dates turned out to be easy enough, what with Amherst, U Mass, and even Harvard nearby. Finding romance in any of the feckless young men who paid for her beer and fumbled with the buckles of her loden coat was another problem. Perhaps it was boredom and frustration that finally drove her into the arms of Luke Walton, for she could never really come up with an adequate reason why she should have chosen him over any of the others to be her boyfriend for a while.

They had met on a blind date in the middle of her junior year. It had been a bitterly cold night, and he had come to call on her enveloped in a vastly oversized army-surplus overcoat and a pair of fuzzy bright-red earmuffs.

"Cute, but three sheets to the wind," was the description delivered to Cassie on the house intercom. "He's having a problem with your name."

"Cashey?" Luke slurred as she approached him. He scratched his head as if he were not quite sure what to do now that the girl was ready to be taken out on the date. "Uh . . . Would you like a drink?" He waved a bottle happily in the air.

"Uh uh," Cassie shook her head, putting the bottle back in his pocket. "No booze in the dorms."

Luke's eyes widened in an "Oh, I get it" look. He took Cassie's arm and led her out into the cold, starry night. Cassie shivered in her coat. She was never warm enough.

"You have a car?" she asked as they walked across the little square outside her dorm.

"Nope. Got a ride down with m'buddy . . ." He paused, probably trying to remember who his buddy was.

Cassie sighed. Swell. Here it was the coldest night of the year and she had a blind date who was blind drunk and had no car.

"You want to go to McGill's or Cavagnaro's?" she demanded, not bothering to hide her annoyance. Luke slowed down to a halt as his mind tried to grapple with the alternatives she proposed.

At last he shrugged his shoulders and grinned down at her, "Hey, Cashey, you mad at me?"

"No!" She stamped her feet in a sudden fury. "I'm cold! I'm not just cold, I'm freezing." And suddenly he caught her up in his arms and enveloped her in the massive tent of his woolen coat.

"S'warm in here," he breathed down at her. "Do you think we can walk?" He held her close, swaying a little, shifting around until their bodies made a perfect fit, and she was surprised to feel a shock of pleasure from this sudden intimacy. Luke was just the right height for her to snuggle her face into the warm hollow of his neck, and his skin had a pleasant, soapy smell. Drunk as he was, there was nothing awkward or tentative in the way that he held her, and it was this as much as anything that allowed her to let down her guard. She knew that they looked ridiculous and she didn't care and all at once she realized that she didn't care about anything at all except that he go on holding her tight and pressing against her in all the right places.

They dated frequently after that and wasted no time on preliminary conversations. On their second date they applied all the ingenuity of their Ivy League educations to overcoming the limitations of a Volkswagen, as a substitute bed. And they passed several passionate, if inarticulate, months proving that neither rain nor snow, not even the restrictions of dormitory life, could deter young lovers from their carnal pursuits.

Cassie frankly enjoyed their uncomplicated and very sexual relationship despite the fact that the mysterious "big O" (as the magazines put it) continued to elude her. The long hours they spent kissing, petting, and exploring were enough for the time being. What Luke lacked in the way of finesse and technique, he made up for with his rough ardor and endurance. The simple, crude passion of their evenings together intoxicated her, and many class hours were given over to an unblushing rerun of their last encounter.

But Luke Walton was hopeless. She'd known it from the start. He was going to get through college by the skin of his teeth, go home to his father's lucrative insurance business in Philadelphia, and, the sooner the better, marry the right girl with the right background and the right fortune. Within a few months, it became clear to Cassie that it was she he had in mind for this role. Luke had naturally assumed that she was a Litton with all the attending endowments, trusts, and inheritances, and Cassie did little, if anything, to discourage those assumptions. It suited her to pass for a rich Litton and seemed to her harmless enough, until she made the liar's mistake of getting carried away with the pretense.

One Wednesday afternoon, his face flushed with excitement, Luke hailed her from across the main quad. As he approached, he shouted breathless but hearty congratulations.

"For what?"

"Well," he said, somewhat taken aback by her blank stare, "maybe I'm not supposed to know, but Dad says he heard at the club about the sale of the *Salem Chronicle* to the guy from England, uh, Stavros. My God! You're a trustee. You don't mean that you didn't know about it? You simply *can't* be unaware of a five-million-dollar sale."

"Wait a minute, Luke. Just wait a minute! You're saying that my uncle just sold the *Winston-Salem Chronicle* for five million dollars?"

"By George, you don't know? Well, that's exactly what I'm saying." He grinned at her, at the same time taking her arm possessively. "Let's blow this dump and really celebrate. Let's go to New York. Hey! Then we can go down to Philadelphia. I want you to meet my folks."

Cassie jerked her arm from his. "Be quiet, Luke. Just shut up a minute and let me think. Who bought this paper? Where did you find out about this?"

Luke looked at her impatiently. "I told you. My dad called me. He was in New York at his club when the word got around. A guy from England bought it. A guy named John

Stavros. He owns a lot of trashy tabloids over there. He's really into buying up newspapers. The rumor is he wanted a respectable toehold in the U.S."

Cassie's mind raced; she felt sick to her stomach. Five million dollars! And Uncle Winthrop, the bastard, the stinking bastard, had it all in his own fat pocket. She stared stupidly at Luke and then all of a sudden she began to laugh—hysterical, choking gasps—until Luke had to shake her hard to get her to calm down.

"There's nothing to celebrate, Luke," she said finally. And then she told him the truth, patiently explaining to him the whole, sordid mess.

Later, there was a tearful call to her mother. Blue was aghast. "I told you over and over again not to let go of those stocks. It was all your daddy had . . . All he had in the world. I don't care what those . . . those pictures looked like. Teenage highjinks, I say, and so what? We ought to get the law on Winthrop. He can't do this to you, honey. You were under age . . . You were coerced . . ."

"Please, Mama," Cassie whispered. "Winthrop Litton's got lawyers who are bigger and better and more powerful than anyone we could hire—"

"No, Cassie, you listen to me—"

"No, Mama. You listen. I've only got one more year left in school. After that I'm on my own. I'm going to New York and I'm going to make something of myself. I'm not going to spend the rest of my life being bitter about Winthrop Litton, no matter how rotten he's been."

Chapter 26

DAHLIA LAY IN bed, awake but not quite ready to face the morning—not just yet. She could hear Dierdre laughing upstairs in the nursery. How, she wondered, did that tiny, hairless blob of an infant become, in the space of—could it be?—less than a year, a golden-haired fairy child, so sweet, so joyously responsive to songs and smiles and pretty things. Dahlia had never felt such a sense of perfection as when Dierdre was born, two weeks early and with no time to get to the hospital. There had only been the maid there, Josephine, who'd done little more than invoke the name of God, and the village doctor doddering about her bedroom, looking as if he needed a drink. Dierdre had been born in four hours, fat, pink, and squealing. Dahlia, though exhausted, had made sure the doctor got his drink and that there was champagne for the rest of the household.

She was tempted to shake off her sleepiness and sneak up to the nursery before Josephine arrived with breakfast. But no. She heard the unmistakable rattling of china and the inevitable rap on the door. Dahlia squinted at the tray Josephine set on her bed: tea, a boiled egg, the newspaper, and the mail. Another day at Glinveagh Castle had begun.

"Good morning, Josephine. What's the day like?" She could tell that things, at least in some quarters, were already in turmoil—not an unusual circumstance.

Josephine was clearly working herself up for a little speech. "It's a saint for sure, Mum, can take that old witch. She's an evil one, she is. You'll not be seein' what I see— she's right smart actin' when you're around up there, Mum, but . . . Well, just now I was having a fine time with the baby. We was laughin' and singin' when, out of the blue, in she thunders, yellin' and shoutin' at me like I was no better than a street girl. Scared me and the baby to death. Mother o' God, I seen the devil lurkin' in her eyes, I have." She crossed herself fervently.

Dahlia neatly cracked and cut the top off her egg, her eyes glancing over the headlines. In fact, she rather agreed with Josephine. Old Nanny, while hardly evil, was certainly as set in her ways as the very stones of Glinveagh. Actually, Dahlia had hired Josephine Muldoon in the hope of packing Old Nanny off to a cottage on the estate. She and Desmond had argued endlessly about it, Dahlia claiming that the old woman's mind was wandering, while Desmond, who had virtually been raised by her, proclaimed her a saint. Dahlia had lost. Old Nanny ruled the nursery wing and would until she expired, a Prince Albert biscuit in one hand and a nappy in the other.

Old Nanny and Josephine, of course, were natural enemies. Josephine, a plump, easy-going girl, believed in ghosts and in having a good time. The latter she did with a seemingly endless assortment of gardeners and tradesmen. Josephine's peccadilloes kept the entire below-stairs at Glinveagh humming with gossip, much to Dahlia's amusement.

"You're looking in the pink today, Josephine. Something to do with that young man I saw you with on the embankment yesterday?"

Dahlia knew very well that it did. Old Nanny had made sure of that the night before. "She was doin' it, Mum—pardon me—right there for God and man to see. And with him! There's not a decent girl in the village would go with him."

Josephine's eyes glowed. "Ooooh. You'll be meaning Michael McGrady, sure. He's a fine lad," she said, pausing to dwell on one or another of his finer points and flushing a bright scarlet—"afterglow," the magazines would have called it.

Dahlia reflected that she herself could use some afterglow. Desmond was kind and sweet—not unlike the tail-wagging, floppy-eared dogs he bred—but of late his love-making had gone from awkward to disastrous. Dahlia tried to remember their sex life when they had first been married, but it was all mixed up in her mind with the excitement of discovering London. Surely there had been some good times then, but she couldn't seem to remember. She had gotten pregnant and come to Glinveagh—and thereafter had been so absorbed with the new life growing inside her and the mammoth job of transforming the house that she had scarcely noticed Desmond's lack of ardor.

But since Dierdre's birth, she had found herself ravenous for sex. It was as if having the baby had triggered some excess of hormones in her body. Desmond, however, though a proud enough daddy, seemed less inclined than ever to be a lover.

For a while she had tried to stimulate him in settings more suited to his outdoor ways. Once, spurred on by images from *Tom Jones* and *Fanny Hill*, she tried to seduce him in the stables, but that had been a definite mistake—Desmond had turned cold and frantic with embarrassment. Humiliated by the rejection and flushed with anger, Dahlia felt more and more like an unsuccessful vamp. Gradually she had given up. Nothing seemed to excite him—not clothes or the lack of them, not food or drink, not atmosphere, not even fetishes, though she tried every variety she'd heard of and a few she'd made up. Oh, there was some sex, if you could call it that—perfunctory couplings at coldly calculated, biologically opportune intervals. He came to her bed only in the interests of providing proper progeny for his lands and title. Their lovely daughter, Dierdre, did not qualify as heir. A son was needed.

"Well, Josephine," Dahlia sighed, "where shall we go today? Mr. Brooks is coming to visit, and we must keep him entertained."

Brooksie now was patiently holding Dierdre's pudgy little hands in his as she teetered and tottered around the nursery, unable to balance alone but wanting so fiercely to walk. Dahlia watched, her pride and happiness in Dierdre tinged by a strange sadness. As time had passed, she realized, she had become a prisoner behind the heavy stone walls of the castle. Desmond had told her once that he had never enjoyed the social life of London, that he preferred the company of his horses and dogs to her friends, and that the rest of the world could go hang for all he cared. And so there were few trips to London and, fewer still, visits from her friends. Carrots, whom she had always counted on for a good gab on the telephone, flatly refused to set foot in Glinveagh.

Only Henry Brooks remained a faithful visitor, venturing to see Dahlia as often as he could. Dahlia watched him with fondness. He and Dierdre, having given up on walking, were building a castle of blocks.

Those long-ago summers at Membland, it had always been the three of them, Dahlia, Carrots, Brooksie—plotting, planning, laughing, always laughing. "The terrible trio," Charlotte had called them. Had they really changed so very much now that they were all grown up? Not really, Dahlia thought. They had just become more clearly defined versions of what they had always been.

Brooksie's hair was as pale as flax, with those funny wire-rimmed glasses that made his blue eyes huge with amazement. But then amazement and curiosity were qualities that he cultivated as carefully as his very dandy appearance. He claimed that his clothes were a necessary tool of his trade, a quirky and brilliant intuition. "No one ever takes a dandy or a fop very seriously, so they let down their guards and say all sorts of things." And it was true. Dahlia found Henry's articles about pop culture devastatingly accurate—and very funny.

"Poor Brooksie, darling." She tried to distract Dierdre. "I think that's enough playing for now. Come, both of you, and have your tea."

"Ah, nursery tea." Brooksie sighed with satisfaction. "The friendly foods of childhood." He popped a watercress sandwich into his mouth and then offered one to Dierdre.

"I used to think that my life would begin when I could graduate from nursery tea to the dinner table downstairs, all those mysterious dishes and endless courses and the pretty, candelit tables with goblets filled with wine. But now that I have, now that I seem to be forever going to or coming from someone's dinner party, I find I really want nothing more than fish fingers, eggy toast, puddings, and buttered cress sandwiches."

Dahlia laughed, agreeing. "Do you remember the time we . . ."

Chapter 27

IT WAS THROUGH her connection with the *Smith Review* that Cassie came upon the chance to take a part-time job working for Gregory Kournos, the revered and honored poet-in-residence at Smith for Cassie's senior year. Now in his seventies, he was one of two or three poets in America whose name the average man on the street might be expected to know, yet he was no pop phenomenon, no Rod McKuen. He was a classicist and a scholar—truly one of the grand old men of American poetry.

Cassie was well aware of several motives when she presented herself as an applicant for the job as his assistant. Certainly money was always to be considered. She needed to take jobs now and then to be able to afford even the smallest luxuries. But in this case she also felt a strong curiosity about the man—whose poetry she had loved for years. She wanted to see how a great poet lived, how he worked; even the smallest details, she felt, would be fascinating.

Kournos, tall and lean, with white hair and piercing blue eyes that looked, Cassie wrote in her journal, "As if they could see through the mists of history," hired her immediately, with very few questions. She was to come several afternoons a week to help with the final organizing of an immense anthology he was compiling.

The actual work was not very different from the clerical tasks she had performed during her summers for Uncle Winthrop—transcribing, typing, filing—but Cassie treasured the experience, feeling that she was in the service of a great man whose books would still be read and loved hundreds of years from now.

They worked in a large study in the back of his house. It was a low-ceilinged room with a row of casement windows on the western wall through which late-afternoon sun flooded its tawny light. The old man and the young girl worked together in comfortable silence, and to Cassie it seemed that he truly lived in another dimension, so absorbed did he become in his scribblings, so faraway was the gaze in his eyes when he stared out at scenes that were visible only to him. She was content to be there, to work and to observe him—she never asked questions, not wanting ever to interrupt the progress of his thoughts.

It was the poet's fancy to keep the room filled, always, with baskets of apples. He had scoured the New England countryside, buying bushels of Pippins, Winesaps, Greenings, Jonathans, and Cortlands, and the room was filled with their heady aroma. She supposed that he lived on apples. Apples, nuts, and raisins. These were everywhere, a bowl on his desk, on her desk, in the hall. Kournos nibbled at them absent-mindedly, pausing now and again to bite into an apple. She never saw any signs of other food in his house, no evidence of real meals. Only apples, nuts, raisins, and endless cups of steaming herb tea.

Their routine continued through the winter months and into spring. Kournos seemed to appreciate her careful attention to the details of his work, and she was extremely pleased merely to be in his calm, grave presence. He was always very polite with her, courtly in his quiet attentions. When she arrived he would help her off with her coat and carefully hang it up. A cup of tea would appear by her elbow as she worked at the files. He was always careful to praise her neatness and efficiency. He took great care to see that she was comfortable. But he never asked her anything about herself. It was as if for him she had neither a past nor any other life outside the confines of his apple-scented rooms.

This suited Cassie very well. With Gregory Kournos, she was not a college girl or a Litton or a rich girl or a poor one or anything else with a name tag and a label. She was herself—in a way she had hardly ever experienced before. They talked of books and poetry and art. He spoke about his work the way some other men might speak about their women. "To work at what you love," he told her, "to dedicate yourself to that which is best in you, is all that matters in the end. All else will wither, all other passions fade away, and only work remains, sustains, succors, and keeps you until you draw your dying breath. Remember that, my dear, when you go out into the world."

There came an evening toward the end of the term when, just as she was preparing to leave, he asked if she would stay for a glass of sherry. They sat by a crackling fire in the two old Chesterfield chairs. Outside, the daylight faded and evening came on in a purple haze. Kournos set out a crystal decanter and two lovely old glasses. The sherry was mellow and soft as velvet in her throat, and slowly a warm glow spread through her body.

"I have wanted to tell you," said Kournos, breaking the silence, "how much I have enjoyed your presence here on these afternoons." Cassie started to speak, but he raised his hand to stop her. "Of course, your work has been of invaluable assistance, but I am speaking of more than that."

Cassie felt her throat tighten. She took another sip of the liquid in her glass. Her hand shook a little. There was something so poignant, so unspeakably tender about this gentle old man.

"You are," he continued, "a very lovely young woman. What I mean to say is that you possess a beauty that transcends the merely physical. There is a light, a grace that shines through you that is the essence of feminine beauty. It has meant a great deal to me . . . Well, it's hard to say this sort of thing, but extremely important, I feel. Your presence has helped me to overcome a great stumbling block in my work, and I will always be in your debt.

"I'd like to read a poem to you, if I may, that I have been working on this winter. I should like very much to dedicate it to you."

* * *

The poem he read was filled with images of Aphrodite and apples, golden-haired maidens in service to Demeter. It was a paean to youth and to fruitfulness. Cassie was overcome with emotion. Never, in her wildest dreams, had she imagined anything as wonderful as this. She came and knelt before him.

"It's simply beautiful. I will never forget this moment as long as I live. Thank you."

He patted her almost absentmindedly on the cheek and sat staring at the fire. Finally he stood up and raised Cassie to her feet.

"Hush," he said. "I want you to do something more for me." He looked deeply into her eyes. "Will you?"

His question hung in the air for a long minute. Cassie nodded. He raised both her hands to his lips and gently kissed her fingers.

"Stand there by the fire," he said. He sat again in his chair, adjusting it slightly to face her. "Unpin your hair. Ahh, yes . . . Her crowning glory . . . Now . . ."

Slowly, piece by piece, Cassie removed her clothes, waiting each time for his request. As she cast off her garments, the radiance of the fire embraced her so that she grew not colder, but warmer. She stood bathed in the firelight, feeling strangely comfortable, as if her clothes had been a hindrance all along.

A sigh of pleasure escaped from Kournos, still reclining in his chair. "Ah, you are extraordinary. The golden girl of every man's dreams." He stood up and went to her. She started to reach for him, but he stopped her. "No. Please. Stand still." His voice was almost harsh. He cupped her large breasts in his hands and bent to kiss them.

Never in her life had she felt like this. Her nipples were as hard and ripe as the apples that filled the room. A fire burned between her legs almost as if tiny licks of flames were darting out of the fireplace and caressing her. She felt her knees begin to buckle.

"I don't think I can stand up any longer," she whispered

hoarsely. They sank down onto the soft Chinese carpet, and he stretched her out at full length, pulling back again to look at her lovely, long body.

"I don't want you to do anything," he said as he placed a cushion under her neck. "Please, let me..." Cassie moaned as his hands moved slowly over her body. He gently spread her thighs, the touch of his fingers caressing her seemed to lift her up, higher and higher, until she seemed to float in space. He held her quietly while she sobbed.

He went on kissing and caressing, his mouth traveling the length of her firelit limbs, lingering here and there with a touch as soft as rose petals. And when his tongue at last arrived to gently taste the center of her being, she felt herself explode with rolling, monumental waves of pleasure. He held her quietly against him.

"I didn't know," she said. "I never..."

He hushed her and went on stroking and caressing her until she was completely quiet, like a child.

At last, she raised herself up on an elbow and looked at him, shyly asking, "What about you?"

He brought her face to his and kissed her on the forehead. "My dear, I have possessed you more intimately than you can imagine. I prefer it this way now."

She slept a while and then bicycled back through the Massachusetts night to her own room.

The next day, an envelope arrived for her. It contained the poem Kournos had read to her the previous evening. Beneath the title were the words, "To Cassandra Litton."

Later that day, Cassie learned that she would graduate with Smith's highest academic honors—a summa cum laude in literature. School days were coming to an end.

BOOK THREE

Chapter 28

IT WAS A short walk from the Barbizon Residence Hotel for Women on Lexington Avenue and Sixty-second Street to the Hathaway Building at Fifty-fourth and Madison Avenue. The express elevator there was closely watched by a uniformed security guard. Cassie stood aside, while her name was called upstairs for clearance, and watched with interest—and not a little envy—as others, those who held the blue-and-gold passes of Hathaway Publications, entered the elevator freely. But once admitted to the dark-paneled car, she felt the distinct sensation of being elevated by something more than the swift upward motion.

In a matter of seconds she stepped out onto the twenty-first floor and into the luxurious and snobbish world of high fashion—the offices of *Style* magazine. Opulent, elegant *Style*. The supreme symbol of fashion for every American woman who had ever dreamed of being frocked by Givenchy, coiffed by Kenneth, rejuvenated at Clinique La Prairie, and set free to wander about in the legendary world of the celebrated smart set.

To the rear of the reception room, a room where everything was lacquered or mirrored so that walls reflected floors, which, in turn, reflected furniture, was a curved corridor that led to *Style*'s editorial offices. Here was where conspicuous consumption got down to serious business. Smells of pomades and powders, expensive creams and exotic scents, permeated the air while the shrill voices of a dozen or more suave, high-strung women reverberated as they cast their practiced eyes on the leggy silhouettes of the models twisting and turning, prancing and parading in a restless quest for "the look," the fashion statement, the style.

The editor-in-chief of *Style* magazine was the sparkling, witty, and ruthless Allanha Davis. Publisher Crosby Hathaway had achieved perhaps the major coup of his career in luring her away from the salons of London and Paris, where for years she had ruled the world of haute monde with an iron hand. A woman of "striking" looks, she might well have been considered ugly had not her wickedly acid tongue, her infallible eye, her inexhaustible energy, and her obsessive interest in and mastery of the subtleties of elegance made such a notion unthinkable. Her crowning genius, however, was her ability to recognize talent in whatever form she found it, and the result was that *Style* magazine boasted the best and most eclectic editorial group on Madison Avenue.

The corridor continued to curve past doors marked BEAUTY, INTERIOR DESIGN, FEATURES, and MODEL PROCUREMENT. Then came a series of cubicles allotted to the "tastemakers," columnists who provided the readers with pertinent guides to what was happening on and off the avenue. Beyond was the literary department.

The high priestess of New York's belles lettres, and the literary editor at *Style,* was Maxine Orlovsky. It was she that Cassie was to see.

"Miss Orlovsky?"

"If you're a writer, you'll be shot!" growled a voice from behind a desk piled high with manuscripts. Cassie saw a pair of stockinged feet propped up on the windowsill.

"Uh . . . no. I'm Cassie Litton. Mr. Kournos, Gregory Kournos wrote to you about me . . ."

"God. Is it Wednesday already? Come in. Find a chair. I'll be with you in a minute."

Cassie looked around. There were three chairs in the cramped office. Each was stacked with manila envelopes. She hesitated, not wanting to disturb anything.

"So." The swivel chair whirled around, and a disheveled and harassed Maxine Orlovsky, a woman of some sixty-five years, peered over her rimless glasses. "Sit, sit. Oh, I see you can't sit. Well, hell, just shove that stack over there on the floor. Okay. right. Grischa's letter didn't make much sense, but I was so surprised to hear from him I decided to see you. I'm curious. The man ignores me for longer than I care to admit and then, suddenly, I'm supposed to see some college girl about, how did he put it, 'a position on my press.' Does he think I'm still up to hand-cranked printing in a dark cellar?" Maxine hooted with laughter. "No matter. You're here. So talk. You got experience?"

Cassie squeezed the now slightly dog-eared copies of the *Smith Review*. "Miss Orlovsky, my experience in New York has consisted of four months of interviews with personnel directors. They seem more interested in my typing skills and the intricacies of the company dental plan than in me and what I can offer. I want to work with writers. I'm not expecting an editorial job to start with. I'll take anything. I'll sharpen pencils and go for coffee if I have to, but I know I have the talent to become an editor." She pushed the copies of the *Review* across the desk. "These constitute my work at Smith. As you can see, we published outside the academic realm. In my senior year alone I published..."

But Maxine held up her hand for silence and was looking through the issues, carefully scanning the tables of contents. "Kenneth Klein? Pretty good. What was he doing? Screwing some coed? No matter. What else you got up your sleeve?"

Cassie began to relax. Maxine Orlovsky seemed actually interested in what she had done.

In fact, as Cassie talked, Maxine was reminded of another fervent young woman. Not a tall, willowy blonde collegiate, but the short, almost plump girl she herself had been in the Paris of the 1930s. The expatriots, they had been called, the Americans who had come to sit on the brink of what they all had considered to be the dawn of a Golden Age in the arts. The young Maxine had exiled herself on the Left Bank, dwelling among the intelligentsia and publishing, with the funds from a small but adequate trust, a literary journal of no small international prestige.

What a time it had been. People from all over the world,

each paying homage to their particular muse. Spanish painters, Italian singers, arrogant Polish actors, dark and brood-
ing Russian emigfes, rich English girls, the American
writers—Hemingway, Fitzgerald, Henry Miller. Sylvia
Beach and her bookstore, Shakespeare and Co., and, of
course, the young, bizarrely handsome Gregory Kournos—
"Hawknose" in his native Russian, and aptly so—sleeping
on the cot in Maxine's studio, where she herself published
early stories of so many of the literary giants of today.

"Okay," Maxine said abruptly. "I could use someone
around here as you can see." She waved vaguely at the
cascading piles of unopened manuscripts. "So. We'll try it,
okay? Just remember, this is no literary magazine. This is
a fashion rag. Upstairs they think they're doing me a favor
if they run one goddamn story per issue. We've got to fight
for every inch of space we can get. Pay's lousy, too. This
is a *furshlugginer* place, but if you can keep your balance
here, you'll do just fine anywhere else."

Chapter 29

CASSIE FOUND HER new job as fascinating as any she'd ever dreamed of. The telephone would ring and she, Cassie Litton, would be speaking, however briefly, with Truman Capote, Kurt Vonnegut, Nora Ephron, Susan Sontag, Philip Roth, George Plimpton, Norman Mailer; it was dizzying.

Maxine had daily lunch appointments at one or another of New York's better-known restaurants, and it was Cassie's job to make all the arrangements as well as her privilege, in some instances, to stand in for Maxine when more than one author needed to be lunched on the same day.

On those occasions she learned to avoid roving hands by sitting opposite, not next to, her author; she learned to order in French, to tip the captain discreetly, and to stick to white-wine spritzers.

At the office, she read unsolicited manuscripts, rejecting most all of them on her own discretion with polite notes of refusal and passing a precious few on for Maxine's perusal.

She typed cover letters for the transmittal of galleys, rights agreements, and Maxine's long, detailed, and often hilarious editing memos. And, of course, she was expected to know whom Maxine wanted to see and who was on her shit list. In short, Cassie was making her transition from the ivy-covered world of the ideal to the glass and aluminum world of the practical. Slowly but surely, her life, her outlook, was changing. All Sammy George did was speed up the process.

Sammy George was *Style*'s highly visible art director, a healthy dose of outrageous bullshit, of real talent, enormous energy, and huge quantities of power. Cassie had heard of him from the very first day of her job, for Maxine and Sammy, a study in contrasts, were brilliant antagonists. The feud between them was legendary. Sammy considered himself responsible for the emotional color, the mood, the attitude of every issue. Maxine's domain was hard print. Sammy begrudged every page that was not visual, and Maxine, in turn, resented every page that was. Maxine and Sammy kept editorial meetings at a lively pitch as they fought page by page for space. And when the battle was done, when Sammy had won and smiled his famous Cheshire-cat smile, or when he had lost and stormed from the conference room, few knew of the subsequent interoffice telephone calls in which they traded compliments and gleefully rehashed the battle like two old, retired generals.

Cassie met Sammy George one beautiful fall day soon after she started working at *Style*. It was lunchtime and the offices were almost totally deserted. She was sitting at her desk with a manuscript before her and a tunafish sandwich on its way to her mouth.

"Tell me," the voice with a slight southern drawl startled her. "What size glove do you wear?"

Sammy George was standing in her doorway and his question was so casual that she promptly answered, "Size seven," before she had time to think about the absurdity of the query.

Then Sammy was around her desk, lifting her hand to his lips, bowing in the courtly manner of a true southern gentleman. "A lady," he grinned, "always knows her glove size. Allow me to take you to lunch."

They walked up Madison Avenue, pausing to window shop, chatting easily about the similarities of growing up in small southern towns. Cutting across to Third Avenue, Sammy steered her into the most beautiful restaurant she had ever seen. The Sign of the Dove was an oasis, a garden, a gilded cage where the scent of flowers and the sound of rushing water managed, somehow, to neutralize the horns, jackhammers, and exhaust fumes just outside its doors.

Over drinks, they talked about *Style,* and Sammy treated her to hilariously catty and probably slanderous sketches of everyone in the office whom Cassie needed to know about. By the time they had finished two drinks and ordered lunch, Cassie felt for the first time since coming to New York the hard shell of loneliness and fear dissolve and melt away. She knew she had found a friend, though for the life of her she could not understand why an important man like Sammy George was taking her to lunch. But as long as he was, she was going to relax and enjoy it.

Of course, Sammy hardly took every new employee at *Style* to lunch, but in Cassie's case he had done some check- ing. Brainy, beautiful, a Litton of the North Carolina Lit- tons—hmm, yes. Worth a second look. And he liked what he saw.

"Look at Serena Howe staring at you," he said. "God. What a cow. She's dying to know who the new face is . . . And speaking of faces, I haven't seen cheekbones like yours since Faye Dunaway. They're classic. Money bones, we call them. How in God's name did you end up working for old baggy buns?"

Cassie stiffened, but Sammy patted her hand. "You're a real babe in the woods, aren't you? I adore Maxine. I do. I promise. But you know she's fighting a losing battle. She's like a piano player in a cathouse. She may be a very good piano player, but nobody goes there to hear the music. *Nobody* buys *Style* to read good literature; they buy it for the clothes and the gossip. Sooner or later, they'll phase out that department, mark my words."

"Sammy, you don't mean it! Does Maxine know?"

"Oh, I tell her all the time, but she says what the hell does a fashion faggot know." Sammy roared with laughter. "You've told me a lot about yourself, but you haven't told me what you're after. Love? Money? Power?"

She looked at Sammy across the table. He was watching her quizzically, a small smile playing on his lips. No doubt the drinks and wine added to her sudden feeling of light- headedness. Nevertheless, there was something about the moment and the bluntness of the question, in the way he looked at her as he waited for the answer, that made her feel as if she were looking into a mirror. When the answer came, she herself was surprised. "I want it all."

Sammy George looked pleased. "You know, sweet pea, people can do anything, have anything, and I mean *anything* in this world just as long as they know clearly what they want. If you know what you want, where you want to go, no matter how high, nothing can stop you. The point is," Sammy carefully watched the effect his words were having on her, "that you, smart, motivated, well-connected, and, let's face it, it never hurts, good-looking, can go way beyond anything Maxine or even Allanha ever dreamed of. If," again he paused, "if you have the guts to jump on the big swing and *if,*" he winked, "you have Sammy George directing the moves, the look, the style . . . Honey, you can have it all."

Cassie felt exhilarated. Had they been lovers openly declaring themselves to each other, her feelings could not have been more nakedly passionate. When she spoke her voice was low and breathy, her eyes green as a cat's. "I want it, Sammy. I swear I do. I want to get to the top. I want the money . . . I want the best, everything. I will not spend my life scrimping, saving, borrowing, being grateful for hand-me-downs . . ."

Sammy's slim, manicured hand floated up to stop her, and, in the drawl that he wore and discarded like a scarf, he began to recite, "As God is my witness . . . as God is my witness . . ."

He seemed not in the least surprised when Cassie, now laughing, joined in to recite verbatim Scarlett O'Hara's sacred oath. "I will never be hungry again."

Sammy became Cassie's teacher and champion. Slowly but methodically he supervised her transformation from an ordinary, pretty career girl into the Grace Kelly of the business world. It was a painful, Pygmalion-like process, but he was determined and she was eager to learn. One by one, she purged her wardrobe of its pleated skirts and cardigan sweaters. He taught her the value of a black velvet Yves St. Laurent jacket, of paisley silk prints, and gold jewelry from David Webb. He took her shopping at Bergdorf's, where they spent two hours and nearly three thousand dollars at the lingerie counter and in the shoe department.

"Whatever did they teach you at that nunnery?" Sammy clucked when she balked at the price of stockings. "You can fake almost everything else, but never your knickers and *never* shoes." He waved away the panty hose, saying imperiously, "Don't! Never give in to mere comfort. Stockings are *always* better. And nothing in the world will do as much for your legs as silk."

He insisted on choosing her shoes as well, again disdainfully dismissing comfort. "Must I spell it out for you?" He heaved a great, impatient sigh. "You've got great legs. Use them. These boots are for construction workers! Here. Try these." He handed her a pair of delicate, brown kid, high-heeled pumps. "Handmade in Italy," he observed with satisfaction. "In shoes like this you'll be traveling by limo soon enough."

And in the end it was Sammy George who helped her find the apartment on the fifteenth floor of a pre-war building overlooking Central Park on Central Park West. The floors were warped and dull through years of neglect, the windows caked with paint and bird glop, the radiator hissed, banged, and whistled each morning at six A.M., but there was a real wood-burning fireplace and French doors that led to a small terrace and a view that took in the whole panorama of the park and the skyline of midtown Manhattan. Cassie finally had a home of her own, and she loved it.

The day she moved in she spent cleaning, scrubbing, and scraping, until she was ready to fall over from fatigue. But as the twilight stole over the city and lights came on like so many burning jewels, she bundled herself up and took a split of champagne out on the freezing terrace. There, shivering with cold and happiness, she toasted herself, her new life, and the drama and excitement of the city that lay spread out before her feet.

Chapter 30

THE GEOGRAPHY OF Glinveagh Castle, as in many old houses, was eccentric in the extreme. The kitchen was so far away from the dining room that by the time platters were raised up the creaking dumbwaiters, transferred onto a trolley, and rolled slowly down the dim, drafty corridors—the roast, the fish, the bird and the inevitable soggy veg—had lost whatever warmth Cook may have originally imparted to them. Dahlia once suggested to Desmond that perhaps it was all a big joke and the food had never been warm in the first place. But Desmond disapproved of jokes about Cook or any of the other people who had been in service at Glinveagh all their lives. At Glinveagh things went on being done as they had always been, as Desmond wanted them to be.

And so they sat, night after night, in the formal dining hall where flickering candlelight and darting echoes of clinking plates and silver always made Dahlia feel like a ghost. At Desmond's insistence they dressed for dinner every night—Desmond in evening clothes and soft slippers while Dahlia most often slipped a long skirt over her blue jeans, in an attempt to keep away the cold.

After dinner they went and sat some more by the fire in the library until promptly at half past nine, when Haskins tapped on the door to ask if there was anything more that was needed. Sometimes Dahlia wondered what would happen if she actually told him what she needed, but her response and Desmond's too was a quiet, proper, *No, thank you*. Did Lady Lovell wish to be called at the usual time in the morning? *Yes.* Then, if all was well, Haskins would bid them good night.

"Desmond," she said after one particularly long and silent evening, "do you ever wonder if the house is alive and we're not."

"Of course not." He peered at her over the breeders' journal he was reading. "What queer things you say."

"I mean Haskins, Mrs. Slough, Old Nanny, Josephine ... everyone. They all bustle about with their schedules and routines and duties, waiting on us hand and foot, and that's all we seem to exist for. We're here so they can do their jobs."

Desmond shook his head. "Darling, I really can't talk now. I've got to make a final decision on the new feeding system by tomorrow morning. We'll talk later, eh? There's a good girl."

Dahlia watched him, his brow furrowed over the weighty question of bone meal for his dogs. Outside the rain beat against the leaded windows. Inside the clock ticked. The telephone rang and Dahlia jumped.

"M'lady, Lady Keyes is ringing from London," Haskins announced on the house line.

"Well, put her through," Dahlia said eagerly. "Carrots!" she exclaimed over the crackling wire.

"Darling," Lady Caroline screamed back piercingly. She loved to pretend that Dahlia was halfway around the world.

"Will you stop screeching," Dahlia laughed. "I can hear you fine and so can half of Ireland."

"Ire ... what? *Iran?* Operator, operator, you've got the wrong country!" Carrots made her voice sound as if it were fading in and out, and that made Dahlia laugh all the harder.

"Darling, you've simply got to get yourself out of that bog and come to London. I need you. Nicky has found out about the little flirtation I was having with his nephew and is raising one hell of a stink. It's too boring. Honestly, men! And don't tell me to come to you. The last time your central heating nearly froze me to death, and that after being hideously mauled by those dreadful hounds. Besides, I've discovered the most divine new restaurant." Carrots paused for a breath. She could talk faster than anyone Dahlia had ever heard—trilling her voice up and down the scales like a diva in rehearsal.

"Of course I'll come," Dahlia answered and then stopped, surprised. She hadn't been to London in ages. It somehow depressed her these days, and she only went for major shopping expeditions. But flying to London for lunch with Carrots was just what she needed.

Carrots was delighted. "Oh, goody. You can help me plan my divorce." And she rang off, leaving Dahlia rather breathless.

Every head in the fashionable restaurant on Beauchamp Place turned as Lady Caroline Keyes made her entrance. She was late, as Dahlia had known she would be, but Dahlia enjoyed sitting there in the hubbub. She was sipping her second Kir and feeling quite mellow. As she watched Carrots weave across the room, dressed in a sweeping Arabian cape and a Moroccan silver collar that would have choked the average neck, Dahlia was aware of a feeling she had had since childhood. Part of her was right there, participating in the whole scene, and part of her was totally outside the situation, watching it as if it were a strange play.

"Darling, I'm late and I could kill myself." Caroline swooped down and kissed Dahlia, "But that horrid traffic matron lays in wait for me every day. And it's such a tiny street. I'll never understand why it needs to be one way, and the wrong way at that. Honestly, I've begged Nicky to see about having the streets changed, but he hasn't done a thing! How was your flight?" Caroline ordered two large martinis from the hovering waiter and sank into her seat.

By the time the food arrived, Carrots was well into the lurid and sensational details of her latest comings and goings. Apparently Nicky had forgiven her and had packed the nephew, "the young scoundrel," off to Canada, where he would toil in the family forestry business.

"Then Nicky suggested we fly to Athens and spend the weekend on one of the islands. He kept referring to it as our 'second honeymoon.' My dear, it was frightful," moaned Caroline, swirling her fork in the fettucine with white-truffle sauce. "God! How can anything so white taste so good? Of course, one should never have gone on the *first* honeymoon with him. Thank goodness his business kept him occupied."

As Carrots talked, Dahlia laughed and clucked along with her. Carrots seemed both gleeful and shocked at her own behavior, and Dahlia wondered what she really thought. Did Lady Caroline Keyes ever wake up in the middle of the night and wonder what it was all about? Or had she escaped the darker side of thinking by throwing herself headlong into living with such vehemence that she never came to cross-purposes with herself? "Damn it!" Dahlia thought, "I'm only twenty-four and my life is passing me by."

". . . imagine my surprise at waking up the next morning and finding the very same Greek waiter in my bed." Carrots paused while she elegantly plucked an arugula leaf out of the salad and popped it in her mouth. Both women seemed oblivious to the fact that at the surrounding tables all conversations had ceased while the lunching crowd strained to hear more.

"But well, a bird in one's bush is worth two in the hand . . . as they say, and it does do such wonders for your skin, especially if one's drunk a bit too much Retsina." Caroline waved away her plate and leaned back on the banquette, glancing about the room to see if she knew anyone.

That afternoon, they went shopping; Caroline forced Dahlia to try on and buy the craziest outfits, so that by the time they had flopped back down at Caroline's elegant Belgravia house, Dahlia was exhausted. Caroline sent away the tea things and had a bottle of champagne sent up. It was like old times, Dahlia thought. But the afternoon's bibulations were catching up with her, and she yawned. "Carrots, sweet, I can't tell you what a splendid day it's been. Really, it's just what I needed, but I've simply got to have a bit of a lie-down. Would that be horribly rude of me? I'm out of practice for the city life, I guess."

When she woke at about eight that evening, she was ensconced in one of the many guest rooms in Caroline's house, and the maid was drawing her bath. A note on the dressing table explained it all:

Darling,

I've sent for your things at Claridge's. We're having a few people for dinner at half past nine and then off for an amusement or two. You're coming, of course. Wear that gypsy thing and brush all your divine hair out of that twist.

Love,
C.

Dahlia appeared in the drawing room that evening having followed Caroline's instructions to the letter. Masses of hair floated down over the layers of red silk embroidered in a king's ransom of gold thread and brocade. The "few people" turned out to be a madhouse of guests. A man who wrote wicked satirical plays kept her in fits of laughter throughout dinner, so that by the time they all careened into the night, Dahlia felt as light, buoyant and carefree as a drifting balloon. At some point in the wee hours of the morning, they ended up in a smoky den in Soho. The dark, cavernous room had once been a strip joint, but there was now an after-hours club where musicians played, not so much performing as experimenting in front of an audience, with new arrangements and sounds. Dahlia's group had dwindled down to a mere five people. Caroline was outrageously drunk, her green velvet turban askew on her head, the folds of her gown flopping dangerously close to completely exposing her breasts, a fact that Caroline seemed to be enjoying enormously.

The lights in the room dimmed just as they had finished placing their drink orders with the waitress. The background music fell away and a solitary spotlight illuminated the previously darkened stage. A tall, slim young man walked out into the smoky blue haze. He wore a plain white shirt open at the neck and tight faded blue jeans. His movements, as he adjusted the mike and tuned the strings of his guitar, were graceful, deliberate, and unhurried. The gaze of his dark eyes was turned inward, and he seemed, if anything, unaware that beyond the light that surrounded him there sat an audience. No one seemed particularly to notice him, except for Dahlia. She was instantly aware of a fierce, animal-like magnetism that emanated from the gaunt-faced young man. And when the first wailing chords broke through the smoky din of the club, Dahlia sat up at attention, feeling every nerve and fiber of her body come alive.

Chris Jones was a serious musician. In concert he was also a consummate showman, strutting about, teasing his audience and wearing outlandish costumes. But in these late-night clubs, his music was simple and sinuous, with a subtlety that would have been lost on his teenage fans. He had only a slide guitar with him this night, and as he played, the sound penetrated Dahlia, and the world around her seemed to recede, leaving her alone and at the mercy of the music, so smooth and erotic. Dahlia felt as if *she* were the guitar and the wailing mournful notes were her soul's response to the skillful fingers, the dark intensity of the musician.

Her layered skirt and flouncy blouse, the fringed shawl, the heavy jewelry, all felt as oppressive as a suit of armor. Inside, her body longed for freedom to leap up and out— to soar wildly while Chris Jones and his music glided in and out and all around her.

When the set was over, he walked off the stage, never so much as acknowledging the presence of an audience. He simply disappeared, and Dahlia was stunned. Slowly she became aware that the once so clever playwright was nodding on her shoulder, quite gone on wine and on the marijuana they had been passing around in the car. Carrots had passed out, but not in her chair. She had crawled up on the table and was now stretched out like a royal corpse in state. Thank God Nicky had left them the car and the driver. As they made their way out of the club, Dahlia looked desperately around, hoping to catch one last glimpse of the musician. A sharp jab of disappointment caught her by surprise, but what surprised her more was the certainty she felt that she would see him again. It was only a matter of time.

"Rise and shine," sang Carrots. She was standing over the large canopied bed. "La, how you country girls do sleep!"

Dahlia mumbled and tried to pull the bedcovers over her head.

"Now, now, dear. A nice cup of Caroline's special tea and you'll feel like a new person." She set a silver tray next to the bed and plopped down. The russet feathers of her dressing gown fluttered about her like a great bird.

"What time is it?" Dahlia muttered.

"Why, it's nearly half past six. High time you were up and about."

"Carrots! You don't mean it. We didn't even get in until five. Whatever are you doing up at this hour?" Dahlia was truly amazed. Carrots, when last seen, was being helped up the stairs by the chauffeur.

"Don't be silly, child. It's half past six P.M. You've slept the whole day and so have I, for that matter. I have thoughtfully brought you a lovely breakfast of bouillon and vodka. Now, there's a good girl."

Dahlia grimaced and pushed the silver cup away. "But I can't have slept all day. I'm supposed to be on the morning flight to Dublin."

"Yes, dear," Caroline cooed, "but we've missed it, haven't we? And dear Desmond has been informed that we were feeling a bit liverish this morning and that we will come home all in good time." Carrots drank down the potion herself and lay down on the bed. "What happened last night? What did we do? Who did we meet? Where did we go? I want all the grizzly details."

Dahlia sighed. "What do you remember last?" she inquired sweetly.

Carrots and Dahlia laughed and talked for about an hour then decided to go around to the Odeon to see *Doctor Zhivago*. But Dahlia hardly watched it. Her mind was racing over the events of the evening before. She felt like a schoolgirl with her first crush. The singer, Jones, was etched in her mind as clearly as if he were sitting with her now. She knew she must see him again. But how? Dahlia squirmed in her seat, trying to sort out her feelings, but all she could actually think of were the sensations, the purely physical thrills and bites that were running through her body.

Carrots was openly weeping at the end of the movie, and Dahlia fished in her handbag for more tissues. They went around the corner to the Great American Disaster for a late-night hamburger, and Dahlia listened patiently while Carrots went on about love, elusive love.

Yes, it was all elusive. One should grab what one could— when one could. After all, life was short, and, in the grand scheme of things, what did it all matter?

Chapter 31

ALTHOUGH MAXINE ORLOVSKY'S annual party was always well attended, it was particularly crowded this year. Perhaps it was the soft spring weather or, perhaps, because the recently defected Russian writer Boris Miklashevski was the guest of honor. Boris, looking arrogant and a little bored, held court on the plum-colored sofa in the middle of the large, high-ceilinged room. "Certainly the hero of the moment," thought Cassie as she watched from across the room, sipping her drink.

The appeal and fascination of the young Russian emigré seemed to cut across all age and sex barriers. Although women were more often favored with a searching look, nearly as many men clamored for his attention. The heavily accented voice seemed to revitalize the profundity of certain current clichés. When he talked of politics, he made Americans feel inexperienced and naive in the face of a man who had been tested in the crucible of tragedy. But what really held his audience was the quicksilver nature of his moods. Just when you thought no face had ever been so gaunt with suffering, so downcast by the cares of the world, a twinkle erupted in his soulful blue eyes, and just for a moment you glimpsed the face of an eager child, a child for whom all dreams were possible and defeat unknown. Those who were privileged to have a glimpse at this other Boris felt as if they had been let in on a well-guarded secret. They inhaled the scent of greatness, and the knowledge of it seemed to lift them out of the ordinary as well.

"I drink cognac," declaimed Boris, taking the offered glass from Maxine, "because it is blood of grape." The way he said *blood* invoked images of Cossacks thundering down on innocent peasants and caused Judy Twilling, the cute editorial assistant from the *New York Review of Books,* to look down at her half-empty glass of red wine with confusion and distaste.

"Grapes . . . are fruit for Dionysus, a pairfect god for our time." Boris flashed his killer smile at the audience. His eyes caught Cassie's across the room.

"Ees troo. Cassie? *You* see how Americans put, how you say, the sugar coating on darker sides of life? Mees Leeton, assistant to my editor, always is called Cassie, never, never, Cassandra, the teller of gloomful, unbeleewahbull trooth!"

Cassie made a wry face and then smiled. It was flattering to have him publicly acknowledge all those hours she had spent getting his story "Englished" enough to be published, but it embarrassed her to feel the eyes of the room swing to her. She smiled again and then, raising her glass to indicate the reason for her departure, walked into the other room.

Maxine's apartment on Gramercy Park was the envy of everyone who had been there. One entered into a large, combination dining room and kitchen as cozy as an old farmhouse. Open shelves held an odd and charming collection of pottery and baskets. There were hooked rugs on the floor and a marmalade cat purring away on top of the refrigerator.

The living room, however, banished all thoughts of rustic charm, for it was, more properly, a salon. The formally draped cathedral windows, the deep aubergine walls, the Oriental carpet, all suggested a European grandeur.

Cassie headed for the dining room, where the food-laden table was an ever bigger attraction than the Russian poet. The huge oak table held baskets filled with golden-brown meat-filled *piroshki,* clever pouches of buckwheat crêpes that enclosed a surprising mouthful of caviar and sour cream, tiny round tomatoes filled with a garlicky purée of white beans, and huge platters of wild mushrooms that tasted, Boris said, "Like a vaulk through Russian forest." It was a beautifully delicious spread, and some version of it would appear in the food pages of the magazine soon.

"So this is how one lives in *style*. Not bad!" These words were uttered in a low, conspiratorial voice, and Cassie turned to look at a casually dressed man who was handing her a freshly made drink.

"Bourbon, right? I've been watching you. You must be one of the models brought in to inspire the writers," he said, looking her over frankly and appreciatively.

"Well, you're right about the bourbon, although I wasn't planning to drink any more. But you're wrong about everything else. I work for Maxine. The only way I try to inspire writers is by writing helpful rejection letters."

"Ah, perfect. The beautiful blond goddess of rejection. And did you learn all about writing 'helpful' rejections at the Radcliffe publishing course?" he said in a teasing way but with a surprising undertone of anger.

Cassie was momentarily thrown off balance. Who was this arrogant man? Why had he been watching her? And, most especially, why did he seem to enjoy insulting her?

"No, I must have missed that course," she replied sweetly. "But Maxine is a very good teacher. Perhaps we've had the honor of rejecting you . . . ?"

"Not that I can remember." His voice seemed filled with insolent amusement.

Cassie didn't like his overbearing manner. He was goading her, and she didn't know how to handle the situation cleverly and with ease. Most of all, she didn't see why she had to. She put down the drink he'd handed her and, flashing a phony, television smile, she said, "Excuse me. I've just seen someone I simply must say hello to." And, without giving him another glance, she walked away.

But the image of his face was imprinted on her mind. She was aware of a strange sensation, one she couldn't identify. It was a disorientation—like seeing a familiar person whose name you couldn't remember coming toward you on the street.

Cassie made her way across the densely packed room

and found Maxine worrying over the rapidly dwindling supply of hors d'oeuvres. "Maxine," she said, sotto voce, "do you know who that man with all the curly brown hair is? Over there by the bar, talking to Gordon Lish."

Maxine peered at Cassie over her half-glasses for a moment, then smiled conspiratorially. "Pete Rossi. Young still, but a *mensch,* if you're asking me. *Esquire* just published the second installment of his Southeast Asia piece. He's the real thing, kid. Go get him."

Women, almost inevitably, found Pete Rossi attractive, though his appeal developed gradually, like the latent image appearing in a developing tray. His features, taken one by one, were pleasant if unremarkable—unruly brown hair, blue eyes, a straight nose and slightly full lips—all serviceable enough. He was of average height but actually appeared shorter because his shoulders were so broad. What was, however, most attractive about him was not so much his physical appearance as it was his supremely unquestioning self-confidence. Pete Rossi never for a moment doubted his appeal, and, as he took Cassie by the elbow and led her to a quiet corner, neither did she.

Cassie felt just a tiny bit tipsy as she stepped out onto the darkened street in front of Maxine's apartment building. Not that she'd had that much to drink—or had she? Pete Rossi had managed to keep their glasses filled even as he'd kept her vastly entertained, making up wild, outlandish stories about the people they had singled out at the party.

She saw a taxi pulling up to the curb. The driver slid over to the passenger side. "Hey, lady, wanna lift?"

Cassie shook her head, then broke into astonished laughter. "Pete! What are you doing in that taxi?"

He shrugged and, opening the door, beckoned her in. "That's my deep, dark secret. What's yours?"

"You drive a cab?" Cassie felt a moment's hesitation.

"Yep. But I'll trow da metah for a dame like you," he said in a Damon Runyon accent.

Cassie slipped demurely into the front seat—and Pete, still chewing on his street-wise accent, said, "Where to, lady? The Stork? El Morocco? 21? Ride wit Rossi and you ride in style."

The taxi squealed away from the curb, and, flipping on the OFF DUTY sign, Pete barreled up Sixth Avenue, hunched over the wheel. Though there was little traffic, he cursed and threw insults out the window at imaginary violators. It was intoxicating. When he had suggested they go from Maxine's to dinner, she had readily accepted. He was fun. He was smart and interesting. And he liked her, she could tell.

At Columbus Circle, he wheeled the car across Central Park South and then drove into the park. It was a beautiful night. All around the park, the city glittered; the lights of the buildings along Fifth Avenue and the West Side blinked through the trees. Pete sped north through the park toward Harlem, then turned off at 116th Street on the West Side and eased into a parking space on Broadway, just south of Columbia University. Cassie had never been this far north in Manhattan. It seemed rather forbidding.

But the restaurant he took her to was a bright, noisy Greek taverna on 103rd Street. After the midtown lunch spots and the gala evenings with Sammy George, this seemed out of another world. The walls were hand painted with badly executed scenes of the Greek isles. The front room was a standard series of Formica tables and red leatherette booths, but Pete confidently greeted the owner and led her through the main dining area, through the kitchen, where waiters, cooks, and busboys waved at him and admired Cassie, to an open-air patio in the back with a corrugated tin roof overhead. On the tables, dozens of votive candles in multicolored holders gave the room a festive look. They sat down, and the owner immediately brought them a bottle of Retsina and a basket of warm bread. Bouzouki music wailed from a scratched record; Cassie fully expected Anthony Quinn to come dancing through the door at any moment.

"Ever been to Greece?" Rossi asked as he poured the Retsina.

"No," Cassie said, reflecting that she'd never been anywhere.

"Well, this is just like being in Greece. All the restaurants, at least the ones where the real people go, are like this. The tin roofs, the painted scenes, the music." He grinned and clinked his glass against hers. "Here's to literature."

Cassie took a sip of wine and made a face. "It tastes like kerosene!"

Pete laughed. "Retsina takes some getting used to, but you'll get to love it."

Cassie wasn't quite sure about that, but the food Pete ordered was wonderful. Flat, round pita bread, oily black olives, anchovies, hot dishes of melted and gooey Kasir cheese, a large salad of feta cheese and tomatoes. Cassie ate it all, and, the more she ate, the more the Retsina came to taste better. Pete kept up a fantastic patter of conversation, mostly telling her about his trip on the overland trail to Katmandu. Soon a large, steaming platter of lamb and vegetables arrived, and Cassie was amazed to realize that all they had eaten had been only the first course. The owner came over to their table to see if all was well. He and Pete launched into a lively discussion of New York politics. Cassie couldn't quite keep up, but she laughed along with them. Theo, the owner, ordered another bottle of wine. The dessert came, a solid pudding with honey dripping over the sides. With it came a glass of Metaxa brandy and a cup of thick, black coffee. The owner rose and took Cassie's hand, saying she was lovely. Cassie beamed.

Pete had launched into a story about an assignment in Tangiers when Cassie realized she was going to be sick. At first she sat with her lips pursed, trying to steady the churning in her stomach. She straightened her back and breathed deeply. Pete was talking on and on. Her eyes blurred and the room began to swim. She smiled again, her hands like lead in her lap. Oh, God! she thought. She looked wildly about her. Somewhere through the kitchen, she remembered, there had been a ladies' room. Her expression was frozen. Pete's story continued. She brought her napkin to her lips.

"Pete," she said urgently, "Pete, I'm so sorry, but I'm going to be sick."

Pete Rossi didn't even blink. He rose and in one motion cupped her elbow and lifted her from the table.

"Hold on," he said.

Cassie could feel herself being almost carried through the room. The kitchen was a blur. Pete ushered her to the door marked DAMES and went in with her. It was a small room, only a toilet and a sink. Cassie stood, unsure for a moment, and then retched violently over the toilet. She retched again. Sweat poured down her face and she felt weak. She wanted to cry.

Pete, standing by the door, reached over and turned on the cold-water tap, wetting a paper towel that he then applied to Cassie's forehead. He asked if she would like a glass of water.

"Oh, yes," she moaned, and he was gone. She gripped the sink, feeling her knees go wobbly, and then splashed cold water on her face. She rinsed her mouth and viewed herself in the mirror, peering at her face, which, while not entirely green, was certainly tinged around the edges. Cassie giggled; she felt better, almost giddy.

Pete knocked on the door, and she opened it a crack and stuck her hand out for the glass. Then he mercifully left her alone. Sitting on the toilet, she took in large gulps of air, and her head began to clear. After fifteen minutes, she felt almost like her old self. But how could she face this man? What must he think?

She freshened her makeup, combed her hair, and then marched out of the ladies' room with as much dignity as she could muster. Pete had paid the bill and was deep in discussion with a man at the bar when Cassie arrived at his side. He rose, slipping his arm around her, and handed her a Coca-Cola. "Just the thing for the whirlies," he said.

Cassie smiled gratefully. He was so *nice*.

When they arrived at her apartment, she tried to apologize, but he refused to listen, teasing her instead.

"It takes a while before you expense-account dames can handle the old hash house," he said, taking her hand.

Cassie, who felt perfectly well by this time, did not want the evening to end. She squeezed his hand. "Would you like to come up for coffee?" she ventured. It sounded like a line from *Cosmopolitan,* and she wasn't sure what she meant by it.

But Pete declined. "Nope. I gotta do another fifty bucks on the meter before I turn in. Maxine's party cost me."

He jumped out of the cab and opened Cassie's door. "Next time, pretty lady," he said and kissed her cheek.

Hours later she could still feel the warmth of his lips.

Chapter 32

CASSIE SAT AT her desk, lost in thought about Pete Rossi. Almost a week had gone by and he hadn't called. All around her, casually gathered members of the senior staff were hashing over the lastest rumors.

"I think our esteemed CEO is scared stiff. Why else would he be running all over the globe? He's trying to raise money. He really is worried about a takeover."

"Well, I want to know who the hell John Stavros is. Up to a year ago no one had ever heard of him. Now he's some kind of press baron, and all you hear is 'John Stavros is trying to buy *Vogue*, no, he's trying to buy the *Post*, or is he buying *Esquire?*' Now he's trying to buy us. Where does this nobody get that kind of money? That's what I want to know."

"Mr. Flash and Trash himself. Jesus! Imagine *Style* magazine turned into a tits and buns rag."

Sammy giggled. "So what do you think it is now?"

"Thanks to you, Sammy. Thanks to you." This from Maxine.

"Listen. From what I hear, he's just shrewd, that's all. It's not his fault that the majority of the population is into cheap thrills. But if he did buy us out, it's ridiculous to think he'd want to turn *Style* into something it isn't. Besides, what are you squawking about? We had 'orgasm' all over the cover last month. Even the tabloids don't do that."

"No, they're too concerned with killer bees and ax murderers." Tim Kennedy, the theater critic, stood up and yawned. "I'm too old and too jaded to give a damn one way or the other, but I don't believe Crosby will let it happen. It's his life."

"I'm with you." Alexandra Richards, the beauty editor, placed two little pads soaked in astringent over her eyelids. "Poor old dear."

Maxine snorted. "Look at you! Listen to you! What the hell do you think we're talking about here? A hemline! I've seen you, in fact, more excited about a hemline. This man threatens everything we've worked for! Everything!"

"What kind of threat, Maxine? I mean, get right down to the point—"

"The threat, Sammy," Maxine's voice was urgent, passionate, "is conglomerate ownership, bottom-line publishing, no concern for editorial values, not the least spark of character. Character is what makes a publication, and *Style* has it. Do you think that happened overnight? Do you think Allanha and Crosby and I all waltzed in here one fine day and produced this magazine on a wing and a prayer? No. It took years. Years of caring and working and reworking. We didn't have formulas and 'marketing skills'—feh. We had talent. Creative talent. More than that, we were dedicated. We were willing to go the distance, to take the risks, to pave the way. *Style* magazine is the highest standard of aspiration and acceptance. It is the arbiter of taste and the first and final word of fashion. Do you really think this magazine should be published by a man whose gutter mentality has brought new lows to journalism? Whose entire empire consists of publications of the most depressing kind?"

"Hear hear." Allanha Davis stood in the door.

"Ahh. The Eva Peron of the fashion industry. Come in, darling," Sammy made a sweeping gesture. "As you can see, Maxine is rousing us to a fever pitch. Stavros, beware. We've just begun to fight."

"Well, you needn't, dear. Crosby, you will all be relieved to know, is in London and has got a whole battalion of investors to the rescue. It seems there are just as many people there who don't want to see this Stavros making inroads in American journalism. Crosby has it all in hand."

Oddly, this seemed to deflate the little gathering, as if one had been promised the most wonderful surprise and then found it to be no surprise at all. Alexandra Richards unfolded her long legs with a sigh. "Wonderful. I knew Crosby wouldn't let us down. So. I guess that means back to the salt mines. Coming, Sammy?" She trailed out of the office. "Who are you lunching with today..."

The inner-office line rang on Cassie's phone. "You've got a note here, hon. Hand delivered by real looker."

Cassie looked at Maxine, knowing she wanted to talk, but with the absolute sureness of a woman's intuition that the note could be from no one but Pete.

It was.

> How about Chinese? Meet me tonight at the Peking Duck. Mott Street. 7:30. No Retsina, I promise. Just tea for two.
>
> Pete

Cassie rode buoyantly downtown on the Lexington Avenue IRT, got off at Canal Street, and stepped onto the swarming streets of Chinatown. The air was rich with the smell of hot oil and spices; goods from the Chinese markets spilled out onto the sidewalks. As she weaved her way through the heavy pedestrian traffic on Mott Street, she saw the sign for the Peking Duck.

Like all restaurants in Chinatown, it was unpretentious, spare, garishly lit. Cassie took a deep breath and pushed her way through the double doors. Pete Rossi was nursing a Kirin beer at a table in the rear. He hadn't seen her yet, and Cassie paused a moment to take his measure. He was unlike any man she had ever known—more intense and with more rough edges showing—but there was a gentleness to his manner that went straight to her heart.

Pete rose when he saw her. "The ladies' room is right down those stairs," he said jokingly. "Just in case."

Cassie slipped into her seat. "Mistah Rossi, ah do solemnly sweah, ah will nevva, nor will any of mah kin, evva, evva be sick again." It was her best Scarlett O'Hara.

Pete laughed. "You southern belles always could run circles 'round us Yankees." He reached over and gripped her hand. He's really glad to see me, Cassie thought.

They ordered sparingly, and Cassie drank only the hot Chinese tea. But they talked and talked. The conversation ranged over a dozen or more topics, from civil rights to the role of art in society to the corporate mentality. And through it all, Cassie perceived in him a virile, righteous anger, uncompromising, perhaps, but just and passionate. There was no subject in which he lacked an opinion, no issue in which he could not find a black and white. For herself, Cassie was more comfortable in the gray areas. He invited her opinions, her resistance, and she gave it. Her mind was agile in the face of his bluntness, dogged where he lost patience. It was an even match, and they were falling in love.

After dinner they walked through Chinatown, holding hands. Pete knew a great deal about ethnic minorities in New York from a series he'd done for the *Village Voice*. He told her about the wrongs done to the Chinese.

"Did you know there was a law that forbade Chinese men from bringing their women into the country? And there was a law against their coming into port on the East Coast. Only the West. So they'd have to work their way east on the railroads. A lot of them jumped ship illegally, of course. They moved into Chinatown and they wound up being bought like slaves by their own people. And they couldn't complain because they were illegal aliens. That's why Chinese food is so cheap. Those coolies work in the kitchens for nothing—just for the privilege of being here."

Cassie shivered. Men and women on the street scurried past them. Pete walked her across Canal Street to Little Italy and they had a cannoli in the very restaurant where Joey Gallo had been gunned down. Then over to the Bowery for a drink at small Ukrainian bar.

"You know, Pete, I've never been anywhere really, but tonight I feel as if I've been all over the world. I'm a little ashamed that all I know of New York is midtown and Central Park West."

"Yeah, I love New York. I love traveling too, but this is the place, man, this is really the place." Pete slapped his hand down on the bar for emphasis. Cassie was thrilled, and the feeling invaded every part of her.

Pete looked at her. "Hey," he said softly, "you want to come over to my place?"

Cassie nodded. Pete paid the bartender, and they walked the few blocks to his building on Second Avenue. It was a derelict, fallen-down neighborhood. On the street level, only one storefront bore a light—the mission house. Cassie trembled as she thought, this is life—gritty and raw. But Pete's arm around her gave her confidence. The building he lived in was as rundown as the rest. A broken steel door faced the street; the hall and the stairs were strewn with litter and lined with graffiti.

But the apartment itself, one large room, had been fixed up nicely. The floors were polished. The exposed pipes were painted an industrial gray. At one end, a grouping of modern stuffed chairs surrounded a low metal table. Industrial metal shelves, filled with books, lined one wall. The kitchen stood in the middle of the room, a colorful array of pots and pans hanging from a rack suspended from the ceiling. The bed was on a platform, six feet off the ground, with a funny set of circular wooden stairs leading up to it.

Cassie exclaimed over the loft, and Pete smiled. He poured her a glass of wine and put Ornette Coleman on the stereo. The room filled with music. Cassie tucked her feet up in the corner of the sofa and sat back with a feeling of intense well-being. She didn't know much about jazz, but this sounded fantastic. Pete moved to the couch to sit beside her now. His hand reached over and began to rub her neck. Gently, but oh so gently. Cassie sighed. His hand seemed enormous as it cradled her neck. She leaned back on the cushion, her head resting on the back of the sofa. Pete's hand reached around and down, across her shoulder to caress the front of her neck. His touch was exquisite, making her feel giddy and lightheaded from the feel of it. She turned her head toward him. His face was so close—his mouth, his breath. Pete leaned to her, and Cassie felt his lips on hers, full and soft. He kissed her for a long time, his mouth moving, opening hers. She felt his tongue, and her tongue.

And all the while he kissed her, his hands moved over her body—hands touching her everywhere, as if defining her shape. At first she was immobile. But when his hand trailed across her knees, lifting her skirt, a surge of energy went through her body. Oh, God. She wanted something strong, even violent, to happen. She wanted to burst free of the confines of her clothes, her attitudes, her life. She looked at Pete. His eyes were on hers. He pulled away and Cassie grabbed his hand.

"Don't stop," she begged.

Pete glanced at the ladder leading to the loft bed. She stood up and loosened her skirt, while he watched her, slightly amused. Her skirt fell away and she waited, wanting a cue from him.

"Take it off," he said, pointing to her silk blouse. "Slowly."

She stood before him, a little unsteady, releasing the small pearl buttons one by one. When she was standing in her bra and panties, he beckoned her to come closer, then reached up and quickly unsnapped the lacy cloth surrounding her breasts. Cassie gasped. Her pink nipples were hard; they ached with longing. Pete drew away, watching her again.

"What is it you want, lady?" he asked in a low, teasing voice.

Cassie's breath caught, and for a moment she wasn't sure she could speak. Finally she whispered, "You."

She felt her knees tremble slightly, and she knelt before him, reaching for his belt and carefully unbuckling it. She unzipped his rough denim jeans, and still he didn't move, still he was watching her. She reached inside, and his hard penis was now in her hand, and then it was free. She felt electric sensations shoot through her body. She looked into his eyes again, and his hand reached out to caress her cheek. His touch seemed to release her final inhibitions, and she caught his hand, bringing it quickly to her mouth, kissing it, licking his fingers one by one, biting—just hard enough. Still on her knees before him, she dropped her head and took him in her mouth; he moaned, caressing the back of her head. Then suddenly he pulled her up to meet his mouth.

"Shh," he whispered, "not so fast." And he was up, leading her by the hand, up the steps and onto the large bed.

She lay on her back, and he knelt before her, removing the last bit of her clothes, the small, lacy panties. He smiled at her. "A real blonde," he said, pleased with his discovery. Then he was teasing her with his hands and his kisses. She felt that she knew his hands, his touch, from many dreams. She lay motionless as Pete looked at her naked body, and she offered herself to his gaze, like a hostage princess, the prize of a great victory.

She was so pale and blond next to the dark tangle of hair on his chest that she might have been a statue, but as he began to stroke her breasts, she grasped him in her arms and pulled him close. They lay pressed together, breathing together, pulses touching as their passion enveloped them ever tighter in its swirling cocoon. Soon they were ravenous with curiosity and need.

Cassie wanted him more than anything in the world, and the painful sweetness of this urgency made her cry out. And then he eased inside of her, filling her up and quieting her for the moment. She felt his strong body on top of her, and she felt her entire soul open to him. She could feel herself melting, melting into him, her legs around him, gripping him tighter and tighter. He paused for a moment, his eyes looking deep into hers. It was a moment frozen and suspended. Then no control was possible.

Her orgasm was sharp and quick. She no longer knew or cared whether her cries were real or imagined. And Pete, hearing her, could no longer hold back. A last thrust and he, too, cried out as he felt himself flow into her.

They lay perfectly still, listening to each other's breathing, feeling their pounding hearts begin to quiet. Cassie felt as if she were floating. Pete's body resting on her felt safe and warm. She loved him. She knew it. She had never in her life felt anything like this. She knew she would willingly surrender everything she had to him. She smiled and reached up to stroke his head. Her fingers slipped through his brown curls.

Chapter 33

CHRIS JONES WAS booked to play at a small but trendy club in Dublin. The Milkmaid had a reputation as a showcase, and anyone who had anything to do with popular music would be found there at one time or another as they were passing through Ireland. For performers like Chris Jones, it was an important place to play.

Dahlia had become an avid reader of *Rolling Stone*, *Cream* and *Variety* in an attempt to find out as much as possible about Jones, and she knew he was considered good but not yet in the star category. Clearly, he could use some support, a plug in the right quarters, whatever these might be. Well fine. The right quarters, the right people, were something about which Dahlia knew just what to do. Even from the wilds of Glinveagh, London, and most especially Carrots, were only a telephone call away.

"We haven't much time. Just five days, to be exact," said Dahlia to Carrots, in the tone of a general plotting of a campaign. "What we need," she went on, "is someone really important in the music business. That's where you come in—you've got to find him and bring him here for the weekend."

Carrots, who loved nothing better than the high drama of a well-planned intrigue, warmed immediately to the task at hand. "Well, now, that shouldn't be too difficult. I'll need a day or two to poke around . . . I know who might be *very* helpful. Brooksie! My dear, his pieces for *Private Eye* are all about these rock musicians. And they're awfully funny. Don't worry, my pet. Just leave it all to Tante Caroline. I'll ring you tomorrow."

The following day was sunny and beautiful, after several days of rain. Knowing that if she stayed home she would sit by the telephone, Dahlia asked Cook to pack some "marching sandwiches" and took Dierdre off for a picnic. Dierdre, looking like a tiny Celtic princess, was good company. Her endless questions and companionable chatter kept Dahlia amused and busy. Around noontime, they flung themselves down, exhausted, beside a large, warm rock and hungrily ate the greasy, delicious bacon and fried-egg sandwiches. They returned home in the afternoon, covered with dust and garlands of wildflowers. Dierdre, reciting a catalogue of birds, beasts, and flowers they had encountered, was led off to the nursery to be bathed and napped. Dahlia rang for tea and was about to bathe and nap herself when Haskins appeared to inform her that Lady Keyes had telephoned four times.

"Oh, goody," thought Dahlia, feeling a pleasant rush of anticipation as she waited for Caroline to come to the telephone.

"It's all settled. I'm having dinner with Alan Leonard and Brooksie tonight," purred Carrots in a voice smug with accomplishment.

"Alan Leonard . . . Alan Leonard . . . Now, wait. Don't tell me. I've seen his name. He's—"

"He's the hottest young producer in town, according to Brooksie. And he's the brains behind Alligator Records. Oh, it's too exciting," squealed Caroline.

"Well, it's unfair," pouted Dahlia. "You're having all the fun while I have to sit here waiting. Just remember, my fate is in your hands, so be good."

At nine the next morning, Dahlia, feeling just a little mean, woke Caroline.

"Oh, my dear . . . oh, my head! Oh, my . . . everything," moaned Carrots. "Alan Leonard is divine! Why didn't I know about short, Jewish men before?"

"Well, tell me. Tell me what happened," urged Dahlia, failing to hide her impatience.

"We had the most marvelous dinner. Brooksie was killingly funny. You know how he is. And Alan—well, he is the most divine creature. His eyes are truly limpid pools, and he's got all this curly brown hair on his head. Well," Caroline sighed, "everywhere, actually. He reminded me of a teddy bear I once had, all covered with furry velvet, and so cozy. And . . . he's the only man I've ever had who can be in three places at once! Uncanny."

"You have been naughty again, haven't you?" Dahlia cut in on Caroline's rhapsody.

"Let's not cross Ts, darling," Carrots said gaily. "After all, naughty is the operative word, isn't it?"

"Carrots! What happened before? I mean, did you talk? Can you bring him for the weekend?" Dahlia persisted.

"Of course. It's all set. Brooksie is coming, too. And it was Alan himself who mentioned going to the Milkmaid. What are you doing about dreary Desmond? Will he be there?"

"No, he's off to America to see about some new spaniels. I'll give him your love, though. He adores you, you know."

"Well, I adore him too. Just as long as I don't have to see him. Adieu, my love." And she rang off.

Dahlia sank back into a pleasantly luxurious reverie. The image of Carrots in bed with a short, Jewish teddy bear made her smile. Irrepressible was the word for Carrots. Not to mention determined. As little girls, hadn't they both promised to devote their lives to *"l'amour, l'amour,"* to have affairs with as many interesting men as they could find? And there was Caroline, true to her sworn intentions, leaping at every amorous opportunity that came her way. Well, the weekend was getting off to a good start. What fun that Brooksie was coming as well. At the very least, they would all be hilariously entertained, for Henry Brooks was good with words. Yes, thought Dahlia, it had every appearance of being a most interesting weekend.

Everything seemed to be working out perfectly. Carrots had arrived, Brooksie was on one arm, Alan Leonard on the other. She was wearing what she called her country costume: a tweedy cape, Irish homespun shooting trousers buckled at the knee, a tattersall waistcoat, stout brogues, and a six-foot Glenurquhart-plaid scarf. She reeked of the moors.

Caroline could walk the fine line between the ridiculous and the sublime. What would have made almost any other woman look idiotic was always, on Caroline, ineffably elegant. They had whiled away the warm afternoon on the banks of the river. Henry Brooks was teaching Dierdre how to fish. Dahlia and Carrots sat comfortably in the shade of a tree, gossiping, while Alan Leonard dozed, his head in Caroline's lap.

Later, dressing for dinner, Dahlia wondered at how intensely happy she was. And with the flood of happiness came the quick realization, almost like a thunderclap, that she had been too lonely, too unhappy, for a long, long time. The thought of Desmond suddenly made her angry. What was the matter with him? Why couldn't he be friendly, easy, companionable? Even if his nature was not a very passionate one, why couldn't they just have fun? But as considerate, polite, and generous as he was, he took no real pleasure in her company. Impatiently, she pushed him from her mind. No, she certainly wasn't going to let him ruin the wonderful time she was having. Chris Jones. She would hear him play again. She would see him. Speak to him, perhaps... She wondered what he looked like up close. As she bent over to brush her long hair forward, she smiled to see her toes all curled in pleasurable anticipation. Quickly, she wound her hair into a knot on top of her head and secured it with a long, ivory Chinese hairpin. She had chosen her dress weeks before—soft, dripping silk, all bias-cut to float around her tiny body, in palest yellow. She would glow softly in the dim light of the nightclub.

Chris Jones was every bit as magnetic and wonderful as she remembered. Alan Leonard was impressed, and, when it turned out that Brooksie knew Jones, he was sent off during a break to fetch the singer to the table.

Up close, Jones was slighter than he appeared on stage. His face was very thin, with deep hollows and prominent cheekbones. His smile as he greeted them was friendly, warm; but his eyes were remote, as if he were looking at something very far away. Only when his glance lingered on Dahlia did he appear to become more aware of his immediate surroundings. But as they all chatted about music and his performance, his songs, he seemed to relax and enjoy himself. When it was suggested that he return to Glinveagh with them and stay for what remained of the weekend, he accepted with pleasure. Everything had gone according to Dahlia's careful, well-laid plan.

Why then was she back in her bedroom, very much alone? All day she had coasted, floated really, on a sense of power. She had felt almost witchy in her ability to make things happen as she wanted them to. But all that was gone now as she stood in the middle of her room flinging off first the yellow dress, and then her jewelry and underwear. She was a failure—a dismal failure. A failure with Desmond and now a failure with Chris Jones. Why was it that Carrots could fall into bed with every passing taxi driver, waiter, or ski instructor if the mood came upon her? Even now she was cuddling up with her Alan bear. But she, Dahlia, had been boringly, interminably faithful to a man who clearly couldn't care less. Her one attempt at adultery, planned, engineered, maneuvered for weeks, had ended pathetically as she had offered Chris Jones her hand and had murmured chastely, "Good night, I hope you'll be very comfortable."

She was thoroughly disgusted with herself. She chewed on a lock of hair and wondered what would happen if she floated through his bedroom door, knowing all the while that she could never bring herself to do that in a million years. Finally, with a stamp of anger and frustration, she slipped a mauve silk kimono over her pale satin gown and headed off to the gardens that were just below.

The night was amazingly warm and soft with moisture. Moonlight glowed through tiny patches of fog that floated here and there like silver cobwebs. It all would have seemed eerie if she hadn't been so familiar with every bush and flower bed. Out of the confines of her empty bedroom, she quieted down and began to enjoy the starry night. She followed the path that led to the reflecting pool—a pool that must now be filled with the image of the moon. The soft, nocturnal sounds, the unearthly light, the gentle air, filled her heart, once again, with longing. Longing for something to happen, something wild and romantic, something that was bigger than she was and out of her control. She started to hurry, as if she were late for an appointment, as if someone were waiting for her, and, as she emerged from the path into the clearing, her heart caught in her throat as she saw the figure of Chris Jones reflected in the gleaming pool. He turned and saw her, but his voice gave away nothing.

"Couldn't sleep. Never can after a performance." His smile was friendly, relaxed.

"I shouldn't wonder," said Dahlia, feeling suddenly that everything, everything was right with the world. She had her power back. Nothing would go wrong now.

"That's quite a thing you do. It's very exciting . . . your music, I mean. So haunting and strong . . . and raw. I thought of Robert Johnson. Even your voice has . . ." She stopped, waiting for the right word, but it didn't matter. Nothing mattered very much.

Jones was looking at her openly—a bemused smile lighting his features. "I'm trying to figure out," he said, coming closer, "how Lady Lovell, who talks like the queen and lives in a castle, knows anything about Robert Johnson."

Dahlia laughed, her voice a silver bell ringing through the moist darkness. "Are you?" She turned and idly plucked a white oleander blossom. "Well," she smiled at him, "a lady never tells. But," she went on, "I suppose that you think a lady wouldn't know anything about Muddy Waters or Otis Span or Willie Dixon or Howlin' Wolf . . ."

"Whoa!" laughed Jones. "Who are you? I thought I was coming out to play with the lords and ladies. Chew on a bit of the upper crust, you know."

Dahlia smiled at him. She stepped closer and tucked the scented blossom into his shirt. He was the perfect height, she noticed, as she raised her eyes a few inches to look more closely at his face.

They stood silently, not touching, looking into each other's eyes, acknowledging mutely the powers that had been set in motion.

"Come," said Dahlia, taking his hand. "I want to show you something."

He followed her to a small side door that led from the garden into the house, down a short corridor, and up the circular marble stairs into the Long Gallery. It was a vast, isolated room running almost the full length of the castle. It housed the furniture and paintings that were the pride of the Lovell collection. But more than that, its perfect proportions created an awesome beauty. As they entered the room, Jones caught her wrist in mid-air to prevent her turning on the lights. White moonlight poured through the enormous, arched windows, bathing the portraits, the furnishings, the vaulted ceiling in pearly luminescence. The room was still and ancient as Jones prowled, catlike, through it, his lips pursed, as if whistling softly to himself. He stood, finally, by the billiards table, his hands softly caressing the green felt.

"Very nice," he said, looking around. "Very nice indeed."

They stood at opposite ends of the big room, enjoying the light, the silence, and the distance between them that was about to disappear.

"Come here, luv. I've got something for you." She walked to him. "But first . . ." He untied the silk ribbon on the kimono and helped her out of it as if he were the butler removing a lady's coat. "Yes," he said appreciatively, looking at the wisp of a satin gown that was held up by two tiny straps. Then he reached over and quickly removed the long ivory pin that fastened her hair. A waterfall of silken curls came tumbling down past her shoulders.

"Perfect," said Jones. "Guinevere waiting for her knight."

It seemed to Dahlia that everything was happening in slow motion. They both knew what was to be. Like underwater swimmers, languid and easy, they drifted to the window, thrilled by the light. She could make out every detail of his face, even a small scar on his chin. He reached into his jeans pocket and removed a small bottle that gleamed white in the moonlight. Into it he dipped a tiny silver spoon and brought the glistening white powder to her nostril. "Ladies love this," he said.

She stood, looking out the window, waiting to see what was going to happen beyond the slightly acrid taste that she felt at the back of her throat. Not much it seemed. Perhaps only a certain kind of clarity, a sharpening of the senses— the pulsing spot in the curve of her neck, her nipples hard against the touch of satin, the sweet, sweet urgency in her loins.

She was almost startled when Jones reached for her and quickly untied the straps that held her gown, but she reached and touched the bare softness of his chest. Suddenly, the tempo changed, as if they were in a film and the musical score was beginning to build. The edges no longer held; sensations flowed into each other like waves in an ocean. She caught her breath sharply as she felt his fingers on her nipples—fingers made hard and rough by the cruel tautness of steel guitar strings. He played her nipples as expertly as he would the opening phrases of a song, so that she almost cried out from the painful pleasure of it. The sensations became more and more jumbled—his tongue, soft, wet, everywhere—her neck, her breast, in her armpit, down her belly, then a sudden swooping up, just as her knees were about to give way. He carried her effortlessly to the billiards table. There she lay, an offering to the gods, moaning softly as he buried his head between her thighs. A huge wave caught her up and lifted her to the crest, carrying her along, now up to the very tip, reaching toward the sky, now plummeting into a canyon of water. Finally he was on her, his mouth pinning hers down, his hands arresting her breasts. He was hard inside her—she was pierced, a butterfly on velvet. They were the ocean now, a roaring turmoil. She felt herself rushing, rolling, plunging like a waterfall, down,

down, down, then spreading gently out, to a soft clear
stillness, until she floated like a trembling leaf on the surface
of a pool.

Chapter 34

"DID YOU EVER think that if our two children, each had two children, and each of them had two children, and this went on for a thousand years there would be a billion new people in this world."

"Pete, what are you talking about?"

"I'm talking about a billion people, but the thing that kills me is that they'd never know about us. You and me. Us. The ones who started it all."

"You're crazy. I'm mad about you, but you're crazy."

Cassie was in love. In love as she had never thought possible. She wanted Pete so much, wanted to be with him so intensely that sometimes her knees would go wobbly and then she would have to sit down and sit very still until she could control the sensations in her stomach and the burning desire in her heart.

It seemed extraordinary to her that they had met by chance. One party, one isolated gathering of people in a city of ten million people, and yet it was that party that changed her whole life. Pete Rossi *was* her whole life, and Cassie's happiness was boundless. When they weren't making love, they were in love. They spent every spare minute together, and Pete handed New York City to her—each mystery, each treasure, each character—as if it were a vast theater created just to amuse and to stimulate her. Pete's New York bore little resemblance to the city Sammy had introduced her to. His were real people in real settings far removed from the glitter, sophistication, and shine that was Sammy.

"That's not sophistication," Pete laughed. "It's snobbery. The 'right' table in the 'right' restaurant at the 'right' time, wearing the 'right' clothes. Who decides these things? Who sets down those rules?"

"*Style* magazine, for one," Cassie said dryly, feeling a tiny bit disloyal to Sammy. "It makes you wonder about people, doesn't it? What are they so frightened of? What do they think is going to happen to them if they have to sit at a table to the left instead of the right?"

The thing about Pete was that he liked women. Really liked them. Cassie didn't have to say a word for him to know what she was thinking and feeling. He seemed to know what she wanted. Not just in bed. Even in restaurants he knew what she wanted. She discovered that she didn't have to finish sentences with him. And sometimes she didn't even have to start them.

They could spend hours together not talking at all—and yet sometimes they would talk clear through the night. Inside of a month she knew more about Pete Rossi than she knew about anyone else on earth. Inside of six months it was as if she'd known him all her life.

He was twenty-nine. He had grown up in suburban Detroit, the only and late-born child of Sylvia and Carlo Rossi. Like the old king and queen in fairy tales who after years of barrenness are suddenly blessed with an heir to the kingdom, Carlo and Sylvia had always regarded Pete's birth as miraculous. As he grew into manhood, Pete, too, was happy to believe, along with his parents, that his was a gifted and special existence.

Sylvia was, he said, a woman of boundless energy and optimism, a high school English teacher who was dedicated to showing generations of adolescents that literature, the best literature, was filled with passion and excitement. An adoring and devoted mother, she encouraged in Pete a love of stories and of storytelling. Each word of his, each scribble, each joke, each observation was praised, admired, and displayed.

Mortar, cement, and bricks made up the stuff of Carlo's daily life. He was a strong man with a passion for building, and he filled his son's life with all the elements of a boyish heaven; machines, bulldozers, and steam shovels were Pete's real-life toys, and construction sites, with all their delicious dangers, were his playgrounds.

Pete conceded that he had not been the best-looking boy in high school. But he certainly had not lacked for girl friends, either. Ah, the girls, the girls. High school had been full of them, clutching their books to their perky little bosoms, flipping the pleats of their skirts as they wiggled down the corridors. Had he gone steady? Cassie demanded to know, hating and envying the girl who had stolen his heart for the first time. No. He hadn't. To go out with one girl had seemed to him such a waste, such an unnecessary abstinence. His father had agreed. "What are you, crazy?" shouted the Carlo of Pete's impersonation. "Play the field. Hey, whaddaya sixteen for?" And then Papa Rossi had gone out and bought his son a car, the kind of car every budding teenage Don Juan dreamed about, a gleaming, red Chevy convertible.

Pete had graduated from the Columbia University School of Journalism at the height of the radical '60s. He had gone to Vietnam as a correspondent for *The Nation* and made quite a name for himself. Now he preferred to work freelance. He liked to pick and choose his own subjects—he didn't want to be typecast as a political activist, or an interviewer, or a critic. He wrote about any and all things that interested him. He was at work on a book now, a compendium of his experiences, his thoughts, his passions.

It was October, a Saturday, and it was raining, torrents sheeting down the windowpanes. Pete sat at his desk, his back to her, working at his book. The sound of the typewriter beat in unison with the sound of the rain until they became one sound. The world at large seemed to fade from Cassie's consciousness, and it was as if they were the only two people on earth. She could not take her eyes from the back of Pete's neck, from the unruly curls of hair that always made her want to stroke him, to caress him. Wordlessly, she reached out her arms to him, and at that very moment he turned to her. She had never felt shy with Pete, but now she felt bold. Bold enough to command him to come to her. Bold enough to undress him and run her hands over him as if he were a statue and she the artist, the creator. Seeing him naked against her fully clothed body excited her. He was beautiful. His skin was taut and the outline of his muscle easy to trace with her fingers. It fascinated her. She watched her hands moving over him, cupping some parts of him, teasing others, controlling the tensions in his body, the small ripples and shivers, as dispassionate herself as if she were a technician in a laboratory. Energy flowed from her hand and into his body until it seemed they were held together by a sheer force of current.

Suddenly Pete took hold of her wrists, and she felt the balance shift as he pushed her to the floor. She struggled to regain her dominance over him, but he was too strong for her. With one hand he pinned her wrists over her head to the hardwood floor while with the other he pulled roughly at the buttons on her dress until it fell away. She was naked underneath, not a bra, no panties, nothing. He stopped, staring at her as if for the first time, but still he did not loosen his grasp. Instead, slowly, he entered her, over and over again in an unrelenting rhythm, until she could feel one orgasm climbing to another and another. At last, as she reached the very outermost limits of awareness, they came together, into one another. They *were* one another.

Minutes, hours later—she didn't know—her legs wrapped around his, her arms cradling his head, they began to giggle.

Chapter 35

TABLOID KING BAGS RAG MAG

After an electrifying boardroom battle for control of Hathaway Publications and its crown jewel, *Style* magazine, John Stavros has launched his American publishing career. Mr. Stavros, known for a gamy history of hostile takeovers, still evidences a large thirst for business challenges. *Shock* was the word in publishing circles, and many doubt the glad rag's take-over will establish journalistic respectability for a man whose empire is based on some fifty scandal sheets worldwide. Fashion soothsayers predict today's Stylish lady will be tomorrow's Fallen Woman.

IT HAD TAKEN John Stavros all of six hours to take control of Hathaway Publications. Despite an intense shouting match and Crosby's last-ditch attempt to get a court order staying the proceedings, Stavros's people had steadily bought out Hathaway's stockholders at outrageously inflated prices until he had acquired more than 50 percent of the shares. At that point he simply declared and installed himself as the new director. It was over before Crosby knew what had hit him. He had no choice but to walk out.

That had been on Friday. On Monday Crosby called the staff of *Style* together and resigned his command "after so many joyful and tumultuous years" in a tearful farewell. Allanha, looking grim, assured them that there would be no immediate changes in the format or the masthead of the magazine and said they were all to "carry on" in the professional manner she had come to expect and respect. But the mood was somber, and afterward the staff gathered in the fashion room to plan, grumble, and commiserate. "It's like a wake, an Irish wake," said the shoe editor, who had apparently never been to an Irish wake.

"Can't you hear it?" Sammy said to Cassie later that evening over drinks at the Four Seasons.

"Hear what?" Cassie asked.

"Opportunity, honey. Knocking loud and clear. The big 'O.'"

Cassie grinned.

"I mean it. This is better than sex any day. In fact, I guarantee you, if you come out on top, it will be the most intensely exhilarating experience of your life. We're talking money, real money. And power, real power. Take a deep breath, Scarlett—things are going to be popping like fireworks in the next few days. Let's you and I hit the beaches running."

The next week, John Stavros formally took control of *Style* magazine. The nervously attentive senior staff stood silently in the large director's room on the top floor. Everyone was concerned for their jobs—everyone except Cassie. Her thoughts were only on seeing in the flesh the man who would have made her fortune had she not so stupidly allowed herself to be duped by Winthrop Litton. She eagerly positioned herself front and center. When, minutes later, Stavros strode into the room, Cassie gaped. The infamous John Stavros was, in a word, awesome. He was young and almost painfully handsome in a way that American men never were, sexy, with dark, Mediterranean coloring and chiseled, angular features. His European manner fit him like an expensive glove, and yet the masculine intensity of the man was manifest. Cassie was astounded. She had expected an English version of her uncle—some pompous, florid businessman who looked as if he'd never been out of a pinstriped suit. But John Stavros—well, he looked more like a movie star than a newspaper executive.

Stavros viewed the room for a moment and then broadcast a surprisingly warm and genial smile.

"People, please forget everything you've ever read about me," he said, his smile widening as a ripple of laughter spread in the room. "I'm well aware that the change in corporate ownership has caused many of you to wonder about the future of *Style* magazine and, more specifically, what your own futures will be. Rest assured, I have admired this magazine for a long time and though a certain reputation for 'house cleaning' precedes me, I have no intention of changing the basic editorial and visual concepts of this publication."

There was a collective sigh of relief.

"However," he continued, "I'm sorry to say that these and many other assurances have not persuaded your editor-in-chief, Allanha Davis. As of today, she has resigned."

The room grew still again. Sammy nudged Cassie. "Strike one."

"I hope that none of you here will be so quick to judge. No changes whatsoever will be effected on issues already in the works. After that you may be surprised, and pleasantly, by the changes that may come about. In any event, I will be assuming Miss Davis's position for the time being and will be meeting soon with each department head in depth."

His talk was brief, but throughout it his eyes scanned the room in swift appraisal. For the brief instant that his eyes rested on Cassie, she felt her breath catch and the hair at the base of her neck prickle, an uncanny but not unpleasant feeling. His eyes were dark and sad. Or were they dark and laughing? It was impossible to say for sure, but in that moment, with his eyes fixed on hers, Cassie felt drawn to the man and to what he represented like a moth to a flame. She smiled at him and felt her face light up.

But despite the smooth assurances about continuity and order, Stavros left a hurricane in his wake. In a matter of days, everything had changed and the office at Hathaway Publications was littered with the debris of shattered careers. The air was thick with fear, anger, firings, resignations, and threats of lawsuits and revenge.

Many of those who were not fired simply refused to work. Press-ready copy and whole sections of layout mysteriously disappeared despite the tight security that everyone was subjected to leaving the building. Finally, only two days before the closing, most of the remaining editorial staff, save Sammy, Maxine, and Cassie, gathered in the cafeteria where they sat drinking coffee and muttering dark thoughts.

"They refuse to budge," reported Sammy after he had gone down as an emissary, "and won't tell where they've hidden the layouts. They've also made it painfully clear that they consider the three of us traitors, scabs, sell-outs, and worse."

Maxine grunted. "What the hell did we need this for? Now of all times! One issue I get control of each year and look what happens. I could cry."

Cassie did cry. They had worked so hard on it. Once a year, fashion stepped down and *Style* focused on writers, publishing, and the literary arts. The issue was, this year, brilliant. Maxie had outdone herself.

"I see that the palace rebellion is not quite as absolute as I was given to believe."

They all three spun around. John Stavros stood in the door. His coat was off, his sleeves rolled up.

"May I assume that you're staying?"

Sammy shrugged. "It's a moot point. Looks like this issue is dead anyway."

"Not if I have anything to say about it." He gave them a smile, and Cassie was struck again by its infectious appeal. "Give me the next eighteen hours of your life and we'll get this issue to bed. You may be surprised that despite my— shall we be blunt and call it 'tacky' reputation—this issue, the literary issue, is the last one I would want to see abandoned."

Even Maxine had to laugh at that one. "But the proofs

are gone and there's not a typesetter in town who can..."

"We won't be needing a typesetter because the proofs are here. Somewhere. They can be found. And we can do it." He looked at each of them in turn. "It will be very hard work, but you're used to that."

Cassie could feel her head nodding yes. Sammy swung his legs down from Maxine's desk, and Maxine leaned forward. "There's no one who wants this issue more than I do," she said grimly, "What's the plan?"

"Turn the place upside-down. Find whatever copy and layout you can. Go through the trash, find the roughs, break open any locked closets and desks, take up carpets, unframe pictures. Overlook nothing. I don't care what gets damaged in the process. Get everything you can find, no matter how sketchy, to my office in four hours. We'll go from there." With that, John Stavros strode out of the office and down the corridor.

It seemed an impossible task at first, but after eight exhausting hours the bare bones of the issue began to fall into place. Stavros worked side by side with his staff of three, hour for hour, idea for idea, and his energy was infectious, his abilities awesome. From rough notes, whole articles were reconstructed. They worked through the night and into the next afternoon, taking cat naps at intervals, drinking gallons of coffee, taking quick, icy showers in the lavish bathroom that had once been a part of Allanha's office suite.

Cassie had been in those offices only once before—when she first came to work for *Style*. Now she was sitting at Allanha's huge, ornate desk, taking a short break to call Pete. She liked the view.

"Oh, Pete, tonight of all nights? You just wouldn't believe what's happening here. Everyone's quit, or threatened to, and the four of us are putting the issue out by ourselves. Everything's been stolen or sabotaged, but we're piecing it back together, it's the most exciting thing. What? Oh, Maxine and Sammy and John and I... John Stavros, the new owner... Well, I thought so too, but he's not at all like that, really... Well, that's my point... I don't know when.

When we're done, I guess. Why don't you go without me and I'll see you at your place after? Well of course I want to see it, but we're crazed here, gimme a break, chum, I mean, this is important stuff and I'm loving it. You can understand that, can't you?... Well how late is it likely to go on?... Okay, sweetheart, if I can. The Bottom Line. Bleecker Street. I got it...If I can I will. I gotta run. Sweetheart? I love you. Bye."

She hung up and hurried back to Stavros's office. She had never felt so alert, quick, smart, turned on. Jesus! Sammy was right. This could be better than sex.

Chapter 36

IT WAS TWELVE-FIFTEEN by the time Cassie left the midtown Madison Avenue offices of *Style* magazine. Cramped and physically exhausted from the day's frantic pace, she hailed a westbound cab on Fifty-seventh Street and gave him her address. By the time they had reached Fifth Avenue, however, she had changed her mind. "I'm sorry, could you make it Bleecker Street, please. The Bottom Line."

The concert was clearly over. The marquee read BLUES TONITE, but the lights were out and small clusters of teenagers in hand-embroidered army-surplus fatigues were fanning out, making their stoned way toward Washington Square. Cassie asked the driver to wait and peeked through the unattended door. Through a haze of blue smoke she saw several black-turtlenecked waitresses clearing the cabaret-style tables. In the far corner near the bar, a cigarette in one hand and a glass of beer in the other, Pete Rossi was engaged in animated conversation with a black man in dark glasses whom Cassie took for a musician. She waved the cab off and entered.

If, as she feared, Pete was angry at her for missing the concert, he didn't show it. "Cassie. I knew you'd make it. You missed a hell of a show, though. Hey, this is Bukkha. Bukkha, Cassie. Bukkha tells me Randy Gleason's backstage. Randy's an old buddy, we're gonna go say 'hi.'"

"Okay, Pete, but I'm really wiped. I'm afraid I'm not up for a late evening."

"No, no, no, nothing like that, I promise. We'll go backstage and say hello, see who's around, maybe just have one drink somewhere if everyone's game. You'll love Randy and you'll get to see a rock star in person, something to chat about at the water cooler tomorrow."

Backstage at the Bottom Line was actually a cavernous, low-ceilinged, dimly lit basement with folding chairs, coils of wire, amplifiers, and transit cases littering the floor. Pete found his friend among a cluster of people loitering under a canopy of pot smoke, and they greeted each other effusively with a slightly elaborate overhand clasp. Cassie was relieved to be offered a more conventional greeting and, exhausted as she was, content to be ignored as the two men hashed over old times with impromptu heartiness.

Around them young people of varying degrees of hipness chatted or shuffled about, waiting, Cassie gathered, for their musical hero to emerge from his dressing room. Cassie dearly hoped he would do so soon so Pete could make his obeisance to the rock celebrity and they could go home and to sleep. When the graffiti-covered dressing-room door finally did open, all thought of sleep simply disappeared from Cassie's mind. In fact, she screamed as if she'd seen a ghost. On Chris Jones's arm was none other than Dahlia de Ginsburgh.

"Cassie?" Dahlia shrieked, "Oh my God! It's Cassie." Dahlia hugged her old friend. "Aren't you going to say anything? Isn't this amazing?" Dahlia kept on hugging Cassie as if she were afraid the girl might dematerialize into a puff of smoke.

At last Cassie pulled herself together enough to disentangle herself from Dahlia's grasp. Her face was pale and she was shaking. Her voice had a tremor as she spoke to Pete, "Pete, this is Dahlia de Ginsburgh. She used to be my closest friend . . . a long time ago . . . And then she wasn't . . ." Cassie turned on her heel and was running up the stairs and out into the dark, deserted city streets. She didn't wait to see if Pete would follow, but ran sobbing through the cold night until she got to Eighth Street, where there were lights and people. She hailed a cab and headed home.

An hour later Pete found her chain-smoking and pacing

the length of the apartment. She glared at him when he walked in and kept on pacing as if he wasn't there.

"Cass, what on earth..." but he was interrupted by the crash of a heavy glass ashtray against the wall.

"How dare she come prancing back into my life like that after what she did! Did you know she was going to be there? Is this your idea of some kind of joke?"

"Hey, hold on, hold up, whoa! Will you just sit down and take it easy for a second. I don't even know who she is."

So Cassie told him. They stayed up into the wee hours of the morning as she recounted the early days of their friendship, how close they'd been, and how much Dahlia's friendship had meant to her. For the first time ever she told Pete about posing for Neil Straker, and as she talked she felt a heavy weight lifting off her heart, a weight she hadn't even known was there. She'd been so frightened and ashamed at the time and she had let these feelings grow and fester like an ugly boil upon her soul. She told Pete all about the way Candy had seduced them and then turned around and blackmailed them; how Dahlia had promised to fix everything but had eloped with Desmond instead, leaving her to face Winthrop Litton alone.

"So she disappeared, just like that, and I never heard from her again. Every time I think of it, it just about kills me. Do you realize how rich I'd be if it hadn't been for those pictures... I'll never forgive Dahlia. Never, ever, ever!"

"Come on, babe, come over here." Pete cradled her in his arms. "You had some bad breaks and got involved with some nasty people, but aren't you being a little hard on your friend? She must have been just as scared and ashamed as you were, maybe more so from what you tell me about her mother. But she wasn't the evil one; it was that girl and your uncle who screwed you to the wall. I think you should call her, Cass... Chris Jones is at the Chelsea. I bet you'd find her there too. Call her, babe."

* * *

Despite her best intentions, Cassie slept late the next morning. Pete had gone out. The phone was ringing insistently.

"Hello?"

"Cassie, please don't hang up, it's Dahlia." Cassie was suddenly wide awake. "I know you're angry with me and you have every right in the world to be furious. I dropped you from my life, I know I did, and it was unforgivable, but when I saw you last night I just knew I couldn't let you slip away again. Won't you please please come and have lunch with me? Cassie, please? Cassie . . . are you there?"

"Oh, Dahlia, I'm here. I've always been here. But honest to God, Dahlia, I've been so angry. I can't tell you how many times I've fantasized this conversation. You'd plead and I'd be ice, then I'd hang up on you. But I guess I always knew I'd cave in in a minute."

"Does that mean we're having lunch?" Dahlia's tone brightened.

"For the life of me I don't know why, but I guess it does."

"Oh, I'm so glad, Cassie, I have missed you, you know, though you couldn't tell from my behavior. There's so much to tell you. So much has changed. How's twelve-thirty at the Four Seasons? My treat?"

"Things have changed more than you think, Dahlia. It's my treat, or it's no deal."

"*Plus ça change* . . . but I love it! I'll pick you up at *Style*."

The girl behind the reception desk at *Style* magazine was chatting comfortably on the telephone, which was cradled in her shoulder. At the same time she was applying frosted-white enamel to her very long finger nails. "One sec, hon. Don't hang up," she told the telephone as she glanced at Dahlia with a bored look. She waved her hand, partly as an indication of the direction and partly to dry the wet enamel. "Models on seventeen," she said and immediately resumed her conversation.

Dahlia, only mildly amused at the girl's assumption, reached over and depressed the button on the telephone, putting an abrupt end to the conversation. The girl started to protest, but something in Dahlia's manner stopped her. Pausing for just a fraction of a second, Dahlia spoke in a measured, polite voice, betraying not the slightest indication of annoyance, "Please be good enough to tell Miss Litton that Lady Lovell is here to see her."

Two beautiful young women were at table. One petite, dark, and casually elegant, the other slightly taller, blond, and very carefully done up, indeed. Dahlia spoke urgently, heedless of the hovering waiter who even now was topping off their champagne glasses. ". . . because I hated myself. If I hadn't done what I did, I think I'd have killed myself, but when I woke up and came to my senses, I mean when I realized what I'd done — to myself, to poor Desmond — it was already months later, and I was so ashamed of myself I didn't know what to say. So I didn't say anything. And then the more time passed, the guiltier I felt. And then there was Dierdre and things were so hectic and crazy and can you really truly forgive me? Because you must. You simply must."

Cassie sighed a deep sigh and smiled. She hadn't thought that letting go of all that anger could be so easy, or feel so good.

"All right. All right. I forgive you. Now what are you doing with Chris Jones, and have you really been married all this time to Desmond, and who on earth is Dierdre? I want to hear it all."

Chapter 37

CASSIE RETURNED TO find a pale and grim-faced Maxine packing up her office.

"Maxine, what on earth is going on here?"

"Push has come to shove, dear. Push has definitely come to a great deal of shoving, and I don't have to take it. I'm too old for this kind of crap."

"You've quit. You're leaving."

"What does it look like I'm doing? Making chicken soup? Of course I'm leaving. Go. You've got messages sitting on your phone. Take care of your business and we'll talk later."

"But . . ."

"Do as I say."

There was, in fact, only one message on her phone, and it was a shaky Cassie Litton who dialed John Stavros's extension and told his secretary that she was returning his call.

Minutes later she was seated on the couch in John Stavros's executive suite. He was choosing his words with care.

"Cassie, you are very fond of Maxine, are you not?"

"Of course I am. And very grateful, too. She's been wonderful to me," Cassie said, so earnestly that she felt herself begin to blush.

"And you are aware that she is, ah, leaving us?"

"Yes, sir, I guess I am. And, frankly, I'd like to know why."

"No doubt you would, and you shall. For official purposes, Maxine has retired three years early because of ill health. But you will recognize that for the nonsense it is. The truth is I fired her, and I want you to know why. It wasn't a personality conflict. I happen to like Maxine. And it wasn't because I am unaware that she is one of the best literary editors in New York. It wasn't because she doesn't work hard. It was purely and simply because she doesn't want to play ball with me."

"But that's not fair," Cassie interjected indignantly. "Maxine's been here for years. She's a huge part of what made *Style* magazine what it is today. How can you do that to her? She's earned the right to have a say around here."

Stavros squinted at her appraisingly. His tone was lightly mocking. "Funny, you don't strike me as the hippie type."

"Of course I'm not—"

"A communist then?"

"I'm not saying anything like—"

"Then you believe in the principles of free enterprise and private ownership?"

"Of course I do." Cassie had never been so quickly put on the defensive. She was sure she was about to get the ax also. But Stavros continued.

"Listen to me, Cassie. This magazine belongs to me. I bought it. I'm not in the business of running a home for literary dilettantes. I'm in the business of making money. I like making money. It's an activity that interests me more than a thousand clever stories by William Gass or Donald Barthelme. I thought perhaps you were interested in making money also. Was I wrong? I was impressed with your work on our first issue, your energy, your intelligence. I've been watching you. But I have to know whether you truly have the ambition to be what I think you can be. I've got to be sure that you're not a loser. I don't abide losers very well."

"I'm not a loser, Mr. Stavros. I may be a lot of things, but I'm not a loser."

"Oh. And what would you call someone who gives away a quarter share of a five-million-dollar newspaper for ten thousand dollars? A winner?"

Cassie's jaw may have lowered, but her dander was up. Without thinking, she said, "I don't know how you know about that, but I can tell you one thing for sure. It is never going to happen to me again. Not ever."

John Stavros was smiling. "I'm delighted to hear it, Cassie, I really am."

"Well, I'm not so delighted. I'd like to know why you're doing this to me. I'd like to know what this is all about."

"I make it my business to know as much about the people who work for me as I can. I set the standards; they measure up. You'd be surprised, Cassie. Most people's lives are open books, easy reading if you know how to look at them. There were no surprises for me with Maxine, or Allanha Davis, for that matter. You, on the other hand, are still a question mark. I like that. I like being challenged. You have talent, you have ambition, but most of all you have—what is it you Americans like to call it?—ah, yes. You have grit. Believe me, those are winning combinations if, *if* you don't let sentiment interfere."

Cassie was flattered by his assessment of her. She could feel her initial hostility and discomfort begin to fade. She *was* a winner, goddamn it. She had been a winner all her life, and here and now maybe it was going to begin to pay off. "You still haven't told me what this is all about," she said carefully, her eyes leveled directly into his.

"This is about a decision you're going to have to make. Especially now that Maxine is leaving and your department is going to be dismantled. You can stay on at *Style* for a while, at least until the department is phased out, you can quit in protest. We can even arrange to fire you if you would prefer to collect unemployment insurance. Or... you can become my assistant, try for bigger things, make something of yourself. The choice is yours. But I warn you, if you decide to work for me, I will expect everything you've got in the way of hard work and, above all, loyalty."

"But, Mr. Stavros..."

"I don't want an answer now. Take a day. Take two. Talk to Maxine. Search your soul. But if you accept my little offer, I want your unqualified support. Nothing less would interest me." Then, lowering his voice, he added, "Oh, and Cassie, I'm hoping you'll want to stay."

Cassie returned to her office on the eighteenth floor deeply confused. Maxine was gone, her office a jumble of hastily labeled cartons. Cassie dialed her home number, but the line was busy. Off the hook, if I know Maxine, she thought. Then she dialed Pete's service. "Ethel? It's Cassie. Tell Pete I'll be home a bit late, will you? Thanks."

If Cassie had expected to find Maxine in a state of emotional disarray, she was mistaken. If anything, Maxine seemed more herself than she had been in quite a while.

"Come in, kid. Sit down. Want a drink?" She poured them each a brandy without waiting for Cassie's response.

"Oh, Maxine, I feel just awful."

"Well, I don't. I've seen this coming since the takeover. What the hell. I'm supposed to be shocked because a schmuck like that doesn't give a shit about literature? I should be so naive."

"But what will you do?"

"Feh. I'll do what I've always done. I'll do some agenting, or maybe I'll start up my own press again. I don't need much. The house is free and clear, thank God. It was just expense-account publishing. You know, I never really thought of it as anything but temporary. I only ever did it as a favor to Crosby and Allanha. All right. So it lasted for twelve years. That's eleven years longer than I expected, and it never was real publishing anyway. Come to think of it, I didn't lose a damned thing this afternoon. Maybe I even got back something I had lost. But I want to know what he said to you. Did he tell you he fired me?"

"Well, yes, he did."

"Ha! I thought he would. Well, it's bullshit. I quit. But what the hell. It comes to the same thing, doesn't it? What else? Did he offer you a job?"

Cassie nodded.

"I thought he would. Gonna take it?"

This was the question Cassie had been waiting for and dreading. What did one say to a loyal friend—and mentor—under the circumstances? So long? Been good to know ya?

Or was it her responsibility to go down with the ship? To allow her first job to end in failure. She tried to think what was right, but her mind would not hold still. "I . . . I don't know. I really don't."

"You're not thinking that you need to turn the job down on my account? Don't be an ass. The gesture isn't going to do a thing for me. You're not going to teach someone like Stavros a lesson. What do you think you're going to accomplish? Do you want the job?"

"Maxine, I'm afraid I do. Is that awful?"

"If you expect me to make moral judgments about your career, you came to the wrong place. You're young, you've got time to make mistakes, take chances. You wanna do it, do it—with my blessing. Truly. But do it with your eyes open. That's all I ask. It's a tough world you'd be getting into, with extraordinary rewards—and extraordinary punishments, too. There's nothing intrinsically wrong with that, Cassie, but if you want an extraordinary life, you have to know that you'll be doing without the ordinary supports that an ordinary life offers an ordinary person."

Chapter 38

CASSIE HAD HALF decided not to say anything to Pete, at least not right away, but the welter of confusing events that day made it virtually impossible to be nonchalant when he asked, over drinks, as he always did, "Well, what kind of day has it been?"

"I think I'm in line for a big promotion."

"Fabulous," Pete said. "Cass, that's wonderful. Maxine's making you a full editor. I knew she would. She's a gruff old bird, but she thinks the world of you. She's told me that a dozen times."

Cassie proceeded cautiously. "Well, it's not exactly that. Maxine's leaving, and—"

"She's leaving? That's a bit sudden, isn't it? Why would she do that?"

"Oh, I guess she wants to get back to small-press publishing. You know, that's what she really likes. That's how she started, back in Paris, doing that sort of thing. The point is—"

"You're taking her place? That's some shoes to fill."

"Well, it's not exactly that either. I think it's something else."

"Like what?" Pete was puzzled, curious.

"I don't know exactly. Something in management, I guess. I'd be working directly for John Stavros. And it's an enormous jump in salary."

"How enormous?"

The figure Stavros had mentioned, so thrilling when she had first heard it, now seemed embarrassing. "Thirty thousand dollars."

"Bullshit!" Pete suddenly exploded. "What the hell do you know about management? Three months ago you were going to be an editor, possibly a good one, and then along comes the Stavros creep and instead of having the sense to clear out, you're climbing to the top of his trash heap!"

Cassie got up from the table and paced the apartment, picking up scattered articles of clothing and emptying ashtrays.

"Why are you so hostile?" she demanded. "I should think you'd be pleased for me. Anyone else would be thrilled. Someone's got to make some real money around here." She knew it was a low blow but couldn't stop herself.

The conversation at that point went from shaky to disastrous. The worst moment came when he accused her of abandoning Maxine, and then her anger was so hot and raw that she flew at him, scratching, punching, screaming like a harridan. How could she abandon Maxine when Maxine virtually told her to do it?

Cassie took the job. She found that life as John Stavros's executive assistant agreed with her, though she keenly felt her lack of experience and worked feverishly to overcome it.

Often her days began at dawn and stretched out into the late evening hours. Many nights she couldn't fall asleep as papers, schedules, voices, filled her mind and could not be turned off. She was constantly exhausted and felt betrayed by Pete, the one person whom she looked to for emotional support. Each day, it seemed, brought with it a new source of friction, a new difficulty, another argument. If she took him to dinner at a good restaurant, he would inevitably sulk, and the evening would end in sullen silence. She tried to cajole him, flirting, flattering, demanding in her best southern-belle drawl, "But honey, what's an expense account for if not to entertain the best writer in New York City?"

Pete remained stubborn. He hated everything that Stavros stood for and told her to save her money and flattery for "the jerks who'll sell themselves to Stavros's scummy rags."

She bought new clothes, and that caused another fight. He was outraged at how much she'd spend.

"Jesus, Cassie! Four hundred dollars for boots!" he growled, tossing them angrily onto the bed.

But what did he know about clothes, sitting around the apartment all day in blue jeans and his old flannel shirts? He refused to wear the Italian shirts she'd bought for him at Meledendri and would not even consider buying a new jacket. He disapproved of everything. And she was growing sick and tired of his moral judgments and righteous pronouncements.

"Oh, Pete," she wailed one night, after an almost wordless dinner, "I don't know what's happening to us. Why are you so angry with me?" And she cried like a baby.

Never able to endure any woman's tears, Pete wrapped his arms around her rigid body. "I think you're the smartest, sexiest, most wonderful woman I've ever met," he said softly, "and I love you. I hate seeing you get so sidetracked by these high rollers."

He held her close, stroked her head while her hot tears soaked his neck. He led her to the bed and undressed her. He brought her tissues, brandy, called her baby names while he caressed her. He rubbed her neck and shoulders, easing away the stiff, hard knots. He rubbed her back, her legs, her feet, her arms, her hands, until she lay subdued and relaxed. He made her drink the brandy, as if it were medicine, and she obeyed. She loved his mastery and, in that light, her own passivity. Then he made love to her, stroking her breasts, his hands circling her stomach, reaching down to her thighs, commanding her to lie still while he caressed her, kissed her, dissolving her will until soon she was filled with unbearable joy. How could another person's touch bring such sheer happiness?

But they could not make love all the time, and it was a relief to Cassie when Pete took the assignment in Chicago for a month. Maybe when he got back the break from each

other would have cleared the air. Maybe some time alone
would do them both good. Maybe.

John Stavros expanded Cassie's field of work. She was
moved upstairs to her own office on the executive floor of
Stavros American Media, a wholly owned subsidiary of
Stavros International Media. Outside her door sat Penny
Lawrence, her own personal secretary. She was given a
portfolio of stock options that she could exercise after a
year had lapsed, her expense account seemed to be unlimited, and almost every other day another credit card arrived
like so much junk mail. "Executive perks," Sammy had
grinned. "Enjoy them, baby doll. I have a feeling we're
going to pay through the nose." In fact, sometimes, she
couldn't help feeling that she was overpaid, that Sammy
was right. But Stavros's demands and whirlwind schedule
kept her too busy to dwell on this or any other inconvenient
truth, and there was, after all, the comforting explanation
that he was grooming her for some future position of great
responsibility.

Chapter 39

STAVROS HIMSELF WAS hard to read. He seemed to think well of her. She had easy access to him, which alone gave her an edge, and yet she was constantly aware of how precarious her position was. Performance, she knew, was everything, and Cassie was proud of the way she organized her day, the hours mapped out and scheduled in fifteen-minute segments. Still, it seemed she was always rushing. Rushing from one deadline to the next, rushing reports, rushing to make appointments, quick drinks after work, a quick change before dinner.

Stavros never gave her a task she couldn't do, although he stretched her capabilities to the limits. He was a genius and she admired him immensely. But with Pete out of town, she found there was more than his business acumen that she admired. The sexual fantasies, held so firmly just below the conscious levels of her thoughts until now, surfaced with a vengeance. She was hopelessly drawn to John Stavros. Everything that had to do with the man became an erotic symbol. The power he wielded, the people he controlled, the lives he influenced all sent waves of sexual desire through her. Desire that reached beyond her experience into darker realms of crude and raw imaginings. At home she couldn't relax, couldn't sleep, and so she stayed later and later at the office.

"I know I'm a slave driver, but I've never been known to work the slaves to death." Cassie's head jerked up. He was leaning in the frame of the open door. "You've been here every night this week. If I didn't know better, I'd think you were planning to take over my company." He smiled, easy and relaxed.

"Oh ... well, I ..." Cassie shifted nervously. She was sitting at his desk bathed in a pool of light from its lamp, the only light on in the immense office. "I didn't like the layout on these charts. You know, for the meeting tomorrow with the cable networks. It seemed easiest to revise them here ..." *He had expected to find her here.*

He sat down in one of the conference chairs opposite her, his face in half shadow. She started to get up. "No, no. Stay there. It suits you. A golden-haired woman on a pedestal. The pedestal of success. Do you feel successful, Miss Cassie Litton? Do you feel you have a future with me?" His eyes were hooded but his voice conveyed another meaning.

Cassie felt almost trapped in the chair. She tried to make her voice light, but it came out soft and urgent. "That's for you to decide, isn't it?"

"Yes. It is." He was silent for a moment, but she could feel his eyes on her. She felt naked under those piercing eyes. "I'm promoting you, Cassie. Acquisitions. Acquisitions is the axis around which the entire international media program revolves."

Cassie nodded, strangely disappointed though a part of her realized what he was offering meant a tremendous leap forward in the corporate hierarchy. She quickly gathered herself together. "Then to answer your question, I feel very successful indeed."

"Good. Success deserves its rewards." He got up and came around the desk. "Come with me then. I have a new toy and I want to show it off."

He held her coat for her, letting his hands rest on her shoulders after she had slipped it on. He was very close to her and she could feel his breath on her neck. Then very carefully he lifted her hair in his hands and let it trail through his fingers. Cassie couldn't suppress the sigh that escaped her lips. He turned her to him with one quick motion, their lips met, hers soft and yielding, his harsh and strong. She felt a wildness in him. And in her.

The "toy" was a gun-metal-gray Aston-Martin DB-6. Stavros seemed pleased with her reaction, and Cassie sank into the passenger seat, letting the rich, soft leather envelop her. He drove expertly and fast through Central Park and then cut across the West Side to the Henry Hudson Parkway. They crossed the George Washington Bridge and turned on to the Palisades, the dark ribbon of road that wound along-side the river.

Stavros glanced at her once and then kept his eyes ahead. His right hand rested on her knee. Cassie sat very still. He seemed to know the effect his touch had on her, but her stillness actually seemed to heighten her awareness of him, the sexual longing she had for him. Each time he moved his hand back to the gearshift, she waited, not moving a muscle until his hand came back to her. And each time it moved higher and higher on her leg, gently caressing the inside of her thigh, teasing her legs apart so that his hand could go higher still. She willed her breath to remain deep and steady, and this seemed to please him.

They reached an open stretch of road, straight and flat. His foot pressed down on the accelerator, and the car shot into the darkness. Now his hand was free from the shifting of gears and it remained between her legs, his fingers prob-ing the part of her that was aching. She was wet, sticky wet, and she let her knees fall apart. The speed of the car was frightening and reckless—they might crash and be dead in a matter of seconds. It didn't seem to matter. What mat-tered only were the searing sensations that controlled her. Her mouth was open, she was sucking for breath, and then she felt her body shaking, exploding into tiny fragments that blew into the night wind. Before she could even catch her breath, he pulled her golden hair and pushed her head between his legs.

Hours later the gleaming gray car pulled to the curb in front of her apartment building. She started to say something, but he put his hand on hers to hush her.

"Things that happen in the dark don't matter. They're like a dream, best forgotten."

She was quiet for a moment, then had to ask, "If this didn't matter, then what does."

"Don't you know?" he laughed harshly. "Surely you won't disappoint me now. Only money matters. Money is everything. There is nothing else."

Chapter 40

CHRIS JONES WAS definitely on his way up. The New York exposure had put him over the top. He was signed with Alligator Records and his songs were climbing the charts on both sides of the Atlantic. Back home in England he was booked in concert almost every week, and as he traveled from city to city, so, incognito, did Dahlia.

Dahlia loved this new role and felt wicked and sultry, imagining herself to be Marlene Dietrich in a smoky, backstage odyssey of passion and illicit sex.

"You're mad," Chris Jones said to her, half seriously but not at all displeased, when she appeared in his dressing room a few days after their New York trip.

"I'm due back on stage in ten minutes." He managed to combine regret with a kind of challenge.

"Then ten minutes it is," she said seductively.

He fucked her on the cot in the dressing room. She didn't bother to undress nor did he. For a time she would be satisfied, but soon enough her hunger would start to grow and she would search him out once more.

Inevitably, that became their pattern. She would find him, be there, no matter where he was. And all he had to do was supply the goods. They never talked much. Their lives were as separate after months of lovemaking as they had been before they met, and Dahlia realized after a time it was because she herself preferred it that way. She didn't want to know about his life, of his family, or where he came from. She didn't want to know anything about him that would make him meaningful. In the most fundamental way, her affair with Jones was based on lust, and lust alone.

There was no sentiment. Sentiment, she thought, was for fools.

To all his "mates" Dahlia was just another girl, though obviously a cut above the usual groupies who swarmed around the singer. No one knew who she was, and Chris didn't seem to care. He called her Doll. "Meet me, Doll," he'd say in an offhand way to the scores of people who surrounded him. Dahlia assumed the arrangement they had was as satisfying to him as it was to her. It never for a moment occurred to her that Jones would tire of the whole scene.

But lately, more and more often, Chris Jones had been keeping Dahlia waiting. She suspected that he enjoyed the power he had over her, knowing that she was waiting for him, that she was aroused almost to a fever pitch, waiting like a prisoner for the release only he could bring her. Then he would be there, his eyes lighting up as he reached for her. And they would embrace hungrily, their passion climbing to excruciating heights.

Dahlia had arranged to meet Jones at his London flat, just off the Kings Road. She had let herself in, into the dark, small, badly furnished room, expecting to find him there. Minutes of glowing anticipation had given way to hours of impatient fury. She had just decided that he wasn't coming when the key turned in the lock.

"Hello, luv. Sorry I'm late." He threw his leather jacket across a chair and opened a bottle of beer.

"Late?" Dahlia mocked. "I wouldn't call four hours 'late.' I'd call it a bloody fucking calculated insult. What am I supposed to do, sitting around this rat hole half the night?"

Jones squinted at her coolly for a moment, as if seeing her for the first time, then turned his back. "Whatever gets you up, Doll."

Dahlia's eyes burned with fury, but she struggled for control. "You arrogant, stupid, ill-mannered, ill-bred, working-class lout," she said, measuring each word with care. "Do you think you're addressing one of your cheap, empty-headed groupie sluts? Do you have any idea what I'm risking by coming to see you?"

"A slut's a slut, luv. You can fancy yourself what you like. It's all the same to me."

Surprised at the vehemence of her own words, Dahlia was amazed at Jones's cool detachment. She charged out of the flat without a further word, slamming the door behind her. She would never, she told herself, ever, degrade herself with the likes of him again. And, fervently, she hoped it was true.

She caught the early plane to Ireland, and, though she was still hurt and angry when the car turned into the drive, the autumn day was crisp and clear, and Glinveagh did look inviting. Perhaps she and Desmond and Dierdre could go for a walk. Their walks had become a most pleasant ritual. Meandering through the countryside, Desmond would show Dierdre the haunts of his childhood, the secret caves and the hidden bridges.

"No, m'lady," Haskins informed her. "His lordship left for London and then France early this morning. He will ring you this evening. And Miss Dierdre and Old Nanny have gone for the day to a birthday party."

Disappointed, she spent the rest of the day alone with her headache. Perhaps it had been the perfect time to end this thing with Jones. Especially if the bastard was going to treat her that way. Who, after all, did he think he was? And, perhaps, now that she had been so awakened to sexual passion, she could awaken Desmond to it as well.

After lunch, she saw Cook and discussed the week's menus, answered a letter, and then walked as far as the gardener's house. She spoke to him about a few matters, then she cut some flowers for the sitting room and took a long turn through the Wild Garden before heading back to the house. It was a beautiful, quiet, and peaceful dusk. The centuries that surrounded the house came alive here, some-how, and reminded her of the generations that preceded her. She stood for a moment at the reflecting pool. It was almost entirely covered with fallen leaves. Yes, she decided. The affair with Jones was over, and she was glad.

She planned that she and Dierdre would have dinner in front of the television and had just ordered it, when the house line rang.

"Lady Keyes, m'lady."

"Yes, put her through. Well, my dear," Dahlia launched in without the usual hellos. "You have rung at a very opportune moment. I have an announcement to make. As of now, I have decided to give up *la vie de l'amour* in favor of a boring country life. Really, I think I've had quite enough of slumming."

There was a long pause. Then Carrots said in a flat tone, "You've seen the papers."

"What papers?" Dahlia asked.

"You haven't seen the papers?" Carrots demanded.

Dahlia started to laugh. "Papers. What is this about papers?" But a curious, nightmarish feeling began to creep over her. "Carrots, what is it? What are you trying to say?"

"Oh, my God, Dahlia. I wish I didn't have to be the one to tell you. It's all over the *Comet*. There's a great, banner headline. 'Shock! Lady Lovell and rock star in love nest! She's his doll, say close friends of singer Chris Jones. Lovely lady and her rising star.' And then there are pictures of you and Chris kissing, *kissing,* in a doorway at some place called the Tic Tac Club in Manchester. Oh, Dahlia, whatever are you going to do? And worse, there are pictures of your mother, and Dierdre and you and Desmond at Ascot. I could cry for you. It's just dreadful."

Dahlia sat holding the telephone, her body frozen, her mind a complete blank. Then her heart rose, beating in her throat, and she could barely speak. "It's not . . . true. It can't be true. There were never any photographers . . ." But she knew she was wrong.

"Do you want me to read more? It goes on and on. The captions are . . . God, Dahlia, has Desmond seen this?"

Dahlia shook her head and then whispered, "I don't know. He was in London today. And then at the airport. He left for France this afternoon, so he may have missed it."

"Wait a minute, darling, I've got another call coming in. Don't move."

Carrots clicked off, leaving Dahlia alone with the hum of the long-distance wires. Worse than anything was being left alone. Dahlia felt a panic rise the longer Caroline was off the line. She bit her lip and prayed for her to come back on.

"Darling, are you there? That was Brooksie, who sends you his love and says stiff upper lip and all that. He'll ring you later, but in the meantime he's gotten Alan Leonard to keep Jones from giving any interviews. Brooksie says that Alan says the record company doesn't want this any more than you do."

The tears, hot and heavy, rose to Dahlia's eyes and spilled over, coursing down her cheeks. Brooksie and Carrots— and Dahlia. The terrible trio. Choking out the words, she said, "I . . . ca . . . can't talk now. I'll ring you . . . later. Oh, Carrots!" And she broke down sobbing into the telephone.

Mercifully, she was alone. She paced up and down her bedroom, crying and twisting her hands, from time to time grabbing one of the posts at the end of the bed and shaking it. "What right! What right do they have to print this? I'll sue them. I'll see that they never print anything about me and my family again. Dierdre's picture!"

She could have killed every last person who worked for those tabloids. They were parasites, vulgar and low. They didn't deserve to live! They had mocked her mother and now they were trying to ruin her. Dahlia went on for nearly an hour before her anger gave way to guilt. She had, after all, been having an affair with a rock star. Of course there had been reporters all around. Chris Jones was news. She had been unforgivably stupid. It was one thing for Carrots to have her little flings. They never amounted to anything, anyway—one, possibly two discreet times with some nobody. But she, Lady Lovell, had been so sure of herself! What on earth had made her think that she could traipse all over England and Scotland and not be found out. What would Desmond do? What would he say?

Dahlia sat numbly on the edge of her bed. The telephone rang again. She jumped. It was Haskins. "I'm sorry to disturb you, m'lady, but Lord Lovell just rang and is returning this evening at nine. Do you wish to wait dinner for him?"

"No, Haskins." Dahlia felt a cold chill. "And cancel mine. I don't think either of us will be hungry tonight."

The divorce proceedings began. Desmond faltered only once, coming to see Dahlia in London. But Dahlia, her eyes swimming in tears, said no.

Chapter 41

CASSIE HUNG UP the telephone. Pete stood waiting for her to say something. "Boy, I've heard icy tones before, but whoever you were talking to must be frozen solid."

Cassie said nothing.

Pete came over to her. "Cassie?" He touched her arm. "What's wrong?"

"Nothing's *wrong*." Cassie frowned. "That was my mother."

"Oh? How is she?"

"Fine. Just fine. And," Cassie practically spat out the words, "newly married."

"No kidding! That's great. I'm happy for her. She's been alone for a long time. Who's...?"

Cassie spun around. "Cut the congratulations, Pete. It's not great. She's gone and married Bud Hurley." Cassie said this as if that said it all. Pete sat on the edge of the sofa.

"Okay. Bud Hurley it is." He waited. "Who is Bud Hurley?"

"Bud Hurley is the man who owns the bowling alley in Winston-Salem. They've been seeing each other for years, but I never thought she'd actually go and marry him. He has an anchor tattooed to his arm. And a five o'clock shadow that makes Nixon's look like baby skin."

Pete laughed. "He sounds cute."

"It's not funny, Pete. I can't believe she did this. He's

so . . . well, common. It's embarrassing."

Pete's eyes narrowed for a moment but he kept his tone light. "What do you care? You've sworn never to set foot down there again. How can your mother embarrass you up here? Besides, I never held Nixon's beard against him. It was just everything else he stood for. Is she happy? That's the main thing. Did she sound happy. Are they in love with each other?"

"It's hardly a question of *love*," Cassie said unreasonably. "Love has always gotten her in trouble. I should think at her age it would be more a question of dignity."

"Well, if you ask me, your mother needs a good man to love her. Christ, even I'd be afraid to face those relatives of yours alone."

"I didn't ask you, and let's not talk about it anymore," Cassie snapped. But clearly she had more to say. "Do you know what they're going to do? Sell up. Sell everything— the house, the furniture, the *bowling alley,* and move to Fort Lauderdale where *Bud* has bought into a marina. My mother acted like that was high adventure. Oh, God, can't you just see them, decked out in leisure outfits, smelling like fish and gasoline—"

"For Christ's sake, Cassie. Can it! Or at least show a little loyalty. What right have you to judge them? Have you ever been to Lauderdale? It's nice. They can have a good life there without a lot of small-town snobs breathing down their necks."

"Are you talking about me?"

"I hope not," he said quietly. "Come on, now. I don't think you're that upset by your mother. Something else is bugging you. Why don't I open a bottle of wine and let's—"

"No, Pete. Just leave me alone, please." She walked over to the window. She felt so pent-up she could scream. The sound of her mother's voice, tremulous and just a little drunk from the champagne, was still ringing in her ears.

But Pete was right. Blue's marriage was not the only thing bothering her.

Pete shrugged, turned back to his desk, and then thought better of it. "I can't work anymore tonight. Let's go down to the Half-Note and listen to Zoot Sims. What do you say?" He was standing behind her now, and he folded his arms around her waist and put his lips to her ear.

"Goddamn it! I said leave me alone!" Her teeth were clenched and her words measured and harsh. The minute they were out of her mouth, she knew it was the worst thing she could have done.

Pete twisted her around in one swift motion, his hands gripping her arms. For a second she thought he was going to hit her.

"Listen to me, Cassie, and listen good. You can play the bitch all you want to with other people, but not with me. Either you tell me what's bugging you or . . . or—"

"Or what, Pete?" She had meant to keep her voice reasonable, but it came out taunting and mean. "Let go of my arms. You're hurting me. What's with you, anyway?"

He stood glaring at her. It was a look that particularly annoyed her—macho and exasperated—as if women were hopeless to reason with. She turned away irritated, frustrated, tired, and thoroughly devoid of any feelings whatsoever for Pete Rossi.

"I really don't want to get into anything tonight," she said. "And I don't want to go hear Zoot Sims. You go. I have a headache and I want to go to bed."

"Alone?"

"Yes, alone. What the hell are you implying?"

"I'm not implying anything. I just know you go to bed thinking of that boss of yours. For sure you spend more time thinking about him than you do about me. You're hung up on him. I'd have to be blind not to see that. I have the right to be upset. I have the right because you're mine. And I don't give up easily on what's mine."

"You don't own me." Cassie could feel the anger mounting in her voice. "You'd like to own me, tell me what I should do with my life, how I should think, what I should feel. Did it ever occur to you that *you* might be the problem? You and," she gestured to the room, "this whole do-good loser's life you lead?" She sat impatiently on the sofa. "You and I want different things from life, Pete."

"Apparently."

She looked down at her hands, debating with herself just how far she intended to go. "Pete, you're harsh and judgmental about people you know nothing about. I think you have a limited and narrow vision. You assume you're right at the onset of everything we talk about, everything we do, everything we plan, and always, always, I'm supposed to come around to your way of thinking. Frankly, I'm sick of it. I'm sick of defending myself. It's no use trying to say what I want. I can't explain it because you just won't listen."

"Try me." Pete's voice was low and controlled, but Cassie could feel the tension between them. It seemed to heighten and exaggerate her thoughts, but she didn't care, and couldn't stop the words from spilling out.

"Ever since I was a little girl I've wanted something big out of life, something important, something that would lift me up and over the billions of people teeming this earth. I don't want to be an average, everyday, cozy kind of person, scurrying around, never wanting much, never expecting much. I want things to happen to me. I want to make them happen. I don't want to leave it up to chance or to someone else's idealistic notions." She didn't look at Pete. "You can say whatever you like about a man like John Stavros, and you can think whatever you damned well please. But he makes me feel larger than life. And no," she hurried on, "I haven't gone to bed with him."

And it was driving her crazy. Nothing even remotely sexual had passed between them since the night in his car. The few times they had talked about anything other than

*business she had felt she blabbered on about stupid things
. . . silly remembrances from her past, gossip . . . oh, God,
she felt guilty about that. She didn't know how she let it
slip about Dahlia and the rock star. She had meant for it
to be funny. Poor Dahlia. But of course what happened to
her had nothing to do with her telling Stavros. Why would
he care?*

She looked at Pete defensively. "John Stavros has given
me the means to move ahead. I won't lose that now, not
when I can see a glimmer of a future for myself. The kind
of future I want. Pete," her voice was almost pleading,
"don't you see? I can't work for that future if I have to keep
apologizing to you for it. It's not that I don't believe in the
things you do. It's just that I can't reprogram myself to fight
for lost causes. I don't want anymore to know what *should*
be or *could* be. I want something real. Something tangible."

"Like money."

"Yes. Like money. And power. And prestige. What's so
terrible about that? I'm ambitious. Men can be ambitious
and everyone cheers them on. But a woman . . . God forbid.
She's still a freak if she wants something more than a second-
rate job and a second-rate life. I tell you, Pete, if I don't
reach for it now, I never will."

"Garbage," Pete muttered. "I'm trying to listen to you,
but we keep coming back to garbage, and it stinks, Cassie.
You're blinded by the price tags, the first-class tickets, and
all the other little trinkets and baubles of that cloying, meaningless, dead-end world you think is so grand. You don't
want something 'big' out of life—all you want is the key
to the front door of the big Litton house up on the hill. Ever
since you were a little girl you've thought of yourself as a
poor relation. You don't know how to measure success
unless you measure it by their standards. Those aren't standards at all. Rich people are rich because they're either
scavengers or criminals, but you refuse to see that. You're
going to play it their way."

He had gotten up and was pacing the floor in front of her. "Well, fine. Have it. Go for it. Get it. And when you think you've succeeded, come back to me and tell me what you've got. Money. Power. Prestige. Listen to those words, Cassie. They're empty and cold. They're lonely and humorless. Where is the love in all of this?"

The agony in his face was so raw and plain that Cassie was almost moved to touch him. But she didn't. She couldn't. She was rooted where she sat on the sofa, feeling only the pulsating throb in her temple. He would never understand. She could never make him understand.

She couldn't give up now. She held her hand out to Pete and he took it, but there was already something cold between them. Her hand felt awkward, lifeless, in his.

"Pete . . . I don't know what more to say. What we had, what we thought we had . . . it isn't there anymore."

He crossed the room to his desk, pulled a piece of paper out of the typewriter, glanced at it briefly, and then crumpled it into a wad. "It's there, Cassie. It's fighting hard for a little nourishment, but it's there."

"No, not this time." Cassie folded her arms, clinging tightly to herself. "Pete, you don't know how badly I feel about this."

"Just tell me you don't love me. None of this matters unless you can tell me that." His eyes were searching hers.

Cassie gripped her arms. "I don't love you."

He didn't speak, and the silence in the room must have gone on for a long time; now she was crying. Still, there seemed nothing more to say. Pete reached for his coat and crossed to the door. Their eyes locked for a moment, and then he nodded, his head cocked to one side, as if he were about to ask a question. Then he shook his head—what was the point? He grinned and made a small comic bow, and then he was gone.

The next day, while she was at work, he cleared his things out. The desk was soon clean of typewriter and paper, his books were gone, leaving gaping holes in the shelves; his razor and his toothbrush, his funny old army jacket with the musky smell when it rained, the glass paperweight she had given him with the vintage red Chevy pictured in the dome, the pack of cards he used to show her tricks. He left the rooms spare and clean again. All smooth surfaces and polished counter tops.

Chapter 42

DAHLIA DIPPED THE cotton-wool pads into the extract of cucumber and leaned back on the Fortuny cushions on her bed. Downstairs she could hear the Portuguese cook and Ron, the rather fey young man she had hired to "manage" things, ranting at each other as they often did. Before long he might very well storm up the back stairs in his sweeping black cashmere cape and fedora and announce that he was giving notice. Ron gave notice on a regular basis. Upstairs, children—Dierdre and her little friends—were thumping on the floor and screaming something that sounded vaguely obscene. Or was it Josephine? Yes, there was the thick Irish accent.

Dahlia watched, suspended, for the next installment of household noises, but all seemed quiet below. No need to entreat Ron not to leave. Bath water running above—so Josephine had things back in hand. Dahlia relaxed and prepared to drift off in the cool, green, scented darkness of her bed.

There was a light tap on the door, and Ron busied himself in with a telephone in his hand.

"Sorry, luv. It's Alistair Buell," he whispered reverentially. "Naturally I thought . . ." Ron's eyebrows completed the sentence more eloquently than any words he could muster. He handed her the receiver.

"Alistair? You're a mind reader. I was just about to pick up the telephone and ring you, and now you've gone and saved me the trouble." Why was it, she wondered to herself, that whenever she spoke with Alistair Buell she suddenly sounded like her mother? Did he recognize the languid gestures and detached amusement that were exact replicas of Camilla's?

Camilla had called him Buell, just that, and they had been great friends. To the rest of the world he was Sir Alistair Buell, a man of legendary wealth and extraordinary charisma. He had spent his life pursuing danger and adventure and had acquired international fame and notoriety as an explorer, big-game hunter, mountain climber, pilot, and sailor. He had traveled to the far corners of the earth and had escaped perils most men never even dreamed of. Now in his sixties, he postured that the world had become too small for him and the only adventure left, the last mountain to climb, the last *terra incognita* to explore, was his own death.

As a child, Dahlia had found Sir Alistair more than a little terrifying. He had come often to Membland and delighted in telling horrifying stories filled with violence, mutilation, and cruelty. He was indeed a great raconteur, but it had always seemed to Dahlia that he reserved the most gruesome details of his adventures for her alone—watching her reactions intently, as if she were undergoing some sort of test.

Camilla and Charlotte had gone on safari with Buell once, and he had taken the two women up in a light plane to circle a boiling, hissing volcanic mountain. Buell particularly relished telling how the sickening, hot fumes had almost overwhelmed them. "Like the putrid stench of a dragon's breath," he whispered down to Dahlia's small pale face. Then he laughed, recalling how the women had begged to go back, how they had gasped for breath and turned green with sickness and fear. But Buell had ignored them, flying the small plane closer and closer to the very heart of the furnace, daring the devil to suck them down. Dahlia had always hated this story; it haunted her nightmares so that she woke screaming and drenched in sweat.

When she remembered him at Membland, she thought of him prowling restlessly, like a big jungle cat, around the house, around the grounds, as if he were stalking something.

He was always particularly ready to pounce on small, defenseless children. Sir Alistair claimed to have a close kinship with children. He preferred their company, he said, to that of most other people. And, indeed, he would seek them out. "Hold them prisoner," Dahlia had once complained bitterly to Charlotte, and tell his awful stories and confuse them with pointed questions. He had stopped her in the courtyard once and demanded, "Do you love your mother?" bursting into paroxysms of laughter at her bewildered, small, "Yes."

Once a year, in the summer, Buell amused himself and provided copy to society editors worldwide by hosting "an entertainment . . . a little garden party for my friends." The invited guests numbered four hundred, and the party was a production as lavish and spectacular as could be brought about with boundless wealth and an inclination to excess. There was never any question about it—Alistair Buell's "little party" was the most important social event of the year, and this despite the fact that it inevitably took place during the awkward and unfashionable month of August and that he autocratically and idiosyncratically insisted on controlling the color of the ladies' dresses. Gentlemen, of course, always wore white tie, but the ladies alternated by year from black to white. No color was permitted, and a famous countess had once protested violently when she had been asked to remove the rubies that decorated her neck and shoulders. But she had complied, not wishing to be overlooked and uninvited the following year.

The guests flocked from the four corners—flying in from North and South America, Australia and Japan—exotic sultans, sheikhs and other minor Asian royals—as well as from the European continent next door. For those to whom such things mattered, an invitation from Buell mattered a great deal. Those who expected one and failed to get it could rightly consider themselves to have been exiled beyond the pale of fashionable society.

This, then, was Alistair Buell.

"Now listen, Alistair. I want you to do me a favor . . . I

want you to put someone at my table... Well, rearrange something... John Stavros. I want him... No, I don't know him, but he's bringing my very dearest friend from America and I want her... Yes, that's it... Of course she's pretty. Now, be an angel and do that for me, won't you... Oh, goody. You are a dear."

Cassie thoroughly enjoyed the flight from New York to London. The other passengers, mostly men, cast covert, curious glances in her direction, but she remained unapproachably aloof and busied herself with the papers she had carried aboard in a soft leather case. She had no fear of flying and she particularly liked the feeling of suspended isolation. For a few hours she was free of responsibilities, telephone calls, any demands at all. She started a letter to her mother, forcing herself to write a few stilted sentences on the velvety writing paper that bore her initials, but her mind kept wandering with pleasant curiosity to the people around her. What did they think of her? Who did they think she was?

She was very well-dressed in a slim skirted suit of unbleached linen—a traveling suit that accommodated wrinkles without losing an ounce of chic. Her straight blond hair had been subtly streaked with ash-pale highlights and styled by Vidal Sassoon; her feet were elegantly shod in new, high-heeled spectator pumps. She was poised, elegant, demure, and she commanded the unspoken admiration of every flight attendant and fellow passenger in the first-class compartment.

At Heathrow a man wearing a navy-blue blazer stood holding a card with her name printed on it in bold black letters. The initials SIM on his breast pocket told her that they were both employees of Stavros International Media. He took her bags and in a very few minutes ushered her into a waiting car, the interior of which was suprisingly cool, the bright morning sunlight tamed and filtered by the tinted glass. The man at the wheel pointed out a cabinet that opened to reveal a small bar with a choice of cold juices and sparkling waters and a second cabinet that became, at the touch of a fingertip, a lighted vanity mirror above a tray holding combs, brushes, tissues, hand cream, and scent.

"I think I'll just move in back here forever," Cassie joked, wondering if the driver could hear her through the dividing glass. He answered immediately and without a trace of humor.

"Yes, madam. Perhaps madam would care for some coffee or tea?"

Cassie declined, thanking him, and leaned back to smoke a cigarette. A large ashtray appeared, rotating out from the mahogany paneling before her. She almost giggled then, feeling like Beauty at the castle of the Beast being waited on by disembodied servants.

The past five months had kept her on the run almost seven days a week and for this she was grateful. Stavros had been right when he said acquisitions was the place to be. Cassie spent a great deal of time on the road, in and out of VIP lounges and lavish suites in top hotels, meeting, researching, snooping, until she felt the information she had gathered would or would not provide Stavros with the means to buy out another company. Whereas many women in high corporate positions complained their sex worked against them, Cassie found this not to be true. Her style and poise, her fresh approach and cultured accent all opened doors for her. People trusted her. She was wined and dined and flirted with and even proposed to by a few quite dazzled admirers, but along those lines her only interest, still, was the elusive man who employed her.

And then, everything changed. Returning from a long two weeks in Los Angeles, she had found a handwritten note from John Stavros on her desk. It was an invitation to dinner that night. Tired as she was, she quickly sent her acceptance and then rushed home to bathe and carefully dress.

Never had she had such a fabulous evening. Dinner at La Côte Basque was filled with stimulating, amusing talk and unlimited bottles of vintage champagne. Afterward they went to the opening of the much-publicized and very chic new uptown club called Night Life. There she met and mingled with the likes of Candy Bergen, the Kissingers, Andy Warhol, Swifty Lazar, Lauren Bacall, Warren Beatty, and Julie Christie. They had drinks at Paley's table, and then she danced with a dark-haired Arab rumored to have a billion dollars in oil. It was fun, more fun than she had had in a long time, and throughout the evening John Stavros was attentive, admiring, and almost gay. Afterward, he had driven her home, and before giving her a chaste but sincere kiss on the cheek he had asked if she would fly to London the following week to attend Alistair Buell's ball.

The next day boxes began arriving in her office. Stavros had picked everything she was to wear—shoes, stockings, lingerie, jewels, a handbag, gold fittings for the handbag, a magnificent cashmere cape, even the scent she was to use. But most extravagant of all was her gown. A long, white Dior gown, a shimmering sheath of a thing hand sewn with a million tiny luminescent pearls.

"Fabulous! Simply fabulous!" Sammy had declared as Cassie modeled the dress in the office. "Mr. Stavros has excellent taste. In that dress ... hmm ... well, I'd say this little trip was going to be ve-ry interesting." Penny, her secretary, let out a knowing hoot, but Cassie ducked back into the dressing room. She didn't know what to think. But there was someone who would. She lost no time in calling Dahlia.

"But darling! How too exciting! You must be at our table ... Don't be silly, Cassie, you can't come all this way and sit with some dreary old business types. I promise your Mr. Stavros will love us ... darling, this is a party not a conference ... Yes, yes, I hear you, but I simply won't take no for an answer. And Cassie, the next day we'll have lunch ... and dinner ... I can't wait to see you."

Cassie grinned from the back seat of the limousine. Outside the window the grimy outskirts of London had given way to the elegant houses of Belgravia. She could hardly wait to see Dahlia, too. Somehow it was very important to her that Dahlia see her in this light, as the woman John Stavros had chosen to be his.

Chapter 43

ALISTAIR BUELL HAD scheduled his party for the night of the full moon—the Blood Moon. He had done this so the menagerie of wild animals housed in cages and islanded behind moats on his estate would be restless—pacing, pawing, and howling as his four hundred guests paraded themselves among the striped tents.

The long drive and expansive grounds were lit by a thousand flaming torches. Masses of exotic flowers were banked everywhere. The air was heavy with the scent of them. The tents, adjacent to the pale-yellow Queen Anne manor house, were all ablaze. From one came the raucous sounds of a Dixieland band flown in from New Orleans, from another the sinuous strains of a tango. Circus people—jugglers, strong men, snake charmers, acrobats—mingled with the swaying, laughing throngs.

Dahlia glanced over at Brooksic as they wandered from tent to tent. He was smiling to himself, his column already half-written in his mind. She spotted Carrots on the dance floor, dressed in a vintage Balenciaga from the late '50s; its skirt ballooned to such a degree that she looked as if she might ascend at any moment. White was the color of the year, and Dahlia was glad she had not tried to compete with the fashion explosion around her.

She had gone to her dressmaker with a few yards of antique silk and a single request. "I want to float." The dress, cut on the bias, clung to her small frame in ghostlike wisps.

Now, walking through the crowds, she searched for Cassie and hoped that nothing had kept her from coming.

"Darling," Carrots waved to her. "I'm having a beastly time rounding up everyone for our table. Oh, God! There's that cow, Mary Rose Somebody-or-other. I once kissed her thinking she was my cousin Roselind, and now I can't stop. She'll realize I don't know who she is..." But the rest of her sentence was drowned out by the persistent and now deafening roar of engines from the sky. Suddenly spotlights lit up the adjacent field and everyone clustered at the edge of the tent to see what was happening.

"It's a helicopter," Carrots exclaimed. "How amusing. I wish we'd come by helicopter. I wonder who it is?"

A man jumped gracefully down from the aircraft and stood for just a moment alone in the glare of the lights. He was lithe and slim, with a strikingly sculpted face that was all planes and angles. He was easily the most attractive man she had seen in a long time, Dahlia thought, but before she could wonder who he was, her hand flew to her mouth and she gasped. "It's Cassie!"

Indeed, the pilot had placed a small set of steps on the ground, and looking every bit the most glamorous of women, Cassie Litton, glittering from head to toe in a white spangled gown, stepped into the light.

"You look fabulous!" Dahlia rushed to embrace her when at last they reached the tent.

"Careful," Cassie joked in her ear, "I might have to return this dress after tonight. Oh, Dahlia, isn't this the most fun!" They gazed at each other with delight before Dahlia turned her glance to the man with her.

"Mr. Stavros," Carrots had taken his arm and was leading him about their circle possessively as she made introductions, "do you know Lady Lovell?" she gushed.

Stavros lifted Dahlia's hand to his lips. "I have the pleasure of knowing Lady Lovell from a previous time... a time when she was the delightfully charming Miss de Ginsburgh."

Dahlia smiled through her confusion. There was something vaguely familiar about this man, but surely they had not met before... she would remember... and yet there was something in the slightly mocking expression on his face—the crooked smile, the jet black eyes, which, at the moment, looked all too amused at her expense.

"What fun!" said Carrots, not hiding for a moment the curiosity she felt. "A meeting with the past . . ."

"Oh dear," said Dahlia, looking to Cassie for some hint, but Cassie seemed equally confused. "You have the advantage. Perhaps we met in America?" She knew they had not, but she wanted a moment to think. Where did she know him from? As she looked into his eyes she felt a faint blush of embarrassment creep across her face.

"No, not America," he said, softly now. He paused, as if remembering something painful.

"Membland," said Dahlia, her voice almost a whisper. She felt as if a bell jar had been placed over the two of them so that they were completely isolated even as they stood in the midst of the swirling party. "It's Yanni."

As if releasing them from bondage, Carrots began to prattle. "But how too thrilling! Our childhood friend. *My*, haven't we grown!" And then, giving Dahlia one last penetrating look, she grasped Cassie in one hand and Brooksie in the other and propelled them to the table.

"Yanni." John Stavros laughed. "I haven't been called that in quite some time." He spoke lightly, but there was a cool, measured undertone to his voice. His eyes seemed to be drinking her in.

Dahlia's heart was pounding. "So you're the terrible John Stavros. I can't believe . . ." She gestured helplessly. "I don't know what to say."

"Then don't say anything." She saw him glance briefly at their table and then back to her. "We needn't sit just yet."

He took her arm and led her away.

Cassie sat at the table between Henry Brooks and Nicky Keyes. There was dinner. There was dancing. Though she talked, and laughed, she would not later be able to remember a word of what was said that night. All she could do was watch Dahlia, gliding in slow circles in the arms of John

Stavros. Her attention was reserved for Dahlia's face, her radiance. Cassie remembered the terrible evening in Washington so many years ago. Dahlia's face then, so small and pale. Cassie's heart had been sick for Dahlia then. She had wanted to take a part of Dahlia's suffering on herself, to share it. She watched her now and wanted her to suffer again.

BOOK FOUR

Chapter 44

A SLEEK BLACK animal with headlights, the Porsche moved quietly along the twisted roads that made up Membland Park. It stopped beside a grove of silver birches, and when the engine died, the night song of a million cicadas rose up to fill the silence. Inside the car, a slim, dark man in evening clothes and a fair-haired woman dressed in white sat looking at the moonlit landscape. Lines of tiny hedgerows ran like stitches on a quilt across a rolling countryside of grazing fields and little woods. Only a gentle breeze disturbed the perfect stillness, making the birches sway and whisper like satin skirts across a floor. Intoxicating fragrance filled the air—sweet, new-cut hay; night-blooming flowers; and something warm and musky from the earth.

"I used to sneak out on nights like this . . ." Dahlia sighed luxuriously. "To come and sit up there under that tree." She pointed to a graceful elm that stood atop a curving rise. "I called her 'My Lady' because of the way her branches open out like arms." Dahlia turned and was surprised to find him watching her. She was amazed to feel the force, the impact of his presence. She wondered, over and over, how a meeting as bizarre and unexpected as theirs could also feel so absolutely right, almost as if it had been meant to be. She never, ever, could have guessed, she told herself repeatedly, that Cassie's famous boss, John Stavros, and handsome Yanni from her childhood days could have turned out to be one and the same. The thoughts of Cassie's eager, happy face made Dahlia feel a pang or two in some remote part of her consciousness, but she dismissed it quickly. It was impossible, improbable, and no one, least of all Dahlia,

253

could have foreseen the accident of their encounter.

"You weren't afraid, alone in the dark?" he asked, still watching her intensely, as if he feared that she might suddenly dissolve and disappear.

Dahlia shook her head and grimaced like a child attempting to be brave. "Certainly not. I felt much safer here away from Mummy's guests. What a madhouse it always was. Do you remember? Endless people and all their intrigues. You played a part in all of that, you know. I'd say that almost all the ladies fancied you at one time or another ... but then, you must have known that!"

"Did they?" He smiled, took up her hand, and brought it almost to his lips. "What an observant little girl you were," he teased, kissing the inside of her palm. She felt a shock of pleasure and excitement. His breath was hot within her hand; his lips were dry as, they lingered in their intimate caress. Then all at once she felt as if a bolt of lightning had brought back the memory of these very lips bruising her childish mouth, as if it had happened yesterday. She caught her breath and let some moments pass before she spoke.

"You must mean what a revolting and obnoxious little girl I was. Oh, do let's walk. I wonder if the house is haunted. Do you believe in ghosts?"

Stavros and Dahlia left the car and walked across the lawn toward the Lady elm. Her high-heeled slippers dug into the earth and she kicked them off so she could feel the cool, damp grass against her feet. She felt at once refreshed and charged with a girlish, restless energy. She lifted up her skirts so she could run. She was a wild thing in the night, wind-blown and free, running so fast it seemed that she was flying, and all the while she knew he watched her and followed. She also knew that she could run as fast as a deer, fast as the wind, fast as a comet in the sky, but that he would catch her in the end, and he would hold her still, clip her wings, and make her his.

They reached the elm on the hill together, and, gasping for breath, laughing and talking, they fell to the ground and leaned against the tree, the same way Dahlia did those many nights ago. A powerful magic seemed to be at work. So many years had passed since Dahlia last was here, so much had happened in her life—Camilla dead and Charlotte, too; a marriage, childbirth, affairs, divorce—they all took on the aspect of a dream, stories in someone else's life. Only this moment, only now was real—the night, the moon, Dahlia and Yanni sitting beneath a tree, their arms entwined, looking at Membland down below.

Camilla's house did not have an imposing look, but rather it snuggled into the landscape, comfortable, inviting, and secure. From where they sat, the sloping roofs, the gray-white stones, the bits of garden, and winding lanes looked like a picture in a storybook. Beyond the house and out of view stood Charlotte's studio, a cavernous stone barn with windows in the roof to catch the light. Between the studio and the house, a series of garden terraces had once grown vegetables and flowers. The ruins of another barn formed the foundation of a hot house for growing figs and grapes and berries out of season and for supplying Camilla year-round bouquets of rare and fragrant flowers.

"Have you changed it much?" he asked and helped her to her feet.

"No. Not at all. I've not been back but once or twice. A caretaker looks after it, although he's getting on. He writes me twice a year, long detailed letters about the rainfall, crops, repairs . . . I'm sure he thinks me quite neglectful."

The main house seemed to grow larger as they came near. The moon was lower in the sky, and all around the night grew darker. Yanni and Dahlia were lost in thought and memories that crowded out the need to talk. He held her tightly by the hand, and there was something childlike in the way they clung together in the dark.

The house was locked up tight. Dahlia swore softly as they made their way around back through the kitchen garden. "Damn!" She poked at another window. "Looks like we'll have to break our way in."

"Unnecessary," he said emphatically and took her wrist, pulling her close. She thought he meant to kiss her, but his lips only brushed the hollow of her neck, and then he whispered in her ear, "I know where there's a key."

In an instant, Stavros had slipped off his shoes and socks, and, grinning wickedly, he climbed easily and nimbly up the old pear tree that had been trained to form an espalier of crosses against the wall beside the kitchen door.

"Why you sneak!" Dahlia was indignant as she watched him scramble across the roof. "Once I tried to climb that tree and you said all sorts of beastly things to me. Where are you going?"

Stavros had disappeared behind the first of five chimneys, then reappeared in seconds triumphantly jangling a ring of keys.

"Why were you always so mean to me?" Dahlia trailed behind him through the cool darkness of the kitchen. She knew she sounded petulant, like a small girl who has been left out of a big boy's game. "All I wanted was a friend, but you were always so aloof, so secretive, so snooty..." Her voice trailed off to a whisper as the silence of the empty house bore down on them.

In the drawing room, French windows opened onto the first of many terraced gardens that overlooked a swimming pool below. It was a large, lushly appointed room, at once romantic, comfortable, and opulent. There was no question but that this was a woman's room, a woman's house—the plaything of a lovely, pampered, self-indulgent woman with exquisite, expensive tastes and with the means to satisfy them.

"Do you want a candle?" Dahlia asked, still whispering. "There always used to be some in the cupboard here—"

"Wait," Stavros said. "Come see the moonlight on the trees." He flung open the doors and all at once the room was flooded with the sounds of night.

"So, you thought *I* was snooty?" His voice held a low, teasing note. "That's good... very good. The noble Lady Dahlia snubbed by a houseboy!"

"There! You see? That's exactly what I mean. Houseboy,

indeed. Why, you're the worst kind of snob—a snob in reverse. Always putting people in their place and keeping them there forever."

"Oh, poor, lonely, little rich girl," he teased her as he slipped his arm around her waist and pulled her close.

When Dahlia spoke again, after he had kissed her, her voice was low and breathless. "I have this feeling that I've been waiting all this time . . . Waiting for you, before I could return to Membland. Oh, Yanni! It all sounds so crazy, but do you know what I mean? It seems so absolutely right that we've come back here together. Don't you feel it too? Don't you feel as if somehow you've always known?"

His eyes seemed to burn in the darkness, and his face looked very grave. He, too, spoke softly when he answered her. "I've never for a moment doubted it."

Yanni's words shot through her like an arrow; she believed him instantly. Long-buried hopes and wild emotions swept her up as every bit of reason left her. Even her memory played sly and wily tricks as she recalled her days with Yanni here at Membland. Those long-gone days when they had both been young and vulnerable, when all their feelings had been raw, their senses and perceptions not yet dulled. Now she could see with absolute clarity that they had recognized a kinship and a bond between them even then— and in a certain way perhaps they had. For they had each known bitter loneliness and isolation, and they had shared a fierce, unyielding pride. These were strong ties between them now. Dahlia knew this if she knew anything.

For Stavros, ghosts were everywhere. Soft voices whispered in the darkened corners or down a corridor, just out of sight. The people who had lived here always spoke in low-pitched whispering voices, as if everything they talked about might be a secret. Oh yes, there had been plenty of secrets in that crowd. Secret lives, secret loves, secret passions. What had *she* thought, he'd often wondered, when she went upstairs that night and found her cupboard ransacked, her letters and her pictures gone, her secrets stolen. Had she understood the meaning of the gesture, that it was then she started to belong to him? A peal of silvery laughter broke the silence. His heart was beating wildly as he looked around, half expecting that she might suddenly make one of her dramatic entrances.

"Look, Yanni, these doors weren't even locked." Dahlia pushed one open and stepped out onto the moonlit terrace. She laughed again, the sound echoing in the stillness. "You didn't need to climb up on the roof after all."

He didn't answer her. The time for talk was over. Instead, he kissed her roughly, pressing her hard against the wall, his hands playing with the flimsy silk that covered her breasts, and then the fabric fell, drooping like petals on a tulip past its prime. He bruised her mouth, just as he had those many years ago, and, once again, she felt excitement mixed with fear.

She kissed him back, matching his passion with her own. Now there was nothing that could stop them. They were abandoned and alone.

She felt her knees begin to tremble, and she clung to him as his hands explored her naked breasts, caressed her thighs, pulled up her skirt, and reached between her legs to pull aside the bit of silk there—so he could touch her with a slow and piercing sureness that made her catch her breath. He caught her up just as her legs gave way beneath her, and he carried her across the room and up the curving stairway. His eyes were fixed on hers, and she felt faint with longing and desire to be possessed by him, to melt away, to have her body merge with his.

He carried her as lightly as a toy, down the long corridor, into Camilla's room, and lowered her, not onto the large, lace-covered bed, but onto the satin white sofa. On the wall above it was a painting framed in antique gold, a portrait of Camilla Baring.

Slowly his hands caressed her as he removed the remnants of her gown and peeled away her panties. He kissed the inside of her thighs and gently pushed her legs apart so he could probe and search with delicate, sure strokes. Oh, she was wet, so wet that he slid a slender finger in and out and spread her open, like a ripened plum, and deftly revealed the throbbing little secret part of her. He used his hands, his mouth, his eyes, to torture her until she moaned aloud, ready to beg but unsure how to find the words. Then he took hold of her own extended hand and used it to replace his own, made her caress herself. He sat beside her and kissed her on the mouth. He watched, waited, playing his hands across her breasts, stroking her belly and her legs, touching her everywhere but there, until she moaned and writhed under the exquisite torture of his touch. Her body was on fire with a craving so intense that she almost screamed her need to him; still he did not release her but watched her, was her audience. He placed her other hand to where her fire burned, then whispered hoarsely, "Oh God, you're beautiful. So young. So perfect. And so lovely. Open yourself to me. Show me your secret parts . . . Come, darling . . . Yes, yes, yes, do it . . . Just like that. Come, baby, bring yourself to me."

Her orgasm came quickly but brought her no relief . . . only loud, choking sobs that wracked her body with pent-up emotion and frustration. Only when she had given up all hope of ever feeling him, knowing him, of getting what she wanted, did he relent. He picked her up, carried her to the bed. Their bodies met and he was in her, surging, pounding, like a restless storm-tossed sea.

Dahlia slept. When she woke up, the morning light flooded the room. The place beside her in the bed was empty. John Stavros stood, dressed, before the portrait of Camilla.

"Were you in love with her?"

He whirled around and in a harsh voice asked her what she meant. His face in daylight was drawn and pale. He looked like he hadn't slept at all.

"Heavens! You needn't look so surprised. You weren't

the only one, you know. Far from it. Everyone was in love with her sometime or another. That was her specialty—making people fall in love with her and turning them into her slaves."

Chapter 45

THE WEATHER CHANGED. The sky was leaden and overcast, and by the time Stavros and Dahlia drove into London in the late afternoon it was through a steady downpour of heavy rain. His mood was desultory, and their conversation during the three-hour drive was as stop and go as the traffic and with as many long, jittery pauses. Stavros looked drawn; his complexion had taken on an ashen pallor. Dahlia herself felt dazed with lack of sleep but unready to climb off the dazzling carousel of wild sensations and euphoria that they had ridden through the night.

She tried to draw him back to the magical rapport that they had shared but hours ago. Gamely tackling one subject after another, she told him all about her life with Desmond—particularly in contrast with her happy life alone in London.

"Well, hardly alone, of course, because there's Dierdre, Josephine, and Ron, of course, to keep us all in line. We're much more like a gypsy camp than a proper household, but at least we're happy and we do as we like..." She paused, watching the raindrops splatter against the windshield. "Poor old gloomy Desmond. I suppose I do feel sorry for him... but honestly! The man's ideas about life were positively feudal. Do you know, it's awfully lucky that Dierdre came out a girl, although Desmond took it very badly. So much nonsense about needing to produce a son and heir. And she's such a sweet, endearing little thing! Oh, it was too ridiculous and pathetic, really. And you see how fortunate I was! Because if we'd had a son, I'd have never been able to leave. I suppose he would have simply locked me away in a tower somewhere, like Mrs. Heathcliff, or was it Rochester? Have you heard a single word I've said?"

Stavros responded with a thin, quick smile and squeezed her hand, but his eyes were blank and faraway. Later he broke the silence only once, surprising her with his abrupt question. "Tell me about your friend. Is she as clever as she appears?"

"Carrots?" Dahlia misunderstood. "Of course she's clever. Whatever made you think of that?"

"No, no. Your American friend, the Litton girl. I've got her working for me now, and I'm impressed with what I've seen so far. She's got a level head and seems ambitious..." His voice trailed off as if he harbored some unspoken doubts.

"Oh, Cassie! Of course. How awful. I'd completely forgotten that she came with you last night. Was it just last night... the party? It seems so..." Dahlia gave Stavros a sidelong, sexy glance to wordlessly remind him of the reasons for her lapse in memory. But he looked straight ahead and did not notice. Dahlia recovered her aplomb and rushed into a torrent of enthusiastic praise about her "dearest friend."

"You simply can't imagine what a treasure you've got. Cassie is absolutely, utterly brilliant. We went to school together you know, and she was always most unbelievably serious and worked ever so hard, because her family was dreadfully poor and so she had to get scholarships and all that sort of thing." She paused to get her breath and then went right on. "Anyway, you would think with all that she might be just a teensy bit dull, but you'd be wrong, because she's awfully clever and amusing and terribly, terribly ambitious. We were just girls, but she always knew exactly what she wanted, and I, for one, never doubted that she would get it. You know I tried to match her up with any number of quite acceptable rich men, because, as I said, she's absolutely penniless, but so attractive, don't you think, that it really needn't be a problem and she could come live comfortably and have as much money as she wanted... But not Cassie! She's quite, quite determined to do it all on her own. But isn't it extraordinary how everything turns out? Here you are, and here I am, and now Cassie!"

"Well, I am happy to hear your high opinion." Stavros rewarded her with a smile. "Very happy indeed, because she seems to fit in well and I have in mind some rather big plans for her."

"Do you mind if I ask you a personal question," Dahlia spoke quietly, tentatively.

"Of course not. What do you want to know? How I got all my money?"

"No," she laughed, amazed. "I never even thought about that. But what I would like to know is why you publish those terrible newspapers. I couldn't believe it when Carrots told me that you were the publisher of the *Comet* and a whole slew of other tabloids like it. They're so awful, Yanni, I can't believe that you would have anything to do with that kind of rubbish."

"Oh come now, surely you're exaggerating." Stavros was cool, unruffled. "Don't tell me that you haven't peeked into the *Comet* from time to time to find out what shenanigans some of your friends or maybe enemies were up to?"

Dahlia blushed but stuck to her guns. "Whether I have or whether I haven't is really not the point. The point is that they're so vulgar, so exploitative—"

"Oh surely not! Why, on the contrary, the *Comet* has just raised ten thousand pounds to help the mother of newborn Siamese twins. You don't find your precious *London Times* doing anything like that."

"You know perfectly well that's not what I mean. I mean that your newspapers pick on perfectly innocent people and drag them through the mud as some sort of entertainment for the masses."

"You mean that we pick on a certain *class* of people, don't you?"

"Well, I suppose I do, even though I hate that word, hate that whole distinction. But all the same, why do you want to pick out a certain class of people and persecute them that way? What gives you the right? Isn't everyone entitled to a decent amount of privacy in their lives?"

"My dear, you're sounding very naive. Certainly I have

the right to publish any stories I choose, as long as they're not libelous. And that's a very murky area. We live in a democracy in which freedom of the press and freedom of speech are two sacred ideals. I choose to publish stories about the privileged classes, the rich and the well born, because I have an extremely sharp sense of what makes newspapers sell and I like, above all, to make money. It amuses me and I'm very good at it."

Dahlia was quiet for a moment. "I suppose you have a point, but I still don't understand why anyone would want to read about what Lady So-and-so was wearing on a certain night . . ."

"And who her lover is? Come, come my dear! Surely you've realized by now that the overprivileged few are able, even let us say, allowed, to keep their privileged positions in a large part because they provide a certain entertainment for the masses of underprivileged people. Once the masses cease to be amused and entertained in this harmless fashion, you have the makings of violent revolution. Think about France, when the masses no longer cared what Marie Antoinette was wearing or with whom she slept, but wanted to see her head severed from her shoulders. They came to watch in droves, you know, and brought picnic baskets. A jolly outing, *'en famille.'* "

"You're very sure of yourself, John Stavros, and very arrogant. I wonder if you have any friends?"

"I have none at all. Only enemies. To be successful, you need friends. To be very successful, you need enemies. I learned that long ago."

The car pulled up in front of her house in Chelsea, and they both seemed suddenly at a loss at what to do next. Although she knew it was ridiculous, Dahlia felt like a schoolgirl, embarrassed and disgracefully late coming home from a date. She was grateful for the teeming rain because the streets were deserted and no one would see the odd-looking couple sitting glumly in the little sports car. Stavros was still wearing his evening clothes, but they were rumpled and undone. She had managed to find an old pair of jeans, a shirt, and espadrilles, but her hair was loose and, with no makeup on, she looked as if she might be just under legal age. Finally, because neither one of them seemed to be able to think of anything to say, she made as if to leave.

It was then that he stopped her, taking her hand and saying quietly, *"Au revoir,* Dahlia de Ginsburgh. It was a lovely night. A most enchanting journey to the past. May I take you to dinner tonight? I'll come for you at eight."

Dahlia was deeply touched and was surprised to feel a rush of tears spring to her eyes. She kissed him quickly on the cheek and rushed out of the car and up the steps to her front door. Her heart beat furiously, like a wild bird in a cage. She turned around to wave, but his car had pulled away, a spray of water in its wake as it sped down the quiet, empty street.

Then, all at once, she crashed, feeling abandoned, tired, wet, and wanting only to get to her room as quickly as possible. She needed solitude and peace—a hot bath, her bed, and some quiet time to think and feel and reassure herself that the last twenty-four hours had really happened.

But inside her chic, cozy cottage, domestic chaos was the *mise-en-scène*. From the nursery three floors above, her daughter's angry, unhappy shrieks issued forth with significant regularity. Dierdre was carefully pacing her strength for a marathon siege of tears.

The loud clanging of someone hammering at a hard metal surface came steadily from the kitchen quarters below her. It was from this same area that Ron emerged, outfitted in denim overalls, his complexion almost as red as the bandanna he had tied around his neck. Ron met his mistress with unspoken disapproval on his tight-lipped face.

"What on earth is going on?" Dahlia found herself having to raise her voice nearly to a shout to be heard over the din.

Ron threw up his arms, rolled his eyes, and plopped down on the settee in an unconscious parody of a housewife at her wit's end. Dahlia, giving up all pretense of authority, followed suit and sat down in the chair opposite, fixing her eyes on the jaunty colors of Ron's red argyle socks, which peeked out from under his rolled-up denim cuffs.

"Grogan," Ron pronounced gravely, "has been found!"

Dahlia stared stupidly at him.

"Miss Dierdre's hamster." His words dripped with patient condescension.

"Oh yes," Dahlia said weakly, recalling that Dierdre's much-beloved pet had left his cage and disappeared some days ago. Another wail of grief and fury came floating down from the upper reaches of the house.

"I'm afraid that Grogan is no longer with us." Ron spoke in somber, melancholy tones.

"Oh no! What's happened to him?" Dahlia looked helplessly up in the direction of the nursery. The hammering intensified in frequency and volume.

Ron shuddered delicately. "They found him in the water tank. We're not quite sure how he got there, but from the looks of him, not to mention the odors that permeated the water..." Ron wrinkled his nose and forced himself to go on, "He must have been there quite a while!"

Dahlia closed her eyes and covered her face with her hands. She looked as though she might be physically ill, but in fact she was trying to fight down a mounting, colossal, and ill-timed hysteria. But Ron was relentless.

"Josephine has put Miss Dierdre to bed, where she is making herself sick crying for her mama because Josephine will not allow her to hold a funeral in the garden until the rain stops."

Dahlia stood up, knowing that she must somehow put an end to this litany of domestic troubles. Ron was not easily put off and followed her agreeably up the stairs.

"*That* will do, Ron," Dahlia spoke sharply, hoping she sounded more forceful than she felt. "If there's nothing else..."

But there was. An endless list of calls and messages. "Lord Lovell rang. Lady Keyes rang. Sir Alistair would like you to dine with him tomorrow. And a Miss Litton has rung *seven* times. She quite refused to believe that you were not in," he coughed accusingly.

Inside the nursery a wild-eyed Dierdre was prostrate with grief, shaking with sobs and hiccups as she recounted the long and gruesome hours that must have preceded Grogan's watery death. She let out an enraged howl when Dahlia tried to comfort her and buried her small, wet face in a mass of pillows.

Josephine stood glumly by. "I said it all from the very beginning. I knew that rat would come to a bad end. It ain't natural keeping them things caged up. It's a wonder we didn't all catch our death of a disease. And Miss Dierdre feeding it little bits of her tea! And now we're reaping the rewards. I knew when we first smelled it there was something rotten in—"

"Josephine, please!" Dahlia begged. "Let's not go on about it. There, there, darling." She patted Dierdre's tangled curls. "We'll get another pet. What about a nice—"

"I don't want another p-p-pet," Dierdre sputtered. "I want Grogan. I loved Grogan, and you're all horrid. Horrid! Horrid! Horrid!" She collapsed again into her pillow.

Dahlia decided that Dierdre too would benefit from a bit of solitary peace and quiet. She beckoned Josephine to follow and together they tiptoed out of the nursery.

She ordered a hot bath and tea, then, changing her mind, she asked Ron to bring up a bottle of champagne instead. "I want some peace and quiet for just one hour. That's all I ask."

"Yes, m'lady. Only what shall I say when Miss Litton rings again?"

"Oh, Christ," Dahlia sighed. "Poor Cassie. What a nuisance. Well, ask her to come around for a drink if she likes. Bring up two glasses with the champagne." And with that she scooted into her room and closed the door with a firm hand.

Chapter 46

IN MANY WAYS, Dahlia's bathroom was the most luxurious room in the house, and except for the deep copper Victorian tub, it looked more nearly like a sumptuously appointed library than a room for bathing. It was here that Dahlia lay stretched beneath billowing clouds of perfumed foam, staring up at the perpetually blue sky of the *trompe l'oeil* ceiling and savoring the thrilling contrast between the very hot water of the bath and the sips of icy-cold champagne.

She was feeling much better, and, when she heard Ron's footsteps ascending the stairs, she found that she was quite looking forward to a nice, gossipy visit with Cassie. That was the great thing about a really good old friend, Dahlia remarked to herself; it didn't matter how much time had passed or all the things that had happened in-between, because, whenever they got together, people and events vanished into thin air, and they could just pick up where they had left off.

The look on Cassie's face, however, as she strode into the steam-filled room, dispelled all of Dahlia's romantic notions about the forgiving nature of old friends and made her wish that she had stuck to her original plan of peaceful solitude and splendid quiet.

"Uh oh! You're furious." She tackled the situation head on with her most engaging and conciliatory manner. "You're not only furious, you're drenched. Oh, darling, I'm so sorry. I know I should have come to you, but as I'd only just got back . . . Here! Have a glass of champagne. You'll feel better in no time." She reached for the silver ice bucket in its stand beside the tub.

"I don't want a glass of champagne." Cassie's response was measured and cool. She looked, Dahlia thought, like a strict governess in her well-cut navy skirt and tailored blouse as she stood stiffly in the doorway, glaring at Dahlia with ill-concealed malice.

"Well, how about a real drink? Bourbon? Scotch? Cognac? Or would you rather have tea? Oh, please, do come sit down," Dahlia continued to plead prettily.

"I haven't come to have a drink and a cozy chat with you, Dahlia. Not this time. Not now."

Dahlia felt all her weariness return. Her blood felt heavy in her veins, the room was suddenly too hot, and she wished desperately that she could just go to sleep. Cassie's rigid stance and the gleam of righteous indignation in her eyes made it all too clear that she was determined to have what Dahlia had long ago dubbed a "major moment."

To Dahlia, these emotional outbursts of frankness seemed both embarrassing and unnecessary. It was something, she had found, that Americans did with great regularity and pride. They liked "to get things off their chests" and to wallow around in what they called "being honest and speaking their minds." It was all so childish, so humorless, and what her French grandmother had called *mauvais ton*. Dahlia looked away, not bothering to conceal her irritation.

"Well, if you don't want a drink and you didn't come to chat, why did you come?" She had thought to keep her voice light, but, instead, her remark had a sharp, cutting edge that sounded unpleasantly familiar. She could hear Camilla—haughty, cold, aristocratic, irritated at having been disturbed out of her natural lethargy by some unreasonable turn of events. She recognized it, and she let it go.

"You know, Dahlia, you are too much. Look at yourself! Lady La-di-dah in her bath!" Cassie was beginning to lose some of her cool manner as fury stole up to fuddle her speech. She poured a glass of champagne and sat down on the couch facing the tub. "I thought you were supposed to be my friend, my best friend," she continued when she had regained some of her composure. "Well I sure would like to know your definition of a friend, because, where I come from, no *friend* would do what you did last night."

"What do you mean, what I did last night?" Dahlia wailed in confusion. "I didn't *do* anything . . . I thought you were upset because I forgot our lunch date!"

"Oh really?" Cassie's voice dripped with icy sarcasm. "It never occurred to you that waltzing off into the night with *my* escort, the man who had brought *me* as his date, the man whom *I* work for, and who is probably the most important man in my life, might make me just a little teeny tiny bit unhappy?" Cassie knocked back her champagne and refilled her glass.

"But, Cassie, that was the most amazing, extraordinary coincidence—"

"Oh come off it, Dahlia! Spare me, for once, your extraordinary this and amazing that! The fact is that you thought absolutely nothing of prancing off with John Stavros as if you owned him and, incidentally, leaving me completely stranded at your wretched party! And if that's your idea of how friends are supposed to treat each other—"

"Listen." Dahlia tried to summon up all the reasonable patience she had heard her father use when engaged in a bit of delicate diplomacy. "I don't know what you're so damned upset about. I didn't leave you stranded. You were at a lovely party, surrounded by perfectly nice people. Anyway, didn't Brooksie—"

"Yes, he did. He was perfectly splendid and fussed over me all evening when he saw the predicament you had left me in. I rather got the feeling that he is used to hanging around and cleaning up your messes. Anyway, he brought me home and then we sat up half the night because he was so worried about you."

"Worried about me?" Dahlia exclaimed. "What on earth is the matter with everyone? Why should Henry Brooks sit around worrying about me?"

"Perhaps he, too, was a little surprised at your behavior."

"I wish you'd stop going on about my so-called *behavior*. You make it sound like some sort of third-rate farce. As I tried to tell you before, I had no idea it was *your* John Stavros or that he was the same person I had known years ago. We certainly didn't plan to go off together . . . But we had a great deal to talk about." Dahlia smiled up at her friend, hoping for some little sign of understanding and encouragement. "And one thing just led to another . . . Well, honestly, darling, you have no reason to be upset with me. Anyway, I thought you, of all people, would understand. We talked about you for the longest time, and I told Yanni how long we'd known each other and how you were my best and dearest friend. Really, Cassie, I told him how clever you are and how terribly ambitious, and I practically made him promise to make sure and pay you vast sums of money and promote you straight to the top. So you see . . ."

But the only thing that Cassie saw was red. She leaped up out of her seat, sputtering with rage. "You what? How dare you meddle like that with my career . . . with my life? Of all the stupid, condescending, humiliating, and insulting things you have ever done, this really takes the cake. What makes you think I need any help from you? I don't need *you* to tell John Stavros anything. What *I* get paid and what sort of promotions I get have absolutely nothing to do with anything you might happen to say about it. Do you understand that, or should I repeat it for you?" Cassie's face was ashen as she towered over Dahlia.

"Cassie, have you flipped? What has gotten into you? You're acting as if I'd gone off and stolen your man, for goodness sakes. John Stavros isn't your lover." She swiped at her toe with a sponge and felt like crying.

Cassie remained standing, her fists tightly clenched, her back as rigid and straight as Granny Litton's. "You'll never understand, will you, Dahlia? You'll never really see how arrogant and truly selfish you are. All your life you've had anything you wanted. You've become so spoiled you think the world is your playpen and that everybody in it exists just to please you. Oh, not that you aren't generous with your toys! After all, what's the fun in playing alone? You've always enjoyed playing Lady Bountiful to poor, deprived

Cassie Litton, haven't you? All those clothes and airplane tickets and costly little trinkets . . . But I don't think that in all the years we've known each other you've ever tried to understand how I might really feel or what I might actually want."

"But, Cassie—"

"Don't but Cassie me! You know it's true. I've just been another one of your retainers. The humble spectator of Lady Dahlia's grand and glorious life."

"Well, Cassie, you said it. I didn't." Dahlia's voice had turned hard with anger. "You must know how much I hate this sort of scene, but, since you insist, let me tell you a thing or two about you. You've envied me for so long that you can't really see how boring and humorless you've become. And I am sick to death of your holier-than-thou attitude at having to work for a living. If you think that my life has been a bed of roses just because I'm rich, then you're the one who is blind. You appreciate nothing and no one. You can't even see what a good thing you had—a terrific man who really loved you, and, on top of that, brains and character enough to support yourself and your ambitions. But you're destroying it with envy and jealousy and some bitter baggage from the past that you can't let go of. Only don't blame it on me, because I've done nothing to hurt you. I'm sorry if I offended you by speaking to John about your job, but I make no excuses for anything else. He may be the man you work for, but he is my lover, and that is true whether you like it or not."

Two angry red spots played on Cassie's pale cheeks, and her eyes glistened with rage. "You're pathetic, Dahlia. Do you really think that one night in bed makes you a man's lover? It only proves that you're nothing but another stupid, little slut!" With that she flung the remnants of her champagne into Dahlia's face, turned on her heel, and dashed straight into Lady Caroline Keyes. They spent a moment struggling to disengage, then Cassie rushed away into the teeming night.

* * *

"Goodness!" Caroline adjusted herself. "Now there's a girl on the go."

"Oh, damn. Bloody, bloody damn." Dahlia smacked the bathwater with her sponge at each word. "What's going on around here? Am I crazy, or has everyone gone completely mad?"

"Not me, darling. I'm just an innocent bystander at the Grand Guignol. You, I think, are currently its leading lady. Mind if I cozy in?" Carrots indicated the bottle of champagne and picked Cassie's glass up off the carpet. She settled down on the loo. "Now, 'you slut,' such a colorful epithet, I want to hear all of it, every little, tiny quiver and shiver of the whole evening."

Dahlia sighed heavily and sank down into the now luke-warm water. Her head was throbbing and Caroline only made it worse.

"I don't want to talk about it," she said petulantly. "Not if you're going to sit there and poke fun at me. It was only the most . . . most extraordinary night of my life and I don't just mean sex. Carrots, I can't begin to tell you . . ."

"Try, darling, try."

"Do you know what you look like? You look like a big vulture hanging over me, all lean and greedy."

"Really? That's nice. I was afraid I'd put on a few pounds lately. I'd all but decided to give up drinking, but now, thank God, I won't have to." She drained her glass with a contented sigh.

"Why are you here?" Dahlia demanded.

"Because, darling girl, I have been sent," Caroline said without guile. "I tell you, Dahlia, you caused such a stir last night that I'm nearly green with envy. The whole table was in an uproar and even Alistair stuck his big nose in it. The lines have been buzzing all day. Finally Brooksie convinced me to come to your side."

"But why? Why is everyone going on so?"

"Well, may I be blunt?"

"You can't help it."

"We've decided that John Stavros is definitely not the

sort of man you should be running around with. He frightens me, my dear."

"Then you *are* all quite mad. I won't listen to any more of this. None of you know what you're talking about. All you can see is the surface, the facade. But I know what's underneath. It's as if I've always known him. And I've waited for him to come to me all my life. Last night something touched me, something reached into the very deepest part of me, and it was like being found. Do you think I'm going to just let that go, like that, just because a few of my so-called friends have to prattle on about something?"

Caroline eyed Dahlia with astonishment. "You're not serious. You've spent a night in bed being gloriously ravaged, and, believe me, I know how that can muddle one's head. We all deserve to be a little satiated from time to time. He's handsome and he's sexy and I quite envied you as you waltzed out last night, but this is not last night. This is today, and the fact of the matter is that John Stavros is a social-climbing little rat."

Dahlia stood up in her tub like Venus emerging from the sea and twirled a towel around herself as if it were an opera cape. "Carrots," she said imperiously, "sod off." She stepped from the bath and progressed to the dressing room, leaving a trail of wet footprints.

Carrots stood up and shouted through the open doorway. "Fine. I'll sod off, all right, but just what do you intend to do now? I ask, of course, only as a so-called friend."

Dahlia reappeared momentarily. "I intend to be his mistress," she said.

Chapter 47

THE NEXT MORNING, Cassie went to Heathrow and took the early flight back to New York. Grim faced and exhausted, she arrived in her office shortly after three o'clock New York time. Her secretary was astonished.

"You're back so soon? How did it go? What was the party like..." But the look on Cassie's face did not encourage conversation. "Uh oh. Zip the lip, huh?"

Cassie nodded. "Sorry, Penny, but I'm in no mood to talk about anything. I'll fill you in later, but in the meantime could you buzz Sammy and ask him to come up here right away. It's urgent."

"Sure... But I'm not sure Sammy's here. You see—"

"He's got to be here! Try him." She stalked into her office and slammed the door. If ever she needed good old dependable Sammy, it was now. He would sympathize with her, take her to dinner, wine and dine her, and make her laugh and forget how humiliated she was, how hurt and lonely and betrayed she felt. She didn't even take off her coat, but paced up and down the room, thankful at least that it was still office hours in New York and she didn't have to go home to that empty, cheerless apartment.

The intercom buzzed. "He's on his way up, Cassie. Want anything? Coffee?"

"No, Penny, thanks. But ask Sammy if he wants anything when he comes through."

He arrived a few minutes later, and, within moments, Cassie was venting her frustration. "... the selfish, mean little bitch. So arrogant, so totally insensitive to anything but her own pleasure. I mean it, Sammy, I could have killed her. She couldn't even see why I was so angry, she was so goddamned nonchalant about it. What he could possibly see in that little twit brain . . ."

Sammy was leaning back in her chair, his feet up on the desk. "Hey, Scarlett, calm down. Strictly off the record, I'd say those two deserve each other."

"What is that supposed to mean?"

"Look, honey, we both knew what was on your mind when you flew out of here. Face it, sugar, you gambled and lost. You lost to your best friend. Now, if that's not a cliché, I don't know what is. It's too bad, though. I had my fingers crossed for you."

Cassie stared out the window. "You mean I'm not as attractive a woman as Dahlia de Ginsburgh. Is that what you're saying?" Her voice dripped disdain.

"Let me tell you something, kiddo." Sammy's voice was soft, almost sad. "You're a beautiful woman, and you've got style and intelligence, too. But face it, Cassie, intelligent women are no longer rarities, style can be acquired, and beauty, well, every generation produces a hundred thousand beautiful boys and girls. But elegance, true, bone-deep, instinctive, world-class elegance, that's disappearing fast. The Dietrichs, the Hepburns—when they die, who will replace them? Jane Fonda? Goldie Hawn? *Real* style, *real* sophistication, *real* glamour, are all becoming as rare as virgins in New York. And do you know why? Because there's no more leisure. Everybody's got a career. There's no time to be elegant. There's only time off from work."

"Oh, you're saying I can't be elegant because I work for a living. Is that it, Sammy? I wasn't to the manor born so I'm condemned to be a working schlep?"

"Well, maybe it sounds like that, but what I'm really saying is that, like me, you're condemned to want to be something you're not, to judge yourself by standards that are not yours. Nobody knows that better than a gay, though we don't like to talk about it much."

"And you think Dahlia's got it? You think she's one of the elegant ones?"

"Well, her mother was. I met her once. I met her with Charlotte Soames. I had just come to work for *Style* and Allanha gave one of her fabulous parties. And there they were. Elegant, beautiful, so extraordinary." Sammy sat staring silently into space, a dreamy look on his face. His gaze came back to Cassie. "You know what was the most amazing thing about Camilla de Ginsburgh? She could sit and do nothing better than anyone I've ever seen. She dominated the fucking room with it—everyone knew she was there but couldn't figure out what she was doing to get their attention. Nothing. That's what she was doing, and that's what no one knows how to do anymore."

"But you think Dahlia does. That she has this . . . this mystique?"

"It doesn't matter what I think. What matters is what you think. You're not Dahlia, you're Cassie. The real question is whether you're going to spend your life regretting that fact or making the most of it."

Cassie looked determined. "You're right, Sammy. I'm a working girl, not a princess. Dahlia said the same thing in a different way. Work is what I'm good at. It's not important how you get to the top. It's getting there that counts. And I'm gonna get there. We'll get there together, won't we? We're a good team."

Sammy grinned ruefully. "We *were* a good team, sweet pea. But I'm afraid you're on your own."

"What do you mean? You're not deserting me, are you? Just when I need you most. Sammy . . . ?"

"I'm not deserting you, kiddo. It's just that the management is so concerned about my happiness that they decided I'd find more of it elsewhere."

"It's not true! They can't fire you just like that. The whole magazine will collapse. Besides, what about your contract, what about—"

Sammy held up his hand. "Contracts are made to be broken. You know that."

"But what are you going to do? Where will you go?"

"You know, I think I'm going to just do nothing. I want

to see what it's like. I've been hustling nonstop since high school. I took the first bus out of Bowling Green and got a job as a model on Seventh Avenue. I went from modeling to photographer's stylist to *Women's Wear Daily*. That's where Allanha found me, and brought me over to *Style*. I haven't had a minute to myself since. But you know what I wanted to do way back then? I wanted to be a set designer. I was going to earn enough money as a model to pay for classes at Cooper Union, but before I knew it I was on the fast track and I never had the time or the guts to get off. Well, now, thanks to Stavros, I'm finally off. Maybe someday I'll thank him. It's a bitch, though." He looked down at his hands, at his perfectly manicured, buffed fingernails.

Cassie hugged him. "I'll miss you, Sammy. I don't know what I'll do without you."

"You'll do just fine, sweet pea. You've got the Sammy George look. You can't go wrong."

"We'll still see each other. Just because we're not in the office together . . . We'll have lunch . . ."

Sammy grinned. "Of course we will."

"Oh, please, don't be that way with me. I mean it. We'll see lots of each other."

"I know you mean it."

Cassie's eyes filled with tears.

He nodded and hugged her again. "I've got to clear out before we get too sappy. I'm going out to the Hamptons tonight and plan to settle in with a big, cold martini and a tawdry book."

"Sounds good," Cassie lied.

"Doesn't it?" Sammy winked and turned quickly on his heel. "Take care, sweet pea." He was out the door before she could say anything else.

She turned back to her desk feeling disoriented, tired, discouraged, and depressed. Now she was alone, as alone as anyone could be. Not even Sammy to jolly her along at work. She put her hand instinctively on the phone, but there was no one to call.

Chapter 48

A WEEK PASSED. Dahlia spent every night with Stavros. She came home for a few hours during the day, bathed, changed her clothes, chatted with Dierdre absent-mindedly, then Stavros came and she was gone again. Dahlia ate little and slept less, yet seemed to have boundless energy. She lost weight, yet still looked radiantly beautiful. She became a creature of the night, sexy and sensuous, available wherever and whenever Stavros wanted her. And he wanted her all to himself. He had no interest in her friends and so neither did she. Certainly she had no inclination to satisfy their morbid curiosity or listen to their silly, stuffy cautions and intrusive disapproval. He had no interest in Dierdre either, and only here she disobeyed him just a little.

"I hate him, I hate him, I hate him! I hope he dies. I hope he dies soon. It isn't at all fair, you know. Why should my poor, sweet Grogan die and he doesn't?" Dierdre's eyes were ablaze with fury, and she was pale and shaking.

Henry Brooks sat quietly on the blue rocker and put his arms around her gently to comfort her.

"There, there," he soothed. "It can't be as bad as all that. Anyway, it isn't worth working yourself up like that. Now come on. Tell me all about it . . . Do you a world of good. Who is this awful, terrible villain? And why do you hate him so?"

Dierdre stared down at her shoes for a few moments, then her serious gray eyes met Henry's in a solid, level gaze. "It's that Mr. Stavros. There are a million reasons why I hate him. But most of all I hate him because of the way he looks at Mummy."

"He's nothing but a common Greek peasant who ought to be off in the hills somewhere tending to his goats or sheep or whatever it is they do . . . Henry, sit down. All that pacing around is giving me a headache." Carrots lit a cigarette and inhaled deeply. "The trouble is," she continued, "that peasants are by far the worst. I know this from painful and bitter personal experience. I once befriended a most beautiful young man from Corsica. He seemed so diffident, so shy, so heartbreakingly young and alone . . ." Lady Caroline gazed through a haze of cigarette smoke as if he might materialize before her even now. Henry continued pacing back and forth across the deep-red Persian carpet. "He had such lovely dark brown eyes, like a gazelle . . ." Carrots sighed. "Well, I invited this poor lamb into my bed, whereupon after only the briefest of embraces that lamb dropped his sheep's clothing and became a wolf. Gone were all the pretty, shy manners and limpid, longing looks, and he was suddenly ordering me about in the most regal manner, commanding me to do all sorts of things I was frankly surprised he even knew about. And he was so strong that he had me quite pinned down on the bed, literally holding both of my hands over my head with just one of his. Then he hauled off and hit me straight across the face! I was, of course, powerless to do anything at all because my sweet little lamb was holding me down. I tell you, Brooksie, he rode me like a jockey rides a racehorse."

Henry Brooks stopped pacing and sat down. "What on earth does that have to do with Dahlia?" He poured some whiskey from a decanter into a glass and handed it to Carrots.

"It's got everything to do with Dahlia because," she took a sip of whiskey, "that was the one time in my life when I completely lost my head and fell head over heels in love. I was totally and utterly taken with an underaged Corsican boy with pretty brown eyes and a wicked left hook. Did I mention he was a delivery boy? For Harrods? Baskets of fruit, I think it was." She lapsed into silence, staring with uncharacteristic intensity at the melting ice in her glass.

"Poor Carrots," Brooksie said fondly, indulgently. "But I still don't see your point. Are we still talking about Dahlia?"

"Of course we are! My *point* is that well-bred English girls have no defense against the wily tricks of unscrupulous Mediterranean peasants. You've seen Dahlia! Have you talked to her?"

"Dahlia doesn't seem to be talking to any of us these days," Brooksie said sadly. "Look, Carrots, I detest the fellow. I loathe and despise what he represents, but I can't quite see that he's keeping Dahlia by force. Yes, I've seen her, and she looks radiant. She's glowing like a light bulb on a Christmas tree." He paused for a moment. "She's a grown woman, after all," he went on quietly. "Whatever we might think, we haven't the right to meddle in her affairs. Anyway, I can't quite see her as a sex slave to Mr. Stavros."

"Oh, can't you really?" Caroline's voice was harsh and serious. "Then, Henry, you are a fool, and that's too bad because I know how much you love her. Unfortunately for both of you, our Mr. Stavros is not a fool, and he isn't going to conveniently disappear because we want him to. He's got money, power, and a very shiny coat of polish. But underneath there's still a rough and angry peasant, and that makes him a nasty piece of business, indeed. You listen to me, Henry Brooks. Dahlia's in trouble and she's going to need help. You can't help her by playing the gentleman and being a fool."

Exactly one week after they'd met at Buell's party, Stavros took Dahlia to dinner. After they had finished with their coffee and their brandy, his limousine drove them to Heathrow Airport. He was in fine high spirits and so was she as he conducted her aboard his private Lear jet. She thought it was a lark, like going for a midnight drive through sleepy country villages.

"Where are you taking me now, oh lord and master?" she asked, camping around a bit.

He helped her with her seatbelt and smiled down at her, "Spetsai."

Chapter 49

CASSIE HURRIED FROM her office and jammed herself into a crowded elevator. She was due at Maxine's in half an hour. Tonight was her birthday, and half of New York's literary crowd would be there to help her celebrate.

Cassie had promised Maxine that she would be there early to help her dress, but as the chauffeured car inched down Fifth Avenue in the rush-hour traffic, she resigned herself to being late. It was a beautiful evening, full of remembrance and hope. Around her, on the sidewalks, in front of St. Patrick's, up and down the promenade of Rockefeller Center, there was a sea of young lovers.

The car turned onto Nineteenth Street and circled the tiny oasis at Gramercy Park before coming to a stop at Maxine's house. A pretty girl was standing on the steps, obviously waiting for someone. There was something in her look, in the way she glanced at her watch and then up and down the street, that made Cassie's heart ache. She looked like a Juliet—romantic, young, vulnerable, hovering on the cusp of her future and waiting so eagerly, so expectantly; surely she was waiting for her lover. Cassie smiled briefly at her as she hurried past on her way up the stairs.

Maxine's bedroom was closed, but Cassie breezed in after only a cursory knock. "Where have you been, everybody's..." she started to say.

Maxine was sitting at her dressing table, staring at a photograph in front of her. Cassie could see that she was crying; her eyes were red and puffy.

"Hell. Just look at me. I'd forgotten what crying does to a face."

"What's wrong, Maxine? Aren't you feeling well? Everyone's waiting downstairs." She instinctively put her arm around her. Then she followed Maxine's eyes to the picture in her lap. It was of Gregory Kournos.

"He's dead," said Maxine flatly. "Got a call an hour ago. I knew he was sick, but he wouldn't see a doctor. I even offered to fly one up to that island of his, but he said no. Then I didn't hear anything more . . . Until now."

Cassie looked at the picture; she had not seen it before. Kournos was young, an arresting face with eyes that seemed to stare into the future, into this very room. She remembered those eyes.

"He was the only man I ever loved." Maxine's voice broke the silence. "You'd think an old lady like me would forget those things. But you don't, you know. I always expected that time and years and work and age would let me forget, but they don't."

"I'm so sorry, Maxine," Cassie whispered.

"It was a long time ago, but when I got that letter from him—about you, remember?—it was the damndest thing. Suddenly I wasn't old anymore and Grisha and I were still the same people we had been in Paris, so busy being young and in love with each other." Maxine closed her eyes. "I can almost *smell* that funny old studio we lived in. Ink from the press mixed with hot borscht mixed with ripe fruit. We had such a good time being poor." Maxine shook her head, weeping quietly. "What happened to us? I've asked myself that a thousand times. Grisha was hopeless. He had no discipline. He was a genius, but he had no . . . no practical side. And I was just the opposite. For me, everything had to be part of a plan, everything had to make sense. He begged me to go away with him. He was restless, he wanted freedom, but I insisted on staying in Paris. I had my press. I had my friends. I was safe. Paris was the place to be, and

I wasn't about to tag along after a wild, would-be poet.
Why should I?"

"Yes. Why should you?" Cassie leaned forward intently.
"You don't regret your life, do you, Maxine? I mean, you
don't regret not going away with him?"

Maxine touched the face in the photograph. "I don't
know," she said slowly, carefully. "I really don't. All I know
is that I've lived with an empty space inside me for a long
time. Sometimes I've been able to live with it, other times
. . . I've wondered if I was really alive at all. When two
people love each other, never mind the differences, they
ought to stick together. But who knows . . . ?" She shrugged.
"Well, I'll never know now, will I?" She brushed a speck
of dust from the picture. "Hell of a day for you to die, old
friend."

The sounds of the party came drifting up the stairs. Maxine got up and moved toward the door. "The last time I saw
Gregory Kournos, it was a beautiful day. But so cold. I
remember the sky, clear and sharp and blue. He used to
wear this big, bulky Russian overcoat. The tails of it were
flapping in the wind and I remember thinking he looked
like a bird in flight. I never saw him again." Her short,
dumpy body paused. "Funny the things you remember after
all these years."

Cassie made no move to follow Maxine. She sat very
still, staring at nothing for minutes on end. Then, slowly,
her eyes focused on the light filtering through the windows.
Long shadows through the panes formed a patterned grid
on the polished wood floors. Cassie remembered another
room, another time. She was eight years old, and she had
been doing her homework in the living room of the cottage
after school. Blue was in the kitchen when the unfamiliar
car had appeared in the drive. Then the knock on the door.

The man from Litton Manufacturing had stood there nervously, twisting his hat in his hand, while she had called
to her mother. She could picture the scene just as it had

been. The shadows cast through the slats in the Venetian blinds had been so sharp that she and the man had been caught like convicts in the bars of light and dark. And she had thought, "This is what it would look like if we were in jail." When Blue had arrived, Cassie only half paid attention to what they were saying.

"He didn't regain consciousness, ma'am. He was gone before we could get the doctor."

Blue had clutched her apron, sitting down on one of the antique "incidental" chairs in the vestibule, those tiny, doll-like chairs that were, Blue said, for "show."

"Where . . . where is my husband now?"

"We took him to Whitehalls, ma'am."

Only then had Cassie's eyes widened with sudden under-standing. Whitehalls! The funeral home down on Main Street. Her daddy. Her daddy was dead.

Cassie sat at Maxine's dressing table and stared at the cool face reflected in the mirror. She hadn't thought of her father in a very long time. Why? It all seemed so remote now, so far away. Her father had been a dreamer, and she had come to think of this as weak. He had been weak—weak in dying, and weak, she had come to believe, in living.

"Cassie?"

She whirled around at the sound of her name—and gasped with recognition. "Pete!"

"I scared you. I'm sorry. Maxine sent me up to get her glasses, and she didn't tell me you were here." He stopped, his face breaking into a half grin of pleasure. "It's good to see you . . . really good."

For a moment, Cassie thought he was going to come to her. But he didn't. She was trembling, and she felt her whole body turn to water, as if her bones and joints had melted. She swallowed hard, feeling her heart thumping like a kettledrum.

"You startled me." Then she started to laugh. "Oh dear. I can't seem to get my breath."

Pete laughed. "I know. I feel like I just skipped a few beats myself. It really is great to see you, Cassie. It seems like a long time."

"Six months," she said and then reddened at how quickly she'd answered. He must think I sit around counting the days, she thought and then realized that, in fact, she had done more or less just that.

"Yeah," Pete agreed. "I've been out of town mostly—"

"Oh? What are you working on?" Her voice was too bright. Tone it down, she told herself. But nothing could keep the tingling off the surface of her skin. She watched him talk, watched his mouth move, the old familiar gestures of his hands; she heard the inflections in his voice, the way he held the soft vowels in the back of his throat for an extra measure . . . the quick, sure laugh—and the warmth of his tone, the easy, caressing warmth. She tried to listen to the actual words, to what he was saying, but she couldn't. This man was her whole life. Why hadn't she realized it sooner? She could hear Maxine's words . . . "Grisha had no discipline. For me everything had to make sense."

"There's something I have to tell you, Cassie." His tone was serious now.

She interrupted before he could say any more.

"Pete, I . . . I wanted to call you so many times. I didn't mean for it to end so badly. I didn't want that. I didn't—"

"I know. I know you didn't. It wasn't your fault. There were two Cassie Littons and I was only able to love one of them. I was the problem, Cassie. And you were right. We did want different things out of life."

Never mind the differences. When two people love each other, they ought to stick together.

Cassie got up and went to him, taking his hand in hers. "I was so wrong—"

"There you are! I've been looking all over for you, Pete."

Cassie dropped Pete's hand. Standing in the doorway was the girl she had seen on the front steps—Juliet.

"I hope I'm not interrupting anything," said the girl.

"No," said Pete. "Not at all. Meet a friend of mine. Cassie Litton."

"Hi, I'm Nell Foster."

Cassie extended her hand, an uncertain smile on her lips. But there was nothing uncertain about the way Nell Foster slipped her arm through Pete's and no doubts either, from the way he looked at her, as to how they felt about each other.

Cassie felt the smile on her face freeze. Nell Foster looked quizzically at her for a moment.

"Cassie Litton. Yes, of course. I can't believe it. I've spent almost the whole day hating you." She laughed delightedly. "Not really. I guess envy is the right word."

Cassie stared at her dumbly. "You what?"

"Esquire. The profile. The *new* American woman. I was so impressed. I *am* so impressed."

"What's this all about?" Pete asked.

"Cassie's the star of *Esquire* magazine. Haven't you seen it? The whole issue is interviews with women all over the country in great jobs. Cassie's the lead, with a color photograph and everything."

Cassie felt weak. She hadn't seen it yet herself. The PR department had arranged it shortly after she'd taken her job with Stavros, and she had forgotten all about it. Nell Foster's face was pretty and eager. The soft curves of her body pressed against Pete. "I . . . I'm sorry, but I think I should go downstairs now," Cassie said softly.

She smiled once more but didn't dare look at Pete. She knew that if she did, she wouldn't make it out of the room before the tears started to fall.

But she did make it out of the room and down the stairs and out the door. She made it all the way home in the taxi and even made it up in the elevator, exchanging small talk with the elevator man about the weather.

And then, only then, in the safety of her apartment, did she cry. It was a wail so foreign to her, coming from so deep a well of misery, that it was frightening. She sat clinging to the arm of the sofa and buried her head in the cushion so she wouldn't have to hear her own sound. She was crying for the whole, crazy, mixed up, stupid, lunatic world now— for all the love that was in her, for the pain of it, for the anger and the pity of it, for the loss. The terrible, terrible loss. For Pete. She was crying for her Pete.

Chapter 50

IN ATHENS THEY went straight to the docks to board an old ferry steamer crowded with islanders and tourists. After the luxury and privacy of the jet, it was irritating to be pushed and shoved by the milling crowds, and Dahlia could barely hide her annoyance. They were still in their evening clothes and were being stared at openly. Stavros was no help. He seemed tense and withdrawn, almost rude, as he led her to the ferry's upper deck.

In the short time she had known him she had come to expect the utmost in opulence and rich abundance. He had squired her about in custom-made cars and showered her with expensive gifts. When she had first seen his London house, a splendid Georgian jewel set in its own private park, even she had been impressed with its sumptuous furnishings, expensive ornaments, and the discreet battalion of servants who treated them like royalty. "I can see the best is quite good enough for you," she had quipped, and he had laughed seemingly delighted by her reactions to everything he showed her. All week long he had been nothing if not the most ardent, most generous, most solicitous admirer, lover, and host.

Now, however, they sat silently on hard wooden benches, the sun already unbearably hot overhead. Dahlia was exhausted but determined that she not put up a fuss at this point. She was curious about their destination. And she was desperately in love.

The island that appeared on the horizon after interminable hours did little to lift her spirits. It was like a great brown arm resting in the middle of the vast blue desert of the

Aegean. It seemed wild and primitive to her, and somehow a little ominous—the barren hills were broken only by twisted olive trees permanently bent by the prevailing winds.

Stavros, however, seemed to revive. His spirits soared from the moment the island came into view. He left her sitting in a small taverna in the busy port with a cooling drink as he went about arranging their transportation to the house.

It was a small cove, almost hidden from the open sea by two giant boulders. John Stavros guided the launch between them. The water, as clear as glass, lapped gently against a stretch of beach. Somehow it all gave the lovely illusion that no one had ever been there before.

"Oh, this is beautiful . . . just perfect. I feel just like Swiss Family Robinson. Wouldn't it be lovely if we were shipwrecked?" Then she laughed. "I take that all back. I can hardly wait to see your house. What I need most is a bath, a drink, and some food. Then I'll be as good as new."

Dahlia viewed the near impenetrable band of pine trees that fringed the beach, and then she craned her neck upward. A solitary villa lay on the headland point of a precipitous bluff. "Up there . . . ?" she moaned. "Why didn't we come by car?"

"There are no cars on the island, darling," he said, the patient native explaining the local customs to a foreigner. "Besides, the house is easy to get to if you know the way. Come."

He turned and started toward a spill of rocks that descended from the cliff down to the beach. He was agile, like a mountain goat. Dahlia tried to keep up with him, but her evening sandals were no help in climbing the steep incline. She slipped, tearing her dress on a limb. He was soon out of sight of her. "Damn," she muttered.

At long last, out of breath and perspiring, she scrambled to a flat open place, and there she stopped to rest. Turning, she gasped aloud at the sight before her. She was high on the bluff and she could see for miles out onto a vast, open, eternal, luminous vista of sea and sky. The pale, golden light seemed to fuse the two together, and she felt as if she were floating in space. The sensation was eerie, unbalancing, altogether mesmerizing and unsettling at the same time.

"Dahlia." His hand was on her shoulder and she fell, shuttering back into his arm as if she had been held by something and then released. He seemed to know exactly what she had experienced.

"Beauty has a hostile touch," he said cryptically and then he smiled. "You're almost there, my darling. Just around the corner..." And suddenly there was the house. It was white, blazing white, and it seemed to mold itself to the side of the hill. Punctuating the gleaming white were terracotta terraces, balconies, and a large central courtyard.

He led her inside the house, which was mercifully cool and surprisingly simple. The furniture was sparse and the stuccoed walls were for the most part bare except for, here and there, icons of ancient religions.

Dahlia sank gratefully on the bed in the master bedroom and looked around. "Darling, I've got to ring London and let them know where I am. They'll never believe it, but at least they won't worry. If I know Josephine and Ron, they're both hysterical right now. Imagine your kidnapping me away to a Grecian island! Where do you keep the telephone?"

"There is no telephone. This is my total retreat from the outside world."

"Well, really. I do think you might have told me this before. Can one of the servants run me into town? Oh, Lord, I forgot, there isn't a car. Well, what about..."

"We're alone here."

"Alone? You mean completely? No servants?" Her tone, though she tried to mask it, showed her irritation.

His smile teased her. "I thought surely you would welcome the chance for us to be completely uninterrupted and alone... no one anywhere to spoil our lovemaking."

Dahlia returned his smile, feeling slightly ashamed of herself to be so lacking in romantic spirit. "Of course, I want to be alone with you," she said enthusiastically. "We'll walk down to the village tomorrow. I'm sure everyone can wait that long to hear from me. This was a charming idea, John. I know we can both use the peace and quiet. I love it and I love you."

She reached for his hand, but a sound, a shadow, a movement from the passage startled her. There appeared in the doorway a boy, a thin, dark boy of about twelve years old. Dahlia looked from him back to Stavros.

"I thought you said we were alone."

"We are, my darling. He is only a serving boy. He doesn't speak English. He will do whatever you like, take care of you." Stavros turned and spoke to the boy in Greek. The boy went immediately to a door at the side of the bedroom. Within seconds, Dahlia could hear water being drawn for her bath.

Chapter 51

DAHLIA LAY IN the tub a long time, letting the hot, scented water soothe away her aches and scratches. When she emerged, the bedroom shutters had been closed against the brilliant day. The bedcovers were turned back, and on the table was a carafe of cold white wine; there were also fresh figs and small, sweet cakes. Dahlia took only a sip of the wine before stretching luxuriously in bed and falling fast asleep. At some point in the hot, still afternoon, she thought she saw someone standing over her bed, but she felt so drugged in her sleep that she could not come fully awake.

That evening, the boy served dinner on the open terrace, and John was a charming and attentive host who told her amusing anecdotes and anticipated her every want. The dinner was delicious, the boy quick and silent, the mood congenial, even gay. But Dahlia could not shake an eerie feeling that somehow the evening did not belong to her. Restlessly she walked to the edge of the terrace, which was the uppermost of a series of sloping gardens. They were perfectly tended, almost English in their precise borders and leveled paths—but there was a wildness, too, in the way the gnarled, twisted olive trees fringed the garden like ancient crones. She took a deep breath, trying to distinguish the heavy fragrance in the air. Unable to, she turned back to ask John what it was, but the question died on her lips. Instead she screamed—in fright, in surprise, in utter amazement.

"The moon!" She pointed, her heart still pounding at what she saw. The moon had risen over the opposite end of the terrace in the short time that her back had been turned.

It was huge, and it hung, a giant, oversized, awesome beacon in the inky sky, heavy and majestic.

All at once she was babbling. "John, John, I don't like it here. I don't know why. It scares me. Nothing is as it should be . . . I don't know whether I'm awake or dreaming. What is happening to me?"

He walked toward her, his body silhouetted in the light of the golden orb.

"Greece. Greece is happening to you. You're frightened because Greece is like no other place in the world. It belongs to the universe, to eternity. You are accustomed to your pale, muted, domesticated landscapes, your thin northern air. But here the land and the air and the light are untamed. Greece is a beautiful, passionate wild creature, and she will make you fall in love with her even as she makes you hate her."

To Dahlia, he was talking about something dark and hidden from her. She could feel the cold, deadly, untouchable center of John Stavros, and she was chilled and frightened. She laughed nervously. "I seem to have experienced that—"

"No. You've experienced very little. You know nothing at all about it. Few people do, in fact. But once they experience it, it is something that can never be forgotten. Your mother knew it, Charlotte knew it . . ." He spoke softly, watching her.

Dahlia was nervous, pacing back and forth. "What on earth are you talking about? I hate it when you get all broody and mystical. What has my mother got to do with anything?"

Stavros laughed, his head thrown back, dry hacking sounds emerging from his throat, but they were sounds that held no mirth. "Don't you feel something familiar about this house? My house? Isn't there a scent, a fragrance that brings you memories? Do you not feel a sort of haunting in the air?"

Dahlia pulled her shawl more tightly around her shoulders as though it might offer her some bit of protection from his strange conversation.

"This was your mother's house once . . . She and Charlotte came and spent a summer here. I was the garden boy. I brought them flowers. I'd never seen a house like this, except from far away. I thought it had to be the most beautiful villa in the world, a villa suitable for Camilla, the most beautiful woman in the world. Now it is mine. Now *you* are mine." He came to her and looked down at her almost tenderly. "Do you know passion? Do you feel passion?" His eyes locked on hers.

"I . . . I feel love . . . But, John, you frighten me . . . Please, don't . . ."

But he gripped her arm and she was unable to look away.

"Passion is love and hate intermingled until they are indistinguishable from one another. To love passionately is to hate. It is terrible. It is to strip yourself to the most base of human cravings, to disown your habits and to release yourself from the bondage of reason. It is terrible and it is dazzling. You felt it today on the path overlooking the sea; you felt it just now seeing the moon. Love and hate, Dahlia. Do you know what I'm talking about?" He brushed a wisp of hair back from her face. She trembled slightly, a shiver of fear and excitement pulsating in her veins.

"Do you dare feel such things with me?" he whispered. "Do you dare give yourself to me as you never have? To let me take you to that terrible place where passion lives?"

It was a question that expected no answer. They both knew what the answer was. She was helpless against him here in the scented, ancient air. She was in a trance, drifting away in an open boat, and would willingly embrace whatever fate he demanded of her. And she had no idea how truly mad he was.

There was only one last tug at her consciousness.

"The boy. Send him away. Send him home. I don't want him here."

"No." Stavros's voice seemed to come from a great distance. "He sees nothing. He is invisible."

Chapter 52

*They are a generation of buccaneers, unprece-
dented, the wave of the future... The rising stars of
America's professional world... The new super-
women of wealth and power.*

WRAPPED UP IN her old flannel bathrobe, wearing the tat-
tered, bunny-fur slippers she had worn all through school,
a damp towel pressed to her forehead, Cassie Litton stared
down at another Cassie Litton, one who was dressed in a
midnight-blue Adolfo dress, whose hair was burnished gold
and fell in easy waves to her shoulders. Behind this other
Cassie Litton, through large windows, the cityscape was
cast in a pale, rosy light.

She reached for another Kleenex as her eyes blurred for
the millionth time. She couldn't read the small print, but
words, certain phrases, jumped out at her. "...her confidence is breathtaking, her energy boundless, her schedule
exhausting..." She reached for the brandy bottle and poured
herself another snifter, glaring malevolently at her own smiling face on the page. Idiot! She read on. But the next
sentence caused her to stop, to lay the magazine down.
"When Cassie talks about her life, she glows—she would
envy Cassie Litton, she acknowledges, if she were not her
already."

For the first time in six months, perhaps for the first time
ever, she allowed herself to think of what she had become,
what she had wanted. Working for Maxine, living with Pete,
had been the happiest time of her life. Why hadn't she
realized it? Why had she thrown it all away? For what?

She couldn't shake the eerie memory she'd had earlier about her father's death. Until now everything about Bobby had seemed so remote, so far away, not just in time but in relevance. But now it seemed very important to her to remember him. Bobby Litton, a dreamer, had not "measured up" to Litton standards; he'd "let them down," "shirked his responsibilities," and "indulged himself" with idealistic notions and an improper marriage. But what had he *really* done. He'd simply married the woman he loved and followed his dream.

She wondered what her father would think of her now. He, who had worked so hard on his newspaper, turning it into a fine, dedicated piece of work. He hadn't cared about the money. He had cared about his wife and his daughter and his work. Not power and prestige. Not money. He would despise her. Just as he had despised his brother, Winthrop, from whom she was no different.

The realization left her more sad than stunned. She sat very still for a long time. Only the sound of the doorbell startled her out of her reverie.

"Pete!"

"I'm sorry to show up like this. I've been trying to call you all night."

"I took the phone off the hook."

"Yeah. Well, I figured something like that. Uh . . . can I come in?"

"Oh, God, yes. I'm sorry. I'm standing here like a dolt. Christ, I must look awful. I wasn't expecting anyone. I wasn't expecting you . . ."

"Well, I guess I figured that, too. You . . . um . . . Jesus, woman! Why did you run out like that? I was half crazy, worrying about you."

"I'm sorry."

"Well, I don't think I can blame you much." Pete shook his head and smiled. "You know, I think Maxine was playing Cupid, sending me up to her room, only she didn't know about my date and I didn't know about Gregory Kournos. So while I was pouring my heart out to Maxine, she was . . ."

"Doing what? What were you doing?"

"Cassie, sit down. No, don't sit down. Come here. Come here and let me hug you. Let me hug my girl."

She went. At first she felt awkward. She knew her face was blotchy and her eyes were swollen. She felt too tall. She felt as though she didn't know how to hug anyone anymore, as though her arms were too long, as though her feet might step on his. But they didn't.

"I love you, Pete."

He stroked her hair; he pressed her to him, and she melted slowly into him. It felt so good to be home.

He rocked her in his arms, tiny, swaying motions, until she sighed deeply, contentedly, from the sheer pleasure of it. Then he led her to the sofa and sat her down.

"Okay. I've got a lot to say to you, so get prepared." Pete took off his jacket. "First of all. Nell Foster. She's a great girl. I know you don't want to hear that, but the fact of the matter is she's been wonderful to me. I can't help myself. I need my creature comforts, especially when I'm miserable, and you made me pretty miserable. It's been a nice, casual affair, but more than that she's been a tremendous help to me in my research. I'll get to that in a minute. But Nell Foster is our friend. All right?"

Cassie nodded.

"I've been working on something for a long time. I tried to tell you about it at Maxine's but you ran out before I had a chance. I told you that night that we split up that you were mine and I didn't give up easily on what was mine. Well, it was a pompous thing to say, but I meant it. I walked out of this apartment, Cassie, but I didn't walk out on you. I've been investigating Stavros International Media. And you don't go very far with that without investigating Mr. Stavros himself. What I've found out, Cassie, is important. Especially where it concerns you."

"What have you found out, Pete?"

"Let's start with the name Candy Lescaux."

"Candy!"

"In the flesh. I met her."

"I don't believe it. Where? How?"

"In Washington. Nell works for the *Washington Post*, and I asked her to nose around Senator Lescaux's office to see if she could come up with Candy's whereabouts. She just laughed. Apparently Candy is notorious. She hangs out at a place called the Sundown Club, and I went there and had a little talk with her."

For the next hour Cassie sat in mute attendance. Pete chronicled one by one the ugly facts of John Stavros's smear campaign on the de Ginsburgh family. It began with the *Comet*'s exclusive story after Camilla de Ginsburgh's death that documented in minute detail a surprising warehouse of intimate information on her life and love affair with Charlotte Soames.

"In the paparazzi world, everyone knew there was a guy in London who would buy anything on the de Ginsburghs for double, triple the going rate," Pete told her. "Candy knew this and sold him those nude shots of you and Dahlia soon after she blackmailed your uncle. I think he used you, Cassie, to get to Dahlia."

"Oh, he didn't need me for that," Cassie said bitterly. "He could have met her any number of ways. But he did use me for information about her. He liked to talk about rich people and I tried to *impress* him with chitchat about my very glamorous friend. He likes to manipulate people and he likes to play games, and I fell right into it. He must have been just biding his time until some juicy bit of gossip about Dahlia came his way so he could publish those pictures. And I gave it to him. I was the one who told him about Dahlia and Chris Jones. I can't believe I was so stupid."

"Honey, you're not stupid. You were in the hands of a master con artist. You wouldn't believe the tricks and dirty dealings Stavros is credited for, but that's not important now. What is important is the fact that the man has a personal vendetta against the de Ginsburgh family, and if, as you say, Dahlia is having an affair with him, I don't think any of this is shaping up roses. It looks pretty murky."

"God, Pete. Do you think it's dangerous?"

Pete shrugged. "I don't know, but it's not doing anyone any good for us to sit here talking. I think you should call someone. Call Dahlia and tell her..."

"She won't believe me, Pete. We had a terrible fight. I said terrible things to her, and she'll just think I'm trying to ruin everything for her."

"Then I'll tell her. Just make the call, Cassie."

Chapter 53

DAHLIA DE GINSBURGH had disappeared, vanished on the arm of newspaper tycoon John Stavros. The last anyone had seen of her was as she stepped into the back of Stavros's black limousine and faded from sight behind the screen of the smoke-colored glass. The driver, when questioned by Henry Brooks, told that he had driven them late at night to Heathrow Airport, where they had boarded the Stavros International Media Lear jet. The airport logs revealed that the jet had flown to Athens and there was no record of a return. They had tracked her that far and no further. Why Dahlia had taken this sudden trip without letting anyone know—not even Dierdre, not even Josephine, not even Ron—was a mystery that remained to be solved. Why she continued to stay away for so long without calling, knowing full well that everyone would be worried, was also a mystery.

"I don't like the looks of this at all," said Lady Caroline to Henry Brooks. "I'm extremely worried and I think something ought to be done. Can't we call Interpol or something like that, or is that only in the movies?"

In fact, everyone was very worried. Cassie and Pete flew directly to London and met with Henry Brooks and Baron de Ginsburgh. The meeting was cordial but extremely tense as they considered the various possibilities of Dahlia's situation.

"This whole thing is unbelievable," said Cassie, "and I could kill myself for having been stupid enough to be taken in by Mr. John Stavros. But I still don't understand . . . Is it possible that he has been in love, if he is capable of such a feeling, with Dahlia all these years? She was only eleven when he left Membland! How did he get to be John Stavros anyway?"

"You know," Henry Brooks spoke, "I don't think it was quite the coincidence that Dahlia thought it was when they met at Buell's party. Although, I must say, it certainly appeals quite strongly to the romantic side of her that John Stavros and the boy who lived at Membland are one and the same. I remember that Yanni Stavropolis left Membland quite suddenly, and of course, there were all sorts of rumors about what he might have done. But whatever he did then, we all know what kind of man he is now—what his business dealings are, the type of scandal sheets he publishes . . . But I tell you, there's something even more murky about the man himself. He's vastly rich, yet no one has a clue to how he got his money. One minute he's the son of a cook, serving at tables, the next he's a big financier . . ."

Henry Brooks got to his feet and began pacing nervously. They all waited patiently for him to go on. He seemed to be searching for the words.

"You see, ever since we realized who Stavros was, something has been bothering me. I couldn't quite put my finger on it. You know, don't you, that I spent most of my summer holidays at Membland—before I went to Eton."

"No," said the baron. "My wife and I usually spent the summer months apart. I only visited Membland once or twice."

Henry nodded. "Well, after my parents died I went to live with my guardians, Lord and Lady Hamilton. It was decided that we, that is Dahlia and I, should spend our summers together. As you can well imagine, we used to get up to no good all the time. And on one occasion, I can remember, we were called on the carpet because something was missing. We were accused, quite wrongly as it happened. It turned out it was a collection of photographs that, of course, didn't sound like much to us, but then Charlotte took us aside and gave us a very severe talking to. Charlotte, as you know, was never very strict with children, quite the contrary, so this talk left a particularly deep impression on me."

The baron stared at the young man, deeply engrossed in what he was saying.

Brooksie thrust his hands deep into his pockets. "She said that certain things, if looked at out of context, could be misinterpreted. She quite went on and on about it. But as we had no earthly idea of what she was talking about, the whole thing more or less built into nothing, you see. I totally forgot about it. Until now . . ." He paused as if weighing his words.

The baron leaned forward, his face somber. "Please don't hesitate to tell anything you know. I, too, am very concerned for Dahlia. I think we all are."

Henry nodded, glancing briefly at Cassie and Pete. "When Camilla and Charlotte died and their story got loose in the tabloids, frankly, I was shocked at the photographs that were printed. These were hardly paparazzi stuff, they were personal and private. I did some research. Those pictures appeared first in the *Comet*—as an exclusive story. And the *Comet* was, still is, a Stavros property. It was his first. I think those pictures were the ones stolen from Membland."

"You're saying he took the pictures and then published them years later?"

"Exactly. For spite. And there's more. Yesterday I took a drive down to Membland myself. God knows what I thought I might find. Only the caretaker was there. He was in an awful state at first, but, thank God, he remembered who I was. In any case, according to him, Dahlia and Stavros spent a night there together, probably the night they met, and then, a day or two later, Stavros showed up again, only this time alone. He had his own set of keys and seemed to know his way around, so the caretaker didn't bother much about him. When Stavros left, the caretaker went in the house and found Camilla's room had been ransacked. Cupboards were open, clothes strewn about the room, and the portrait, the portrait Charlotte painted of Camilla, it was . . . slashed. Slashed to ribbons."

A hush fell over the room. The baron turned his back, his hands clasped behind him. There was some urgency in his voice when he spoke.

"Much of what you have told me I have known or suspected. You see, I, too, have quite a dossier on this John Stavros, on his past, on his finances. There are so many facets to this man, so many interwoven threads, that it would take a great deal of time to unravel all the mysteries of his character. And time, I'm afraid, is what we have very little of. But there are certain things you all must know before we proceed. John Stavros has been under investigation by the World Bank for many years in regard to certain transactions, dealings of enormous magnitude. It has taken us all this time to piece together his career, but we have finally been able to confirm what we had suspected all along.

"It was only recently, shortly before my daughter met this man, that our investigators turned up the information that our man had once been a servant in my wife's house. As far as the World Bank is concerned, this information is of little interest, but I was stunned. To me it has become the central part of a dangerous and disturbing puzzle. I might have predicted that he would seek out my daughter, for he is a man obsessed with memory, but what I could not predict, indeed what has taken me months to accept, is that my Dahlia would be obsessed with him!"

They were all silent—Henry, Cassie, and Pete, and even Caroline Keyes, who for once seemed without brightness or animation. The baron suddenly looked very old, very tired and worn.

"It is a sad and complicated story, and now, I fear, it has turned ugly. But I digress. You see, it all started innocently enough. There was a boy who adored his mistress. He was clever, bright, accomplished in every way, but he was on the outside and the outside can be a very cruel place. He was resentful of his position, infuriated; he was ashamed of the way he was treated. In the end his anger boiled over and he was sent away, disgraced and dismissed. But it was this very anger that gave him the motivation to do what he did next.

"He went to Africa, to the colonies. There was a civil war going on, anarchy, a grand opportunity for so clever a young man. Soldiers of fortune, they were called. He made himself valuable to the general of the winning side, who, when the fighting was over, proclaimed himself 'president.' I've seen it so many times before. The new 'president' denounced the communists, murdered a few socialist professors for effect, and then he asked the Americans for money, relief money.

"But the money did not go to rebuild the country or to aid the victims of the war; it went instead to Switzerland, to a numbered account. And who arranged this? You know the answer. Within months the general was dead, the victim of an assassination that, according to some, was the work of a rival—assisted, of course, by a white mercenary and funds from a Swiss bank. The remainder of the funds? Gone. A very formidable amount, all gone. And now a young financier appears in London. No one knows quite where his money is coming from, but he buys one newspaper after another. He is hungry for power and even further wealth. He must have his fortune; he must prove himself smarter, more clever, wealthier than the rest. The boy's infatuation has become the man's obsession. But the object of his desire—she dies. And now a sickness comes over him."

Pete stood up. "Dahlia then . . ."

"There is the cruel irony. Dahlia knows nothing of this man's obsession. I believe that she actually means very little to him, but she is the one and only and last link to the woman he has carried always in his heart."

Henry, too, got up. "We must get to Dahlia, before it is too late. Who can tell what this man is capable of!"

"But where are they?" asked Cassie hopelessly. "We know they got as far as Athens, but what good does that do?"

The baron looked around, and a glimmer of hope seemed to show up on his tired features. "No. They are not in Athens. But Athens is only a short distance from the island of Spetsai, the island he lived on as a boy. Come! We go to Spetsai! That is where she is, now I am sure of it. I only hope it is not too late."

Chapter 54

THREE, MAYBE FOUR whole days had passed before Dahlia began to suspect that all was not quite right in Stavros's beautiful white villa high on the bluff, away from all civilization. Stavros insisted that they stay within the confines of the villa and would not even let her go to the village telephone to call Dierdre. He assured her that the boy had sent a cable, assuring everyone that she was fine. But there was no question that far from relaxing and enjoying this impromptu vacation, she was as nervous and jumpy as a cat a great deal of the time. Her moods and anxiety were very closely linked to Stavros himself, who was by turns attentive and loving and then moody, angry, and combative for no reason at all.

She was amazed to discover how well he had prepared for her stay in this remote corner of the world. She had come with nothing but the clothes on her back, and yet he provided her with an entire wardrobe of well-chosen, beautiful clothes. There was nothing she could ask for that he did not provide, except, she slowly came to realize, the freedom to leave. This he would not grant her, and every time she asked when they would go back home or in any way bring up the question of traveling on, a black mood came over him and he accused her of not loving him enough, not wanting him, not being satisfied. He could become so unpleasant, almost violent, that soon enough she avoided the subject altogether and hoped for the best.

The days and nights blended into one another, punctuated by long hours of passionate lovemaking that left her exhausted and in a druglike stupor.

Over and over again he would summon her, and again and again she would go—until their responses to each other took on more and more the form of an erotic pageant, a wild masque. She seemed to be an actress playing a part; there were even props—a book, a special chair, a vase of flowers from the garden, and costumes. Beautiful things, soft, treasured objects to adorn her and accessorize the pale, flowing gowns he bade her wear.

He liked to bring her down, down to a place where she was nothing, where she sweated until she was slippery and wet all over, and her body was no longer hers. And yet she responded without question or reserve. His sense of her was beyond understanding, beyond anything she could fathom. And still he would want more, relentlessly twisting her this way and that, watching her, beckoning her down paths she had never dreamed of—and always, always, surprising her, eluding her, filling her up only to starve her ultimately into more submission.

They slept, they ate, they made love again.

"Tell me, Dahlia," he asked, his voice low, insinuating, "have you ever been made love to by a woman? Would you like me to bring a woman to the house? Someone as lovely and soft as you are? Who do you want, Dahlia? Tell me."

She thought he was teasing her, making things up, like telling her that this had been her mother's house. "I don't want anyone, darling. You're quite enough for me."

"Really? What about your friend. Cassie. I could get her, you know. You could have her right here, touching you, kissing you, licking you . . ."

"Stop it." She was indignant. "Sometimes you go too far."

But he pulled her roughly to him and held her prisoner on the bed. "Oh, what fine innocent indignation! But you know, you can't fool me. I know everything about you that there is to know, my pretty, pretty Dahlia. You are your mother's daughter, after all . . ."

In a flash her hand flung out and slapped him hard, and in a flash he overpowered and subdued her, roaring with laughter. Then his hand was between her legs and it teased her until she moaned, gave up the struggle, gave herself to him.

She hated him and yet could not resist him. He frightened her and yet she could not leave. He bullied her, and yes, she was his prisoner.

"What a delicate flower. What a fine scent it gives. So fragile, so perfect." His hands moved to her throat, to her breasts, to her belly. They were rough and quick, and suddenly she felt the full rush of fear. It was as if without any warning they had crossed over the fine line of reason. She was more scared than she had ever been. Every nerve in her body called for her to run, scream, cry out.

"I am going to do anything I like to you. I am going to possess you in any way I like, and you will not utter a sound, not one word. Do I make myself clear?"

Dahlia closed her eyes. Her fear was complete. He was mad. She was entirely at the mercy of a madman, and no one knew where she was. She was lost and alone and so desperately afraid.

"Do you know where you are, Dahlia?" His lips were close to her ear. "Do you know whose house you are in? Whose bed?"

She looked at him but did not utter a sound. He seemed pleased with this.

"I own this house, yes. But it isn't mine. I bought the house many years ago. I bought it for a particular woman to live in." He looked around the room with a pleased expression. "Nothing has been changed, nothing has been altered. And she has lived here. All these years she has lived in this house. She wears these clothes, she reads these books, she breathes the scent of these flowers, and she waits. She waits for me. It is your mother's house, Dahlia. It is Camilla's house."

Dahlia held her hands to her ears and screamed, "Stop it! Stop it! Your're mad! You're totally insane. Let me go. Let me out of here. How dare you do this to me? I want no part of you. I want no part of your sick fantasies! And that's what you are . . . sick, sick, sick . . . "

The first blow was a surprise. She reeled back but she could not escape. His blows kept coming until she felt herself starting to lose consciousness.

He lifted her up and carried her out into bright sun, his steps sure, away from the house and down the path to the sea. She was going to die. She knew it.

On the beach, in the cove, with only the sounds of the cicadas in the still, silent heat of the day, he laid her on a rug, a bright carpet. She held her breath, expecting another blow, expecting . . . She didn't know, but Stavros stood away from her.

The boy! He was there now. He was so thin and young, and there was something akin to fear in his eyes, as well. He lay on top of her. He was inside her. And then it was over.

It was nothing, nothing at all. But Dahlia felt the ache in her jaws, clamped tight so she would not retch. She felt the bile of pain and disgust and horror in her throat.

The boy was gone now, and she felt the burning rays of the sun on her flesh. She knew she must move to cover herself, but her arms were like lead. A shadow fell over her face and she squinted up into it. John Stavros loomed over her—a faceless black shadow. He paused only for a moment and then he turned away and walked to one of the giant boulders that framed the cove. Up, up, he climbed. Then, lightly, gracefully, like a bird, he sprang away from the rock and dove into the deep azure-blue sea.

Chapter 55

THE VIOLENT SHOCK of cool water on his burning skin took his breath away. He waited for a moment to allow his eyes to adjust to the green underwater world, and then he swam to the ocean floor. Beauty was everywhere. Shells glistened and shone like jewels, sea urchins undulated their purple, porcupine quills as he swam by, and a shower of tiny, silver fish darted past him like shooting stars. The sandy bottom was like a soft carpet on which a king's ransom was now displayed.

He was home. Here in this watery world he felt a sense of peace and calm that could never be had on land. He pushed himself further out to sea, where it was cooler still, and darker. Up ahead he could see the outline of large, gray boulders that seemed like a fortress, but there were chinks and dark crevices that beckoned him to enter.

He pulled himself hand over hand along a stony corridor until at last there was an opening, a grotto, and he quickened his movement. Soon he had to go up for air, but there was still time. He knew his body, and the capacity of his lungs. Shadows of light and dark danced hypnotically about him, creating in his mind an illusion of devastating clarity: a boudoir. He could not believe what he saw and yet—there, a dressing table. And there, a chair plump with cushions. A bed, and on it . . . His heart strained loudly in his chest. His head began to throb, but he felt only ecstasy in his body. *She* leaned back on the bed and beckoned to him. His lungs were bursting, but he could not take his eyes from her. He must have air. He must breathe. He must go to the surface, to the light. He jerked his body, twisting it this way and that, but he could not find the way back out of the enclosure. He was clawing at the rock and his body screamed for air.

But now there was a sound. A light, musical silvery laugh. It soothed his terror. Relief surged through his body. Peace and calm returned. She came toward him now. Her body floating gently in the current, her golden hair billowing about her in soft, sensuous motion. Her mouth was wet and open, smiling, calling to him. He swam to her. She moved away—teasing him. He felt the blood in his veins and in his groin. A seductress of the deep. She was the rapturous deep itself. And at last, before the darkness, she was his.

Chapter 56

SHE WAS AWAKE. A sound? A voice? Dahlia dragged herself to a sitting position. But she was alone. There was no one. Carefully, she looked around her. The long shadows from the trees told her it was late in the evening. She had been asleep for hours. She tried to stand up, but a wave of dizziness swept over her, and she doubled up. The bright colors, the woven threads, the repeating curves in the design of the carpet riveted her attention until the dizziness and nausea passed. Her mouth felt parched and swollen, and her skin was taut, stinging with the burn of the sun. Stiff, aching, the pounding in her head making her unsteady, she struggled to her feet and made her way to the water's edge.

Cool, so cool—the gentle lapping of the soft waves soothed her, and she sank gratefully down in the wet sand. She brought handfuls of water to the throbbing spots of pain, on her forehead, the back of her neck, her temples, until at last her head began to clear. Then her eyes filled with helpless tears. Most painful of all were the vivid recollections of this day. The degradation, the fear, the violence, the sickness, the perversion—she sobbed until there were no more tears in her.

She heard it again! A voice calling, and she strained to listen but heard only the eerie whistling of the wind. Her pulse began to race. She was afraid. Afraid of this place, afraid of him. She must get out. She must go home.

And the thought of home brought new terror, the very real terror that he would never let her go. He would keep her here, force her . . . She shuddered with sickening panic.

The only way off the beach was up the hill to the house.

She was trapped here on the beach, unless . . . unless—there must be other houses, another path at the top, a road to the village, something, someone!

Crumpled at the edge of the gaudy beach rug was the dress he had forced her to wear. She grabbed it and put it on. Was it her mother's? Yes, yes, she remembered it now, she even remembered her mother wearing it long ago. Or perhaps it had only been in a photograph. She could not distinguish what was real, what was imagined—perhaps this very day had been a nightmare, it was so like one.

She tried to move quickly, but her movements were leaden and heavy as if she were trapped in amber.

Again, the wave of dizziness and an unbearable thirst. If only she could swallow, if only she could have a tiny glass of water. When had she last eaten? It was all in a haze, a blur of events whirling out of control. She must have water. She dragged herself to the foot of the path. Every muscle screamed its protest; her feet were bleeding from the sharp pebbles and rocks. She tripped and fell as she made her way up the hill, but her thirst galvanized what strength she had left. The inside of her mouth felt like sandpaper, and every few feet she stopped to cling, swaying, to the branch of a tree.

She heard her name again. Yes, yes. This time it was clear, calling to her on a breath of air. Someone wanted her, a voice so familiar. She started moving toward the voice, her thirst forgotten, the pain magically dissolved. She felt light and buoyant, almost as if she could float, drifting toward the lovely voice that called to her. It was her mother's voice. Her mother calling to her, and Dahlia was going home to her mother. Camilla would lay her cool hand on Dahlia's forehead and brush the tangles of hair from her face, and Dahlia would be safe and no one but her beautiful mother would ever touch her again.

She came to a clearing in the path. The house was just a few steps more, around the bend, but . . .

It was a powerful compulsion that made her stop—she felt drawn, forced, to look out once again into the limitless space of sea and air, and a craving, deep and raw, tugged at her. She stood poised at the very edge of the cliff. And then a sob choked its way up from her belly. She was not going to her mother. Her mother was dead. Standing on the edge of the cliff, looking out to sea and air, she felt the earth give way beneath her. She could float, float into space. Fall, plummet, down, down to the sea, to the rocks. Death. Death . . . sweet, terrible, lonely death. Dahlia teetered on the edge, unable to move, unable to save herself, her eyes wide with terror and fascination. She was spellbound, mesmerized—

"Dahlia! Don't! Don't move!"

She froze. A hand grabbed her arm. Another hand was on her shoulder. The strong, firm hands snatched her back from the edge. She was safe, alive—she turned, choking back the sobs that were tearing at her throat.

"Br . . . Brooksie?! How did you . . . Oh God, oh God, I almost fell, I almost fell into the sky. I was so afraid . . . I . . ."

Over his shoulder she saw someone coming down the path. Cassie and a man. She tried to speak, and then she was in Cassie's arms.

Cassie held on to Dahlia as tightly as she could.

"Dahlia. Poor Dahlia."

Chapter 57

HE WAS DEAD. There were no sensational headlines. No shocking stories to titillate the public. PRESS LORD DEAD BY ACCIDENTAL DROWNING. The obituary pages chronicled his life—what was known about it—and listed his holdings. Then most of the world went about its business and forgot him. In London a hastily convened board of directors elected a new chief executive of Stavros International Media. It was announced that Stavros American Media would be dissolved, its holdings sold to the highest bidders. In New York, Cassie had not waited to see what would happen to her job. She had quit. In France, Dahlia sequestered herself in her father's château.

And in Spetsai, a lone woman dressed in black, her figure stooped with age and grief, followed a donkey-drawn cart with its polished ebony coffin to a small walled hillside cemetery. Now she was rich. Rich enough to buy all the tavernas and tourist hotels her heart might desire. But it did not matter anymore. Nothing did. Her beloved boy was dead.

Father and daughter sat opposite one another in the small, exquisite dining room the baron reserved for his intimate dinners. In the week Dahlia had been with him she had taken her meals in her room, but tonight she announced she was coming down. It was a quiet dinner and Dahlia looked thin, perhaps, and pale, but in the glow of the flickering candlelight, the baron thought he had never seen her looking more beautiful. Her hair was pulled away from her face and secured in a simple chignon at the base of her neck. She wore a deep-burgundy Indian caftan shot through with tiny gold threads that caught the light. Yes, he thought, the girl is gone. The woman has emerged.

Throughout dinner and afterward, over brandy in his study, they talked of many things, each knowing, waiting for the right moment to talk of what needed to be said. At last the baron spoke.

"He was buried today."

Dahlia said nothing for a moment, then nodded. "I knew it was to be today. I feel . . . perhaps I should have done something . . . though I don't know what."

"There is nothing to be done. Such a tormented, complicated life. A living hell, I should think. Perhaps he has found his peace at last, in death. I admit as one approaches that time of life myself, I find I look at death in a new light. And life, too. This man, what he has done and what has happened, has given me much to think about. I wonder if I might share these thoughts with you."

"Of course," Dahlia said, but she felt her muscles tense. She didn't know how ready she was to talk about John Stavros. To talk about him was to have to explore some truths about herself, and she was afraid of them.

"You know, as your father I would have liked nothing better than to have been able to protect you from all of this. It's every parent's instinct to shield our children from ugliness and harm. But as a person who has a great many years behind him, I know with a certainty that it is only in the extremities of experience that we learn about ourselves. To plumb the depths of emotion, however painful, can be the very thing that gives us strength. You may hate this man now. Indeed you have every right to. But in time you will be able to temper your feelings with understanding."

"But I don't understand. I want to understand, but I don't."

"Try then to think of what happened to this man as a boy. You know, had he been left alone, untouched by our culture, left to grow in his own way by his own means, think what perhaps might have come of his life."

"You mean leave the savages in the jungles and don't try to civilize them." Her tone was bitter.

"I mean let the dead bury the dead. He was a man, a very intelligent man, perhaps a genius. He would have gone far in his life had he not been possessed by the very thing that he wanted to possess. He was caught, trapped, seduced, if you will . . . You and I can probably never fully understand." He stopped and spoke again quietly. "Your mother was quite the most extraordinary being I have ever known. Extraordinary."

Dahlia looked at her father. "You know I used to think I knew her so well, but all I really remember are feelings . . . the way her hand felt so cool on my cheek . . . the particular softness of her scent . . . the way her hair fell on her neck. Do you know, I saved, well, hoarded is the right word, bits and pieces of things that had come from her, little silly things. But after she and Charlotte died, I started to feel as if I hadn't known her at all. I certainly knew nothing of their attachment to one another, and I tried not to care. After a while I rather thought I didn't care but," she took a deep breath, "on the island, in the face of his madness over her, his obsession, I realized how much I wanted to know about her. I *want* to know what she was really like."

The baron smiled gently at his daughter. "That I can surely not say. But I will tell you how she was in my eyes."

Dahlia nodded. "Yes, please."

Pausing to let his mind reach for the right words, the baron let his thoughts drift back in time.

"One of the great sadnesses of my life has been that you never knew my friend, Oliver Baring, your grandfather. He was a grand man and the greatest friend of my life. He and your grandmother, India Jane. She has always remained to my mind the most beautiful woman in the world."

Dahlia was amazed, both at his words and the particular tone in his voice.

"I am not," the baron continued, "a romancer, and do not know how to weave *les histoires,* so it is difficult to draw a picture of your remarkable grandparents. Oliver was a very large man, very handsome, *très, très gai*. India Jane..." He let out a deep sigh. "Yes, India Jane had a *joie de vivre*, an enthusiasm that made one feel no matter what one was doing, it was the best in the world. Nothing could be better than to be in the company of India Jane. Ahh, and when she laughed, it was life... champagne... clear, seductive..."

Dahlia was fascinated. "Papa, really, you sound as if you were in love with her. Were you?"

The baron looked at his daughter. "You young people today... for you everything is so simple, and most simple of all is—love. You fall in and out of love as easily as you fly around from country to country." He shook his head. "I could not 'be in love' as you say, with my best friend's wife. We were gentlemen. It was not done. But you see... I could, and did, worship her.

"Well, so. The Barings... they were quite a *famille*. Oliver and India Jane were the last of the true English adventurers. They traveled everywhere... they were like dancers, always in motion.

"Mon dieu, Oliver was the happiest family man I have ever met. He adored his wife, not only with the passion of youth but with increasing depth over the years. If a man loves his wife, then to have daughters... a daughter," the baron raised his glass in salute to Dahlia, "then one's happiness is complete. The four Baring girls were each as beautiful as the flowers for which they were named. Your aunts Violet, Iris, Delphine, and, of course, Camilla. Perhaps because Oliver was so rich in family he never quite noticed his slipping financial fortunes.

"Well, as the daughters became young ladies, India Jane took it upon herself to prepare the girls for suitable marriages. She was, as with everything, extremely successful, and the three eldest did not let their seasons in London come to a close without achieving this goal. Strange to say, my friend Oliver, who should have been delighted to see his girls well settled, grew more sad with the marriage of each daughter. You know, I think that if he could have kept them all, financially and emotionally, he would have.

"And so, we come to Camilla. You must understand I knew her from the time she was a baby. Does that shock you? She was, as you know, the youngest, and she was, oh yes, the most exotic beauty in the family. But it should have been perfectly clear to all of us that she would always go her own way. She was of her own kind, and she followed her own path, your mama. Never the guilt, never the regret.

"It had always seemed to me that she enjoyed her own company above all else. There was always an aloof . . . a rather remote look about her as if she carried inside a secret that was far more fascinating than the world around her. It was true, however, that she quite liked the company of writers and artists. She enjoyed dipping her toes into the swirling streams of *la vie bohème*. Paris in 1939 was the perfect place for such a creature as Camilla. Of course, she could move easily on the Right Bank, in the fashionable salons, but more and more she was drawn to the most dangerous and exciting life of the artists on the Left Bank. Ah, what a grand time it was. People from all over the world were here, each paying homage to their particular muse—writers from America, painters from Spain, singers from Russia. It was an exciting time. And in this great garden of creative talent, Camilla Baring caused a sensation. There were men all over Paris, rich and poor, young and old, who were madly in love with her. She was a walking muse, and more poems, stories, pictures, and études were dedicated to her than she could remember.

"Alas, no man interested Camilla for long. As a 'friend of the family,' I had her complete trust and confidence. Since she was a tiny girl, we had always been and remained to the end the greatest of friends.

"For me it was amusing to escort her here and there and watch the effect she had on people and to see who, if anyone at all, would spark her interest. They all seemed to hold such promise, such allure for her. I would ask her how it goes with one or the other of them, and she would answer,

sighing deeply, I can hear her voice now, 'Really, de Ginsburgh, why are they *all* so predictable? Do you know I can
always foretell the exact moment when they're going to tell
me how beautiful I am and confess their undying adoration.
I feel as if I'm drowning in a great ocean of ennui.'"

The baron paused to see if Dahlia had anything to say,
but his daughter sat silently waiting for him to continue.

"Well, to proceed. It was at a large party that we both
met Charlotte Soames. She already had quite a reputation
as a painter. She was a striking woman, as you know. She
never changed much over the years, though she was a trifle
leaner when we met her. But always the straight hair, and
those piercing green eyes that could slay a cobra. She watched
people. She told me once the world was to her a vast Kabuki
drama. She derived her considerable wisdom not from what
people said but how they moved. The little gestures repeated
over and over again, the wave of the hand, the little pout,
the tilt of the head just so before the laugh."

"Oh, I know what you mean," Dahlia laughed. "I could
never hide *anything* from Charlotte, but then I never felt as
if I wanted to, either. She always made me feel rather
special." Dahlia's eyes traveled to the portrait of herself
when she was nine years old. Her hair was neatly braided.
She was wearing the somber gray of a French schoolgirl's
uniform, but the look on her gamine face proclaimed to all
the world that here sat a child ready for any kind of mischief.

"Oh, Papa. It breaks my heart that Dierdre will never
know Mama and Charlotte. What a pair of grandmothers
they would have made . . . But please, go on. I'm shame-
lessly curious about how this strange, ah, triangle came
about."

"Well . . . then I must continue about Charlotte, because
I believe there is no understanding your mother without also
understanding Charlotte. As I have said, when we met her
she had quite a reputation as a painter. It was clear that
great talent lay in her portraits, most especially those of
women. There was in her work a kind of, yes, eroticism

that was breathtaking. Charlotte was never a romantic. She loved women . . . but she painted *la verité,* the truth, in a most disturbing way.

"You know, I don't believe Charlotte spent one moment of her life wondering why she made love to women. And I daresay she was better at it than most men. It is, after all, not so much a question of technique as of—"

"Papa, really." Dahlia couldn't help feeling a little shocked.

"Come, my dear," he said with no levity in his voice. "You are, alas, no longer a child, and although I confess I am slightly surprised to find it so, it has become important to me that you understand how it was. Is is not better that we speak of these things here, now, over cognac than to leave them to the pages of the vulgar newspapers." Dahlia nodded. Then added, "I do think you are the most amazing, wonderful father. How lucky we all were to have you."

He clucked her into silence. "But, you see, if a man has as his rival in love another woman, he has a formidable rival, indeed. Fortunately for me . . . perhaps for everyone, it never occurred to me to enter into such a competition for Camilla's, ah, favors. I had seen her break too many hearts.

"In any case, it was immediately clear to me that Camilla was strongly drawn to Charlotte. You know, Camilla was so accustomed to turning heads with her beauty that Charlotte must have been quite a novelty. So frank, so direct, and not a trace of flirtation or flattery. She saw another Camilla, not the aloof, self-possessed lady but," he shrugged, "the restless undercurrents, the longings. Yes, I am sure of it. It was Charlotte's triumph—and her undoing—to have such a vision.

"Naturally enough, Camilla agreed to pose for Charlotte, despite Charlotte's warning that the picture might not be at all what she expected.

"The painting that emerged, you know all too well. It is a remarkable portrait—although difficult for us—you and me—to comfortably assess. Yet, I believe it holds the key . . . bah, I too am mincing words. It tells the entire story of their love, for a great love it was—lifelong and strong. Unusual? Yes. Uncomfortable in many quarters? Certainly. But as undeniable and uncontrollable as elements of nature."

"But I don't understand how it was for you?" Dahlia sat forward in her chair. "Are you telling me that Charlotte and Mother were lovers even before you married her? Why did you marry her? Did you know Charlotte would always be there?"

"Ah, my dear. So many questions, so many answers, but the truth is so elusive. Who knows what would have happened if Oliver had not suddenly died, leaving a legacy of debts and ruined finances? Who knows how the world would have been if the holocaust of war had not put such a quick and ugly end to the playground that was Paris. If? If? If? If I hadn't loved India Jane and if I hadn't been, shall we say, maturing in years, if I hadn't wanted a child? *Enfin*, we struck a bargain, your mother and I. I wanted a child, she needed financial security. There was no question of romantic love to muddle up the arrangement. It was, I think, except for some details, not as unusual an arrangement as it may sound. Marriages have been arranged since time immemorial, and most of them with far less happy results.

"I will tell you something else. There has always existed between me and Charlotte a great bond of sympathy. I think we both knew that no one could truly possess Camilla. She possessed herself. We were the fortunate ones with whom she shared some part of herself. There were very few of us, only Charlotte, and me, and finally—you."

Epilogue

OUR STORY ENDS, as all stories should, with a wedding. Pete proposed to Cassie one hot, muggy afternoon in the parking lot of the White Castle hamburger emporium on the Major Deegan Expressway in the Bronx. Cassie accepted immediately.

The wedding itself will take place at the de Ginsburgh château in the autumn, just after the harvest of champagne grapes has been completed. It has been a good year for the grapes, and the entire village is in a mood to celebrate both the harvest and the wedding of the charming American couple

Baron de Ginsburgh has prevailed upon the mayor to officiate at the ceremony, and old Maurice, an honored son of Epernay, has marshaled the combined forces of the *char-cutière*, the *boulanger* and the *pâtissière*. Oysters are coming from Normandy, *foie gras* from Strasbourg, and the ripest brie from the neighboring village of Vernon.

The ceremony itself will take place in the old north garden where the roses tumble over a small ornate marble folly built by an earlier de Ginsburgh who lived in a more baroque time. Cassie will wear a soft summer cotton dress cut in the style of an Edwardian morning frock. It is a pretty, modest dress with its skirt falling well below the knee and yet revealing ankle and leg to show off the embroidered white silk stockings. The bodice is gently pleated with a large collar that sweeps across her shoulders and is trimmed with intricate handmade lace. The dress reminds Cassie of southern ladies in old photographs sitting on shaded verandas. She will carry the silk handkerchief her father gave

Blue on their wedding day, and she has borrowed Dahlia's pearl necklace as her only piece of jewelry. On her head will be a garland of blue wildflowers, flowers that Dierdre Lovell will pick for her in the morning. Dierdre is to be Cassie's only attendant and will lead the procession through the little pine forest and into the old rose garden.

On the eve of the wedding, the guests have gathered— guests who have arrived throughout the day from London, New York, and Paris. There has been a large country dinner at the village inn to honor the bride and groom with many toasts and a great deal of champagne. By midnight everyone has gone to bed. Every quarter hour the deep chimes of the church bell ring out into the placid, warm night. The bells seem to echo the song of the nightingale whose single, tremulous note fills the air.

Lady Caroline Keyes turned off the light beside her bed and inhaled, deeply savoring the perfumed air. She let the darkness of the night envelop her like a silken coverlet, and at last she allowed the torrent of hot, salty tears to stream down her cheeks, making large damp spots on the linen pillowcase. Weddings always made her cry. She cried before, during, and after, abandoning herself totally to an ecstasy of sentiment and emotion.

She had come alone and was not happy about it. Ever since she had turned a new page in her life and embraced virtue and fidelity as her guiding principles, she found that whenever she was any distance from her husband she missed him. Enormously! She loved entirely the vision of herself as a lonely tragic without Nicky Keyes to protect and shelter her.

It had come to her in a flash shortly after Dahlia returned from Spetsai the notion that virtue could be the newest, hottest, most radical idea to hit the London scene. Carrots had begun her new life, naturally enough, by changing her entire wardrobe. She had reshaped her image to include subdued ladylike dresses and shapeless cardigans over tweed skirts—kind of a cross between Wallis Simpson and Virginia Woolf.

But only this morning Saunders, her maid, had brought her a note from Nicky on the breakfast tray:

Poor Loopy Pet!
    How roundabout and subtle you've become. As if I would deny you anything! Please, please stop all this moping about in dreary gray jumpers and hideous maiden-aunt frocks. Wherever did you find them? Of course you must have new dresses.

Your devoted Nicky

Enclosed was a very generous check.

Carrots drifted off to sleep, her head filled with visions of her new look for summer. Oh, how right she had been. Virtue paid handsome dividends indeed!

Across the hall, Pete Rossi's room spun around wildly as he struggled to maintain his equilibrium. His mind was a jumble of impressions—the beauty of the French countryside, the vast quantities of champagne he had consumed during the evening, the visions of the impending ceremony in the morning. He thought about Cassie, about their lives stretching out before them, and he thought how lucky he was to have found a woman who suited him perfectly—beautiful, proud, smart, ambitious, and just a little crazy. As desire for her filled his veins, he thought about the subtle, secret smell of her, the perfect rounded arc of her hip, the way her body curled against his—but sleep overtook him and soon he was snoring softly in the song-filled night.

Blue sighed happily and snuggled deeper into the hollow of her husband's arm. Bud's deep breathing was uninterrupted as he pulled his wife in closer to his side and caressed the luxurious mound of her breast. Tired as she was, Blue still fought off the delicious waves of sleep that tugged and pulled at her consciousness. She was too happy, too excited about her darling Cassie's wedding day, to give herself up to ordinary necessities like sleep. All her life she had watched Cassie strive for and achieve her goals one by one and seemingly all on her own. She had turned herself into an educated, successful, and prosperous young woman, but in her mother's eyes she had also acquired a hard-bitten, driven quality and a lonely aloofness that broke Blue's heart and made her feel that despite all the outward signs of success, her private life was sad, indeed.

Blue liked Pete Rossi and she liked the changes in Cassie, who was more relaxed, less guarded, less angry, less determined to be in control. For the first time she seemed unconcerned about her unemployment and even laughed about it. "So what if we're broke," she had said, squeezing Pete's hand, "you always told me that being happy was more important than having money in the bank, didn't you, Mama?"

Blue could hardly believe that she'd managed to keep her big secret all to herself for this long. Well, not all to herself—Bud knew and, of course, the baron knew because he was the one who'd insisted on helping her in the first place. He had found the right law firm and had put the weight of his own position and bank account at her service. After that everything had worked like a charm. Winthrop Litton had put up almost no kind of fight at all when confronted with a battery of Yankee lawyers who accused him of tampering with a minor ward's finances, and he'd agreed to their suggested settlement terms eagerly—almost happily. Tomorrow she would tell them—her new son and her beloved daughter . . . It would be Blue's own special wedding present, her setting to right what had gone wrong. Cassie and Pete might never get to be truly rich, but they would always be amply provided for by the generous monthly check that was to be paid to Cassie for the rest of her life from her share of the Litton fortune.

Blue smiled, remembering how Bud had patted her knee only that morning as they toasted each other on the flight to Paris. "See, honey," he said, "I told you everything would turn out fine!"

In the west wing of the old château, Cassie and Dahlia sat in the large, cushioned window seat of Dahlia's bedroom. They weren't a bit sleepy and in fact had vowed to stay up all night. The casement windows were flung open and they could smell the lovely scent of stock and mignonette.

"It's funny, here I am getting married tomorrow, but I don't feel at all grown up. Somehow I feel younger and less sure of myself than I did when we were back in school."

"I think that's what happens. I think we reach the extent of our maturity when we're seventeen or eighteen and then it's all down hill from there. I've been married and divorced and God knows what, and I certainly don't feel older. I'm just totally amazed when Dierdre looks up at me with that look that I remember so well, the one reserved for grown-ups, and I can see that she thinks that I'm as old as the hills."

"Remember that feeling when you couldn't imagine, in your wildest dreams, that there would be a life for you beyond the life of childhood?"

"Mmm. Why were we in such a hurry to leave it, I wonder? One seemed so much wiser then. Why do we have to do so many stupid, hurtful things just to find out what we really knew all along?"

"I don't know. Maybe growing up is just a kind of coming back, you know, a homecoming..."

"The return of the prodigal daughter and all that..." They were both silent for a few minutes, then Dahlia asked, "Have you and Pete finally decided where you're going? You know, for your wedding trip? And after?"

"Sort of. We've got the car, and we're just going to go. Drive down through France and then into Italy. If we find a place we like, we'll stay there. I think we'll take our time, sort of hang out in the old country until we find ourselves and decide what to do with our lives next . . . what about you?"

"Didn't I tell you? It's too exciting! Brooksie is taking Dierdre and me to Disneyworld. I don't know who's more excited—me or Dierdre or Brooksie. After that, well . . . we thought we'd stay in America for a while, until we find ourselves, decide what we should do . . ."

Baron Guy de Ginsburgh sat in his private chamber, a combination dressing room, library, and office, watching the darkness of the night slowly giving way to the coming dawn. He was smoking one of the rare cigars he still permitted himself, despite the fact that his doctor had disadvised him even this small indulgence. He slept only three or four hours a night, whether out of habit or increasing age he did not know, but he enjoyed the solitary hours. It gave him the leisured time for random, drifting thoughts.

But at last he stubbed out the cigar and rose. He made his way silently down the long hallway and up the stairs into the tiny dormer bedroom to once again gaze at the lovely shut-eyed face of his granddaughter, Dierdre, and gently, needlessly he adjusted the blankets around her sleeping form.

And what is Dierdre Lovell dreaming? She is six years old and her life stretches before her like a sandy beach waiting for footprints. Soon enough she will grow up and experience the tumults of love, passion, friendship, and ambition, and she will look at her fading, slightly tired mother and scarcely be able to imagine that she, too, once had, not very long ago, a life as intense as her own. Even less will she be able to see that the silken strands of life's web are stitched through generations and centuries. And then one day perhaps she, too, will realize that everything she thought was hers alone is part of a larger tapestry and that no one can ever entirely break free from these invisible ties to the past.

But, of course, little Dierdre knows none of this. Tonight she dreams of weddings and happy endings.

Bestselling Books from Berkley